By Charles Todd

A FALSE MIRROR
A LONG SHADOW
A COLD TREACHERY
THE MURDER STONE
A FEARSOME DOUBT
LEGACY OF THE DEAD
WATCHERS OF TIME
SEARCH THE DARK
WINGS OF FIRE
A TEST OF WILLS

Forthcoming in hardcover

A PALE HORSE

CHARLES TODD

A FALSE MIRROR

AN INSPECTOR IAN RUTLEDGE NOVEL

HARPER

An Imprint of HarperCollinsPublishers

This is a work of fiction. The characters, incidents, and dialogue are products of the author's imagination and are not to be construed as real. Any resemblance to real persons, living or dead, is entirely co-incidental.

HARPER

An Imprint of HarperCollins*Publishers*
10 East 53rd Street
New York, New York 10022–5299

Copyright © 2007 by Charles Todd
Excerpt from *A Pale Horse* copyright © 2008 by Charles Todd
ISBN: 978-0-06-078674-8

First Harper paperback printing: January 2008
First William Morrow hardcover printing: January 2007

Printed in the United States of America

Visit Harper paperbacks on the World Wide Web at
www.harpercollins.com

10 9 8 7 6 5 4 3 2 1

For Bonnie and Joe,
and everyone at The Black Orchid.
In addition to a well-deserved Raven,
a Todd award in gratitude for
friendship, book parties, chocolate-covered
raisins, and the most exciting sidewalk
conversations in New York. With much, much love.

1

It was a bitterly cold night of frost, the stars sharp and piercingly bright overhead.

He pulled the motorcar to the verge and settled to watch the house that lay directly across the black expanse of water. It stood out against the sky, amazingly clear. Even from here he could tell there were lamps burning in three of the rooms. He could picture them in his mind: at the rear of the house—the sitting room, very likely. In the entry, where the pattern of the fanlight over the front door shone starkly against the deep shadows there—behind it the staircase, of course. And one on the first floor, under the eaves.

Their bedroom, surely.

The sitting room lamp went out after half an hour. He could see, for an instant, the grotesque silhouette cast for a moment or two against the drawn shades as someone reached out to turn down the flame. And then the silhouette reappeared briefly in the fanlight just as the second lamp was extinguished.

He leaned forward, his concentration intense, then swore as the windscreen clouded with his breath.

Were there two people in the bedroom now?

He couldn't bear to think about it. He couldn't bear to picture her in another man's arms, wrapped in the warmth of the bedclothes, whispering softly, her hair falling over his shoulder and across his chest. . . .

His fists pounded angrily on the steering wheel as he tried to force the images out of his mind.

And then the last lamp went out, leaving the house in darkness. Shutting them *in*. While he sat there, like a fool, in the windless night, cold and wretched.

It was the fourth time he'd driven into Hampton Regis. He had promised the doctor he'd do no such thing. But the temptation was too strong, overwhelming his better judgment. Haunted by the need to know, he had told himself that *once* would do no harm. But once had become twice. And now here he was again.

Dr. Beatie had said, "Stephen—you aren't healed yet. Do you understand? Emotional distress could put you back here, in a worse state than before!"

Both of them knew it was a lie. There could be no worse state than the one he'd somehow, miraculously, survived. He had had to kill the Captain before Dr. Beatie could set him free. He wished now it had been Matthew Hamilton who had died.

He caught himself, knowing it was wrong to wish such a thing. But God, he was tired, and alone, and sometimes afraid. He wanted things the way they had been in 1914. Before the war—the trenches—the nightmares. Before Matthew Hamilton had walked into the clinic waiting room to comfort Felicity and told her—what? Lies? Or the sordid truth? That her fiancé was a coward.

After a time Stephen got out to crank the motorcar, the sound of the powerful engine roaring into life and filling the cold silence. He would freeze to death if he sat here, uselessly mourning.

Setting his teeth, he turned the motorcar and without looking again at the darkened house behind him, drove back the way he'd come.

He couldn't see behind the silken white curtains that covered the window under the eaves a pale face staring out into the night, watching the puff of exhaust whip across the rear light, a wraith shielding its brightness until it was out of sight.

Matthew Hamilton rose early, quietly throwing back the bedclothes and the counterpane that covered him, then tucking the ends around his wife's bare shoulder. Looking down at her, he marveled again at his luck. Then reminded himself that it wasn't his luck at all, but someone else's misfortune, that he had married this lovely, loving woman in his bed.

Wryly turning away, he dressed quickly and then set about making up the fire so that the room would be warm for her. When it was drawing well, he went down to the kitchen and blew the fire there into life for the kettle. While he waited for it to boil, he raised the shades and looked out at the clear, cold morning. The sun was not yet up, but a pale rose had begun to streak the winter-brown lawns spreading to the cliff face overlooking the sea. The water beyond was still, waiting for the sun, and farther out there was a soft mist blanketing it.

To the west, across the harbor below, the land rose up again, running out to a point a little higher than the one on which his house was set. The pair of headlands formed two arms embracing the Mole—the medieval stone pier that jutted out across the shingle to the tideline—creating a haven for shipping along England's south coast in an age when sailing ships made Hampton Regis rich.

There had once been a watchtower on the far headland, built to keep an eye on Napoleon. Only ruins stood there now, overgrown at the base, a few feet of stone still reaching upward like pleading fingers.

Two days ago he'd seen a vixen and her kits romping there, and he'd been touched by their exuberance, wondering how any man could hunt them down. Farmers were often a backward lot, though it was an unkind thing to say. But foxes kept vermin down, and like the old owl in the belfry at the church, deserved a better character than they'd been given.

The kettle whistled behind him, startling him, and he moved quickly to lift it off the plate. He enjoyed these few minutes alone, before the maid arrived, before the house was a-bustle. He also enjoyed spoiling his wife, doing such small things for her pleasure. A far cry from his long years of exile in other countries, alone and often distrusted, the voice of London when often London had left him to his own devices. It was over, and he called himself happy.

Felicity was standing by the window when he brought her tea, her robe belted tightly about her waist.

"Watching for the foxes?" he asked. "They should be active again this morning." He handed her a cup as she turned.

But she hadn't been watching for the foxes. He could see that in her face. Why was love so perceptive? It would be better off blind, he thought, pretending not to notice her guilt.

She was saying, "We ought to have a fine day. Just as well—I've a thousand things to do!" She smiled up at him, then reached out to lay her free hand against his cheek. "I do love you, Matthew," she told him softly.

He covered her fingers with his own. "I'm glad," he responded simply. "I don't quite know how I managed to live so many years without you."

She set down her cup and walked over to the blazing fire. "Shall I take the dogcart or the motorcar?"

"The motor, of course. It will be warmer."

She nodded, thinking about her errands. Then she said, "Must you call on Miss Trining today? She'll have something to say about you arriving in a dogcart. Far beneath your dignity."

He laughed. "Yes, I know. I shall never live up to old Petrie's standards. Queen Victoria herself couldn't have found fault with him."

"I should hope not. She *knighted* him," Felicity answered, laughing with him. "But just think—the next important man who chooses to reside here will be held up to *your* standards." She lowered her voice. "Not quite the man Matthew Hamilton was, you know," she said gruffly in imitation of Miss Trining. "I don't know what the Foreign Office is coming to these days!"

It was perfect mimicry.

"It would never do for you to attend a vestry meeting. I'd see your face down the table, know what you were thinking, and lose any reputation I ever had for being a sober, God-fearing civil servant. They'd chuck me out on the spot for unseemly levity."

"Not you," she said quickly. "God knows, they're lucky to have someone under eighty willing to serve. I on the other hand would be burned at the stake, before sunrise. Like Guinevere."

She bit her lip as she spoke the name, wishing she could take it back. She put her arms around his neck, her eyes closed. "Hold me," she begged.

And he did, her tea forgotten.

2

Chief Superintendent Bowles sat at his cluttered desk, chewing on the end of his mustache, staring at his subordinate.

"Time off?" he said. "What on earth for?"

"A—personal matter," Inspector Rutledge answered, unforthcoming.

"Indeed!" Bowles continued to stare. The nurse who'd sent him a copy of this man's medical file before Rutledge returned to duty last June must have lied.

Rutledge was still thin for his height, and his face was drawn as if from lack of sleep. But the eyes, dark and haunted, were intelligent and alert. So much for cowardice. And he hadn't shown a yellow streak in the north, over that nasty business about the child. The local man had complained of him, of course, and Mickelson had been angry over the outcome of the case. But the Chief Magistrate had told Bowles in no uncertain terms that the investigation had been brilliantly handled.

And the Chief Magistrate had Connections. It wouldn't do to ignore that.

Rutledge had also done well in Northamptonshire, though it had been a grave risk sending this man to see to Hensley. But then he'd trusted Hensley to keep his mouth shut, and it had turned out all right. There was no proof to be found that he'd known what Hensley was up to. Or none that he knew of.

His thoughts returned to the letter from the clinic.

Bowles had half a mind to bring that fool nurse up on charges of incompetence. For the past six months, Rutledge had somehow managed to turn every test into a small success. What was he to do about this man who refused to destroy himself? The nurse had sworn she'd overheard him threatening suicide time and again, she had sworn he wouldn't survive the rigors of the Yard for more than a month, two at best. What's more, how did Rutledge manage to carry out his duties in such a way that others protected him? Protectors who were unaware that Rutledge had come out of the trenches with shell shock and must have killed who knew how many brave soldiers through his own lack of moral fiber!

Bowles would have given much to know who had pinned medals on this man's chest and called him a hero. That officer deserved to be shot, by God!

Better still, *Rutledge* ought to have been shot, he thought sourly, and not for the first time. It was the least the Germans could have done, after their rampage across Belgium and France. A nice clean bullet to the heart crossing No Man's Land. If Rutledge had ever crossed it, of course— very likely he'd cowered in the trench out of harm's way while his men died. And no German fire could reach him there, however hard the guns had tried.

His already bleak mood was turning into a nasty head-ache—

Bowles suddenly became aware that he'd been glaring at Rutledge in silence. He cleared his throat, shifting in his chair to give the impression he'd been preoccupied with other issues instead of sitting there like a fool, daydreaming.

"There's the Shepherd's Market murder still to be solved. Not to mention that business about the men found dead in Green Park. I don't see how I can spare you. Or anyone else for that matter."

Rutledge said, "It's rather important."

"So is peace and order!" Bowles snapped. "Or do you think yourself above the rest of us? Jaunting about the country-side attending to personal affairs indeed, while there's work to be done here."

"Neither of these cases is mine," Rutledge reminded him, his voice neutral. But something in his eyes warned Bowles that this leave he'd requested was a more serious business than Rutledge was willing to admit.

Bowles brought his attention back to his inspector's face. Was Rutledge on the brink of breaking down? Was that what made him so anxious to get away for a bit?

The more Bowles considered that possibility, the more he began to believe in it. What else could it be but a recognition on Rutledge's part that time was running out?

"You're to stay in town and work with Phipps, do you hear me? You'll help him find out what's behind the Green Park murders. And there's an end to it."

He sat back in his chair and studied the fountain pen in his fingers. "An end to it!" he repeated forcefully. "Request denied."

Chief Inspector Phipps was a nervous man whose effi-

ciency was not in question, but whose personality left much
to be desired. He seemed to feed on his own anxieties to
the point of aggravating everyone around him. Inspector
Mickelson had sworn the Chief Inspector could drive God
himself mad.

What would close contact with him do to a man facing a
breakdown?

Satisfied, Bowles picked up a file on his desk and opened
it. Rutledge was dismissed.

Chief Inspector Phipps walked into Rutledge's office without knocking, his fingers beating a ragged tattoo on the back
of the file he was carrying.

Rutledge looked up, his gaze going to the file.

The Green Park murders, so close to Buckingham Palace,
had drawn the attention of the press. Two men had been
killed there, a week apart. So far nothing uncovered in the
investigation indicated any connection between them. But
each had been garroted and left in the bushes. An early
riser found the first victim when his dog was drawn to the
shrubbery and began barking. Children playing hide-and-
seek with their nursemaid had discovered the second victim.
Their father—titled and furious—had appeared at the Yard
in person, demanding to know why his son and daughter had
been subjected to such a gruesome experience. They were
distraught, as was his wife, he'd told Phipps in no uncertain
terms. And the Yard was to blame for allowing murderers to
roam unhindered in decent parts of town. No mention was
made of any anguish the nursemaid had suffered.

Phipps set the file on Rutledge's desk and began to pace
the narrow office as he spoke.

"Bowles has given you to me. Anything in particular on
your desk at the moment?"

Rutledge said, "I've closed the file on George Ferrell. This morning."

"Good, good!" Phipps wheeled and paced back the other way.

"Each of our victims," Phipps went on, "was found on a Sunday morning. Tomorrow is Saturday. I want Green Park covered from first light to first light. You'll be given a police matron dressed as a nanny. She'll be pushing a pram, and you're her suitor, a young clerk from a nearby shop, who urges her to sit and talk for an hour." He paused to consider Rutledge. "You don't really look like a lovesick young clerk. I'll ask Constable Bevins to assume that role, instead, and you can walk Bevins's dog several times during the day and early evening. I want an inspector close by at all times, you see. You'll have the damned dog on your hands until Bevins is off duty. See the beast doesn't annoy the chief superintendent, if you must bring it back to the Yard."

"With so many people in the Park, it isn't likely that another murder will occur there," Rutledge pointed out.

"And that's what I'm hoping, don't you see? We throw our man off balance, make it difficult for him to plan." Phipps paused long enough to crack his knuckles, one by one. "Once the killer has lured his target into the park, it won't be easy to shift him to another site."

"What if he's already killed the two men he'd intended to murder?"

"Oh, I don't think that's a very likely possibility! We've got ourselves a trend here, don't you know. He'll come to the Park, all right. Wait and see. And he'll have told his victim where and when to meet him, I should think. Safer than arriving together. Someone might see them and remember." He was pacing again, rubbing his jaw with the back of his nails. "Very well, then, we're looking for two men, arriving separately, then meeting. They'll go off together toward the shrubbery, for privacy. That's when we'll have them. Bevins is to bring his dog to the Yard at six o'clock tomorrow morning. Be here and make certain that you have a change of clothes—we shan't want to be noticed!"

Hamish said, "Aye, but the dog will be the same dog."

But Rutledge's mind was elsewhere. It was cold, the trees bare, the wind brutal coming down the Thames. Huddled in a greatcoat, he thought, who would know whether he was wearing a blue or a gray suit beneath it? But a change of hat and shoes might well be in order. . . .

Phipps was at the door, tapping the frame as he changed his mind again.

"No, perhaps you ought to be the policeman on foot—"

"I hardly look like a young constable. The dog and I will manage well enough."

"Unless he decides to bite you. I've heard that Bevins's dog has a nasty disposition."

And with that he was gone.

Rutledge, leaning back in his chair, wished himself away from this place, away from London. Away from the wretchedness of torn bodies, bloody scenes of crimes. Although he suspected Frances, his sister, had had a hand in it, he'd just been invited to Kent, to stay with Melinda Crawford, whom he'd known for as long as he was aware of knowing anyone other than his parents. As a child, Melinda had seen enough of death herself, in the Great Indian Mutiny. He could depend on her to keep him amused and to thrust him into her various projects, never speaking about what had happened in November, not twenty miles from her. Even a long weekend would be a godsend. But there was nothing he could do about it.

As it happened, Bevins's dog was a great, heavy-coated black monster with more than a little mastiff in him. He slavered heavily as he greeted Rutledge and then trotted scdately at his side as the two of them left the Yard and headed for Green Park.

In the back of Rutledge's mind, Hamish was unsettled this morning. The voice was just behind his shoulder, clear in spite of the traffic that moved through the streets even at this early hour or the jostling of people as they hurried past or stepped aside with a murmured comment about the dog on its leather lead.

"Ugly brute," one man said, and as if the dog understood, he raised his massive head and stared back. The man turned into the nearest shop, out of reach of the strong white teeth grinning malevolently almost on a level with his throat.

Hamish was saying, "Ye've been reduced to this, then. A distraction any green constable on probation could ha' provided."

"Not by choice," Rutledge answered curtly, under his breath.

"Aye, he's a bad enemy, yon chief superintendent. M' Granny would ha' found him in the bowl of water, and put a curse on him."

"I wonder what my godfather would have to say to that."

"He's no' a Scot. He wouldna' be told what went on below the stairs."

The voice was not really there—although Rutledge had never dared to turn his head to see. It was in his own mind, deep-seated since July 1916, when both he and Corporal MacLeod had cracked under the stress of the ferocious Somme Offensive. But it was Hamish MacLeod, the good soldier, the caring young Scot putting his men ahead of himself, who had faced the hastily collected firing squad intended to keep order in the midst of the bedlam of battle. The charge was refusing an order, but the order had been to lead his men back into heavy fire for one more hopeless attempt to reach the German machine gunners—one more suicidal command sent up from the rear. Hamish had continued to refuse, and Rutledge had had no choice but to execute his corporal. For the greater good, for the men who would have to die anyway, whether their corporal was with them or not. Military necessity. He himself had delivered the coup de grâce, refusing to leave to any of his men that last horror—only to be buried alive moments later by a British shell fired too short.

And Rutledge knew then, and in all his waking moments since that dreadful half-death, that one more night—one more day—would have seen him refuse orders as well, refuse to be a party to more ungodly slaughter. Instead, he'd been patched up at the nearest aid station and sent back to the trenches, a man emotionally destroyed, trying desperately to protect his men, and all the while, the voice of a dead man ringing in his head and in his dreams and in his ears.

Rutledge said, "There's the park." He wasn't aware that he'd spoken aloud, but the dog turned its head as if the words were meant for him. "Good dog," he said, and then considered Hamish's remark. Rutledge's godfather, David Trevor, had shut himself away in his Scottish hunting lodge after the death of his son Ross at sea. There had been times when Rutledge had been sorely tempted to confide in Trevor about his own war, about what he had done, but Scotland held too many memories now. And however much Trevor had wanted Rutledge to befriend and guide Fiona, the young woman who was foster mother to Trevor's grandson, it was not possible. She was the girl Hamish had intended to marry after the war, and she still grieved for her dead fiancé. Every time Rutledge looked into her face, his own wretched guilt closed his throat.

It should have been Hamish, not himself, who had come home at the end of the war.

He could feel himself losing touch with the present,

the London street he was crossing in the midst of traffic. His surroundings faded into images of torn and bloody young bodies lying in the mud, and the sounds of men who screamed in agony as they were mortally hit, or begged for their wives and mothers to help them. He could hear the bolts on the rifles of the firing squad as a round was chambered, and see his men shivering in a trench, deathly afraid of going over the top one more time, too exhausted to fire their weapons, and yet driven to climb the ladders out of the greater fear of letting their comrades down.

" 'Ware!"

A motorcar's horn blew in his face, jolting him into the realization that he and the dog were in the middle of the street, vehicles swerving to miss them.

Rutledge swore, pulled the dog's lead closer, and managed to get them to the far side of the road as Hamish told him roundly to mind what he was about.

And what would Chief Inspector Phipps think of half of London staring at the madman and dog intent on getting themselves killed on The Mall? If that didn't attract the attention of the murderer, nothing Phipps had planned would distract him.

But the shock of what had just happened reminded Rutledge that it was cowardly to ask another man, even his godfather, to hear what no one should have to hear, just to buy a little peace for himself. He'd managed on his own thus far. He could manage a little longer. But dear God, it was lonely!

Round and round it went, the circle that had nowhere to end.

They had reached Green Park, he and the dog, and Rutledge could see Bevins courting the police matron in her demure nanny's uniform. The hardness of her face betrayed her, but Bevins was the epitome of a lovesick young clerk, leaning earnestly toward the woman, as if pleading with her. His Welsh charm was evident.

Thrusting his wretched mood aside, Rutledge slowly walked the dog through the park, giving the animal time to explore the smells frozen in the grass. The very image of a man with time on his hands, an ex-soldier, perhaps, down on his luck, the greatcoat and an old hat betraying his reduced circumstances. He made himself stoop a little, to change his appearance and fit his role.

The dog caught sight of Bevins, but the constable was prepared for that, leaping to his feet and coming to kneel by the animal, petting it while looking up at Rutledge, asking questions about the breed. When Rutledge called the dog to heel, Bevins got to his feet, touched his hat to Rutledge, and went back to his wooing. A good man.

During the interlude, Rutledge had glimpsed someone entering the park. It was Phipps, walking too fast for a man strolling, his eyes everywhere. He took in the nanny and the constable, looked across at a corporal who was leaning against a tree, smoking a cigarette, and a heavyset sergeant in a checked tweed coat, seated on a bench casually reading the morning papers. But the Chief Inspector passed through without speaking to anyone. It was clear he had come to judge the authenticity of his actors, and was satisfied.

Rutledge finished his tour of the park and returned to the Yard, the dog thoroughly pleased with its outing.

He met Inspector Mickelson on the stairs, and they passed without speaking. Mickelson was dressed as a banker, furled umbrella, hat set squarely on his head, on his way to take his own part in Phipps's play.

The dog growled deep in his throat as Mickelson went by, and Rutledge patted the massive head. Mickelson was a stickler for the rules, and one of Bowles's favorites. He had also nearly got Rutledge killed in Westmorland. It was with some satisfaction that Rutledge accepted the dog's judgment corroborating his own.

After half an hour, Bevins also returned, his face flushed with the cold wind.

"Any luck?" Rutledge asked, meeting him in the corridor.

"No, sir." Then he grinned. "I'm a chimney sweep next. Got the clothes off a man we took up for housebreaking last week. Pray God there's no lice in them."

Rutledge had walked the dog the third time, glimpsing the sweep working on his brushes as if something about them troubled him. The nanny was now unrecognizable as a shopgirl flirting with a young army private. Another man was arguing with a friend, and Rutledge caught part of what Sergeant Gibson was saying so earnestly—his views on the Labor Party and what the government ought to do about people out of work.

We've got the same number of actors—Rutledge thought, bringing the dog to heel again after allowing it to explore among the trees along the edge of the grass. *It doesn't vary.*

No murderer worth his salt would walk into such a carefully managed trap.

And then Phipps was there again, carrying his umbrella, a folded copy of *The Times* under his arm. He looked like a retired solicitor, his nose red from the cold, his attention fixed on the distant traffic, just barely heard here in the park.

It was a waste of time, Hamish was saying.

Rutledge answered, "One of the murder victims sold pipes in a shop. The other was a conductor on an omnibus. What did they have in common, that made them a target?"

"It wilna' be how they earned their living."

"True enough." Rutledge let the dog walk ahead to the base of one of the great trees that had given the park its name. "This was a place where men dueled, once. A long time ago."

"Oh, aye? But to use a garrote properly, you must come from behind. No' face-to-face. It's no' an honorable encounter!"

"A woman, then?"

Hamish answered, thoughtful. "There's no woman, else yon Chief Inspector would ha' had her name by now fra' someone eager to turn her in for prostitution."

"A gaming debt?"

"A warning," Hamish countered.

And that, thought Rutledge, was very likely the case. A warning to stay in line—or die.

But for what? From whom?

He had come to the end of the park, Buckingham Palace gleaming in soot-streaked glory in the late-afternoon sun. His father had brought him here as a child to watch the Changing of the Guard. The ceremony had impressed him, and for a week he'd wanted nothing more than to be a soldier, with a bearskin hat. He smiled at the memory. He'd fallen in love with pageantry, not war. Just as so many young men had done in August 1914. And they'd learned the difference soon enough in France.

There was a man leaning against a lamppost, his face shadowed by his hat. Rutledge saw him but kept walking. From where this man stood, he could watch the comings and goings in Green Park, the bare limbs of the trees offering none of the protection of summer's shade.

Rutledge passed him by, ignoring him. A hundred yards farther on, he found a constable and surprised him by handing over the dog to him. And then Rutledge cut through St. James's Park, made his way back again to The Mall, and found a bench from which he could watch the man still leaning against the lamppost.

A low profile.

The wind was cold, and he could feel his feet growing numb, but he sat still, his hat tilted over his eyes as if asleep.

When the man finally left his post and turned away, Rutledge followed at a discreet distance.

3

Felicity never discovered why Matthew went to walk on the shale beach below the breakwater that morning. He enjoyed strolling by the sea. It was, he'd often said, a way of clearing his mind. The fact that he'd made it a habit of late had begun to worry her.

She'd heard nothing by breakfast, and ate her meal in anxious silence, pretending that it was normal for her husband not to join her when he had business of his own in the town. By ten o'clock when there was no word, she began to grow uneasy. She went to find his diary to be certain he'd had nothing scheduled for the day. She couldn't settle to anything, moving from task to task, humming to herself to pretend all was well. But it was a farce, and failed to comfort her.

While Nan, the maid, was dusting the stairs, Felicity slipped out to look for the motorcar, and saw it was still in its shed. The horse that drew the dogcart had been fed, the stable mucked out, chores Matthew always dealt with before breakfast. The cart was there where it always was. Nothing had changed.

He couldn't have returned from his walk. If there'd been someone at the door, she'd have heard it.

Matthew wasn't in the gardens. He wasn't in the house. A mist still concealed the Mole from view but she thought it was beginning to lift.

And no one had come to tell her that something had happened to him.

He couldn't simply disappear—could he? She remembered those frightful landslips that occurred from time to time along the coast just west of here, when an entire cliff face could vanish into the sea. She shivered at the thought of never knowing what had become of him. Then scolded herself for letting her imagination exaggerate her fear.

By eleven, she was verging on real anxiety, pacing the floor, listening for the sound of the latch lifting or a familiar footfall in the hall. Listening for the knocker to sound.

Where was Matthew?

She had just gone up to her room for her coat and hat when she heard the knocker clanging hard against the plate on the door.

Felicity stood still for a moment, her heart thudding. And then, calling to Nan that she'd see to it, she flew down the stairs, almost flinging herself at the door, pulling it open with such force it startled the constable standing there.

"Mrs. Hamilton?" he said, as if he didn't know her at all.

"Yes, Constable Jordan, what is it? I was just on the point of going out—"

He cut across her words. "It's your husband, Mrs. Hamilton."

His tone of voice as much as Matthew's name stopped her in her tracks, one hand outstretched as if to ward off the blow that was coming.

"He's dead." She said it so flatly that Constable Jordan stared at her.

"No, madam—"

The relief was almost more than she could bear. "No," she repeated.

"Here!" For an instant he thought she was going to faint before his eyes, and he reached out for her arm. "Steady on! He's badly injured, but he's not dead." *Yet,* he added to himself. "They've sent me to take you to him, I can drive if you like."

"Drive. Yes, he doesn't have the car, does he?" She was bewildered, trying to understand. "Where is he? At Dr. Granville's surgery?"

"Yes, madam."

"Stop calling me madam!" she told him irritably. "You know my name, I'm not a stranger! Wait, I was just getting my coat—"

"Where were you going, if I may ask?"

"To look for him, of course. He hasn't been home since early morning." And she was already on her way up the stairs, ignoring what Jordan was saying to her back. In a flash she was back with her coat, and it wasn't until she stepped into the motorcar that she realized she'd forgotten her hat.

Inspector Bennett knocked on the door of the house that was set above the little stream meandering down to the town through a broad valley. It had once been a major river, this forlorn little stream, but over the centuries it had silted up, and farmers had taken advantage of the fertile soil to carve out pasture and tillage. More a pretty cottage than a house, really, Bennett found himself thinking as he stood there, left behind when one of the more prosperous farmers had built his family a grander home upstream. Restored in the

1890s by a man retiring from service in India, it was what all ex-patriots seemed to dream of: wisteria-covered doorway, sweetly blooming in the spring, thatched roof hanging low, whitewashed stucco over stone, and behind a white fence, a front garden that in summer was filled with flowers that loved the cooler English weather—lupine and roses and sweet william and larkspur, with hollyhocks towering over the lot. The kind of garden his own grandmother had had, come to that.

There was no answer to his knock, and he tried again.

The cottage was actually outside Bennett's jurisdiction, set a good half mile from the town's inland boundaries. He was within his rights to be here, due to the nature of events, and the charge would be murder soon enough.

The door seemed to open reluctantly, and Stephen Mallory stuck his head out. He was unshaven, and smelled of whiskey. Bennett made a mental note of that, examining Mallory's eyes. They were bloodshot, and there was a cut on his cheekbone under the left one. But Mallory was fully dressed.

"That's a nasty cut, sir. How did you come by it?"

"I don't know. I think I fell out of bed. What do you want?"

"It's in connection with a body we found this morning. Might I come in, sir?"

"A body?" Mallory seemed to gather his wits. "Here? You mean in Hampton Regis?"

"Yes, sir."

"Not the war, then . . ." He wiped a hand across his mouth, relief evident. He'd dreamed—but let it go.

"No, sir."

Mallory stepped out onto the vine-covered porch, his eyes wary now. "What body?"

"I'd rather talk inside, if you don't mind, sir."

"Why? There's no one here to listen, saving the occasional sparrow. What body?"

It was Bennett's turn to feel reluctance. "An early riser found the body of a man down by the breakwater."

Mallory seemed to relax. "Washed ashore, you mean?"

"No, sir, though the tide had nearly taken him. He hadn't been in the water long, as far as we could tell."

"What's it to do with me, then?"

"You sometimes take an early walk along the water or the cliffs. Did you do either today?"

"You mean, did I see the body and not report it. No, I didn't walk this morning. I was—under the weather. Does this body have a name? Or do you want me to identify him, if I can? Is that why you're here?"

Standing face-to-face with Mallory, Bennett found it difficult to measure his man. It would have been more useful—and more comfortable—inside, where he could have sat across the room and watched the play of emotions.

"We've identified the victim, sir. But I'd like to ask you a few questions first, if I may. Can you tell me where you were last evening and early this morning?"

Mallory was nothing if not quick. The truth began to dawn on him, and there was something in his eyes that startled the inspector. Relief? Anger, certainly, and then something else. A very real fear.

"He's dead, you say?"

"I haven't said," Bennett responded. "If you'll just answer my questions—"

"It's Matthew Hamilton they've found, isn't it?" For an instant Bennett thought Mallory was going to take the lapels of his coat and shake the answer out of him. *"Isn't it!"*

"Why should you think that, sir?" Bennett asked, keeping his tone level, unchallenging.

But Stephen Mallory was already out the door, shoving him aside and racing toward the bicycle that Bennett had left against the gatepost.

He caught the handlebars, dragged the bicycle with him,

and opening the door, tossed it high and into the rear of his motorcar. He wheeled to reach the crank, but Bennett was there, trying to catch him around the shoulders and wrestle him to the ground. Mallory threw him off with the strength of a madman, Bennett thought, as he found himself hitting a fence post with a crack that made his head swim.

It was all the time Mallory needed. He'd brought the engine to life with the crank and was already stepping into the motorcar when Bennett charged him again, tackling him around the hips. Mallory kicked out with his free leg, bracing himself with the frame of the door and the steering wheel. Bennett's breath came out in a long *whoosh!* Then Mallory was free and throwing himself into the driver's seat, reaching for the gears.

He had just time enough to swing the door shut when Bennett, still game, though breathing hard and struggling to keep on his feet, leaped for the door.

Mallory gunned the motor, shifted into first and then as fast as he dared into second, dragging Inspector Bennett with him as the motorcar jumped forward like a horse under the whip. Fighting for control of the wheel, Mallory drove on, weaving at first and then more smoothly as his tires hit the lane and caught.

Bennett, holding on for dear life, was being dragged, his grunts of pain and anger jerked from his body as he bounced beside the car. But then his grip slipped and Mallory hammered with his fist on the other hand still clinging to the door.

Bennett fell off with a wild yell, and then screamed as the rear tire bumped over his foot.

Mallory didn't stop. There was only one thought in his head now. Reaching Felicity before she could hear the news from anyone else.

4

Felicity sat by her husband's bed in the small examining room near the garden door of the surgery, where Dr. Granville treated his more serious cases.

Next to the bed were rolls of bandaging and a pan filled with bloody water, a sponge on the floor beside it and a pair of scissors next to that.

Matthew Hamilton, lying naked on the sheet, seemed to be wrapped in gauze and tape. His face was covered, although she could just see the cut lip and the thickening bruise on his chin. One arm was entirely swathed, and there was more bandaging around his chest and on one thigh.

His color was ghastly, she thought, catching his good hand in hers and holding it tight.

"Matthew," she whispered, trying to keep her voice steady against the shock of seeing him like this. "Matthew, it's me. Can you hear me? *Oh, darling, can you hear me!*"

But there was only silence from the quiet figure on the bed. Dr. Granville, behind her, said impatiently, "I told you not to come in—"

She whirled on him, her face twisting with fear and anger. "He's my *husband*!"

As if it explained anything. Anything at all.

"Come sit in my office." Granville was trying persuasion now. "Until I've had a chance to finish my examination. You mustn't interfere. There could be internal bleeding, for one thing—" He caught himself before he added *brain damage*.

"Why can't he hear me? God in heaven, you'd think he would know *my* voice, no matter how hurt he is!"

"He's not conscious, Mrs. Hamilton. I've tried to explain—it was a severe beating about the head. One arm is broken. There's a deep bruise on his thigh. At least two ribs cracked as well. That's as far as I've got. For his sake, he's better off out of his pain just now. I can't administer any other relief until I know how his brain is affected. If you'll just sit there in my office . . ."

She held on to Hamilton's hand as if it were a lifeline. "I want to be here, not somewhere else. He's going to be all right, isn't he? And I want to be here when he wakes up."

Granville thought, *She's hardly heard a word I've said to her.* Aloud, he went on, "I don't need two patients on my hands, Mrs. Hamilton. Think what's best for your husband."

Still she refused to let go.

He ignored her then, concentrating on running his hands over the broken body in front of him, watching the thin trickle of blood that had begun to appear at the corner of Hamilton's mouth.

There was a commotion out front, and Mrs. Granville came to the door. "Doctor. Inspector Bennett is here. I think you ought to have a look at his foot—"

Granville glanced at her. "I'm busy!" he snapped.

"All the same," she answered, and was gone.

After a moment, he sighed and walked quietly out the door. When his wife insisted, he had learned to pay heed.

In the examining room behind his office Granville found Inspector Bennett hunched in a chair, his face gray with pain, his eyes blazing with what appeared to be impotent fury.

Dr. Granville looked down at the man's foot, and his attention sharpened. His wife had removed Bennett's boot, and the stocking was humped with the swelling. *Broken*—

He knelt by the inspector and his wife handed him a pair of scissors to cut away the policeman's stocking. Bennett was biting his lip, forcing down a groan of pain. "Had to drag the bloody thing half a mile before I could find help," he managed at last, then glanced at the doctor's wife. "Begging your pardon, ma'am."

"What happened?" Granville asked, looking at the discolored ankle and twisted metatarsals.

The constable standing woodenly beside the inspector, his face without expression, waited.

Bennett said in a growl, "That bast— That devil ran over me!"

"Motorcar?" The inspector nodded, and Granville went on, "It will hurt, but I need to run my hands here—and there." He began gently, and Bennett all but screamed when the doctor pressed on the raised area just ahead of the big, calloused toes.

"Dislocated, I think. Your foot must have been on its side when the tire compressed it. Into sand, I would guess— any harder surface and the entire foot would have been crushed."

"Yes, sand," Bennett answered between clenched teeth.

"And I think *this* bone took the brunt and is probably

broken." He looked up, nodding at his wife, and she disappeared into the back, reappearing almost immediately with a basin of soapy water and a cloth.

Dr. Granville began to bathe the injured area, keeping his hands away from the part that hurt the most. Then he proceeded to bandage the entire foot, glancing again at his wife as he worked.

"For right now, swollen as it is—and will be—it's most important to stay off your feet entirely. But if you can't—" He turned, and his wife set a pair of crutches into his hands. "If you can't, then use these. Don't walk at all until the swelling is down. I'm quite serious. Elevate your foot on a stool, and soak it in this—" His wife passed him a small packet of crystals. "Bandages and all, every two hours and again before you go to bed. After that we'll see. I'll come round to the house after my dinner and have another look at that bone."

Mrs. Granville stood smiling at her husband's back, as if he'd worked a miracle for the inspector.

"Crutches?" Bennett demanded. "Can't you just set it, put some plaster over it, and let me be about my business?"

"You're not to put your weight on that foot, Bennett. Do you hear me? Not until I can look at it again. Who did this to you? Mrs. Blackwood?"

Mrs. Blackwood had learned to drive her husband's motorcar when he hadn't come home from France. She was a terror on the roadway, her control minimal and her attention seldom on the mechanics of driving.

The silent constable smothered a grin.

"Mrs. Blackwood?" Bennett said, almost snarling. "What has she to do with it? No, it was that—that—" Words failed him. "I was trying to bring in Mallory, in connection with Mr. Hamilton's thrashing. Mrs. Granville tells me Hamilton's still alive but not speaking. More's the pity. All he has to do is nod his head to a question or two, and I'll have my man."

Granville said sharply, "You think Stephen Mallory is behind this beating? Surely not!"

"Then why did he nearly break my neck, and run over my foot in his hurry to get away from me? When I set eyes on him again, it's charges he'll be hearing, assaulting a police officer with intent to do bodily harm, suspicion of attempted murder, and anything else I can think of. I'd almost wish Hamilton dead, to make it murder."

"You don't believe that!" Granville answered him, indignant. "Why should Mallory want to kill Hamilton—I understood they were friends."

"Because," Bennett exclaimed, his voice raised in fury, "he covets Hamilton's wife. Didn't you *know*? It's the gossip all over town."

Granville saw the inspector, hobbling unsteadily on his crutches and in a foul temper, out of the surgery. For a moment he watched the man down the walk, then cautioned the hovering constable to keep out of Bennett's way. His face thoughtful, the doctor turned and strode back to Hamilton's room.

He stepped across the threshold, an apology for the delay on his lips. And found his patient alone.

Mrs. Hamilton had gone out through the garden door, leaving it half ajar.

Granville bent over Matthew Hamilton's broken body, listening to his uneasy breathing. To the doctor's practiced eye, his patient's condition remained unchanged. And if his wife's voice hadn't roused him, it was safe to say that no one could, for several more hours at the very least. The body found its own methods of healing, often enough, and a wise medical man learned to leave it to work its own miracle. He was almost grateful for Bennett's injury, to keep the man out of the sickroom with his loud, badgering demands for answers and information.

"You have twenty-four hours of peace. Make the most of them," he added softly to the silent, bandaged man. "After that, I shall have to find another way of keeping the inspector at bay."

Straightening, Granville looked toward the open door just behind him. Bits of conversation reached him down the passage. Two women in the midst of what must have been a lively discussion in one of the other rooms. His wife speaking to someone in his office, though he could only make out every other word. There was a rumble of a reply, then as the man raised his voice, Granville caught the end of the sentence. ". . . if you wouldn't mind, Missus."

Had Mrs. Hamilton overheard any of his exchange with Inspector Bennett? The man had all but shouted at times, his anger getting the better of him. Had she heard Bennett accuse Stephen Mallory of trying to murder her husband? Was that why she left so abruptly, after hovering over Hamilton, nearly in tears?

He silently repeated Bennett's last comment. *He covets Hamilton's wife. Didn't you know? It's the gossip all over town!*

Dr. Granville found himself wondering how much of that was true.

Felicity Hamilton walked quickly through the streets without taking any notice of where she was going. First one shock and then the other. She wasn't sure she could deal with either of them. She couldn't stop thinking about Matthew lying there on the narrow bed of the doctor's surgery, looking like a dead man. Bruised, battered, his bones broken—it hurt to imagine what he'd endured.

She hadn't thought to ask who had discovered him lying on the strand. Why hadn't she gone searching for him herself? Everyone knew he enjoyed walking along the tideline after a storm, looking for treasures washed ashore. Not that he ever found many—but he'd bring home a bit of driftwood or a smoothed shard of brown glass with the wide grin of a boy who had been out without leave, offering his tokens in the hope of avoiding a scolding. Wrapped in a sea mist, he particularly liked to stand at the edge of the sea listening to the waves break and roll toward him. And there had been a sea mist this morning, filling the gardens with a soft white veil, smothering all sound as it swathed trees and walls with a pale dampness.

People would say she ought to have known—

Tears ran down her face. She loved him more than she'd ever told him. And if he died, and didn't know, it was her fault.

She refused to consider Bennett's claim that Stephen had attacked him. It was too bizarre, too unbelievable. And yet she *had* almost believed it, in the first shock of hearing Inspector Bennett's bold accusation. It had torn at her heart and the icy truth of guilt had swept her.

You can't love two men. Not in the same way. For God's sake, it's not possible!

The gates to the drive loomed ahead, small things, decorative, hardly intended to keep intruders out or love inside. She had no recollection of how she had got this far, or how long it had taken her. Her feet had guided her home. That was all that mattered. Had anyone spoken to her? She'd been deaf and blind, absorbed in her own misery.

Home.

The graceful tiled plate on the gatepost mocked her. *Casa Miranda.* The name of a house where Matthew had lived in one of his postings. He'd liked it, he'd told her, and had carried it with him ever after. She had wanted to name the house on the hill *Windsong*, but he'd laughed and said that was commonplace and she'd soon grow to like Miranda better. It meant Vantage Point, he said, but it still sounded foreign to her, like a woman's name. Wasn't there a Miranda in one of Shakespeare's plays?

She all but ran up the drive, her gaze on the door, and then stopped short.

Why had she come back to the house? Why hadn't she gone to search for Stephen?

She didn't know the answer to that. Except that she'd run home like a hurt child to hide her face in her mother's skirts.

Or—yes, she did know why she hadn't searched—she hadn't wanted to look into his face and read shame and guilt and love there.

For an instant she debated going back to the doctor's surgery, but her feet were once more carrying her toward the front door, not down the way she had come. After what she'd heard, she couldn't bear to face any of them. She was sure Granville's wife had never liked her. This would only give Mrs. Granville more fodder for gossip. What Bennett had said would be all over Hampton Regis before the day was out. If no one believed it before, everyone would believe it now.

Opening her door, she realized it was Nan's day to clean—she'd forgotten that Nan was here when the constable had knocked. Well, she'd just have to send the maid home, she couldn't bear having someone there, in the house, moving about. She needed to think.

Stepping from the bright morning into the dimly lit foyer, she once again stopped dead in her tracks.

"Matthew?" she said to the ghost of him sitting at the bottom of the staircase. A sudden fear swept her. *Had he died without her there to hold his hand? Had she left him to die and he'd come to chide her?*

But it wasn't Matthew's ghost, it was Stephen, very much alive.

She watched his face crumple as he read the shock in her face. "How is he?" he asked, his voice husky. "For God's sake, tell me he's still alive?"

"He's alive," she heard herself saying. "But he's so—*I've never seen anyone that badly hurt.*"

"Thank God. Bennett told me they'd found a body—I thought—"

Felicity shut the door and leaned against it, her legs refusing to hold her up. "What are you doing here? The police—Bennett's foot may be broken, did you know that?"

"I'm sorry. He tried to stop me, it was his own doing. I had to come here, I had to tell you that I didn't harm Matthew. I didn't touch him, Felicity! I would never have touched him. Tell me you believe me?"

He got to his feet, standing there with such pain in his eyes that she couldn't bear to see it.

"Felicity—"

He put out his hand, begging.

"Please, Felicity. *I didn't hurt him!*"

She took a deep shuddering breath. "I don't know what to think anymore. If you were innocent, why didn't you let Bennett question you? Why did you run him down?"

"I didn't run him down. He was clinging to the door of the car, and wouldn't let go. When he couldn't hold on any longer, he dropped the wrong way. I couldn't have stopped if I'd had angels holding the motorcar back. All I could think of was that I had to see you, had to tell you that I didn't touch Matthew."

"Then who did?" she asked wearily.

"I don't know. I'm going to find out, I promise you that."

"Oh, Stephen—" Her voice broke.

He stepped forward, intending to comfort her, and then turned away. "For God's sake, don't cry."

"Don't cry?" she repeated through her tears. "Matthew's probably dying, and I'm *here*, instead of *there*, and I love you both, and I don't want anything to happen to either of you. Why can't we just be happy, and not think of anything else but that?"

"Because I love you," he told her bluntly. "And God help me, I can't stop."

5

Rutledge, following his quarry through the busy London streets, kept a good distance between himself and the man who had been leaning against the lamppost.

Old Bowels would have his head on a platter if he was wrong. Hamish was busy reminding him of that. But instinct told him he wasn't wrong. The man's interest had been too intense. Too personal.

His quarry moved briskly, but without the illusion of hurrying. They were into Kensington now, shops and flats on one side, the palace grounds on the other. At length the man turned down a side street, walked four houses from the corner, turned up the steps, and let himself in the door.

Rutledge stayed where he was. It was an old trick, walking into a building and waiting to see who was behind you. And if someone *was* there, he was often gullible enough to keep on going, right past the window where you watched. And you simply stepped out when he was past and went quietly in the opposite direction.

But after half an hour, no one had come out the front door, and Rutledge was swearing with certainty that his quarry had gone out the back and disappeared.

He had resigned himself to losing the man altogether, just as his quarry stepped out of the door again, looked both ways, and then came toward Rutledge.

"Whist!" Hamish warned in his ear.

There was nothing for it but to disappear into the door at his shoulder, and Rutledge found himself in a tobacconist's, the aroma of cigars strong in the confines of the small, paneled shop.

"May I help you, sir?"

He turned to find an elderly clerk behind the counter, staring at him.

If he confessed to being a policeman, Rutledge thought, it would be all over the neighborhood before tea.

And then his quarry came around the corner and opened the door to the shop.

Rutledge quickly said to the clerk, "I'm looking for a Mrs. Channing—"

It was the first name that came into his head.

"Channing? I don't believe I know any Channings hereabouts. Mr. Fields, is it a name you're familiar with?"

And Rutledge, turning, found himself confronting the observer at the lamppost.

His face was scarred, giving it a bitter twist, the slate blue eyes wary, the mouth tight.

"Channings? No, I can't think of any. Sorry."

Rutledge had no option. He thanked the man and the clerk and went out the shop door into the street. He made a pretense of standing there, looking first one way and then the other, as if uncertain what to do next. Hamish, in the back of his mind, said, "Ye canna' loiter."

Rutledge snapped, "You needn't tell me." He turned back

the way he'd come and moved on, wondering where the constable whose patch this was might have taken himself.

He found a pub one street away, and went inside.

"Do you know where I might find Constable—" He left the name open.

The barkeep's face was closed. "Constable Waddington? May I ask why you're looking for him? Is there trouble?"

"There's been a break-in at a neighbor's house, I've been sent to find him."

"Well, then—he's just stepped over to Mrs. Whittier's house, sir. He—er—he looks in on her from time to time."

"And where do I find Mrs. Whittier?" Rutledge asked patiently.

"On Linton Street, around the next corner but one. You can't miss it, number forty-one. If I may ask, whose house has had a break—"

But Rutledge was gone before the man had finished his question.

The Whittier house was no more than a stairwell-and-a-room wide. He went up the front steps and knocked firmly at the door.

A woman answered the summons, her face a little flushed, her curling fair hair more than a little mussed.

"Mrs. Whittier?"

"Yes?" Her voice was rather breathless, and her manner dismissive, as if he had no business knocking at her door at this hour of the day.

"I'm looking for Constable Waddington. Will I find him here?"

The flush deepened. "Oh—yes. He was just—he was just helping me with the—attic door. I couldn't shift it at all, and my trunk is in there—"

But Rutledge was already moving past her into the house.

"Waddington!" he bellowed, and the constable came hurrying to the top of the stairs, buttoning his tunic at the neck.

"Who are you?" the constable retorted. "And what do you want of me?"

"Inspector Rutledge, Scotland Yard. Come down here and get on with your duty."

Waddington moved swiftly down the steps, straightening his tunic as he came, and brought up short at the foot of the stairs. Braced for a reprimand and worse. The skin around his eyes was tight with apprehension. He was a short, thin man, with a ruddy complexion, as flushed now as Mrs. Whittier's.

Rutledge said, "I need you to identify someone for me. Hurry!"

Relief flooded Waddington's face, and he cast a swift glance at the woman watching anxiously. A wordless warning.

Rutledge was out the door with Waddington at his heels, and they had hardly reached the bottom step before the house door swung quietly shut, the latch turned.

"I'm sorry, sir. Mrs. Whittier is a widow woman and—"

"—the attic door wouldn't budge."

Waddington trotted beside him, attempting to keep up. "Er, yes, sir."

"There's a man called Fields who appears to live on Swan Street, the fourth house down. The tobacconist knew him by name. Do you?"

Waddington responded, "Scarred face, tall?"

"Yes."

"That's his sister's house. He's been living there since her husband was killed last month. A widow, three small children—"

"What happened to her husband? What's his name?"

They had nearly reached the tobacconist's shop on the corner.

"Greene, sir. He was murdered. By person or persons unknown."

Someone had known. Whether the inquest had been aware of it or not.

"Any reason for the killing?"

"Money, sir. A scheme that went wrong, one that was to make his fortune. Only he was taken advantage of and lost everything instead. All his savings. This according to the widow at the inquest. All the same, she couldn't name the man who tricked him. Greene had kept his dealings to himself, wanting to surprise her, he said. She begged him to go to the police, but the next day he turned up hanging from a tree along the Thames. His killer tried to make it look like suicide, but it didn't wash. He'd been garroted first."

And the men in Green Park had been garroted.

They had stopped at the corner, and Rutledge indicated the house in question. "Is that where Greene lived, and Fields now lives with his sister?"

"Yes, sir."

"Then let's walk on, shall we? As if we're looking for someone else."

As they went on up the road, Waddington said, "What's this in aid of, sir? Why are you asking about Mr. Fields? Do you think *he* committed the murder?"

"No. But I think he's been out for revenge."

A cab came along and Rutledge hailed it. "I want you to maintain a close watch on Fields for me. If there's any change in his circumstances, call me at once. Or Sergeant Gibson, failing that. Meanwhile, keep this to yourself. I don't want gossip in the canteen or the shops. Do you understand?"

"Yes, sir. Am I to do anything else?"

"Yes. Stay away from Mrs. Whittier while you're on duty."

When he reached the Yard, Rutledge learned that Chief Superintendent Bowles was well on his way to an apoplexy, and screaming for Rutledge's blood.

6

Stephen Mallory stood there at the foot of the stairs, staring helplessly at the woman weeping in front of him. "No, I didn't mean that. I've put that all behind me. Felicity!"

Before she could answer, the maid, Nan, appeared at the top of the steps.

"Mrs. Hamilton?" she asked. "Is everything all right?"

"No—yes—" Felicity said, wiping her face with her gloved hands. "Thank you, Nan. I've just had bad news, that's all."

"Not your mother—" Nan said, her strong face registering alarm. "Oh, not your mother, ma'am."

"She's—it's Mr. Hamilton. I'll explain later. Could you find some tea for us, please? We'll be in the sitting room."

She walked briskly toward the rear of the house, and into a room that looked out on the sea. It was filled with windows, two pairs on the front and one pair on the side, and seemed to glow with the reflected light of the sun on the water.

Vantage Point. It was certainly that.

Sinking into a chair, she said, "Shut the door. What are we to do? Bennett will be here before we know it, after your blood. Casa Miranda is the first place he'll look. And I must go back to Matthew." Her voice broke again. "I don't know whether to believe you or not. Matthew hasn't an enemy in the world, I can't imagine why anyone should attack him like that, except in anger." Looking up at him, she added irritably, "Do sit down, Stephen! I'm not accusing you, I'm just terribly confused, and worried and frightened. What have you done with your motorcar?"

"It's in your shed, where Bennett or his men can't see it from the road." Stephen took the chair farthest from her. "Felicity, what good would it possibly do me to hurt Matthew?" He cleared his throat. "Look, even if I did away with Matthew, do you think I'd be fool enough to believe I'd have you then? That you'd forget him and walk off into the rainbow with me? What good would it do me to hurt Matthew, for God's sake—it would be like hurting *you*."

"Bennett won't believe you. You ran, Stephen; it was the worst thing you could do."

"I told you, I ran to you, not from him. That was uppermost in my mind, making sure you didn't believe what he was saying. I'll find Bennett now and apologize and let him ask me whatever it is he wants to ask me."

"He'll take you into custody. And there'll be no end of fuss. They'll drag our names through God knows what scandal, and in the end, it will be impossible to show our faces anywhere. I *heard* him raving in Dr. Granville's office—" She stopped, unwilling to repeat to Mallory what had been said. "You can't imagine how furious he is, how determined he is to blame you."

"When Matthew comes to his senses, he'll be able to tell them what happened—who did this to him."

She looked at him. "What if he didn't see his attacker? What if he doesn't remember what happened? What if he dies without waking up? What then?"

Stephen wheeled to the window, blind to the distant sea glimmering at the bottom of the lawns, and gulls wheeling above a fishing boat pulling for shore. *What would Matthew do when he was in his right mind again? And if he couldn't remember, what would he think? Whom would he believe? Bennett?*

He turned back to Felicity, trying to stifle the fear rising in him. He said, with more force than he felt, "He's bound to remember. He's a stubborn old bird, he'll come through this, Felicity, wait and see."

"I must go back to the surgery. What will you do—"

She broke off as Nan came in with the tea tray. The woman's eyes were busy, moving from her mistress's face to Stephen Mallory's as she tried to make sense of the strained relations between them. There was an avidness as well, and Stephen frowned. What he saw worried him, and his first thought was that Nan would go rushing off to the police, given the chance.

He got up hastily and took the tray from her, saying, "Thank you, Nan, that will be all for now."

The maid reluctantly withdrew, and after she had gone, Stephen went silently to the door and pulled it open suddenly, expecting to find her there, listening. But she was not in the passage.

Felicity was trying to pour the tea with shaking hands and sloshed half of hers into the saucer.

Stephen gently took the teapot from her, dabbed at her saucer with his handkerchief, then gave her the clean cup, adding sugar and milk to it.

She drank it thirstily, as if it was a panacea for her problems.

"I can't think. My mind's a blur," she said, setting her cup down at last. "I wish none of this had happened, I wish it was all a bad dream and there was no truth in any of it, I wish—"

There was a pounding at the front door.

They stared at each other.

"Bennett." Stephen said the name with despair, then added rapidly, "Felicity, if *you* believe I'm telling you the truth, that's all that matters."

But she was at the sitting room door ahead of him. "Never mind, Nan, I'll see to it," she called. And then turning back to Stephen, she said, "There's the revolver in Matthew's desk. Top drawer. *Quickly!*"

Stephen turned to the desk under the windows at the side of the room, opened the drawer, and found the weapon lying there under a handful of papers.

"Come with me," Felicity added, all but pulling at him. "Hurry, to the door!"

The pounding was louder, filling the house with noise.

"I'm not shooting a policeman."

"No, come on, Stephen, *hurry!*"

Nan had stepped out of the kitchen passage, half hidden by the morning shadows in that corner of the hall, her inquisitiveness narrowing her eyes as she peered toward the door. Then she saw the weapon in Stephen's hand and cried out.

Felicity said rapidly, "Hold the revolver against my back. *Do as I say!*"

But Stephen was already there, the weapon pointed at her even as he prayed it was empty. Driven by the strident pounding, he refused to think beyond this moment, beyond the need to protect Felicity from any appearance of collusion in the tangle he'd made of things.

She reached the front door and called out, "Who is it?"

Her voice quivered, but she had herself under control. Mallory marveled at her.

"Inspector Bennett. Open the door, Mrs. Hamilton."

"I can't," she cried. "I can't. Please go away before he shoots me!"

Stephen flinched, unprepared for her dramatic pronouncement. He kept his finger away from the trigger, bile filling his throat with a fear that had nothing to do with Felicity or the inspector. Put the barrel into his mouth and end the torment, that's all he had to do. . . . But not here, not in front of *her*.

There was silence on the other side of the door. Then, "Is Stephen Mallory with you, Mrs. Hamilton?"

"Yes, he's right behind me."

"Is he armed, Mrs. Hamilton?"

"Yes—yes, he has my husband's revolver. Please don't open that door!"

She could hear Bennett speaking rapidly to one of the men with him, then heard them speculating among themselves. Stephen seemed turned to stone behind her.

"My maid is here too. Please go away. *Please.*" The anxiety in her voice was genuine, her need to be rid of them pressing her into real fear.

"Very well, Mrs. Hamilton," another voice said. "But we'll be back. And I'd advise Mr. Mallory that it would be in his own best interest to give himself up quietly. There's no need to subject you to more horror."

"I understand."

She thought she could hear them moving away to the drive, still talking among themselves. Bennett would be furious at being thwarted a second time, he wasn't a man to take frustration in his stride and try to deal with it sensibly. She could feel her heart thudding in her chest, realizing only then that she'd made matters worse for herself and for Mallory.

Behind her Stephen was exclaiming hoarsely, "What have you done? In heaven's name, Felicity, do you want to see me hang?"

They locked Nan into one of the rooms in the servants' quarters, where a butler had kept a cot, then went up the stairs into the sitting room again.

Stephen, drained, sat down heavily in the chair by the window. Realizing he still held the revolver, he gingerly set it on the desk and leaned back again.

"Stephen," Felicity was saying gently, "Stephen, no, listen to me. They aren't going to treat you fairly. Bennett is vindictive at best. He'll have you up on a charge of attempted murder, and if Matthew dies—"

She broke off, her face horrified. "I can't go back to Matthew. I can't go back to sit with him."

"You should have thought of that before you got me into this muddle."

"But Nan had seen you. I couldn't pretend you weren't here. She'd have told them everything she knows and made up the rest. You don't know her. All I could think of was that Nan must surely have heard you say you still loved me. It's all they needed to be told, Bennett was already saying at the surgery that you and I—" She stopped. "What have I *done*?"

"I don't see any way out of this." He glanced toward the revolver. "It would solve everything if I just went into the garden and ended it, and let them think what they like."

Felicity was out of her chair, picking up the revolver and shoving it into the desk drawer again, turning the key and then putting it in her pocket.

"No, don't ever say that again. We'll find a way. Matthew's man of business—we can ask to speak to him, and tell him the truth."

"He's never liked you, Felicity. You know that as well as I do."

It was true. Mr. Caldwell had had his hands on Matthew's fortune for years, managing it while Hamilton was out of the country. He blamed Felicity for the fact that Hamilton had retired early and demanded an accounting. She'd always wondered if he had made free with the funds from time to time, when his own accounts were in arrears. If that was true, he'd covered his tracks by the time Matthew resumed management of his money.

He would like nothing better than to watch Matthew Hamilton's wife begging him to defend her former lover. And then refuse her pleas.

"Where else can we turn?" She considered the rector and the vestry members, rejecting them one by one. They would hardly defy the police on her account.

For the first time she realized how foolish she'd been to antagonize the people Matthew had tried to cultivate in his new circumstances. Unaccustomed to the narrowness of village life, she'd been quickly bored by the people here, and with them, and had told herself that soon enough Matthew would be as well. That this would become their country house for the summer months, not their year-round residence. In which case they needn't concern themselves with Hampton Regis's dull pretense at Society.

She had slowly come to understand that he liked this part of England, that he intended to live here because it was where he'd hoped to live in his retirement. It had been too late then to undo the first impression she must have made, and her pride kept her from acknowledging her error to the likes of Miss Trining. But she should have swallowed her pride and made the effort, if need be she should have walked on hot coals barefoot for Matthew's sake. Instead, Matthew's charm had become the key to her acceptance here, and she had no illusions about that now, when she was in need of kindness.

The Restons and Miss Trining and the others would relish watching her being dragged through the mire. It was what happened to older men who lost their heads and married unwisely, they would say. A beauty, perhaps, but look what such beauty came to, in the end. So sordid.

Desperate now, she added, "Someone in London, do you think? Friends of your uncle, the bishop?"

But his uncle the bishop had died in the autumn.

"No, they'd be useless." He paused, then said with obvious reluctance, "Scotland Yard." Even as he did, Stephen Mallory knew what Dr. Beatie would tell him: *Don't open that wound again. You aren't healed yet, you can't take the risk.*

He got to his feet, unable to sit still.

He wouldn't have to deal with the man, surely?

He could just put his case to the Yard, and they'd send someone.

No, they wouldn't, not when they heard what Bennett had to say.

He could feel his body tighten and his mind shut itself away. Even if he sent for the Captain, the man wouldn't come, not when he realized who was asking for help. Yet where else could they turn, he and Felicity, after what he'd done and she had compounded this day?

But not the Captain—please God, not the Captain!

He stood there looking down into Felicity's face, despair sweeping him with such force he felt sick.

For her sake, he had to do something. He must get her out of this nightmare unscathed, whatever the cost. And then he could go into the garden. It wouldn't matter anymore.

He couldn't hide behind her skirts much longer. He shuddered to think what half the town was whispering already.

"Stephen?" Her eyes were pleading with him. "I don't know anyone at Scotland Yard. Do you?"

He held out his hand for the key to the desk. "There's someone—I need stationery, an envelope."

She handed him the key reluctantly, uncertain what he was going to do with it.

He rummaged in the drawer, ignoring the weapon, and drew out several sheets of stationery. Matthew Hamilton's family crest stared back at him, but he ignored it. Felicity pointed out the pen and ink, and he began to write.

After a moment he stopped, tore up the sheet, and began again.

On the third try he appeared to be satisfied. He handed her the sheet while he wrote a direction on the envelope.

She held the sheet of paper like a lifeline, reading and rereading it:

> *Bennett, I refuse to surrender to anyone other than Inspector Ian Rutledge of Scotland Yard. Bring him to me, here, as fast as you can. I won't be had with promises.*

And he'd signed it, simply, *Mallory.*

"Who is this man Rutledge?" she asked, frowning. "A policeman? He'll be sure to side with Inspector Bennett. There must be someone else? Someone in the Foreign Office—they'll take Matthew's side, won't they?" She rubbed her eyes with her hands. "I daren't tell my mother. She's not well. It will kill her."

"You wouldn't know this man. We—we served together in France. And just sending for him will give us a little time, don't you see? When Matthew comes to his senses and tells Bennett the truth, I won't need the Yard or anyone else." It was sheer bravado. His reward was a tiny flicker of hope in her eyes. It faded as quickly as it had flared.

"But will this man travel all the way from *London* just to let you surrender to him? And what if he does? And Matthew is dead and can't ever speak? There must be some other way. We've got to find a *way*."

She looked at him, her face flushed with distress and her eyes filling now with tears. He wanted more than anything to take her in his arms and tell her it would be all right.

If Rutledge wouldn't come, there was always the revolver in the drawer. He had seen the lock. It was flimsy, it could be broken. And when he was dead, Felicity would be safe. She could tell them whatever she pleased, and it wouldn't matter how she must blacken his character.

He said none of that to her. But there was bitterness in his voice when he finally answered her.

"There isn't another way. You should have thought of the consequences before you stopped Inspector Bennett from coming in. It's too late now, we don't have many choices left to us."

7

Bowles was livid.

"Where have you been? Not where you ought to be, that's certain. I sent men to the park to find you. You were away from your *post,* damn it!"

"I think I may have—"

"I don't give a dance in hell what you think, man! You're off the case."

"If you will listen to me—sir—"

"Look at this." Bowles shot a sheet of paper across the desk. "Know this man, do you?"

Rutledge scanned the message. It had come in as a telephone call from the south coast.

> One Stephen Mallory holding two women at point of gun, refuses to surrender to local authorities, will speak only to Inspector Rutledge. Wanted for severely

beating one Matthew Hamilton and leaving him for dead, for assaulting a police officer in the course of his duties, presently threatening to murder his first victim's wife and her maid, if Rutledge does not come in person.

Stephen Mallory. His memory rejected the name. Drew a deliberate blank.

But Hamish said roughly, "Lieutenant Mallory." Reminding him against his will.

The war. So many things came round to the war. He couldn't escape it, no matter where he turned. For him it had really never ended.

He could feel himself sliding back there again. To the trenches, to the Somme. And Lieutenant Mallory, standing in the summer rain, cursing him, cursing the war, cursing the killing. Rutledge could smell the foulness of the mud and the fear of his men, heard the noise that threatened to deafen him—the constant rattle of machine-gun fire and the sharpness of rifle fire and the heavy pounding of the shelling. Men were screaming all around him, and the dead or dying were everywhere he looked, along the top of the trench, under foot, out in the wire and in shell holes. The first day of that bloody battle, when so many men died. Twenty thousand of them *in one day*.

Hamish brought him out of the nightmare, his voice loud in Rutledge's ears. "He was wounded, but they sent him back to the Front."

"Yes," he answered silently.

They had been so short of men. The medical staff had cleared anyone who could still hold a rifle as fit for duty. Days later Rutledge himself had taken his own turn at the aid station, resting a few hours, then getting to his feet and stumbling out of the tent, like a man sleepwalking.

Rutledge remembered Mallory's dazed eyes, the stiffly bandaged shoulder, the fearlessness that had bordered on recklessness. It had turned his salient against the lieutenant, and there had been whispers about him. That he was bad luck. That he got men killed. And Mallory had been hell-bent on proving he was no coward, whatever the doctors had murmured about possible shell shock.

"Missed the bone," he'd told everyone, making light of it. "Still, it aches like the very devil. But nothing for the pain until I've won the war."

And four days later, he had been found crouched in a shell hole, crying softly. This time the wound was in his calf, and he couldn't walk. The stretcher bearers had got him back to the rear, while rumor debated whether he had shot himself or been picked off by one of the new German snipers. Or—by his own men.

They hadn't seen him again.

Bowles was still waiting, searching Rutledge's face.

Dragging himself back to the present, Rutledge looked up at him.

"He was in France."

It was a reply brief to the point of curtness, but it was all he was prepared to say while the Chief Superintendent glared accusingly at him as if he bore the responsibility for whatever had happened along the south coast.

"So was half the male population of Britain in France. Why should this man Mallory summon you in the circumstances? With the war well over?" The suspicion in Bowles's voice was palpable.

"I can't answer that, sir. We weren't—close friends, if that's what you are suggesting. I can't imagine why he should wish to see me now." It was the truth. Rutledge was still recalling more details about Mallory, details stuffed long ago into the bottom of the black well that was nightmare and the war: a gifted officer, yet he lacked the common touch that made tired and exhausted soldiers follow him over the top. Hamish MacLeod had possessed that touch . . . and so, although he had hated it, had he himself. He had felt like a charlatan, a pied piper, using his voice and his experience in command to lure unwilling men to their deaths. A Judas goat, unharmed while so many were slaughtered around him, like cattle at an abattoir.

But Mallory had got out. He had deserted his men and got out.

"Hmmpf." Bowles slammed a drawer shut, taking out his impotent anger on the unoffending desk. "So you say. Well, you'd damned well better get down there and see what this is all about. And you're not to play favorites, you understand me? The man this Mallory is said to have attacked—he's got friends in high places. They'll be howling for my blood and yours if his wife's made free with. You understand me?"

"Are you sending me to—" He glanced down at the message again. "To Hampton Regis?"

"I don't have much choice, do I?"

"Who is the victim, this Matthew Hamilton?" The name was not uncommon.

"Foreign Office, served on Malta before he resigned. Went uninvited to the Peace Conference in Paris, I'm told, and wasn't very popular with his views there. But he's still too bloody important to ignore, and if his wife wants you, she's to have you."

"I thought it was Mallory who asked for me?"

"Don't quibble, Rutledge. Just get yourself down there as soon as may be. I don't want to see your face until this business has been resolved."

"I must speak with Phipps before I go. Sir. There's something he ought to know about the Green Park killings—"

"Phipps is perfectly capable of drawing his own conclusions. I want you in Hampton Regis this night. And I expect you to get to the bottom of this business as fast as you can."

"Sir, there's a man in Kensington—"

"Are you deaf? Leave Phipps to his own affairs and see to yours. That's an order. Good day."

Rutledge turned and walked out of the room.

He'd have given much to know whether Fields had had a hand in the Green Park killings. And for a moment he considered going in search of Sergeant Gibson. But if Bowles got wind of that, the sergeant would find himself caught in the middle.

Rutledge went back to his own office, collected his coat and hat, and made his way out of the building to his motorcar.

If he wrapped up this business in Hampton Regis quickly, he would be back in London in good time to look into the possibilities himself. And he had a strong feeling that Fields wouldn't kill again unless he was pressed.

Rutledge had hoped that chance would throw Sergeant Gibson in his path before he'd left the Yard. It would have been better for both of them if the encounter had come about naturally. He'd taken his time going down the stairs, out the door, listening to voices here and there. But the sergeant was nowhere to be seen. Or heard.

"What if ye're wrong aboot Fields?" Hamish asked. "Ye canna' put him at risk, withoot better proof."

A hunch wasn't proof. A gut feeling wouldn't stand up in court. But in hasty hands either could send an innocent man to die on the gallows. Bowles was right, it was best to step aside and leave the case in Phipps's hands. For the time being. Rutledge turned away from the Yard and drove to Kensington to find Constable Waddington.

If Fields was guilty, he'd still be there when Rutledge got back. And it wouldn't do for Waddington to become the third victim of the Green Park killer simply because Rutledge had put the fear of God into him about Duty.

It was time to call him off. Until there was something he himself could do about Fields.

The drive to the south coast was long and cold. This part of England held bitter memories for Rutledge. He hadn't been to the West Country since last summer. He caught himself thinking about those ghosts in his past, cases he'd dealt with even while he struggled to cope with Hamish MacLeod driving him nearly to suicide. He tried to shut the ghosts out by filling his mind with familiar lines of poetry, then realized that from habit most of them came from a single author. O. A. Manning had been an echo of his war, her poetry locked in his brain because it had touched a nerve at a time when he was grateful for any understanding. He had found that in the slim volumes he carried with him in the trenches, a voice of sanity in the middle of a nightmare. O. A. Manning had reached many men at the Front, though she herself had never set foot in France.

Hamish was taunting him. "You were half in love wi' her."

He wasn't sure whether it was half in love—or caught in her spell.

Still, ever since then, he'd found himself measuring other women by her memory. That had not always been a wise thing to do, for it had drawn him to one woman in particular. And memory had been a false mirror, as he had learned to his sorrow.

Hamish said, his voice unforgiving, "In France I lost Fiona forever. What right do you have to be happy now?"

It was unanswerable. They drove in silence for miles after that, Rutledge forcing his attention to stay on the road ahead and then as night fell, on the sweep of his headlamps marking his path. Traffic had thinned, and at times his vehicle was the only one he saw for long stretches. He passed a lorry once, and later a milk wagon trundling on its way. An owl flitted through the light that guided him, and later what looked like a hunting cat darted to the side of the road, startling him awake.

He kept reminding himself that two lives hung in the balance in Hampton Regis. If he failed, two women might die. And he couldn't be sure—he couldn't be absolutely certain that Mallory would spare them. Not if he was driven to the point of desperation.

Because Rutledge had no idea how Mallory had changed in the past three years. For better or for worse.

He heard a church clock striking the hour as he drove the last winding half mile into the heart of Hampton Regis. Although it was quite late, he found a furious Inspector Bennett waiting impatiently for him in the police station off the harbor road.

"What took you so long? I expect the train would have been quicker."

Rutledge, his shoulders tight from pressing as hard as he had on the roads, said only, "I'm here now." He'd refused to take the trains since he'd come back from France. They were crowded, claustrophobic, leaving him shaken and frantic to get down as soon as possible. A hurtling coffin of metal and wood. He doubted if Bennett would understand that.

"Yes, and I'd like to know what you intend to do about Mallory. Made me look a fool, having to send for you. I manage my own patch, thank you very much, without outside interference."

"I intend to do nothing at the moment." Rutledge glanced down at the man's foot, in a thick and unwieldy cast. "That must be hurting like the very devil. How did it happen?"

He'd been intent on changing the subject but was taken aback by the vehemence of Bennett's retort. "Mallory ran me down, that's what happened. When I went to arrest him, Flung me off the damned motorcar, directly into its path. If I hadn't been quicker, I daresay he'd have been glad to see me dead under his wheels."

The note had said something about Mallory assaulting a police officer, but Rutledge had assumed there had been a brief exchange of blows or a shoving match.

Such violence put an entirely different complexion on the coming confrontation. And it seemed to underline Mallory's guilt in attacking Hamilton.

He'd hoped to wait for daylight, for his own sake as well as to give Mallory time to rethink his position. After all, there had been no set timetable for his arrival, and darkness often put fears and decisions into uncomfortable perspective. Men brooded in the night, and were grateful for sanity in the morning.

"Are you up to answering questions?" he asked Bennett now. "I'll need a better picture of events than was available at the Yard. For one thing, has anything changed in Mallory's situation? Are the women still safe? Has he tried to harm either of them?"

They walked back to Bennett's office. Bennett sank into his chair like a man in pain, easing the injured foot out of the way of his single crutch. Rutledge took the only other chair.

It was a tiny room, hardly wide enough for the desk, the chairs, and the two men. From the scatter of papers across the desktop, Rutledge could see that his counterpart was not a tidy man, more impetuous than organized, and likely to have a temperament to match.

Bennett shuffled irritably at the papers, turning some, shoving others aside, creating a small avalanche that he caught just before it went over the edge. The near mishap did nothing for his mood.

Hamish said, "He'll no' help you, if he isna' forced to."

"A facade," Rutledge answered silently. "That's all I'm expected to be. But we'll see about that."

Bennett was saying, "There's not much to tell. Matthew Hamilton—you probably know the name, coming as you do from London—was walking on the strand early this morning in a heavy sea mist. Apparently it's something he does to help him think. That's what one of the other vestry members told me. Miss Trining, that was. At any rate, someone came up behind him, footsteps no doubt muffled by the incoming tide, and struck him down. While he was still dazed, his attacker hit him repeatedly with something heavy, a stick, a cane, a bit of flotsam—who knows? By the time someone saw him lying there and summoned help, Hamilton's feet were awash, and all tracks had vanished. If no one had seen him in time, he might well have drowned in another quarter hour."

Matthew Hamilton . . . Rutledge cudgeled his tired wits. His sister had spoken of the man from time to time. Or one of her friends had done. Rutledge had paid scant attention, but he possessed a good memory and he managed to dredge up a few details. Hamilton moved in good circles, but he wasn't particularly enchanted with London and soon after his marriage he'd disappeared from the social scene. That accounted for the move to Hampton Regis. But why had he chosen to close up his flat as well? London gossips had looked for an answer to that and failed to find it.

The information Bowles had given Rutledge was lean to the point of skeletal: that Hamilton had been at the Peace Conference in Paris, coming unbidden from his station on Malta, and was sent back there posthaste.

Wasn't it this same Hamilton who had been against stiff reparations from Germany? French vengeance he'd called

it. And hadn't he railed against the American president
Wilson's belief in self-determination, publicly branding it
foolishness in the extreme? Wilson had been tired, ill, his
idealistic pronouncements according to Hamilton failing to
take into account the realities of world politics and setting the stage for grave consequences down the road. The
British and French delegations had been intent on ignoring
the American president, palming him off with his precious
League of Nations. Hamilton had tried repeatedly to convince them all that they were sowing the seeds of disaster
which another generation would reap in blood. It hadn't
been a popular stance.

The British had all but disowned him, as they had disowned Lawrence and others with a clearer vision. Rutledge
had been in hospital during most of the Peace Conference,
his knowledge of it secondhand. But the displeasure of the
Foreign Office hadn't sent a man of Hamilton's stature to a
backwater like Hampton Regis. Small wonder the gossips
had been busy.

Given Hamilton's history, what scandal or past indiscre-
tion might have caught up with him here? Stephen Mallory
had had no role in Hamilton's diplomatic career. Yet that
had covered at least twenty years of Hamilton's life.

Bennett was still speaking, his voice sour. "And how is
it you're acquainted with this man Mallory? Does *he* have
friends in high places?"

"Hardly high places. I expect the Yard was more concerned about the Hamiltons and their maid than any connection I might have with your suspect."

"Then you won't mind telling me how it was you came to
know him."

"In the war," Rutledge answered him, and changed the
subject, though he knew Bennett wasn't satisfied. "Any improvement in Hamilton's condition?"

"Not according to the doctor." Bennett grimaced as he shifted his foot again. "He's been close to consciousness a time or two, but he never quite wakes up. That doesn't bode well for his ability to recall who attacked him."

"Yes, I see that. What happened next?"

"I sent my constable, Jordan, to the Hamilton house to fetch Mrs. Hamilton to him, and I went to Mallory's cottage myself. It lies inland, a few miles up the Hampton River. My intent was to question him about where he'd been that morning, but he lost his head and went directly to find Mrs. Hamilton. She was at Dr. Granville's surgery. He waited until she came home, and took both Mrs. Hamilton and her maid hostage. When we went to try and talk him into surrendering, he threatened to kill both women if we didn't summon you directly."

"Since then, you haven't tried to—er—persuade him to surrender?"

"I had myself driven up to the house shortly before nightfall, and called to Mrs. Hamilton. Mallory answered for her and reminded me that their safety depended on you coming down from London." He considered Rutledge, his eyes hostile. "I still can't see why he should have sent for you by name. There must be more to it." His posture was insistent, as if he were determined to get to the bottom of the connection.

"I've told you. We served together in France, and I expect I'm the only policeman he knows."

Bennett took out his watch. "I've posted two men near the house, out of sight but where they could hear the women scream or a shot fired. It's time to relieve them. I expect you'll want to come along. You can speak to Mallory yourself."

They went out to the motorcar, and Bennett beckoned to two constables who had just arrived at the station to accompany him. They nodded to Rutledge and stepped into the rear seat, where Hamish usually sat. The familiar Scots voice rumbled with irritation.

All the while, Bennett was still pressing, eager to wrap up the inquiry. For him, the matter was very simple. Rutledge was here, therefore Mallory ought to surrender himself to the police. It needn't drag on any longer.

Rutledge didn't interrupt, understanding the pent-up frustration that drove the man. But the harangue also served to fix his own actions. Bennett was using the listening constables behind him to make certain that the man from London couldn't avoid doing his duty.

Fate was never kind.

He wasn't prepared tonight. No more than he expected Mallory to be prepared. His mind needed to be fresh, and in the dark, Mallory would be on edge, expecting trickery.

Hamish spoke just behind his shoulder. The voice seemed much nearer, as if the Scot had leaned forward to whisper. "Mayhap he willna' open the door."

And Rutledge answered silently, "He'll want to see what I've become."

Hampton Regis was fitted inside the curve of its tiny bay with the snugness of centuries. Houses along the Mole—the ancient harbor—were timeless, their facades much the same, Rutledge thought as he turned the motorcar, since the days of Drake and the Duke of Monmouth. The later houses— and they were barely later than the last century—had been built along streets set perpendicular to the waterfront, like newcomers handed second best.

Bennett, suddenly aware that he'd lost Rutledge's attention with his barrage of advice, dropped the subject of Mallory and nodded toward the western end of the Mole disappearing behind them. "The river was broader once, and the shipyards and fishing industry lined its banks. Once the river silted up, Victorian money leveled the ground and built there. Now the Hampton's hardly more than a little stream passing under a stone bridge." Then he added with the satisfaction of the working-class man, "My grandfather always said fish scales make the slopes of social climbing rather a slippery business."

He waited for Rutledge to smile at his grandfather's plebeian sense of humor, but the man seemed to be intent on his driving, as if feeling the miles he'd already come.

Instead, Rutledge was struggling to marshal his thoughts, wondering in another part of his mind if anything remained of the authority he had once exercised over the lieutenant under his command in France. And whether he could wield it now.

The Hamiltons lived out on the road he'd come down from London, the one that ran in a gentle bend down into the town, traced its way along the water, and then rose softly to the far headland, following the coast for miles before vanishing into Devon. Bennett was telling him now that the western stretch of cliffs was prone to landslips, and from time to time over the centuries had sent houses and farms and churchyards down into the sea. Matthew Hamilton on the other hand had chosen the more stable eastern heights, living in one of the larger houses there on the seaward side, with sufficient property around them to give them privacy.

The view of the water as the motorcar climbed was stippled with faint moonlight, like a tarnished mirror. Bennett pointed and Rutledge paused to drop off the pair of constables. Then he turned through gates into a trim garden. The drive made a loop through the flower beds, ending at the steps.

Time had run out. *What was he to say to Mallory?*

He looked up at the house, wondering what emotions ran rampant behind that late Georgian front, upright and gracious, its weathered brick surely a lovely rose in the daylight. Very much the sort of classic design a career foreign service officer might have yearned for in his long exile abroad in the heat of some godforsaken island or busy, overcrowded capital. An England that existed now only in homesick dreams. The war had changed all that.

There were no lights that Rutledge could see. He hoped the household had gone to bed, where he wished he was now. But it would not be a peaceful sleep for the two women imprisoned there with a possible killer. And he was their only hope.

He tried to picture Mallory creeping up behind Hamilton as he walked along the strand, and striking him hard across the back of the head. He wanted to believe it was impossible that a man he'd known in the trenches could do such a thing. But then they'd been taught to kill by masters, and what was one more life in the long rolls of the dead? Bennett had been treated with equal callousness. There had to be a reason. And why, if he'd had the chance to run, had Mallory come here instead?

And that brought Rutledge to Hamilton's wife. What was her relationship to Mallory? Or his to her?

Without warning Hamish said, "You should ken how he feels."

Rutledge caught his breath on the realization. In spite of the promises they'd made to each other at the start of the war, Jean had left him, to marry a diplomat serving now in Canada.

Had Mallory been Mrs. Hamilton's lover once? Was that the key?

Bennett was staring at him, waiting for him to act.

Rutledge forced himself back to the present.

"Stay here," he said to Bennett, and left the motor turning over quietly as he went to lift the knocker

After a time a male voice called warily, "Who's there?"
He didn't recognize it.

"Rutledge, from Scotland Yard," he answered carefully. "It's very late, I'm aware of that. I drove straight through, after the summons. I wanted you to know I'm here."

"Stand in your headlamps, so that I can see you."

Rutledge turned and did as he was asked. After nearly a minute, a curtain twitched in an upstairs room.

Then the voice was back at the door, calling, "You've changed. But then so have I. Come back in the morning. Alone. Keep Bennett out of this." The tension behind the words was clear even through the door's wooden panels.

"I told you," Bennett jeered. "Wound like a spring."

"I won't leave until I'm certain the women are safe," Rutledge responded, returning to the door himself to listen for whatever sounds he could hear from inside.

Someone had a candle, its brightness wavering as if in an unsteady hand. Had Mallory been drinking? That was a bad sign. Rutledge tried to recall what they'd talked about in the lines, and what the man's weaknesses were. The problem was, they hadn't been close. Mallory, like Rutledge himself, had had other things on his mind. Rutledge had had more in common with Hamish, though they had come from vastly different backgrounds. Both had possessed an instinctive understanding of tactics and strategy, and that had drawn them together.

Over his head the fanlight was elegant, reminding him of Georgian houses in London. It had been crafted, he thought, by a master hand. But all the candle's golden light showed him was a shadowy flight of stairs and the lamp hanging in the hall. Venetian, he thought in one corner of his mind.

Hamish was saying, "He broke, Mallory did. Only you didna' shoot *him*." And that summed up more than Rutledge was prepared to deal with tonight.

The voice inside the house went on, "They're safe. I had promised as much, if Bennett sent for you. They'll be safe until the morning. I swear it."

"I want to speak to Mrs. Hamilton myself."

"Damn it, man, she's asleep."

"Nevertheless. I've kept my half of the bargain."

There was a silence broken only by Bennett's grumbling from the motorcar.

Finally a woman's voice, nervous and uncertain, called, "Inspector? He hasn't harmed us. Please do as he asks. We'll be all right tonight."

"Mrs. Hamilton?"

"Yes. Have you news of my husband? I've been so worried about him."

"He's resting, Mrs. Hamilton. So I'm told. But you need to be with him. If Mr. Mallory will allow it, I'll take you to the surgery myself, so that you can be reassured your husband is going to live."

From the motorcar Bennett called, "It's not her we want out of there, it's him." Rutledge ignored him.

"I—I can't leave," she answered. "I—in the morning, perhaps?"

"Mallory? Surely you'll relent for Mrs. Hamilton's sake?"

But there was only silence from the other side of the door. After a time, Rutledge returned to the motorcar and climbed into his seat. He could feel the tension of the last few minutes smothering him, until his head seemed to thunder with it.

"You should have pressed him," Bennett told him in no uncertain terms. "While you had the chance. God knows what state those women will be in, come morning."

Rutledge said, "Mallory is tired. He won't be thinking very clearly. Anything that strikes him now as interference on our part will only make their situation worse. I can't believe he'll harm them tonight. Not after he'd got what he wanted. We'll leave him to wonder about tomorrow and how he's to explain himself."

"That's foolishness," Bennett retorted. "You're coddling a *murderer*."

Hamish said, making clear his opinion of Bennett, "He's no' thinking sae verra' clearly himsel'. He hasna' considered that yon lieutenant would gladly see ye deid."

"Why do you so firmly believe Mallory attacked Hamilton?" Rutledge asked the fuming inspector beside him as they drove out of the gates. He could see that a new face had replaced the watcher he'd glimpsed earlier in the shadows of a large tree. He presumed that while he was speaking to Mallory, distracting him, there had been a swift changing of the guard and the other constables had already walked back into Hampton Regis.

"Jealousy," Bennett said baldly.

"Mallory was involved with Hamilton's wife?" He considered the ramification of this. "Or only infatuated with her?"

Hamish, derisive in his mind, demanded, "Does it make any difference?"

"I can't say," Bennett added grudgingly, "how much *involvement* there has been. If gossip is to be believed, certainly on Mallory's part there was the desire to step into Matthew Hamilton's shoes. Or bed. How Mrs. Hamilton felt about it, no one seems to know."

"What else do the gossips whisper?"

"There's a difference in age between Mr. and Mrs. Hamilton. Twenty years, at a guess. Mallory on the other hand can't be more than three or four years older than Mrs. Hamilton. The rest is plain as the nose on your face, isn't it? She wouldn't be the first woman to see a young sweetheart off to war, and then have second thoughts about waiting for him. Especially when her head's turned by the attentions of someone of Hamilton's standing. It explains why, when young Mallory is mustered out, he comes straight to Hampton Regis to live, not all that long after the Hamiltons take Casa Miranda. He's got no family here, nor any connections that we know of. What else could have brought him?"

"Mallory returned to England in 1916."

"Did he, now? Then where's he been since then?" Bennett shook his head. "I don't see how it matters either way. He's in love with her, that's clear enough, whenever it was he came to know her. Why else was he in such a hurry to see her, once he knew he was caught out?"

"Why, indeed?"

"Where there's smoke, there's bound to be fire."

The road was quiet, the town dark, asleep.

"And so Hamilton was struck down, beaten, and left to drown. But no one saw the attack."

"No one has stepped forward."

"I'd like to look in on Matthew Hamilton," Rutledge said.

"It's well after midnight, man. You can't go dragging the doctor out of his bed at this hour."

"I doubt he's in his bed."

"Oh, very well." Bennett gestured toward the first turning as they reached the Mole. "Down that street to the next corner. The house with the delicate iron fencing along the back garden."

But the doctor's house was dark, and although Rutledge went to tap lightly on the surgery door, no one came to answer his summons. He tested the handle, and it turned in his hand. Did no one in the country lock their doors?

He stood in the opening, listening intently. But the dark passage before him was silent, and he could feel Inspector Bennett's eyes boring into the back of his head.

If the doctor wasn't sitting up with his patient, it was very likely a good sign that he was not expected to die this night.

They drove back to the Mole, where the sea beyond the harbor wall was a black presence, restless and whispering as the wind picked up. There they took the second turning, and Bennett pointed out a small inn set back from the street, a black and white Elizabethan building with a slate roof where once there must have been thatch, and outbuildings in the yard behind it. A small garden had replaced the yard in front, and daffodils were already in bloom in sheltered patches. This morning would be the first day of March, Rutledge reminded himself. The winter had seemed endless, unrelenting.

"That's the Duke of Monmouth Inn," Bennett told Rutledge. "I've taken the liberty of putting you up there. But I'd be obliged if you'll drive me as far as my house, which is down the end of the street and on the next corner. Damned foot!"

Rutledge went past the inn and on down the street. "You believe that Mallory ran from you because he's guilty. Why didn't he keep going, either into Devon or toward the port towns? It would have been a smarter move on his part."

Bennett said, "I told you, it was a matter of jealousy. What's the sense in killing the husband if you don't succeed in getting the wife to yourself?"

"Hardly to himself, if the hangman's knocking at the door."

"Yes, well, I don't suppose he'd expected to find himself the prime suspect so quickly. Nor her so hesitant about running off with him while her husband was still alive. If the sea had taken the body, it'ud been a different story." Bennett hesitated and then added, "I'd led Mallory to believe Hamilton was dead. It seemed best at the time. He must have been shocked when he learned his victim was still with us."

"And that's my point," Rutledge countered, pulling up before the small house that Bennett was indicating. "You're looking at the connection between Mallory and Mrs. Hamilton as a strong motive. Instead, Mallory might have gone to her for fear he *would* be blamed. You've told me of no direct evidence linking him to what happened."

"Except that he ran," Bennett answered simply, reaching into the back of the motorcar for his crutch. "Add to that, he had no compunction about killing me as well. And now he's holding those two women at the point of a gun. Does that cry innocence to you?"

Rutledge found he was holding his breath. The rear seat of the motorcar belonged to Hamish—

But Bennett's fumbling was successful, and he retrieved the crutch, nearly striking Rutledge in the face with the rubber tip.

"I'd not heard it myself," Bennett repeated, swinging the crutch out into the road and gingerly lowering his bad foot after it. "The worst of the gossip, I mean. But one of my men, Coxe by name, brought it to my attention. He's cousin to the housemaid, Nan Weekes. Just as well he told me. That gave me a jump on Mallory, or so I'd thought. Nearly had the bastard. But I'll have him yet."

With that he hobbled up to his door and went in without looking back.

Rutledge waited to see Bennett safely inside, and then, easing his stiff shoulders, he turned the motorcar toward the hotel. Even Hamish was ready to call it a night, his presence heavily silent in the rear seat.

The Duke of Monmouth Inn was named for the illegitimate but favored son of Charles II, and there had been many people when Charles died who preferred him over the Catholic Prince James, the king's younger brother. A short but bloody rebellion centered mostly in the West Country had come to grief on the scaffold at the hands of Bloody Jeffreys, the hanging judge of the Bloody Assizes, and that was the end of the duke.

And so history had taken a different turn. The intolerant James had assumed the crown, only to face his own trouble in less than three years. That had swept in his daughter Mary and her Dutch husband, William. There were not many inns named for *him*, Rutledge thought, making the turning.

The building appeared to have been a coaching inn during the early 1800s, hardly the duke's era. Still, there was a portrait of him in velvets, a wig, and a plumed hat on the sign hanging from an iron frame above the door. If the artist was to be believed, Monmouth had been a rather handsome young man who bore no resemblance to the long-faced Stuarts.

The sign creaked on its hinges as Rutledge walked around to the door after leaving his motorcar in the yard behind the inn. He could feel the sea's breath, salty and damp, as he lifted the latch and stepped into the dark lobby.

A lamp bloomed from the door into the office, and a sleepy night porter stepped out, wary but curious.

"Inspector Rutledge," he said to the man, setting down his valise and moving to the desk. "Inspector Bennett has taken a room for me."

The night porter reached inside a drawer and handed him a key. "First floor, to your left. Number fifteen."

Rutledge took the key, retrieved his case, and went up the shadowy stairs.

Hamish said, as they made their way down an even darker passage, "I wouldna' be astonished to see a ghost outside yon door."

"As long as he doesn't rattle chains as I sleep, I've no quarrel with him."

Hamish chuckled derisively. There were other things Rutledge feared in his dreams. The rattle of machine-gun fire . . .

He opened the door to number 15, and discovered that it was large enough and pleasant enough, with a view toward the sea through rows of chimney pots. But standing at the glass, careful not to place himself where he could see his own reflection—or Hamish's behind him—he could just make out the rooftop of Hamilton's house on its gentle rise above the harbor and the sweep of the drive as it reached the gates and turned in.

And it intrigued him that the house, sheltered in its garden, was so visible from this angle. It would be easy to wait here and watch the comings and goings to the door. He made a mental note tomorrow to look in the other rooms on this side of the inn, to see if the view was as clear.

8

After conferring with the desk clerk after breakfast, Rutledge learned that the rooms to either side of his were not presently occupied, and he took the opportunity to look out their windows. But the inn's chimneys blocked any view from the room to his right, while to the left a clump of trees in the rear garden of a house across the way broke up his line of sight sufficiently to shield most activity at the Hamilton home.

Number 15 offered the clearest view.

"Aye, but to what end?" Hamish asked him bluntly.

"Someone must have watched Hamilton leave his house on the morning he was attacked. Without necessarily being seen. As far as I can tell, other than the church tower the inn offers the best vantage point."

The night desk clerk slept in his little room behind Reception. Anyone could step quietly through the inn door without waking him. And the stairs are only a stone's throw away, carpeted and dark as pitch.

Rutledge decided to walk to the Hamilton residence this morning, a quieter approach than arriving by motorcar. The air was damp and cloudy, the sea a wintry gray and the tang of salt strong on the wind, mixed with the reek of the tide-line. Gulls wheeled, dipping and calling raucously where a man sat cleaning his catch over the gunwale of his boat.

As he climbed the road, Rutledge turned to look at the headland across the bay. The woman waiting tables at breakfast had told him there had been landslips there in living memory. It no doubt explained why no one had built there, but five minutes later showed him the stone foundation of what appeared to be an ecclesiastical building rather than a house.

Hamish said, belligerent this morning, "You canna' be sure."

But he thought he could. The pattern of the stones seemed to indicate a round small chapel, perhaps once called St. Peter's after the Fisherman, its tower a beacon to returning ships. Or dedicated to St. Michael, since that militant saint seemed to fancy the high ground.

And then the other side of the bay was cut off from view, and he could look down into the harbor and far out to sea. A fishing boat bobbed in the near distance, taking the weather in stride, but a man in a rowboat, coming around the cliff face and pulling for the Mole, was battling stiff currents.

Rutledge reached the Hamilton gate, nodding to the damp constable huddled under his cape beside a cedar that seemed to drip constantly, its own waterfall.

The tiled plate announcing *Casa Miranda* caught his attention. An exotic name for a stately Georgian house. But Hamilton might have wanted a nostalgic reminder of another life.

Rutledge went directly to the door and lifted the brass knocker, letting it fall heavily, like the stroke of doom.

It was daylight now, he thought. Such as it was. He prayed the ghosts would stand more easily at bay.

After a moment a weary male voice called, "Who's there?"

"Rutledge. I'm alone."

"Give me five minutes to be sure of that."

Finally satisfied, Mallory let him inside but kept the door between himself and the gardens beyond, as if expecting a sniper waiting to pick him off.

"He's haggard," Hamish said, not without satisfaction as Rutledge and Mallory confronted each other in silence, both taking note of changes since they had fought together in France. Both searching for a middle ground that had nothing to do with France.

Mallory, looking at Rutledge, could see more clearly the toll the war had taken and the peace had not replaced.

Rutledge could read all too well the long lines of pain in the other man's face, the dark circles of sleeplessness and strain under the eyes. How much of it had been put there by the past few days, Rutledge could only guess. But Mallory was tall and English fair and still handsome, and it was easy to see that he might be very attractive to women.

Hamish, reminding Rutledge, added, "The men didna' like him."

Crossing Hamish's words, Mallory was saying, "Neither of us has prospered since France, it would seem."

After a moment Rutledge said, "No. Few of us did."

It was as if the empty words summed up four years of war for both men, neither willing to admit to the personal shadows that dwelled under the surface of the mind, neither wanting to bring any of it back. And yet the very act of standing here opened the nightmare in ways neither had foreseen.

For Rutledge it was the sound of a firing squad slamming a round home with nervous, ragged precision. And the memory of men lifting wooden stocks to their shoulders, sighting down the steel barrels at one of their own.

All for nothing—*all for nothing.*

For Mallory it was the voice of Dr. Beatie shouting at him, urging him to do what had to be done to end his suffering. Driving him to kill.

The awkward silence lengthened, and Mallory was the first to turn away, abruptly gesturing toward the drawing room. "In there. Where we won't be overheard."

His voice cracked on the words, and he cast a backward glance toward the stairs, as if expecting to see someone standing at the top of the flight.

Rutledge reminded himself of the task he'd been sent to accomplish. "Where is Mrs. Hamilton?" he asked, not leaving the hall. "And her maid? I shan't bargain with you until I'm certain they're safe."

Mallory grimaced. "Damn it, they're well enough. Felicity—Mrs. Hamilton—is still asleep. The maid—her name is Nan Weekes—is threatening me with God's curse if I touch *her.* She might well be the best cleaning woman in Dorset, but she's safe enough from rape, even in the dark. A few more days of the rough side of her tongue, and she'll stand in greater danger of murder." He'd meant it facetiously, but it hung in the air like a threat and he cursed himself for a fool.

"Mrs. Hamilton has made no effort to escape?" Rutledge asked, listening to the undercurrents in the quiet voice. For signs of instability, building forces that could end in murder-suicide.

"And leave Nan to my tender mercies? She's not that sort. Are you coming into the drawing room or not?"

Rutledge followed him into the pretty room facing the gardens and the road, its walls covered in a shell-colored silk, the drapes and chairs a pale green striped with a soft

shade of lavender. But the room's feminine air didn't detract
from its ornaments, which appeared to reflect Hamilton's
years abroad in the Foreign Service. Olive and other Mediterranean woods framed pen-and-ink sketches of places
Hamilton must have visited on his travels, and on a table by
the window there were tiny figures that looked to be Greek
or Roman, many of them wearing masks and each of them
elegantly made, reminding Rutledge of stage sets. African
carvings in ebony, Hellenic gods in marble, and other exotic
statuettes in clay and stone and wood were set out on the top
of a cabinet containing two shelves of small ornate boxes
in every imaginable material. Together these objects gave
the room its masculine character. One figure, taking pride
of place, was a fat woman with pendulous breasts and enormous thighs—but no head.

Mallory sat down heavily, as if he were on the verge of
falling asleep where he stood. If he was armed, Rutledge
could see no sign of it. But then it would be wise not to have
a weapon where it could be taken away in a surprise move
to disarm him.

"I heard about Corporal MacLeod's death," Mallory said
into the silence. "Long afterward. I wish it had been me
killed in that attack. But I wasn't there, was I? I was behind
the lines in that bloody hospital tent, trying to remember
where I was and why I was strapped to my stretcher. You
never told me how you'd survived."

You weren't there to tell—

Rutledge, caught unprepared, nearly spoke the thought
aloud, but managed to say without inflection of any kind,
"I'm not sure I did."

Mallory nodded. "I hated you, you know. You kept going,
no matter what happened. Like a dead man who hadn't got
the word. I hated that discipline. I hated your courage. I felt
diminished by it."

Rutledge found he couldn't answer. *If you only knew—* After a moment, when he could trust his voice, he said, "It wasn't courage, it was necessity."

"Yes. Well." Mallory looked at him for a moment and then said again, "I hated you. The only way I could get a grip on my own sanity was to face that."

"I didn't come here to talk about the war."

Mallory ignored him. "I didn't leave France by my own choice. You must know that. My uncle, the bishop, had influence in high places. He pulled me out when my father died. Compassionate leave. Then he saw to it that I stayed in England. He was my mother's brother, he must have believed he was doing the right thing. She could have got on very well without me, but there you are. I didn't handle it very well. I wasn't very good at teaching bumbling tenant farmers and green shop clerks how to kill. I kept dreaming about them torn and dying, and you standing over them, blaming me for failing them and you. I wanted one of them to kill you. In the end, I had to do that for myself."

"I don't want to hear your confession. I have no *right* to hear it."

"You heard our confessions often enough in the trenches," Mallory retorted, his voice tight. "But I didn't desert. I didn't *desert*."

Hamish growled deep in Rutledge's mind, a wordless rejection of Mallory's denial.

Rutledge stood there with nothing to say, and in some far corner of his being, he could hear the guns again, a perfect morning for gas, and he had to stop himself from putting up a hand to test the direction of the wind.

He couldn't think of a way to deflect Mallory's need to exonerate himself, and tried to shut it out, withdrawing from the insistent voice almost as he found himself withdrawing from the man.

"I just wanted to make it clear that I'm expecting no favors," Mallory finished. "Spare me your pity, or whatever it is you feel toward me. Understand this. The only reason I sent for you is that stubborn bastard, Bennett. He wants my blood. And he'd have had it, if I hadn't fended for myself."

"You ran him down," Rutledge pointed out, grateful for the shift in subject. He sat down on the other side of the room. "His foot is probably broken."

Mallory sat up. "Did he tell you that?" He laughed harshly, without humor. "Yes, well, he would, wouldn't he? The truth is, he was clinging to the motorcar, wouldn't let go. When he fell off the door, it was bad luck that his foot was in the wrong place. It wasn't intentional, and don't you let him tell you it was."

"Nevertheless—"

"No. Listen to me. I don't know why he came to arrest me without any physical evidence and no eyewitness to put me at the scene. But he did. Someone must have told him I was once engaged to Mrs. Hamilton and would have been glad to see her husband out of the way."

"It looks now to be the truth."

"No, I tell you. I had nothing to do with the assault on Hamilton. The first I knew of it was Bennett standing in my doorway going on about a body found on the strand and asking me to come with him." His voice was earnest as he leaned forward in his chair. "I didn't even understand that it was Matthew he was talking about until he began insisting that I go with him. And then all I could think of was Felicity—Mrs. Hamilton. I had to see her, to tell her I hadn't harmed Matthew. If Bennett believed it, he'd try to convince her as well. You weren't *there,* you weren't in my shoes—he'd already made up his mind, he had no intention of looking anywhere else. Once I was in custody, I'd be facing trial."

He was protesting too strongly, Rutledge thought. And yet he sat there, with no weapon visible, speaking to Scotland Yard as if he had nothing to fear. Truth? Or a well-planned fiction?

"You must look at it from Bennett's viewpoint. You were the one person most likely to benefit if Hamilton died of his injuries. And therefore a strong suspect."

"Benefit? Oh, yes, I could woo the grieving widow, couldn't I? But she loves Matthew, and I don't think I'm likely to step into his place even if he dies. I just didn't want her to hate me, or believe I could hurt her in any way."

"Then why did you threaten the two women? Surely by the time Bennett was knocking at the door here, you'd had a chance to explain yourself. Why go the next step?"

Mallory started to answer, thought better of it, and then finally said, frowning, "I'm not really sure myself how it happened. It just—did."

"Let them go. That will be in your favor. I'll see them safely away from here, and then we'll take you down to the station to tell your side of the story."

Mallory laughed without humor. "I'm not a fool, Rutledge. As soon as I set them free, I've nothing to use as a means of bargaining with you. I want you to find out who did attack Hamilton, and bring him here to tell Mrs. Hamilton why. I'm owed that, and when you've done it, I'll give myself up."

"Mrs. Hamilton ought to be with her husband. If you hold her here against her will, and her husband dies, she'll never forgive you. Don't you see that? For her sake, you have to take the chance that you'll stand trial. Let her go, and I give you my word I'll do everything I can for you."

Mallory got to his feet and began to pace. "I can't let her leave. Bennett would never allow her to come back here again. And if Matthew dies, who's to speak for me?"

"Then let the maid go."

"I can't, don't you see? If I'm shut in this house for days with Mrs. Hamilton without a proper chaperone, her reputation is ruined."

"I hardly think the maid, locked away as she is, can speak on behalf of your honor or Mrs. Hamilton's."

"Yes, well, Nan's staying. You don't know the women in this town."

"What if I offer myself in Mrs. Hamilton's place? She can go to the surgery, look in on her husband, comfort him, and then come back again."

Rutledge could see how torn the man before him was. A range of emotions flitted across his face before he said, "I can't be sure Bennett will agree to that. He'll leave you here to rot because you've invaded his patch, and you won't be free to argue when he doesn't make any effort to get at the truth. No. We keep things as they are. You'll do what you can to learn who wanted Matthew dead, and I'll give you my solemn word that both women are safe with me. In God's name, why should I harm either of them?"

"Why did I drive all the way from London, if you're unwilling to make any compromise now that I'm here, or show good faith? That's foolishness."

Mallory's pacing stopped. "The trenches were foolishness. A stalemate within a stalemate. I'm just taking a leaf from the war's book. Right now, it's the only weapon I have."

And then Rutledge asked the question that had been in the back of his mind all the way from London. "Why did you turn to me? Why didn't you ask the bishop, your uncle, to help you?" It was flung at Mallory almost viciously, welling up out of Rutledge's own anguish.

"He's dead." After a moment Mallory went on, the words wrenched from him. "I had promised myself I'd never have to see you again. Do you think I wanted this? *Any of it?* If there had been any other way?"

Rutledge stood up as well and took a deep breath, attempting to break off the unforgiving savaging of each other. Throughout the exchange, Hamish had been ominously silent, a dark presence like thunder in the distance. Like guns in the distance . . . Rutledge made an effort. "Let me speak to Mrs. Hamilton, before I go."

"She's in her room. Matthew's room." There was a bitter twist to his voice at the words. "At the head of the stairs, turn right toward the sea. It's the last door but one."

Rutledge climbed the stairs at a steady pace, neither hurrying nor taking his time. When he reached the passage at the top, he turned right, found the next but one door and tapped lightly.

There was no answer. He opened the door gently and looked inside.

The bedclothes were a tangle, spilling half off the bed. In the midst of them was a tousled fair head, buried in a sea of dark rose coverlet that matched flowers in the draperies and the fabric of one chair by the hearth. Her face was to the wall and out of his line of sight. He'd have to go round the bed to see it.

"Mrs. Hamilton?" he called quietly.

But she was deeply asleep. Or pretending to be. He couldn't be certain. He wasn't close enough to the bed to see how she breathed.

Hamish said, "If she sleeps sae soundly, there's naething on her conscience."

But women sleep deeply after love. What role had Felicity Hamilton played in the events of the last twenty-four hours?

After a moment, he closed the door and went back the way he'd come.

Mallory was waiting for him, and without a word led him to the kitchen precincts.

The maid, Nan, was wide awake and choleric. A thin woman with weather-reddened skin and pale hair that showed streaks of graying, she sat rigidly in her chair in a small pantry off the servants hall, her eyes alive with fury.

"Who's that, then?" she snapped at Mallory as he brought Rutledge in. He ignored her.

But Rutledge answered her, identifying himself simply as a police inspector.

"You haven't kept her locked up like this all this time, have you?" Rutledge asked, turning back to Mallory. There was no food or water in the room, no sign even of a chamber pot.

"Good God, no. But she was banging on the door of the servants' hall at six this morning and I couldn't have that. I think she broke that other chair against it." He gestured to the chair flung against the wall, the splat shattered.

"And who wouldn't be making a racket, kept here by the likes of you?" she demanded. "I've a cousin at home. A policeman. He'll be wanting your blood if you lay a hand on me!"

"I haven't touched you," Mallory retorted, "except to shut you up down here so that we could have a little *peace*."

Nan was on the point of answering him, when Rutledge asked quickly, "*Has* he harmed you in any way?"

"He'd not dare to. But who can say what he's done to Mrs. Hamilton?"

There was something avid in her face that told him she wished for it. As if there was little love between herself and her mistress, and whatever Felicity Hamilton suffered, she had earned. So much for Nan as chaperone. Mallory was right, she'd blacken his character with a vengeance. And Mrs. Hamilton's as well, relishing the chance.

Rutledge wondered how she felt about Mr. Hamilton, whether her loyalties lay there—or with neither of her employers.

She hadn't asked about Matthew Hamilton. How he fared,

whether he was alive or dead. Did she even know why she and her mistress were being held against their wills?

"She's no' concerned for them. Only for hersel'," Hamish replied. "But her tongue will clack once away fra' here."

"You can't leave them like this, you have to feed them, you know," Rutledge said to Mallory. "It's going to be a bigger problem than you think, keeping them here."

"I'll manage," Mallory replied stiffly. "I can prepare food, tea. It won't be fancy, but it will be edible. I've even mucked out the stables this morning for the damned horse. All right, you've seen both of them."

They turned toward the door, Rutledge promising Nan Weekes help before very long and getting the sharp side of her tongue for letting "that man" get round him so. "Poor excuse for a policeman you are."

It was as if she'd expected him to overpower Mallory in front of her, and set her free, and held it against him for failing to try.

Hamish remarked, "There's the thorn in this dilemma."

It was true. Mrs. Hamilton might sleep soundly under the circumstances, her door not locked. But Nan was another matter. Rutledge found himself more worried for her than for her mistress. Mallory's stability would be fragile after days of strain and Nan's belligerence.

Outside, as they walked to the back stairs, Rutledge said, "Look. Tell me what it is you want me to do? This has to end, you know it as well as I do. Tell me what it will take to set the women free." It was an appeal to Mallory's better nature, but even as he spoke the words, he knew they were empty.

"That's simple," Mallory answered. "Find out who nearly killed Matthew Hamilton."

*   *   *

Rutledge went to Dr. Granville's surgery next, greeting the doctor's wife and asking for a few minutes of the doctor's time. The waiting room behind him was crowded, and he could feel every eye on him as he introduced himself to Mrs. Granville.

Mrs. Granville said doubtfully, "He's got his hands full just now. What with Mr. Hamilton and his usual hours. I don't know if there's been an epidemic of sore throats and unsettled stomachs or if people are hoping for news of poor Matthew."

"Perhaps you could take me to see Mr. Hamilton, then. And I shan't have to disturb the doctor."

"Well, I'm not certain Mr. Bennett would agree."

He smiled. "I'm handling the matter for Inspector Bennett. Until he's fit to do more on his own."

"Yes, poor man. In that case, then." She let him into a passage that ended in a door that was half glass, with fenced lawns and bare trees beyond. He followed her past a series of closed doors to the last but one. "He's in quite a bit of pain, isn't he? The inspector. But he wouldn't hear of anything to help, you know."

Now he could see through the glass into the tidy garden just beyond, and a table under a tree, with chairs around it. He had a picture of tea set out there on a summer's day, and children running through the grass, laughing. The England he and Mallory and so many others had fought for. Bleak now in winter, cold and quiet. As if war had drained away the color and reality, not the seasons.

Hamilton's tiny room was windowless. He lay there on the cot bed, the lamp beside him lit but shielded to keep the light out of his eyes.

But Matthew Hamilton's bruised eyes were closed, and his breathing was labored, as if it hurt to draw too much air in at a time.

Rutledge, looking down at him, took his measure: a tall man, broad shouldered, with dark hair silvering at the temples, long sun-bronzed fingers lying idle on the coverlet, slender body. He could have put up a good fight, if he'd been attacked face-on. A match for Mallory or anyone else, physically.

Hamish said, "It was a vicious beating."

And that appeared to be true. His ribs were wrapped tightly, the broken arm set, and lumps under the coverlet indicated bandaging on his legs as well.

To kill? Or simply vengeful, without much caring about the outcome.

"I'm told he was found near the tideline," Rutledge commented quietly.

"Oh, his clothing was soaked with seawater," Mrs. Granville replied. "It's a wonder, cold as he was, he didn't die of exposure. But Anthony—the doctor, that is—feels that the cold may have prevented massive internal bleeding."

"One good thing, then. No sign of returning to consciousness?"

"He's moaned a time or two. The doctor is reluctant to administer anything to help with the pain, at least for the next few hours, because of possible brain injury."

"But he's not conscious enough to speak, as far as you know? When he begins to moan?" He reached out and touched one of the hands on top of the coverlet, and raised his voice a little. "Mr. Hamilton? Can you hear me? I've brought a message from your wife, Matthew. Do you understand what I'm telling you? Grasp my hand if you do."

There was no response.

"How is Mrs. Hamilton?" Mrs. Granville asked him, leaning forward a little, as if eager for news. He turned to look at her, seeing her now as one of the village women rather than just the doctor's assistant. "She hasn't been back to see him," she continued. "I've heard that she's under—er—constraint at the house."

A thin face, thinner lips, gray eyes alive with curiosity.

"Mrs. Hamilton is safe where she is," he answered carefully. "I don't think you need to fear for her or the maid. I'd hoped to bring her with me. Perhaps the next time. Could I see Mr. Hamilton's clothing?"

Surprised, Mrs. Granville said, "Well, yes, of course, if you like. It's all in the cupboard there. I dried the woolen things as best I could."

He was already opening the low cupboard at the foot of the bed. The coat and trousers Hamilton had been wearing were still dampish, and had that odd feeling that salt water gives to fabric, heavy and slightly stiff. No hat, as if the man had enjoyed the wind in his hair. Or had lost it in the struggle.

"Boots," Hamish said, and Rutledge saw the Wellingtons under the neatly folded pile of undergarments.

"He was planning from the start to walk by the sea," Rutledge responded silently. "He wasn't lured there."

Mrs. Granville was saying, "The contents of his pockets are in that small box. I was going to offer it to Mrs. Hamilton yesterday, but she left so suddenly."

Rutledge took out the box and opened it. Wallet, in some unusual leather now stiff and water stained. Several pounds in bills. A handkerchief. A handful of coins. Keys on a ring. A pipe and tobacco in a pouch. And a watch, the fob on the gold chain an enameled shield with the cross of Malta in red and white. The watch must have been cleaned and wound, for it was ticking softly.

Nothing unusual or unexpected. Save for the keys, he returned the items to the box and set it back where he'd found it. Then as an afterthought, he put them back as well. As long as Hamilton was alive, they should be left for him.

Just as he was closing the cupboard, the man on the bed groaned in pain, then stirred uncomfortably before subsiding into silence once more.

"If he speaks at all, no matter how trivial his words may seem to you, write them down and summon me at once. Leave word at the station or at the Duke of Monmouth."

"Yes, of course, Inspector." She followed him to the door. "I'll tell the doctor you came, and if he has any need to speak with you, he'll reach you."

He walked down the passage and was almost at the outside door when a woman came out of the surgery waiting room, nearly colliding with him.

"Miss Trining," Mrs. Granville said, in the tone of voice reserved for someone of substance.

"I shan't wait any longer," Miss Trining said. "I feel better now, anyway."

"Are you sure you oughtn't stay until the doctor sees you? Indigestion is sometimes—"

"I know my own body best," Miss Trining said shortly, then looked Rutledge up and down. "Who are you?"

He gave her his best smile. "Inspector Rutledge from Scotland Yard," he said. "And you are . . . ?"

"Charlotte Trining. I'm a member of the vestry, along with Matthew. Have you been to see him? Dr. Granville won't let me near him."

"And rightly so. Rest is the best cure, sometimes," he said. "I've my motorcar outside. May I drive you somewhere?"

Over Miss Trining's head, Mrs. Granville shot him a grateful look.

"Yes, thank you." She nodded to the doctor's wife and let Rutledge hold the door for her.

He said good-bye to Mrs. Granville and followed Miss Trining to the car, opening the passenger door for her.

He had met many women like her over the years. Imperious and self-important, accustomed to having their way, and as often as not a force in any community out of sheer natural gall and ferocious, driving energy. The sort of women who had *connections* and were never shy about alluding to them.

Her dark blue eyes were scanning him as he turned the crank and then climbed in beside her.

Hamish said, "'Ware!" and was silent again.

Miss Trining said, "I shouldn't have thought Bennett's foot injury was sufficiently serious to summon Scotland Yard to his aid."

"I expect he felt he couldn't remain objective," Rutledge answered. "And rightly so."

"I never liked that man, Mallory," she went on. "I'm not surprised he attacked Matthew. What does surprise me is that he didn't finish the job while he was at it. Lack of moral fiber, I expect. I'm told by a cousin in Sussex that he suffered shell shock during the war. I don't hold with cowards. Watch where you're driving, young man. You nearly hit that cart!"

He had. Her words had struck him like a physical blow, and he had swerved without realizing where he was.

Saying nothing, he fought to regain his composure, and she looked at him sharply, turning her head to stare at him.

"Don't tell me you feel differently on the subject."

"I was at the Front, Miss Trining," he answered after a moment. "I saw firsthand what men had to endure. I can't stand in judgment of them now."

"I should have thought you would know, better than most, how they let their friends and comrades down."

It was harshly said and harshly meant.

He remembered a line from O. A. Manning, the war poet who was in reality Olivia Marlow.

Without looking at Miss Trining, he quoted,

> *"Courage is not measured by*
> *Marching bands and banners in the wind.*
> *If you have not walked*
> *The bloody lines and seen the faces,*
> *You have no right to describe it so.*
> *We die here to keep you safe at home,*
> *And what we suffer*
> *Pray you may never know."*

"Yes, yes, I know the poem. What does it say to anything?"

"That you weren't there, Miss Trining. And have no right to judge."

She turned away in a huff. "You can let me down here, if you will," she said, pointing to a milliner's shop to his left.

But when he drew up to the shop, he said, "You appear to know the Hamiltons well. Tell me about Matthew."

"There's not much to tell. He's been a valued civil servant, he came back to England, married a much younger woman, and seems to have settled into his new life without looking back."

"Did you know him before he came to Hampton Regis?"

Something in her face belied her response. "No. I must say that he's been an asset to us here, recognizing his responsibility to set a good example for all of us. I admire that."

"And Mrs. Hamilton?"

"She could do far more than she has, to be frank. I don't think she realizes how she lets her husband down at every turn. Refusing to serve on committees, refusing to take up charitable work, refusing to entertain in the style that I'm sure Matthew was accustomed to abroad. After all, a senior foreign service officer does have a certain social position. But that's what comes of marrying someone so much younger, you know. No sense of what's due a man of Matthew's stature."

"Does Matthew Hamilton have enemies?"

She stared at him again. *"Enemies?"* Her emphasis on the word was noticeable. "I shouldn't think anyone in Hampton Regis has any connection with his past. Why should they? Most of them have never been abroad, unless they were in the war. Much less to Malta and Sicily and Crete."

"I was thinking more specifically than that. Here in Hampton Regis."

"You are entirely too young and inexperienced to handle this inquiry," she said flatly. "I shall have a word with the Chief Constable about that when he comes to tea." And without waiting for him to come around and open her door for her, she did it herself and stepped out. "Good day, Inspector."

9

When Felicity wandered down for breakfast, there were dark shadows under her eyes and she seemed distracted.

"Rutledge was here again," Mallory said. "You were asleep."

"Just pretending. I heard him knock at my door and panicked."

"I don't think he believed the hostage story. But Nan gave him an earful."

"Yes, I'm sure she did. I wish we could let her leave, just to be rid of her. I don't feel comfortable when she's in the house. I never have. She adores Matthew." She hesitated. "Did he say—is Matthew all right?"

She was asking if he still lived. Mallory could feel his heart turn over. What would she do if Matthew died? Turn on him, slip out of the house in the middle of the night, when he finally sank into deep sleep, unable to keep his eyes open any longer? And then he felt guilty for even considering such a cruel betrayal.

"Still unconscious." He didn't tell her that Rutledge had offered to let her visit her husband. He wasn't sure how she'd respond to that.

Felicity shook her head and pulled her shawl closer, as if she felt cold. "You don't suppose we could build a fire in the study or the sitting room? It would be so much cozier."

"Felicity." She looked up at him, then looked away. "What are we going to *do*?"

"I thought this inspector was here to sort it all out for us. That's why you wanted him to come, isn't it?"

"The question is, will he be strong enough to stand up to Bennett?" He hesitated. "He wanted to know if we'd had an affair."

"Hardly an affair. I was in love with you long before I met Matthew. I was going to marry you. Only you didn't want to marry *me*. Not then." There was a hurt expression on her face, as if she remembered the past more clearly or, at the very least, differently.

"Dear girl! I told you, I didn't want to come home to you a lame beggar—"

"But you didn't, did you?" There was accusation in her voice, as if he had tricked her somehow. "You came home *whole*."

"I couldn't know that. It was you who refused to wait. Who didn't have faith in the future."

"How could I, when you'd painted it so bleakly?" She stood in the doorway to the dining room. "I don't suppose you could make a pot of tea. Matthew always brought me my morning tea."

He hesitated, and then said, "Yes, of course. Breakfast!" as if it had just struck him what time it was. "We've got to feed Nan, as well."

Felicity frowned. "We'd be so much better off without her. I wish she was gone."

"No, we shouldn't be. She's your chaperone."

"Little good she is at chaperoning. Locked up below-stairs."

He smiled. "Appearances, my dear, appearances," he said, in a voice that was so like Miss Trining's that she laughed. Nan must have heard it as well, for she began to bang ominously on the door of her prison.

"I wish she was dead!" Felicity said in anger, and then covered her mouth with her hand. "I didn't mean that, truly I didn't." She waited to be forgiven, like a child.

"No, of course you didn't." But he turned away, his appetite gone, and went on to prepare a meal he couldn't swallow.

Bennett was in a foul mood. His foot had kept him awake most of the night, and this morning Rutledge had proceeded to act without him. It was unprofessional, and in his present state of mind, unforgivable. He sat in his office hunched over his desk like a poisonous toad, waiting for Rutledge to appear.

Then he said, with understated anger, "I hear you've been busy."

"I couldn't sleep," Rutledge said blandly, his face giving nothing away. "And so I went to the house. The women are safe, but their situation isn't the best. I'd like to bring this business to a conclusion today."

And so would I, Bennett thought, *if only to be rid of the likes of you.*

His feelings were so clear in his expression that Hamish said, "Watch your back. He doesna' care how it ends."

"Yes, at least Mallory is right there," Rutledge answered silently. And to Bennett, "Perhaps it would help if we could go over the evidence against Mallory again."

"I've told you. Twice before. There was reason to believe he might have had a hand in the assault, and I went to confront him. He ran me down and fled. What more do you want in the way of evidence?"

"I believe you, of course. But what I'd prefer are witnesses, some sort of direct proof at the scene that he might have been there. I daresay Mallory can afford a decent barrister. We had better be prepared for that."

"The only tracks were ours, the ones we made coming down to have a look at Hamilton. We didn't know then he'd been beaten, did we? First thought was, he'd walked too far and his heart had given out. Dr. Granville was with us, I'd sent for him straightaway. And he was anxious. Hamilton's had malaria, dysentery, and God knows what other diseases out where he's been," Bennett retorted, easing his leg in front of him. "Bones are the very devil! You'd think they'd have no feeling in them. At any rate, I cast about for footprints, a weapon, some sign of a struggle—and I came up empty-handed. Here was a badly injured man, he had no enemies that we knew of, and the only person with any reason to see him out of the picture is the man now hiding behind the skirts of two frightened women. That should tell you something. If he's innocent, why didn't Mallory stand and take questioning like a man?"

"Because," Hamish was pointing out, "Mallory didna' trust the police to be fair."

Rutledge tried to quell the voice in his head. "Who were Matthew Hamilton's friends? He served on the vestry. What does the rector have to say to this business?"

"I haven't asked him. When have I had the time?"

"Then perhaps we should see him now. I'll drive you," Rutledge went on as Bennett was on the point of protesting. He stood by the door waiting, and Bennett had no choice but to get to his feet and clumsily adjust his crutch under his arm.

Rutledge had passed the church coming into Hampton Regis last night and heard the clock strike the hour. It stood not far from the turning to Casa Miranda, a tall, rather austere stone edifice well set out in its churchyard. To the west of it behind a massive Victorian shrubbery, this morning he glimpsed the sunlit windows of what must be the rectory.

The rector wasn't a man to take sides. Slim and frail, he looked to be older than he was, a man so trodden down by life that only his faith sustained him.

When they found him in the church, staring at the baptismal font as if expecting it to break into speech at any moment, he seemed surprised to see them.

Bennett made the introductions and said without further ado, "Mr. Rutledge would like your opinion of Matthew Hamilton."

"Matthew?" Augustus Putnam faltered. "Is he dead then? I've been remiss, I haven't been to see him."

"He's still very much alive," Rutledge responded. "Shall we sit down over there?" He gestured to the chairs at the back of the nave. "Inspector Bennett would appreciate it."

"Yes, yes—by all means." Putnam led the way to the chairs and waited as if the host until both men were seated. Then he sat down heavily as if worn out by the interview to come.

"Matthew Hamilton," Rutledge reminded him.

"Ah. Well, you probably know his history. Foreign Office and all that. He's been so helpful with church affairs. I've been grateful. Sometimes the vestry board can be. . . ." He hesitated, looking for the right word, then smiled. "Obstreperous," he ended.

"Too many demands and not enough money?" Rutledge asked.

"Yes, exactly," Putnam agreed gratefully. "We have to make do—the war, you know. It changed so much."

"The rector lost his only son at Passchendaele," Bennett

told Rutledge with some bluntness, as if that explained the
rector's situation.

"I'm sorry," Rutledge's voice carried more than the usual
polite murmuring of sympathy.

Putnam nodded in acknowledgment.

"Thank you. It's still amazingly raw. The loss." His
thoughts seemed to wander away, as if searching for some
explanation for why his son had been taken. After a moment,
he came back to the present. "I've the greatest respect and
admiration for Matthew Hamilton," he said. "There's been
much comment about his interest in foreign gods, but I can
tell you he's a fine example of what a good parishioner ought
to be. Kind, considerate, intelligent, compassionate."

"Foreign gods?" Rutledge asked.

"He was something of an amateur archaeologist in his
spare time. Part of the collection he brought home with him
has—er—stirred up some confusion in the minds of a few
people. Especially the goddess."

For an instant Rutledge found himself wondering if the
reference was to Mrs. Hamilton, and then he remembered
the headless figure in the drawing room. "Have you seen
this collection?" he asked with interest.

Putnam smiled. "Yes, I was particularly asked to view
it. George Reston was most insistent about that. He was
shocked, you see. I expect Matthew had enjoyed a little
amusement at his expense. We aren't very worldly, here." He
cast a swift glance toward the silent Bennett, then added to
Rutledge, "Have you been to Malta, Inspector? Or to some
of the other early sites in the Mediterranean? I've read a
little about them, and I must confess they tend to be extraor-
dinary in their perspectives."

Rutledge held back a grin. In so many words Putnam had
told him more than Bennett had understood. Putnam, he
realized, wasn't quite as childlike as he appeared. It was a

facade developed over time to shield himself from the wrath of the Restons and the Trinings among his flock.

"And Mrs. Hamilton? Do you know her well at all?"

"A lovely young woman," he said. "We've been saddened by the fact that she doesn't come to services as often as we'd like. But she seems sincere in her faith."

Hamish said, "The auld biddies must ha' driven her away."

"Yes, I'm sure," Rutledge answered aloud, then winced.

Bennett put in, "We're here to inquire if you can think of anyone who might wish Mr. Hamilton ill."

Putnam considered that for a moment, then shook his head. "I would say he's universally liked."

Which left the impression that no one felt that way about his wife.

"And Mr. Mallory?" Rutledge asked.

"Ah. Mr. Mallory. We've had long talks, you know. On the nature of faith. He lost his in France. Not too surprising, I'm told. But not lost forever, one hopes."

Translated, it seemed to say that Putnam had enjoyed very little success with Mallory. But there was an undercurrent of compassion that spoke of understanding and sadness.

Sometimes, Rutledge thought, reading between the lines was a skill a policeman ought to develop early on. But Bennett, sitting there with righteous stolidity, was not listening to the nuances. He was a blunt man with little imagination, and his foot must have been hurting him after the exertion of getting in and out of the motorcar. There was a grim downturn to his mouth, as though he was consciously suppressing the pain.

And then Putnam commented, as if reminded by something only he could see, "I should like to know what you think of our bosses. Will you take a moment to look at them?"

Bennett opened his mouth to say that they had other calls to make, but Rutledge was before him, intrigued by the rector's shift in subject.

"By all means," he told Putnam with enthusiasm infusing his voice. "I've a fondness for architecture." He turned to Bennett and said, "It shouldn't take more than five minutes."

Bennett said stiffly, "I'll just wait in the motorcar then." He adjusted his crutch and walked off, clearly put out by the distraction.

Putnam led Rutledge down the nave, where they could look up into the darkness of the high vaulted ceiling. Pointing to the ribs of the vaulting where what appeared to be flat stone buttons pinned them into place, he said, "If your eyes are younger and better than mine, you can just pick out the devices on each boss." The rector's words echoed above their heads, as clear to Bennett as they were to him.

And Rutledge could. As the west door closed behind Bennett, he stared upward into the shadows. The bosses were from Henry VII's day, he thought, with the white rose of Lancaster and the red rose of York melded into the Tudor rose, healing all wounds of the long bloody wrangling among the descendants of Edward I. Or such was the hope. Henry Tudor had certainly done his best to rid himself of any opposition. The device of the portcullis was there too, and while they were both of interest, they weren't unique to this church.

But Rutledge waited patiently for Putnam to explain the significance of them. After a moment he said, quietly, "One morning Matthew Hamilton was standing where you are now, as we were discussing a vestry matter. The subject turned to mistakes we've all made in our lives, and he said to me, 'There's a Miss Cole who could tell you much about a mistake that altered my life. I've carried more than a little guilt about that over the years, and I've wondered how to make amends. Only I've put it off too long now.'" The rector shrugged diffidently. "I recall almost his exact words because whatever he had done still greatly distressed him. I asked if he'd care to tell me more, and he said it was his own cross to bear. This may have nothing to do with the attack on him. But you did ask if there might be someone who wished him ill. I would be grateful if you kept this to yourself. It could cause needless pain if I'm wrong."

"Did he ever mention this woman again?"

"It was not a subject I cared to bring up myself."

"I appreciate your advice," Rutledge answered slowly. "And your wisdom," he added after a moment.

Putnam smiled. "One learns diplomacy in many arenas, Inspector. I'm sure the police and the foreign service have nothing on the Church when it comes to treading with care."

He escorted Rutledge up the aisle to the west door and added as it swung inward, bringing in the cold air, "Some things are best left unsaid. And then there is no necessity for explanation or retraction."

They shook hands and Rutledge left. Hamish said, "Yon's a canny man."

Bennett, fuming in the motorcar, demanded, "What's so unique about the bosses, then?"

"Putnam takes pride in them," Rutledge answered simply. "And sometimes it's wise to give a lonely man a few minutes of one's time. It may encourage him to remember something we ought to know."

Grunting, Bennett let Rutledge crank the motor on his own. As the other man stepped behind the wheel, Bennett said, "In my view, finding our man is more important than pacifying the rector."

"You live here. You know best," Rutledge said without emphasis.

"Standing around on those cold pavestones has made my foot ache like all the imps of hell taking hot tongs to it. I'll have to rest it." It was obvious that the man was of two minds, torn between putting up his foot and staying the course.

"I'll drive you home. After that I'll call in again at the surgery. With any luck there should be news."

"If he's going to live, you mean. Hamilton. I've got a bad feeling about that. You could tell Mrs. Hamilton that her husband is dying, in the hope Mallory will let her visit him."

"And if he won't, she'll be distressed to no purpose."

"Her feelings aren't our concern. Winking Mallory out of there is."

"In good time," Rutledge promised, driving through the town and turning down the road to Bennett's house. "And Nan Weekes is still there, remember."

"If Hamilton lives, Mallory won't hang," Bennett commented, ignoring his reply. "It's a pity."

He clambered down with an effort and hobbled up the walk to his door.

Hamish said, "He wants his revenge."

"And I'm here to see he doesn't have it."

But there was no news, although Matthew Hamilton seemed to be breathing less stressfully.

"As if he's coming up from the depths," Granville said, "although it might be the body and not the mind that's healing." He examined Rutledge with some curiosity, and Rutledge found himself flushing under the scrutiny.

What did the doctor read in *his* face? Shell shock? Nightmares?

"I don't quite see Scotland Yard's interest in this business," Granville commented. His blue eyes were concerned. "Was it Mrs. Hamilton who sent for you? Are you a friend?"

"I've never met her before this."

"I'm worried about her, to be truthful." He ran a hand through his hair. "If Mallory will allow it, I'll be happy to come to the house and make certain she's holding up well under the circumstances. Something to help her sleep might be in order. She's a strong woman, but even the strong can break under the weight of anxiety and fear."

"I'll see what I can do. Meanwhile, I'll be here again," Rutledge said, "as often as I can, until there's news."

"Is there any hope that Mallory will allow Mrs. Hamilton to come here to speak to her husband? He might respond to her voice, if not to ours. It's worth trying." His words seemed to fall flat in the small room.

"That might well depend," Rutledge answered him, "on whether Mallory believes Hamilton will clear him or condemn him, once he's awake." He looked the doctor over in his turn, seeing the competent hands, the strong face, the dark hair prematurely graying at the temples. It gave the man a distinguished air, one that patients must find comforting, he thought, when they were very ill. He was wasted, here in Hampton Regis.

Granville said, "If you want my professional opinion, you'll be wise to convince that young hothead to come to his senses. This is as vicious a beating as I've dealt with in many years. My guess is, Mallory's unstable, and God knows what he intends to do with Mrs. Hamilton. If she rejects him, he may turn to murder and suicide as his only way out."

"What are Hamilton's chances? I need to be told."

"Worst case? He could very well be helpless and in a wheelchair for the rest of his life. That's my greatest fear."

Hamish said irascibly, "He isna' dead. Ye shouldna' speak o'er him as if he were."

And yet, it seemed that Matthew Hamilton had no reality, his bruises like Caesar's wounds speaking for him. What would he have to say when he opened his eyes? Would he know where he was—or even who he was? Or would he lunge upright and swear at the memory of his attack?

What had Miss Trining had to say about Mallory? That he was a coward—and as far as anyone knew, this attack had been cowardly too, from behind. It was easy to see why guilt had been assigned so quickly. Mallory was the perfect scapegoat. . . .

With a last look at the injured man, Rutledge left and this time openly drove to the Hamilton house. Mallory answered his summons reluctantly. "What now?"

"I'd like to speak to Mrs. Hamilton, if you don't mind."

Mallory frowned. "Is he—have you come to say he's dead?"

"No. But the doctor feels it would be a good thing to have his wife speak to Hamilton, encourage him as it were, something to cling to in the darkness."

"For God's sake, don't tell her that, she'll be frantic."

"As she should be," Rutledge replied. "She's *his* wife, man, after all."

Mallory shook his head. "I can't let you talk to her. I can't—it isn't something that will work. Get me out of this, if you can. It's the best solution for all of us. Matthew Hamilton included. *I didn't harm him.*"

He shut the door firmly. But inside, Rutledge could hear voices, raised as if in anger.

Hamish said, "It's no' sae simple."

"No. It never is. I have a feeling it will get worse before it gets any better."

But how best to find this Miss Cole whom the rector had mentioned? Without asking questions and giving half the town something more to discuss behind their hands?

He went back to the hotel and stopped at the desk to ask if there had been any messages for him.

The clerk assured him there had not been, and Rutledge started toward the stairs, heading for his room. Then he turned back to the desk. "Friends in London," he said, "asked me to look up someone here. A Miss Cole. Do you know where I can find her?"

But the clerk shook his head. "Are you sure of the name? The only Cole here was a friend of my father's and long since in the churchyard."

"It's not important," Rutledge replied, and went on his way.

Hamish, in his mind, reminded him that he should have asked the rector where to find the woman.

"If he'd known it, I rather think he'd have given me her direction," Rutledge said, walking into his room and coming to stand by the window, looking out on the street. "I'm not sure why he was quite so guarded. That interests me. He may believe that Hamilton spoke of her in confidence."

Below him in the street he glimpsed a knot of women talking, their hats close together as they stood there in deep discussion. He rather thought the subject was Matthew Hamilton and his wife, a prisoner of Hamilton's alleged attacker.

He wondered how any of them—Mallory, Hamilton, or his wife—would manage after the fact, when they must live here in spite of gossip and suspicion of what might have transpired in that house while Mrs. Hamilton was held against her will.

Or was she? He remembered the tousled head among the bedclothes. How many women in Mrs. Hamilton's situation could sleep so deeply and so free from anxiety?

"She knows Mallory," Hamish offered. "She mayna' believe he's guilty."

And that was a good point. "But why isn't she by her husband's side, even if she had to fight her way out of that house?

Mallory can't stay awake forever. He can lock doors but he can't prevent her from trying to climb out her window. Or even stop her from standing there screaming for all the world to hear. It would go a long way, that screaming, toward making the neighbors aware that she was held against her will."

"Would it please her husband, if she makes hersel' a spectacle?"

"If I were married to her, and couldn't get there to help her, I'd have liked to know she wasn't taking the separation without some effort to defend her honor."

"Aye, but then you havena' a wife."

It was a blow that Rutledge hadn't expected. He'd spoken without thinking, considering the issue theoretically.

Jean was in Canada, married to *her* diplomat. What if he, Rutledge, had gone there after her, and held her against her will? What would she have done then? But she would know, of course, that he'd do no such thing. He hadn't been able to fight for her when she released him from their engagement. He'd been too ill in his mind to find the strength to defend his love for her or explain that he was haunted by what had happened in France, by the dying and the turmoil and the horror of watching men he knew fall with appalling wounds. He hadn't been able to tell her what it was like to know with certainty that carrying out his orders had killed so many of them. Never mind that the orders were only his to give, not his to change. He'd failed his men in a way that no amount of argument or reason or excuse could alter. He'd held their lives in his hands. And he'd let them slip through his fingers. It was as simple—and as complicated—as that.

How could he have explained Hamish? Come to that, how could he explain to any woman what war had done to him and to so many others? How could he describe watching Hamish fall, how could he tell anyone how the man had lain there, trying to speak to him, begging for release? And how could he ever condone drawing his revolver and delivering the coup de grâce, the blow of grace, to put Corporal Hamish MacLeod out of his pain and torment?

Jean would have despised him, walked away in disgust long before he'd finished telling her half of it. And so he had let her go without a struggle, knowing that he was abhorrent to her in his battered state, knowing that he couldn't ask her to love him, when Hamish MacLeod owned him, body and soul. Better to let her go, let the last hope of his salvation walk out the door of his hospital room and never come back again. Better to let her think that he was a pathetic remnant of the man she'd loved, rather than believe he was what he truly was—a man who had killed other men, including his own. A common murderer, come to that.

Rutledge straightened up from the window and turned around to look at the room, the draperies beside him, the desk to the other side, one chair and a chest with drawers, a bed. A room in a hotel, a man without roots, without a home, without any ties of love.

He and Mallory . . .

In an attempt to shrug off the mood that had swept him, he tried to think what to do next. Where to turn in this investigation that had been thrust upon him.

For one thing, what did he know about Matthew Hamilton, the face behind the diplomatic mask? Where had the man served besides Malta? Had his career been blameless? A civil servant doing his duty through long years of exile.

And why had Hamilton chosen exile? That was something that would require an answer too. To serve abroad took a willingness to sever ties and rely totally on one's self. Even on precious weeks of leave, it must be difficult to reestablish intimacy with friends and family, to fit in again when he knew so little about the ordinary lives of the people he'd left behind. When he hadn't been there to be a part of the small events, the everyday trials and hopes and dreams of people who hadn't spoken with him for years? What had he found to take back with him to his station, to fill the empty weeks and months and even years of absence? An outcast at home—and an outcast in the field, for all intents and purposes.

Rutledge went to find a telephone, and once shut into the tiny room where it stood, he put in a call to Scotland Yard.

It took all of ten minutes to bring Sergeant Gibson to the telephone. The deep gruff voice sounded tense, unwelcoming.

Rutledge thought, *And this is how it must have been when Hamilton called to say he was in London for a few weeks, and would like to meet a friend.*

Aloud he said to Gibson, "I'm calling in regard to one Matthew Hamilton, Foreign Office, stationed in his last years of service in Malta. There must have been earlier postings. If he was successful in his position, why did he end his career in the foreign service equivalent to Coventry? Why not in a better posting?"

But the answer to that was already in his mind. *The war.* Half of Europe was a battlefield. There were no gracious capitals available to reward senior civil servants for long years of doing their duty. And Matthew Hamilton hadn't distinguished himself at the Peace Conference in Paris.

"I'll look into it, sir," Gibson answered, that wariness still apparent.

Rutledge was on the point of asking how the search for the Green Park murderer was progressing, and thought better of it. Wariness from Gibson was a form of warning. And he didn't take that lightly.

Chief Superintendent Bowles was no doubt in a foul mood, and everyone was walking clear of him, whenever possible.

There was a pause, lengthening, and nothing more was

said. "That's the lot," Rutledge added, into the silence. "Call me here when you have something."

And the connection was broken.

Whatever was happening in London, even Gibson was apprehensive. It didn't bode well for the inquiry he'd left behind.

10

Rutledge forced himself to return to the Hamilton house, knocking at the door, and going on knocking until finally Mallory answered.

He said, irritation in his voice and in his face, "Go away. If you haven't come to tell me I'm free to leave, we have nothing to say to each other."

"I thought," Rutledge retorted, "that you'd sent for me to help. How can I, if I'm shut out? I need information, and with luck, you can give it to me."

Mallory, surprised, said, "What kind of information? I can't tell you who it was struck Hamilton down. I wasn't there. I didn't come into town yesterday morning. If you want the truth, I'd finished a bottle of whiskey the night before and was still asleep when Bennett came pounding on my door."

"I need to speak to Mrs. Hamilton, then. There may be something she hasn't told either you or me. Something she may not consider important or has forgotten in the stress of events. We may not have a great deal of time. If Hamilton dies, Bennett will have his way and bring you in for trial, whatever the cost."

"Yes, well, that was his intention from the start. I've only delayed him for a little while," Mallory replied moodily. "I don't like being in debt to you or anyone else. I should have ended this while I still could."

Rutledge could almost feel Hamish, behind his shoulder, alert to something in Mallory's quiet voice.

"It isna' the same. *He* isna' the same."

It was true. Reality setting in with morning light? Or had something happened between Mallory and Mrs. Hamilton this morning? What if she no longer believed his protestations of innocence?

Murder followed by suicide . . . time was running out faster than even Rutledge had expected.

The door was suddenly pushed wider. "You wanted to speak to me, Inspector? Is it Matthew? Is he all right?" The woman standing there was quite beautiful, in a fragile and defenseless way. The kind of woman, in his experience, who brought out protectiveness in men, the need to shield and guard. Rutledge had found such women to be very capable of looking after themselves.

Jean had been fragile too, until her own needs had driven her to strength.

"You ought to be with him, Mrs. Hamilton." Rutledge spoke directly to her. "He needs to feel your presence there beside him."

"Then you must do something to end this silly business," she said fiercely.

Even her voice was intriguing, low and gentle. It enhanced the helpless image. She was like a child, he thought, but by no means childish. He could see her mind working behind the pretty eyes focused on his face.

When he said nothing, she looked from Rutledge to Mallory, pulling her blue woolen sweater closer about her, almost to the point of wrapping her arms about herself. She added quickly, the anger gone and worry in its place, "Are you lying to me? Is he better and you aren't telling me, just to frighten me? Or is he truly worse, and you're afraid to let me hear it?" She stood there, waiting for him to commit himself to a lie or the truth.

"There's little change," Rutledge told her finally. He was suddenly afraid to pit her against Mallory and add to the man's agitation. "Which may not be a very good sign. The doctor feels he ought to have come round by now. And he hasn't."

Something stirred in her eyes, fear coiling and uncoiling. "And if I wanted to go to him? What then? Who would take my place here? And would you let me come back again?" She glanced quickly at Mallory, then away. "I must come back, you see. For—for Nan's sake. I can't leave her in this predicament all alone."

"I could stay here, in your place," Rutledge offered for a second time. "I think Mr. Mallory would accept that."

"No!" The word was explosive, angry. "I warned you not to bring it up, damn you. You're no use to either of us caught in Bennett's trap with me." Mallory had stepped in front of Felicity Hamilton, as if half expecting her to push through the door and run out to the motorcar or down the drive, before he could stop her. "Get out of here, Rutledge, and don't come again until you've got news. I've had enough of your meddling, do you hear me? Help me by finding the man responsible for this, or stay away from me."

"But, Stephen," Mrs. Hamilton said, turning to him, pleading. "It's not meddling. I wouldn't be long—I'd go and sit with Matthew for just a little while, and then come straight back here. I promise you."

"Felicity. They wouldn't let you come back. Don't you understand? They're using Matthew to make trouble. Frightening you so that you'll rush down to Granville's surgery and—" He broke off. "Don't look at me like that," he pleaded. *"This is none of my doing."*

"You didn't see him lying there, Stephen. You didn't see the blood and the bandages. I did." She whirled back to Rutledge. "You'll give me your word I can come back, won't you?"

"It's not his word that matters. For God's sake, Bennett won't have given *his,* and so he's free to do as he pleases. I don't want to hang for something I didn't do. Even if Matthew dies—"

"No, don't say that!" she exclaimed. "I won't let you even think it."

Rutledge could see the anguish in Mallory's face and the intensity in Mrs. Hamilton's, each with a need the other couldn't meet. A confrontation neither had anticipated at the start of this debacle.

Hamish said, "It's no' a very good thing—"

And Rutledge cut his words short, saying quickly to Mrs. Hamilton, "He's right. Bennett won't be bound by my promises. If you leave here, there's no turning back." He looked over her head to Mallory's tight face.

"We needn't stand here on the steps quarreling. Let me in—"

"No!" Mallory said again. "You've already made matters worse. Why haven't you done as I asked, why haven't you got to the bottom of this business? I don't understand what's taking so long. It's not as if Matthew had other enemies—"

He stopped, and then tried to change his own words. "Someone hated Matthew Hamilton enough to give him that beating. Someone you haven't found yet."

"But not for lack of trying," Rutledge retorted, his impatience getting the best of him. And then he added rapidly, before Mallory could move to the door to shut it, "Mrs. Hamilton, you must tell me about your husband's work in the Mediterranean. Who it was who envied him? Who it was who resented his skill in carrying out his duties or was angry about what happened in Paris? *Who it was who caught up with him on the strand and tried to kill him?*"

She stared at him. "But I don't know what Matthew did. I don't know that part of the world, I met him after he'd come back to London. I asked him once if we could travel to Malta and let me see the places he knew there. And he wouldn't hear of it. He said that part of his life was finished, done with, and neither of us should dwell on what had gone before."

"Then who would know? Who might have seen him at work, who might have been to Malta and understood what he was doing there?"

Mrs. Hamilton's face crumpled, tears heavy in her voice. "Don't you see? I believed he was telling me that my engagement to Stephen was closed, that the bargain was, neither of us would look back, and so I never pressed him, because I didn't want him to press me. It never seemed to matter, not really, though sometimes he would grow quiet and stand there in the drawing room, his hands on that ugly female figure, and I knew his thoughts weren't in the room with me. And it hurt to be shut out, because I'd have liked to ask him about her, where he'd found her, and what he knew about the other figures he kept there. But I was afraid it would open Pandora's box for both of us, and I couldn't bear it. I don't *know* what's in his past."

It was a difficult admission to make, that the marriage had had its secrets. But had it been a true bargain? Rutledge wondered. Had her own guilty memories made her believe that Matthew Hamilton was deliberately concealing something from her? His silences might have been no more than a deep and abiding fear of one day losing his wife. By the same token, Felicity Hamilton had no way of judging, young as she was, the breadth of Hamilton's experiences in foreign service. What secrets he was privy to, what mistakes he had made.

There was anguish in Mallory's eyes as he watched her cry, and his hands moved once to comfort her, and then drew back.

"Surely there was someone at the wedding, someone who came to call when you were in London—a place for me to start?" Rutledge pressed her.

But she shook her head, and Mallory said protectively, "She's told you. She can't help."

And then he shut the door, as if raising a shield between Felicity Hamilton and the world outside.

It was a tender gesture, in a way, an odd sort of moment between captor and captive.

As he stood there, staring at the brass knocker and the solid wood panels of the door closed in his face, Rutledge found himself thinking that this was more a wretched triangle than what it had seemed in the beginning—Mallory's desperate effort to stay out of prison.

Over Hamish's objections, Rutledge drove back to Dr. Granville's surgery, let himself in quietly through the back garden, and sat down by the bedside of the wounded man.

"You mustna' do this," the voice in his head warned him, and he shut it out.

After a time Rutledge began to speak to the unconscious Hamilton. At first about that island in the Mediterranean that had been such a large part of Hamilton's life, and then of his marriage, and finally, running short of material to fill the gaps in his knowledge of husband or wife, about the war.

Rutledge found himself back in the trenches as he spoke, his body tense and his mind distracted not by fear of dying but by the unbearable fear that he wouldn't die.

Hamish rumbled in the back of his mind, emotions filling the narrow room and spilling over into silences that grew increasingly longer as Rutledge tried to avoid the personal and keep to an objective view of the war.

Except for what he'd read or been told since, he knew nothing about the peace that had been fought over and turned into punishment for Germany, each participating nation stretching out greedy hands for what they wanted out of the shambles of dead men's suffering. He'd been locked in his own private hell while Wilson and Lloyd George and Clemenceau created the new world in their own images. The defeated Kaiser was gone, shut in his tiny estate in Holland, and the Tsar, deposed and dragged around Russia like a trophy until he was no longer of any value to anyone, was dead.

Wilson had been fixated on his League of Nations, and he was willing to trade like a tinker for anything of value in return for support. Ill and heartbroken, he'd been defeated in turn, carrying the League home like a dying comrade. And the concept of self-determination had brought Arabs and Slavs and Africans and Indians to the table to plead for their tiny patches.

What did Hamilton know about any of this? Why had he gone to Paris uninvited, and then been sent away as sharply, as if he had overstepped his bounds? If the Foreign Office hadn't named him to the official delegation, he had no business there, and certainly no right to speak his mind as he had done. Or did the war have nothing to do with Hampton Regis and what had happened on the strand below the Mole?

Rutledge brought himself sharply back to the present and, for want of any other topic, began to talk about the case he'd left behind in London.

Hamish, receding into the shadows only a little, was crowding him now, seeming to block the door and shut out the very air with his ominous presence.

Why were there no windows in this wretched room? Why was there no sunlight to brighten it, or a wind from the sea to refresh it? It smelled of antiseptic and death and pain. Hardly an encouragement to live.

Increasingly claustrophobic and uneasy, wishing himself anywhere but here, Rutledge at first didn't hear the grunt as Hamilton moved a little on his narrow bed. It was followed by what sounded like a word, garbled and twisted by the bruised lips. Rutledge turned to stare at the bandage-swathed patient beside him.

And this time Hamilton said, quite clearly, "Water."

Rutledge reached for the carafe standing on the small table next to the bed, and in his haste almost knocked the glass onto the floor. He half filled it and knelt by the cot, holding up Hamilton's head so that he could try to sip the water.

It was difficult at first, clumsily done, but then Hamilton seemed to find the knack of drinking without hurting his mouth or spilling the contents of the glass down his chest. He was thirsty, but after a time, exhausted by sheer effort, he closed his eyes and lay back again on Rutledge's arm.

Rutledge lowered him gently back to the pillows and set the glass aside. Hamilton seemed to be breathing quietly, and for a time Rutledge thought he must have lapsed into unconsciousness again.

But then he said, hoarsely, "Felicity?" And after that, "Who's there?"

Rutledge answered, "I'm from London. I came to investigate what happened to you. Do you remember? Can you remember?"

He groaned again as he moved a little, then touched his

bandages lightly, as if not sure what they were or why they covered him. "Do I know this place?"

"You're in Dr. Granville's surgery. In Hampton Regis. Someone found you—"

Hamilton interrupted, saying fretfully, "You came all this way from London? But I've resigned, you know. It's finished. I've only to close up the house in Valletta."

And then, as if there was a crack in the confusion, he added roughly, "Felicity? *Forgive me!*"

Rutledge waited, trying to decide what to say to him about her circumstances, and in the end saying nothing.

But the injured man had tired himself, slipping easily into sleep or into unconsciousness, Rutledge couldn't tell.

He waited there for another five minutes, but there was no further response. After that, he went in search of Dr. Granville.

The doctor was not impressed by Rutledge's account of Hamilton's brief period of apparent wakefulness. Rutledge could also feel the man's unspoken condemnation for interfering with the welfare of a patient. But he believed he'd done no harm and stood silently beside the doctor, looking down at Hamilton as Granville examined him.

"He made sense, you say?"

"Of a kind, yes. I've told you. He was thirsty, drank a little, and twice spoke his wife's name. He wanted to know who I was, and then there was something more about closing up the house. He touched his bandages but didn't ask how he'd come by them. He wasn't rambling. At the same time, he wasn't fully aware of his circumstances."

"I wish you'd called me straightaway, so that I could have judged for myself."

"There wasn't time."

Dr. Granville was considering Rutledge as if he'd deliberately delayed in calling for help, in the hope that Hamilton might say something that would shed light on the beating. He turned back to the bed as Hamilton started moving his head from side to side on the pillow in silent distress.

Hamish said softly, "He's reliving the blows."

Granville gestured toward his patient. "Look, you can see for yourself he's at a level of consciousness now where he's beginning to feel the full force of his pain. I shall have to sedate him, and that's dangerous. It's never wise to push head injuries too soon. Leave well enough alone. That's an order."

After a moment, Rutledge said, "Still, he should begin to recover now, wouldn't you think? Having come this far?"

Granville was busy. "He's warmer than he ought to be. A degree or two of fever, in fact, if I'm not mistaken. Did you upset him, telling him why his wife wasn't sitting here with him?"

"Most certainly not. I said nothing about Mrs. Hamilton."

"And nothing about Mallory?"

"Nothing."

Granville opened the door and gestured for Rutledge to precede him from the room. "We'll leave him to rest. If his fever continues to rise, I'll give him something for it later. And I'll see that there's some broth to hand, in the event he wakes again."

"Someone should be here. You can't hear him while you're busy with your other patients," Rutledge pressed, following Granville down the passage. "Or for that matter, from your house."

The doctor said, "I'll have to find someone I can trust."

"As soon as possible. If I can walk in here without being seen, anyone can. Lock that garden door for starters."

"I can't. My wife and I use it regularly." Granville ushered Rutledge out and went to sit at his desk, his fingers laced on

the blotter in front of him. And then after a moment, he got up
and went back to where Hamilton lay, silent and vulnerable.

Rutledge returned to the inn for a late luncheon, and sat
there quietly by himself in a corner of the small dining
room. On the walls were photographs of sailing vessels,
usually in full rig, sails billowing out and the sea breaking
as the bow cleaved it. One was a Chinese junk, another a fe-
lucca on the Nile, a third making its way up what appeared
to be the Amazon, the rain forest bending out over the river,
spreading deep and ominous shadows across the water. The
technique was good, and the photographer had had a nice
eye for composition, using it subtly and to great effect.

The woman who was serving him was a little flustered,
as if this wasn't her normal duty. She smiled ruefully as his
soup spilled onto the plate under the bowl, and said, "Sorry!
Becky usually does this, but she's not been well enough this
week. I'm a very poor substitute."

"Not at all," he responded politely. "She's recovering, I
hope?"

"Mumps," she said with a sigh. "And at her age! Dr.
Granville tells me that one can have them again, if the first
time was long enough ago and quite mild. I look in my
mirror every morning, wondering if I'll come down with
them next. The doctor is a good man. He sat with her most
of Sunday night, when her fever was so high. And we're not
allowed to visit. One of the maids looks after her."

"She's here, in the inn?"

"In the servants' wing. It's the only home she has."

Rutledge tried to remember when he'd had mumps.
Bowles would call for his head, if he got them now. Measles
had spread through the trenches. That had been nothing
compared with the sweep of the influenza epidemic.

When the woman brought his next course, he asked, "Is there anyone living in or near Hampton Regis by the name of Cole? A Miss Cole?"

"No, sorry. I don't believe there is. Perhaps it would help if you knew her married name?" But he didn't, and she was off to the kitchen once more.

For once even Hamish was quiet. There were only a handful of people in the room. Two women who looked enough alike to be sisters. Two men having an earnest discussion at a table by the window. Three women nearer the door who cast occasional glances in his direction as if they knew who he was. Their low-voiced conversation had about it the intensity of gossip. But it was one of the men by the window who came across to his table as they were leaving. The shorter one, with graying hair and a scar across his face.

"I'm George Reston," he said, not holding out his hand. "I serve with Matthew Hamilton on the vestry committee. Is there any improvement in his condition?"

Reston . . . who held the goddess against Hamilton, or so the rector had told him.

"He's in guarded condition," Rutledge responded.

"Such a pity." But the cold expression in his eyes belied his words.

Hamish's voice rumbled through Rutledge's mind. "He's of the opinion Hamilton came by his just reward."

Rutledge had to agree with that. Aloud, he said, "Yes, assault usually is."

Reston stared at him. "I beg your pardon?"

"He was struck from behind. A cowardly way of settling a score, as I'm sure you'll agree."

Reston said only, "We are praying for him." And he turned on his heel to go.

But Rutledge stopped him, rising to stand looking down

at him. "We're asking everyone in Hampton Regis to tell us where he or she was early Monday morning."

Reston retorted tightly, "Are you suggesting that I'm a suspect?" His jaw was flexing with his anger.

Rutledge replied blandly, "We're looking for witnesses. Anyone who might have seen anything, anyone who might have heard something. Perhaps unwittingly able to give us a small piece of information to solve the puzzle of what transpired there on the strand. I'm sure you'll want to assist us with the inquiry?"

Reston seemed taken aback. "I was probably having breakfast with my wife."

"When do you have breakfast?"

"When? Er, seven o'clock, I should think."

"And when do you leave the house—as a rule?"

"I'm in my office at the bank by eight."

The women at the other table had turned to stare, absorbing every word to repeat later to friends. Reston cast them a dark glance over his shoulder.

"I don't pass the Mole on my way to the bank," he went on, collecting himself. "If that's what interests you."

"Did you know Matthew Hamilton before he went to his posting in the Mediterranean?"

Something in Reston's face changed, so swiftly that Rutledge wasn't sure what it signified. "I'm afraid not. My first contact with him was through correspondence, when he was in search of a house along this stretch of the coast."

"Thank you, Mr. Reston. I appreciate your cooperation." Rutledge retrieved his serviette and sat down again, ending the conversation.

It was on the tip of Reston's tongue to say something more, but he stopped himself and this time took his leave. His companion for lunch had already gone out, and Reston seemed annoyed when the woman serving tables told him as much.

Rutledge went back to his meal and made a point not to look at the three women who had been eavesdropping. After a time, they resumed their low-voiced conversation.

Hamish said, "Will ye speak to them as well?"

"Not now," Rutledge answered. "I don't think one of them could have overpowered Hamilton. Someone took a chance, striking him from behind. The first blow might not have been enough to stop him. But I'd wager whoever it was was prepared to finish what he'd started, if Hamilton did turn."

"The youngest lass has a cane." It was an observation that Rutledge had failed to make.

He quietly examined the woman more closely. She was indeed younger than her companions, perhaps in her early thirties. And taller. That was food for thought. He nodded to the woman serving, settled his reckoning, and went out to the desk in the lobby.

The middle-aged clerk was still there, reading a book that he hastily closed and put away when he saw that Rutledge was coming toward him.

"Can you give me the names of the three women seated together in the dining room?"

The clerk was surprised. He repeated, "The three women?"

"Yes," Rutledge answered impatiently. The clerk took a sheet of paper from a drawer behind the desk and carefully printed out three names.

"How do I tell them apart?" Rutledge asked.

"Mrs. Jordan is in black. She's a widow. Mrs. Tibbet is in blue, the one with the graying hair. Miss Esterley uses a cane since her accident."

"Accident?"

"Yes. Mr. Hamilton struck her bicycle one night during a rainstorm, as he was coming down from London."

"I see. Could you give me her direction?"

The clerk stared at him. "She's still in the dining room, if you'd care to speak with her."

Rutledge smiled. "In front of her friends? I think not."

He was waiting by the gate to Miss Esterley's front garden when she walked around the corner on her way home. She hesitated. Then, after a moment's consideration, she continued in his direction, and as she came up with him, she said, "I'm to be favored by a visit from the man from London. I wonder why?"

Rutledge smiled and gave his name.

"Yes, yes, everyone knows who you are. Come in. There'll be gossip enough as it is. We might as well sit and be comfortable."

He followed her up the walk and into the house. It was small, comfortable, and nicely set up. The parlor, to the right of the door, was uncluttered, and a gray cat was curled up on a mat by the small fire in the hearth.

Rutledge had noted her stride. She seemed to manage quite well, and he found himself wondering if the cane was now an affectation. It was of rosewood, with a silver figure for a handle. A swan, he thought, although it was mostly hidden by her gloved hand. Feminine, and very elegant.

She ushered him into the parlor as a maid appeared from the back of the house and took Miss Esterley's coat and gloves.

"That will be all, Nell," she said, dismissing the girl. "Now, Inspector, why should you be standing at my gate? Has someone told you that Matthew Hamilton put me in hospital for three months? I hardly think that's cause to batter him to death. But you may look at my cane, if you wish."

He met her smile with one of his own. "I'm interested in

anyone who has a connection with him. How did the accident happen?"

"It was my fault, actually. I'd stayed late with a friend who was ill. Reading to her. The storm came up rather suddenly, and I made a dash for it. Unfortunately, I didn't dash soon enough, and the rain caught me halfway home. It was dark as pitch, wind lashing the trees, and I should have stopped. But I thought, Only a little farther, and I'm safe. His motor came around the next bend and struck me before he even knew I was there. I'd seen his lights but thought I had time to pull across the road and into the shelter of some trees. Ridiculous to be worried about being splashed, I was already as wet as I could ever be. But you don't always think rationally, do you, on the spur of the moment?"

She had an interesting face, square jawed with a straight nose and deep-set eyes. The kind, Hamish was saying, that could lie well, without betraying the thoughts behind the words.

"Were you badly injured?"

"My knee took the brunt of the blow. It was weeks before I could walk on it again, and then it was stiff for ages after that."

"Who was your doctor?" he asked, intending to verify details of the accident and how she might have felt at the time it occurred.

"Dr. Granville, of course, and I must say he worked a miracle." But it was clear she preferred to talk about Hamilton. "It was my claim to fame, you know. Meeting Matthew Hamilton on his very first visit to Hampton Regis. I have first acquaintance. It quite puts Miss Trining's nose out of joint."

He smothered a laugh. "When was this?"

"Last year. I was disappointed to discover that he was married. We're short of eligible bachelors here." He thought she was mocking him.

Miss Esterley was, in fact, striking, while Felicity Hamilton could be described as beautiful. But there were attractions other than beauty. Intelligence for one, character, spirit. A shared background. "Are you on good terms with Mrs. Hamilton?"

"I have no reason not to be. I don't dally with married men."

"I didn't mean that you did—"

"What you were asking, Inspector, was whether or not his wife was jealous of me. I doubt it. Was I jealous of her? No. I enjoyed Matthew Hamilton's visits to hospital immensely, and later at the convalescent home. He has a very pleasant manner, and it passed the time. I've traveled a little, and we shared an interest in that. Otherwise, he came out of kindness and a sense of duty. He felt responsible. And as I had no one else to look out for me, it was rather nice to be taken care of." Before she could stop herself, she cast a wistful glance at a photograph on the table at his elbow. An artillery captain, he saw, smiling at the camera with a devil-may-care expression. He didn't need to ask Miss Esterley if the captain had come home from France.

Hamish said, "Aye, but she wanted you to notice."

Rutledge responded silently, "If she was jealous of Hamilton, it would have been his wife struck down on the strand."

"A woman scorned," the Scots voice retorted.

Almost as if she'd heard Hamish, she said, "I grew up in Kenya, Mr. Rutledge. Matthew Hamilton hadn't traveled to Nairobi, but I'd been to Crete and Malta and Cyprus on holiday with my parents. We could only afford the slow steamer, not the fast packet, you see. And that was our good fortune, because we enjoyed exploring. It was what took my father out to Kenya in the first place."

"Do you know Matthew Hamilton well enough to tell me who might have wished to see him die?"

"Whispers say it must be Stephen Mallory. But I doubt it." She frowned. "It's going to make it difficult for all three of them when Matthew Hamilton is recovered. Even if Stephen didn't harm him, he's destroyed Felicity Hamilton's reputation here."

"There's the maid—"

"Yes, well, you don't know Nan as I do. She used to work for a friend before the Hamiltons came. If it had been Felicity who was attacked, I'd have thought of Nan before anyone else. It's a terrible thing to say about someone you know, but I see her stooping to murder if she thought it would free her employer from his wife's spell. And spell it is. Make no mistake."

11

As they were leaving the Esterley house, Hamish said, "What's the secret of Matthew Hamilton, then?"

"Miss Trining is jealous of him in her own fashion," Rutledge answered thoughtfully. "Miss Esterley enjoyed his company more than perhaps was—suitable, for want of a better word. If she'd been as fond of the doctor responsible for seeing to it that she walked again, I'd find that more commendable. And there's Miss Cole. I expect the rector heard something in Hamilton's voice that betrayed more than he'd intended to say, when he brought up her name. I wonder what Frances would make of him?"

His sister was a very good judge of people and often better than most when it came to understanding the roots of relationships.

The trouble was, the force of character and the vitality of the helpless man lying on the cot in Dr. Granville's examining room were obscured by bandaging and silence. It was hard to tell whether his charm was real or merely cultivated through years of diplomatic necessity. Even Felicity might not know the answer, even though she had married him.

Hamish could be right, that what people wanted to see in him, they did see. The eye of the beholder.

Rutledge threaded his way through the busy streets, intent on going to the police station, but he paused briefly to look out across the Mole toward the open sea. The view beckoned, the day clear enough to see for miles, the water lapping softly at the strand of shingle where Hamilton had been walking. There were boats there now, drawn up out of reach of the tide, and gulls sat on the jutting pier, calling to one another. He had always loved the water. And this afternoon it was a mirror, deep blue and peaceful. But the sea was not always so quiet.

Inspector Bennett was waiting for him, demanding to know why Mr. Reston had been questioned like a common suspect. "He's respected in these parts," Bennett pointed out. "A man of business."

"Even men of business commit murder," Rutledge said blandly. "More to the purpose, he might well have been walking to the bank that morning and passed someone hurrying away from the Mole. I'd have thought a prominent citizen would be more than happy to help the police with their inquiries. Instead he complains to you."

"That's as may be. I've already put my men to questioning the fishermen and the loungers who hang about the Mole. They're a more likely source of information."

"Have they had anything to tell you, so far?"

"They saw nothing, worst luck," Bennett admitted. "There was a mist that morning. Some people like walking in mists. I don't see it myself, quickest way to lose your bearings and find yourself in trouble."

"Yes, well, set your men to questioning the shopkeepers along the Mole, the man who sweeps out the pub, the milliner who comes early to work—anyone who might have seen Hamilton before he reached the Mole. Or noticed someone following him on Monday morning."

Sourly, Bennett said, "This isn't London, with limitless resources."

"If someone was going to come forward of his own accord to tell us what he saw, he'd have done it by now. What we're after is what people don't realize is important."

"And what's more," Bennett went on, moving to his next grievance, "I'm told you woke Hamilton up, questioned him, and *then* summoned the doctor to him. What was that about?"

"It was hardly questioning him. He came to his senses on his own, spoke a few words that indicated he was only just aware of my presence, and that was the extent of it."

"So you say. How do I know that was all that took place?"

Irritated, Rutledge said, "Good Lord, Bennett, why should I keep such information from you?"

"If it didn't look good for your friend, you might not wish to tell me."

Rutledge let it go, aware that anything he could say would only make matters worse. "How was Hamilton? Did you see him after I did?"

"We were there, Granville and I, in the room, trying to rouse him again." It was a reluctant admission.

"Any luck?" Rutledge wondered just how they'd gone about it.

"None. It looked to me as if he was in a deep sleep. What's to be done now?"

"I don't know," Rutledge confessed. "Until Hamilton can talk to us, we're at an impasse. It might be just as well to set a watch over him. Did Dr. Granville mention that to you? Not only to write down anything he may say. It's possible someone might decide it was prudent to finish what began yesterday morning."

"Hamilton's no danger, with Mallory clapped up in the house with the women and under guard himself."

"But what if it isn't Mallory who attacked him?"

"How many men do you think I have? Two are watching the house in turns. I've got two more questioning the loungers and fishermen along the harbor, and now you want to set a watch on the doctor's surgery. He's calling in a woman to sit with Hamilton. That will suffice."

But would it, Hamish was asking as Rutledge left the station.

"It will have to" was the clipped reply.

The afternoon was unproductive. Rutledge went to find the rector to learn more about Miss Cole, but there was no answer to his knock.

He was walking back to his motorcar when he saw Miss Trining coming out the door of a neighboring house. She lifted a hand in recognition.

Hamish said, "She watched you go to yon rectory."

"Very likely," he murmured in reply, and waited for her to reach him.

"Good morning, Inspector. Are you in need of the rector? I'm afraid he's been called away. Mrs. Tomlinson is not well." She stood there, as if expecting him to tell her his business.

But he said pleasantly, "Thank you, Miss Trining. I'll come again in the afternoon."

"I understand you've been questioning Mr. Reston. May I know the purpose of your interest in him?"

"Mr. Reston's bank is just off the Mole. I'd hoped he could tell me who was on the street that morning."

Her attention sharpened. "And could he?"

Rutledge smiled to take the sting out of his response. "I'm afraid I can't answer that."

Her mouth tightened. "Indeed. I thought perhaps you were curious about his past. But since you don't choose to confide in me, I feel no compunction to confide in you. Good day, Inspector."

He watched her walk away, her back stiff and straight. Now what, he wondered, had possessed her to cast doubt on Mr. Reston's past? Whatever it was she knew—or thought she knew—Bennett was unaware of it. And that was intriguing.

He found the Reston house after asking the shy girl behind the counter at a flower shop near the Mole for directions. The shop smelled of dried lavender and lilies. The girl, a brunette in her early twenties, was dressed in a white shirtwaist and a dark blue skirt, her hair pulled back becomingly to a knot at the nape of her neck. She smiled at him as he entered, the obligatory smile of someone hoping to make a sale.

When she recognized him, she was suddenly wary, as if he had come to question her.

"I've already spoken to Constable Jordan," she said in a soft voice. "I didn't see anyone out and about the morning that Mr. Hamilton was hurt."

"Did you see the doctor and the police removing him to Dr. Granville's surgery?"

"Oh, no, I looked away. It was upsetting."

Hamish said, "It must ha' been. But why was she no' curious?"

"Did you know it was Mr. Hamilton they were bringing up from the strand?"

"Not then. I—I thought someone had drowned."

"Is drowning common, off the Mole?"

She shook her head. "Not very. There's no bathing here, not with the currents. But sometimes, especially in the war, seamen washed up along the south coast. A good many were never identified. Which is sad—no one to mourn for them, and perhaps a wife or mother somewhere waiting and waiting for them to come home."

And no one to buy flowers to put on their graves, he thought. He asked her the question that had brought him to the shop and thanked her.

The banker lived in what Bennett had called the fish scale side of Hampton Regis, an imposing gray stone edifice with a mock turret and a battlemented porch over the drive that looped past the side of the house.

Mrs. Reston, he was told by an elderly maid in a prim starched cap that was more suited to an Edwardian household, was not at home this morning.

Feeling thwarted, Rutledge retraced his steps and went again to Casa Miranda, asking to speak to Mrs. Hamilton. Mallory, he noted, looked haggard.

She came to the door with red eyes, as if she'd been crying for some time. Her first words were, "Is there news? If it's bad, tell me quickly."

He couldn't bear the distress in her voice. "Your husband was briefly awake, Mrs. Hamilton," he said gently, then added with a glance toward Mallory, "Not awake long enough to know where he is or why he is there. I must tell you he spoke your name, and we must take that as a good sign. Dr. Granville is doing all he can."

"Please tell him I'm grateful." Felicity Hamilton began to weep, her face in her hands. He thought, Tears of relief. Both men looked away from her, uncertain how to comfort her.

After a moment Mallory said quietly, "What do you want, Rutledge?"

"Let me in for ten minutes. If I'm to help, I need more information than I have now. Anything that you can tell me—"

"No."

But Felicity, finding her handkerchief, said emphatically, "Don't be foolish, Stephen. If it will somehow help."

Reluctantly Mallory stepped aside to allow Rutledge into the hall.

The house already had a dismal air, as if without someone polishing and cleaning, without an ordinary schedule for the day, it was deteriorating.

They went to the sitting room, where the luncheon dishes still stood on trays. Rutledge thought they'd had sandwiches of some kind, and tea. Makeshift meals.

"Tell me about Miss Esterley," he began as they sat down, Mallory anxiously watching Felicity Hamilton.

She said blankly, "Miss Esterley? But surely you don't think—I mean, it wasn't Matthew's fault that she was injured."

"I'm not suggesting anything. Still, she *has* come in contact with your husband under difficult circumstances, and I must ask what effect her accident might have had on their relationship."

"There was no 'relationship,' as you put it," Felicity replied irritably. "He felt responsible for her, he saw to it that she had every care. And she has no problem with her knee now, she still uses that cane because she's grown accustomed to it."

Or to make sure Hamilton didn't forget. He could feel Hamish's presence behind him, the thought leaping across the space between them as if it didn't exist.

"That may be true." Rutledge hesitated, trying to choose his next words carefully.

Felicity was there before him. "If you're asking me whether she read more into Matthew's attentions than he intended, I shouldn't be surprised. It doesn't trouble me. Matthew is mine, he always will be—" She broke off in embarrassment, casting a quick glance over her shoulder at Mallory, standing behind her chair, and was suddenly rattled. "I meant to say, his affections aren't likely to stray in that direction."

But Rutledge wondered if she was protesting too strongly. A man could love one woman very deeply and still be unfaithful to her in his mind. As Felicity Hamilton herself could have loved Matthew and still dreamed of Stephen Mallory.

"Wi' the right weapon, a woman could ha' knocked Hamilton doon," Hamish reminded Rutledge softly. "It doesna' have to be a man."

"Do you by any chance know a Miss Cole? I'm not sure if that's her name still, or if she's married now."

"Cole?" She shook her head. "Should I?"

"The name had come up in another interview. I had the feeling she might live nearby."

"Ask the rector, he should know. I haven't heard of any Coles in Hampton Regis. Have you?" She turned to Mallory.

He said, "No, I don't recognize the name either. Although there are a number of Coles in Kent, I think. I was in school with a Hugh Cole."

Rutledge posed his next question. "What do you know about the Restons?"

She smiled grimly, her pretty face suddenly cold and hard. "He's not what he seems, I can tell you that. He raised such a *fuss* about the goddess. As if he'd never set foot in a museum. And the rest of Matthew's collection as well. Obscene and disgusting, those were his exact words. Insufferable little man. He thinks he's the arbiter of morality here in Hampton Regis, but I happen to know for a fact that when he was an officer in a London bank, he had a vicious temper and nearly—"

She stopped, her hand over her mouth. "Gentle God. I'd forgotten. He struck down a man during a disagreement outside his London club. It was hushed up, of course, but the man was in hospital for days. *He could have attacked Matthew!* Over that stupid, stupid clay figure."

"How do you know about this?" Rutledge asked her, breaking in.

"The mother of a friend of mine. When I told Clarissa I was coming to live in Hampton Regis, her mother said, 'But that's where that awful man went, the one your father saw, Clarissa, outside his club. Shocking to say the least.' " Her voice unconsciously took on the tones of the older woman speaking, giving force to the words.

"What weapon did he use in this beating?"

"He had a weighted cane. For protection, he claimed, since he often carried large sums of money for the bank. The other man wouldn't press charges, he'd apparently said some very inflammatory things to Mr. Reston that he didn't wish to be made public. But *there's* your murderer, Inspector, you've only to arrest him, and our ordeal will be finished." There was an expression of such hope on her face.

Behind her, Mallory's lips tightened and his eyes met Rutledge's in mute appeal.

"It isn't that simple, Mrs. Hamilton," Rutledge told her. "But thank you. I'll look into this and see what comes of it."

"I don't see why it isn't simple. Go to his house, inspect the cane, and you'll have all the proof you need," she pleaded. "And I can sit with Matthew."

Mallory winced but said nothing.

"Yes, as soon as possible. Can you tell me who Clarissa's mother is, and how I can find her? I'll need to speak to her."

Felicity Hamilton went flying from the room and came back with a sheet of paper bearing a name and an address. "Here. Call on her, whatever you must do. But today, please! I can't bear any more of this."

"Yes, thank you, Mrs. Hamilton. If there's anything else you can think of, just ask Mr. Mallory to call to the constable standing near the gate. He'll see that I get word."

She seemed to have bloomed into brightness, her face flushed with the prospect of resolution, her hopes high. Like a child waiting for a treat, he thought. Would this soon grow tiresome to a man like Matthew Hamilton? Or was he still enthralled with his wife's beauty and brightness and waywardness?

Hamish had no answer for that as Rutledge asked Mallory to allow him to look in on Nan Weekes.

She was still angry and resentful. After a time, he was able to calm her tirade sufficiently to say, "I'm here to ask if you've thought of anyone we might question or investigate. Someone who may have come to the house and quarreled with Mr. Hamilton, or someone who upset him in any way."

"You know who it was struck down Mr. Hamilton. He's standing there behind you. Or if it wasn't him, it was her. You'd do well to arrest both of them before I'm murdered in my bed."

"You think he might harm you, rather than Mrs. Hamilton?"

"He's barged in here, hasn't he, and had his way with her. When he's tired of that, he'll likely rid himself of both of us. And she'd like to see me dead now, so there are no ears in this house to hear what goes on."

Mallory was already objecting vociferously, his voice

rising in fury above hers. "No one has touched her, and if you say I have, then you're a liar—"

Over his shoulder Rutledge ordered him to be silent. "This must be done, and you know it."

Mallory turned his back on both of them and slammed the door behind him.

"He's got a temper on him. It's just a matter of time before he kills again," Nan said spitefully. "Mark my words!"

Rutledge said, "Listen to me, Miss Weekes. Your anger does you credit but it won't serve you here. Do you understand me? You'll only antagonize your keeper. If Hamilton dies before he can speak, we may never get at the truth. And whether you like it or not, your life may come to depend on something you can tell us, something you may know that we don't." He tried to keep his voice level, reasonable, in an effort to break through the maid's stiff resistance. "Put aside your feelings and help me. There must surely be others in Hampton Regis who had a reason to dislike Hamilton, or even his wife. You keep house for people, you overhear conversations in the course of your duties. You have friends who clean for other families and who gossip with you."

"We were God-fearing people in Hampton Regis, before he brought *her* here. A good Christian woman wouldn't have let him put those idols up in plain sight in his drawing room. She encourages him, if you ask me. All very well in parts of the world where people believe in such nasty things, but not here, rubbed in our faces. And when she tires of that sport, she lures her lover here. If she didn't wield the stick that struck down her husband, she drove that man into doing it for her. If that isn't true, tell me why she and her lover plotted this business of keeping us locked up here? Oh, yes, I saw it with my own eyes! You'd think if she truly loved her husband, she'd want to be there, sitting beside him, and nothing would stand in her way. That man has to sleep some time."

"You're telling me that it was Mrs. Hamilton who devised the plan to hold you both at gunpoint?"

"I heard them, didn't I? And I'll testify to that in a courtroom. See if I don't." With another spiteful glance at the closed door where Mallory must be listening, she added, "Ask anyone. At night he'd drive to the headland across the way and watch this house. He doesn't think people know about that, but they do. They whisper behind his back. He's been plotting to murder Mr. Hamilton for months, if you want my opinion, but as long as the poor man is breathing, she won't leave with him."

"Because she loves Hamilton, after all?"

"Because he's better off than Mr. Mallory. She's a little hussy, that one, and she married Mr. Hamilton for his money. Ask anyone, and they'll tell you the same."

And if Hamilton was dead, she'd inherit that money . . . assuming she came through this ordeal unscathed.

It was, Hamish commented as Rutledge left Nan sitting there and rejoined a very tense Mallory in the passage, a very good motive for murder.

They walked through the house in silence. Then, at the door, Mallory asked Rutledge quietly, making certain that his voice didn't carry up the stairs or into the drawing room, "Are you keeping something from me? *Did* he say anything?"

"Why should I lie to you? He was in no state to answer questions. But we can hope that by tomorrow the news is better. Mallory, listen to me, encourage Mrs. Hamilton to remember the names of wedding guests and friends she and Hamilton visited in London. It could be your salvation if Reston is in the clear."

With that he stepped outside and walked on, without turning back.

12

The child began to scream at two in the morning. When Nanny failed to comfort the boy, she went to his mother's room and knocked.

"He's hysterical. I don't understand why, there's nothing amiss that I can find." The anxiety in her normally calm voice was a counterpoint to the heartbreaking wails issuing from the nursery.

"Should we summon Dr. Granville?" Mrs. Cornelius asked, quickly knotting her dressing gown around her. "Is he feverish, you think? Has he been sick?"

"He's very well. It was the window, you see. He insisted I close it and put down the shade. He said something out there wanted *in*."

"Was the shade raised? Whatever for?" Mrs. Cornelius followed Nanny down the passage and opened the nursery door. She could hear her son before she got there, sobbing

inconsolably now and calling for her. She crossed to the bed
and put her arms around him. He clung to her, burying his
face in the dark hair that tumbled down her shoulder.

"What is it, my love, what is it?" she repeated in a sing-
song voice, ignoring the hovering nanny. But he shook his
head with some force, as if he didn't want to tell her.

Nanny said softly, "Sometimes in the night, he'll wake up
and go to the window seat. It looks out to the sea. He likes
that. He's learned to lift the shade for himself."

"Was it the sea that frightened you?" she asked the clinging child. But he shook his head again. "Or the mist? You've
seen mists before, haven't you, my love?"

Nanny had closed the window but had not pulled down
the shade.

Mrs. Cornelius turned to peer out. This window looked
down on the street but she could see the water just beyond
the next house but one. Or could have done, in the moonlight. A sea mist had crept in, a filmy white wraith that made
the street and the rooftops and the outlines of houses seem
unfamiliar and unfriendly.

Cradling the child in her arms, she shivered. Anything
could be out there, she thought. What had Jeremy seen? And
it was in just such a mist that Mr. Hamilton had been struck
down.

What if someone lurked in the shadows, watching this
lighted window, perhaps knowing it was her son's nursery?
What if he had lured the boy to slip down and open the
house door?

They were wealthy enough to pay a goodly ransom.

She had caught her son's fear.

She said to Nanny, "Rouse Mr. Cornelius, if you please.
Ask him to send for Inspector Bennett. It may be nothing,
but on the other hand, better safe than sorry. Tell him to take
Benedict with him." The footman, she thought, would be

protection enough. "And beg him to remember to lock the door behind him. *Hurry!*"

When Nanny had gone, she said, soothingly, "It's all right, Jeremy, there's nothing to worry you. Would you like to sleep in my bed for a bit?" Anything to take him away from here and the lighted window.

She could feel his head bob against her breast. "Then you must stand up like the little man you are, and take my hand. You're far too big for me to carry."

After a time, he sat up and then got down from her lap, but held tightly to her hand as they went back along the dark passage and into her room.

Watching him climb into her bed and snuggle under the bedclothes, she thought, *He might be going on seven, but he's still a baby.*

She took the precaution of locking the bedroom door until her husband returned.

Moments later, Cornelius, sitting in his dressing room, was dragging his trousers on over his nightclothes and searching for his stockings and shoes, all the while grumbling under his breath. But he was accustomed to doing his wife's bidding, and pulling on his heavy coat and finding a scarf, he set out in the darkness for the police station, two streets over.

He had rejected as foolishness taking Benedict with him but had sensibly brought his cane.

He didn't like the sea mist any more than his son had done, and he listened to the muffled echo of his heels, thinking that Matthew Hamilton had been walking out later than this, and someone invisible in just such a mist had nearly killed him. Had Jeremy's terror somehow been intended to bring another prominent man out into the dark streets to be assaulted? Nonsense, he told himself briskly. The child had had a nightmare, and his wife had been frightened by the unexpected intensity of it. Nevertheless he found himself looking over his shoulder whenever there was a sound behind him, and he walked a little faster.

Why the devil did a street appear to be so different on a night of mist? The shrubbery in back of Mrs. Pickering's house looked like hunched monsters brooding over a pool of cotton wool shrouding their feet. And a chimney atop the Reston house sported a gull that floated in midair. When a cat ran out of a doorway on the Mole, it startled him so badly he nearly dropped his cane. A black cat, he was certain of it.

Whatever Jeremy had seen, by the time he reached the police station, Theo Cornelius had convinced himself that something indeed was abroad, and his heart was pounding from a sense of being watched.

The police station was empty. A lamp stood on the desk in the main room, and beside it a note that sent him on to Bennett's house, growling as he went. All for a silly child's nightmare, he told himself now. Otherwise he'd be at home in his own bed, sound asleep. Jeremy had been begging sweets in the kitchen again, and Cook spoiled him recklessly.

But bravado did nothing to stop the hairs on the back of his neck from prickling as he stepped into the street again.

It took him several minutes to rouse someone at Bennett's house. The inspector came to the door, his crutch propping him up as he looked out at the man on his step.

"Mr. Cornelius," he said, instantly recognizing his caller. "What's to do, sir, is there any trouble?"

"My son is having a nightmare. My wife insisted that I summon you." It sounded ridiculous, putting it that way, and he took a step backward. "Er—she felt that since Mr. Hamilton had been attacked on a morning when there was sea mist, it might be important to discover what had upset my son."

"I see." But it was evident Bennett didn't. He cleared his throat and said, "You must fetch Mr. Rutledge at the Duke of Monmouth, sir. He's in charge of the inquiry into what happened to Mr. Hamilton."

"Look," Cornelius began irritably, "I've been to the station, and I've come here. I'm damned if I'll spend what's left of the night—"

But Bennett was there before him. He pointed to his bandaged foot and said, "It's all I can do to walk down the stairs, sir, much less as far as your house. We're spread thin, and that's why Mr. Rutledge has come. You'd do better speaking with him. He's from Scotland Yard, you know. A *London* policeman." He smiled grimly.

Cornelius turned away, angry and feeling a worse fool. He was of half a mind to go home and to bed, be damned to alarums in the night. But his wife would simply send him out again, and so he went instead to the Duke of Monmouth Inn. The sense of danger had faded, replaced by anger and resentment. What he should have done was hunt the fool down himself! Not come for the incompetent and unhelpful police. The Chief Constable would hear about this—

It seemed to be the middle of the night when Rutledge came out of a deep sleep to hear voices in the passage outside his door.

He listened for a moment or two, and recognized the desk clerk's as one of them.

By the time the man knocked, Rutledge was on his feet and reaching for his clothes.

Rutledge opened his door to the desk clerk, his hair disheveled and trousers thrown on with haste. Behind him was a taller man, fair and flustered but well dressed.

"Mr. Rutledge? This is Mr. Cornelius. Inspector Bennett has sent him to you." He turned slightly to include Cornelius in the conversation.

The man said, "There's something wrong at my house. My son's had a shock, and my wife sent me to fetch you. Will you come?"

"What kind of shock?" Rutledge asked, swiftly finishing dressing.

"I don't know. He was screaming the house down half an hour ago. There's a mist coming in. My wife was concerned about that, what with the assault on Mr. Hamilton." He stopped, seeming at a loss for words. His story hadn't come out the way he'd intended it should.

But Rutledge followed him without argument, with Hamish alert and awake in his mind, quarreling and taunting during the silent walk to where Cornelius lived.

The mist had grown denser, and it was a strangely quiet, soft world, the sea itself hissing somewhere to his left instead of rolling in with its usual thunder.

The Cornelius house was on Mercer Street, which curved away from the center of town but still allowed a very nice view of the water. More prosperous residents lived here—Reston's house was just down the road—and the Victorian flavor of money and respectability was reflected in the size and style of the dwellings.

Rutledge was reminded of Bennett's comment that fish scales made for slippery social climbing.

They went up the walk to Number 4 and Cornelius let them in with his key. There was a lamp at the foot of the stairs, but the ground floor was in darkness. Carrying the lamp, Cornelius took the steps two at a time to the first floor, and Rutledge followed.

The man was annoyed that his wife had locked the bedroom door, and knocked briskly.

She came out to them, shushing them. "Jeremy's just gone to sleep again."

She stared uncertainly at Rutledge, and her husband hastily presented him, adding, "He's here in Bennett's stead."

"What seems to be the trouble?" Rutledge asked her.

"It's probably a wild-goose chase," she began apologetically, confronted now with this stranger from London instead of Mr. Bennett. She was beginning to wonder if she'd been wise to call in the police. But the memory of her son's distress kept her from making light of her fears. "Nanny tells me my son sits by his window late at night, and tonight there was something in the mist that frightened him. He began to cry and it took me some time to calm him down again. But after what happened to Matthew Hamilton—"

"Yes, you did the right thing," Rutledge replied, cutting short the apology. "Did he describe to you what he'd seen?"

"A hunchback creature stumbling along the road at the head of the street. He believes it was a monster of some kind, but of course that's only a child's interpretation. I can't think what it might actually have been." She glanced at her husband. "Jeremy is possessed of a lively imagination, and his grandfather encourages him by reading to him books that are, well, perhaps a little *mature* for him. But he doesn't make up stories. Something was there. I'm convinced of it."

"A fisherman carrying his nets down to the boat?" Rutledge took out his watch. "When do the fishermen set sail? Before dawn, surely."

"I hadn't thought of that—but why should that frighten Jeremy? He must have seen them dozens of times. And this—this creature wasn't walking toward the Mole but away from it, following the west road."

"And yet," Hamish put in, "she didna' fear to send her husband out in the dark."

Which was an interesting point. Mr. Cornelius was a

prime target, if someone was intent on distracting the police from the attack on Hamilton by hunting other likely prey in the night. Rutledge shifted his emphasis slightly but that was in effect his next question.

"If you were concerned about who or what was out there, was it wise to send Mr. Cornelius to the police?"

She stared at Rutledge. "But he took Benedict with him. And besides my husband has no enemies."

Over her head Rutledge and Cornelius exchanged glances. In silent agreement that she needn't be told her husband had gone out alone.

"Neither, apparently, did Hamilton have enemies," Rutledge answered her.

Mrs. Cornelius refused to wake the boy for Rutledge to question further tonight. "The problem is out there, not in here. I've told you everything my son told me. There's been enough time wasted already, Inspector. If this 'monster' is to be found, you'd best hurry."

In the end, he didn't press, and Cornelius saw him out again with heartfelt apologies.

Walking back through the mist, Rutledge could understand the sense of unease that had triggered the boy's fear. Nothing appeared to have its normal shape in this white shroud. A cat skirting a garden walk loomed large as it rounded the corner of a wall, as if magnified by the murky light. And a small boat, putting out to sea, seemed to be sailing into a milky curtain that clung to it and draped it until it vanished, a captive of some voracious sea monster. Rooftops appeared and disappeared, chimney pots were heads poking out of the swirls as if strange creatures were dancing there high above the street. A wandering dog knocked over a pail, and the noise of it rolled among the houses with waves of echoes.

He spent half an hour searching for whatever it was young

Jeremy had seen, but there was nothing to account for it.

"The lad should ha' been abed and asleep."

And if the Nanny had caught Jeremy disobeying rules, he might have invented a monster to distract her. It had to be considered.

Rutledge had circled back to the head of Mercer Street and now stood still, looking down it toward the Cornelius house. The windows were dark, everyone settled in his bed. He found himself wondering who would see him if he raised his arms high, threw back his head and howled silently.

Chances were, no one. Perhaps whoever had passed here, briefly crossing Jeremy Cornelius's line of sight, had counted on that. And in the mist, everyone was all but invisible.

A straying husband hurrying back to his wife. A drunk, hoping to find his bed at last, or a housebreaker taking his chances?

"Or yon doctor, on his way to a confinement," Hamish put in. "It needna' be more out of the ordinary than that."

Rutledge turned toward the inn, grateful for his heavy coat against the night chill.

Odd that Bennett had sent Cornelius to him, he found himself thinking as the inn came into sight. The sign was disembodied, a floating man high above the street, catching the light from the lamp that Rutledge had left burning in his room.

Even with its tenuous connection to the Hamilton matter, Jeremy Cornelius's ghostly figure was not a case for the Yard. Bennett had hoped to make him look like a fool, chasing a child's hobgoblins in the middle of the night.

A not-so-subtle attempt to show the outsider that the local man knew what he was about, and at the same time, placating a prominent citizen in need.

Rain came an hour later, a downpour that went on until the eaves were dripping and the dawn was lost in the heavy clouds that seemed to rest on the very rooftops, replicating last night's fog.

Rutledge awoke some forty minutes later than he usually did, the darkness in his room and the regular pattering of the rain blotting out nightmares, allowing him for once to sleep deeply.

The dining room was empty, his breakfast set out on the long table by the kitchen door. He filled his plate and sat down, Hamish seeming to hover behind him in the shadows. The woman who was now serving at meals brought him his tea and stood by his table for a moment looking out the windows at the weather.

He thought to ask about Becky and was assured that she was expected to resume her duties by early next week.

"Thank goodness this wasn't a busier time of year," she went on, and then nodded toward the rain, coming down harder as they watched. "My grandmother told us last night this was coming. Her knees ached something fierce. The barometer bore her out, but we didn't know, did we, that it would be such a stormy morning." She sighed. "Poor daffodils, they'll have muddy faces now."

He offered a smile, and she went back to the kitchen. It was a depressing morning, true enough, and Hamish was vigorously reminding him of the rain in the trenches, the sour smells of unwashed bodies, wet wool, mud, and despair in equal measure.

Finishing the last of his toast and tea, he rose and walked out to the lobby, opening the door to a gust of air so heavy with moisture it seemed to have come from the sea, not the sky.

He had expected to go back to Matthew Hamilton this morning, to sit there again and talk to the man, hoping to bring him back to the present once more. He had the feeling that Hamilton had understood more than Rutledge or the doctor realized, and that the words flowing around him had partly roused him out of the pain and blackness that engulfed him. But it was late, and his first duty must be to Mrs. Hamilton and her maid.

The situation there was unstable enough to change by the hour.

He fetched his hat and coat, and with a sigh dashed through the downpour to the motorcar, feeling his shoulders and his shoes taking the brunt of what was pelting down and swirling in puddles under foot.

He turned the crank and ran for the driver's door, nearly colliding with a man half hidden behind a large black umbrella. He seemed to appear out of nowhere from the boot of the motorcar.

The umbrella flexed as it struck Rutledge and dumped a shower of water into his face as he ducked away from the points.

The man holding it swore, and then as it shifted a little so that he could peer under the dripping edge, he said, "Rutledge?"

It was Dr. Granville.

"Are you looking for me?" Rutledge asked, and then added, "For God's sake, come inside before we're both wet through." Leaving the motorcar running, he urged the doctor through the yard door into the inn.

They found themselves in the narrow, flagged passage that led from the back hall, and Granville left his umbrella outside, taking out a handkerchief to wipe his face.

"What is it? Has Hamilton taken a turn for the worst?" Rutledge asked when the man seemed to hesitate.

"Or is he dead?" Rutledge went on, staring hard at the doctor.

"I don't know." The doctor's voice was diffident, as if he were embarrassed to say what had brought him here.

"You didn't put a guard on him, is that it? After I'd warned you. Well? What has happened to him now? Come on, man, speak up!"

The doctor looked up at him. "He's gone," he said simply. "Just—gone."

At first Rutledge took that to mean that Hamilton had died in the night, alone and without regaining his senses. But then he realized that the doctor meant what he said quite literally. The shock in his eyes was unmistakable.

"Gone? When? *Where?*" Rutledge demanded.

"I don't know. For God's sake, I don't know. His bed was empty when I went to check on him half an hour ago."

"Are you quite sure he hasn't passed out in another room as he tried to find help?"

"I've searched the premises. He's *gone,* I tell you."

"To the house. To find his wife." Rutledge swore, and wheeled toward the door. "Come on, man, we've got to search for him."

"He can't have made it far, it's not a climb he can—"

But Rutledge had the sleeve of his coat, pulling at him, and the doctor came reluctantly behind him, catching up his umbrella but with no time to open it.

They made for the motorcar and climbed in, bringing the miasma of wet wool after them, steaming up the windscreen with the heat of their bodies.

Rutledge found a cloth under his seat and scrubbed at the inside of the glass, swearing again. Then he tossed the cloth to the doctor, put the motorcar into gear, and turned in a shimmering fan of spray.

They came out of the inn drive and went toward the street that ran along the Mole. "Have you spoken to Bennett?" Rutledge asked, taking the next turn far too fast, feeling the tires slipping sideways in a spin. He brought the vehicle back under control and headed to the east.

"No. I couldn't face him. I came straightaway for you instead. I thought perhaps—look out, you fool, there's a bicycle ahead!—damn it, we're no good to Hamilton or anyone else if we're dead."

But Rutledge paid him no heed. Every second counted now. Three minutes later, he found a very wet constable standing under a tree some distance from the drive to the house, where he'd taken what shelter he could find against the trunk.

"How long have you been on duty?" Rutledge asked, lowering the window.

"Since six, sir," the man answered, looking as wretched as he must feel. "It's been all quiet at the house. Not a sound out of them."

"And no one has come in or out?"

"No, sir. No one."

But if the earlier watcher had been standing where this man was, it would be hard in the dark to know who had come. Or gone.

Rutledge thanked him and drove up to the door.

The shrubbery by the drive was as wet as a rain forest, he thought, getting out to hammer on the house door. And the downpour had hardly lessened since it began.

Mallory came to answer his impatient summons, looking as tired as Rutledge had ever seen him. "What do you want now?" He glanced over Rutledge's shoulder and saw the doctor in the motorcar.

"For God's sake, why have you brought *him*? I've done them no harm."

"Hamilton has disappeared," Rutledge told him bluntly. "He may have come here. I want to search the house, and after that the grounds."

"It's a trick. He's dead, isn't he? Well, you aren't bringing any of your men or Bennett's here on a pretense to search. I'll use the revolver if I have to. Do you hear me?"

"He's *missing*," Rutledge said grimly. "You'd better listen to me, Mallory. I'm not here to play at cat and mouse. If he's been out in this rain for hours, he'll be running a fever by now, or he could have bled to death from his internal injuries—God only knows. Will you let me in to search or not?"

Mallory called out to Dr. Granville. "Is this true? Is Hamilton gone?"

"In the night," the doctor confirmed. "He must have come here, man! Where else would he go? In his condition?"

Mallory swore. "He isn't here, I tell you!" But his gaze moved toward the dark, silent house behind him. "I'd have *known*."

"Stay here if you like, and guard the door. But let me search," Rutledge said rapidly. "I'll do it alone, and I give you my word now that I have no other motive. I won't leave a window or door unlocked, I won't frighten either of the women. It's his *house*, Mallory, he knows it better than you do."

"I thought he was too badly injured to know where he was, much less walk away. *You told me as much, damn it,*" he retorted accusingly. "You lied to me!"

"We believed it to be true. But you know as well as I do that badly injured men are capable of heroic effort. We saw that often enough in the war, for God's sake. If he's determined to know why his wife hasn't visited him, he may have tried to reach her, for fear something has happened to her as well. Or he may be out for revenge. It's better if I find him first, before you come on him in the dark."

The other man stood there, undecided. And then he opened the door wider and let Rutledge step inside, watching the water dripping relentlessly from his coat and his trousers to puddle on the floor.

Mallory gestured to it and said ruefully, "I can't even call the maid to clear it up. Just stay away from Nan, and from

Mrs. Hamilton. And don't linger. I don't trust you, and I'll be searching the house again after you leave. I'm quite serious, Rutledge, don't drive me into a corner."

He said to Mallory, "If Hamilton managed to make his way here, pray that his mind is clear. It could be your salvation."

And with Hamish behind him, alternately warning and driving him, Rutledge set about his search.

It would be to Mallory's advantage to bring the wounded man to his wife, Rutledge kept telling himself, since she couldn't go to him. And yet—

He went into every room belowstairs and on the ground floor, testing the window locks, looking for signs of a break-in while Mallory slept. He searched for wet footprints on carpets and felt for damp draperies where windows might have been thrown open during the heavy rain. And he listened intently for any sounds that might tell him that Hamilton was here, and also a prisoner.

But a quarter of an hour later, he had found nothing except the irate Nan, demanding to know why she hadn't been set free long since.

Passing Mallory where he sat on the staircase, Rutledge moved on to the first floor, methodically going from bedroom to bedroom even as he began to realize it was hopeless. Looking under beds, into wardrobes, behind screens, even behind the stiff brocade draperies that hung at each window, he tried to think where Hamilton might have gone if he hadn't come here to Casa Miranda. But there were still the grounds to search.

The only room he didn't enter was Mrs. Hamilton's.

When he'd finished in the attics, he stood outside her door and tapped lightly on the panel. He had the feeling she was cowering inside, unwilling to face him.

Without Stephen Mallory's knowledge, had she gone to

the doctor's surgery during the night and somehow managed to bring her husband back with her? It would have been a disastrous act of courage and determination even to try, and she couldn't have moved Hamilton if he'd been unconscious still.

Mallory had to sleep sometime, although he looked as if he'd never closed his eyes. Was that her solution to the need to know how her husband fared?

And if it was, then he himself must now tread with care.

"Mayhap she doesna' know who is at the door," Hamish pointed out.

The room must look out to the sea and the headland on the other side of the Mole. She may not have heard his motorcar with the rain making such a racket. "It's Inspector Rutledge, Mrs. Hamilton. No one else is with me."

Except for Hamish, he added silently. But how would she know?

After a moment, he called to her again, more insistently this time.

And she said, her voice tremulous, "What do you want? Is there news?"

"Are you alone in there, Mrs. Hamilton?"

There was a pause before she came to the door, opening it a crack. She too looked very tired, her face already losing some of the soft vulnerability he remembered.

Warily she said, "What do you mean? Of course I'm alone."

"May I come in and look around your room, Mrs. Hamilton? I won't take more than a moment or two."

"Look—what is it you're looking *for*?"

"I want to see that all is well with you, as Mr. Mallory has assured me it is."

But with the intuition of a woman, she could sense that something wasn't right.

"Have you interviewed George Reston?" she demanded suspiciously. "What has he said to you?"

"I'm looking into that, I promise you. Just now—"

Pulling her shawl closer, as if trying to warm herself, she said, "No. I don't want to see you or anyone else. Go away."

"Mrs. Hamilton." He studied her hair, but it appeared dry to him. Yet out in this storm, nothing stayed dry for very long. Had Matthew Hamilton been moved before the rains began? Under cover of the mist?

"I'm not feeling very well this morning. I want to be left alone. Don't disturb me again until you can bring me good news." She looked away from him, tears filling her eyes. "I can't bear much more."

She closed the door in his face, and he heard the key turn in the lock.

Hamish said, "She didna' ask how her husband was, this morning."

There was nothing for it after that but to search the grounds. And the heavy rain hadn't let up. Rutledge briefly explained to Granville what he was doing and why, then asked to borrow his umbrella.

The doctor said before he handed it over, "I really ought to look in on Mrs. Hamilton while I'm here. When she hears what's become of her husband, she'll be distraught. If you'll have a word with Mallory—"

Rutledge cut him short. "Stay out of it. If you want to be useful, think where we ought to look if Hamilton isn't here." He took the umbrella, effectively stranding Granville in the motorcar.

The umbrella turned out to be all but worthless, and after a time he gave up and furled it. There was no sign of Matthew Hamilton on the grounds or in the outbuildings. No sign, even, that someone had been there, no muddy marks on floors in the garden shed or the small stable that had been partly converted to a garage. Rutledge put his hand on the bonnets of the motorcars there—they were cool to the touch—and hunted for deep footprints in the soft wet earth. The lone horse nickered as he leaned into its stall, and blew as he offered his hand to it. And he used his instincts as well, lifting rain-heavy branches, burrowing under shrubs, putting himself in the shoes of a man desperately tired or overcome by weakness. He even poked a hand around the iron seat in the back garden, now draped in a tentlike covering of oiled cloth to prevent rusting over the winter. Mrs. Hamilton and her husband must have sat here and watched the sunset of a summer's evening. Today the sea and the sky seemed to have merged, a gray mass that was nearly indistinguishable behind the curtain of fresh squalls on the horizon.

Rutledge was just turning away when he realized that closer to hand there was a gathering of men down along the Mole, Bennett among them, leaning on his crutches. They were all getting into a line of carts and carriages and motorcars, hurry evident even at this distance.

Hamish said, "They've found him, then."

13

Mallory was once more sitting at the bottom of the staircase, this time with a whiskey glass in his hand. He was staring at it morosely and barely glanced up as Rutledge stepped through the door. Then something in Rutledge's face brought him to his feet.

"What? What have you found?"

"Nothing. Here. But I think perhaps Bennett has been more successful in the village. I must go."

He turned away toward the motorcar but Mallory called him back. "Did you tell her he was missing? I must know—*did you tell her?*"

"No," Rutledge said, standing there looking closely at him. How much more would it take to make this man break? He was grateful now that he hadn't discovered Matthew Hamilton hidden in the house. "I saw no point in adding to her distress. But if we find Hamilton has crept out and died—or has been left somewhere to die—it will be hard to stop Bennett from wanting your liver nailed to the police station door."

"Damn you!"

The curse followed Rutledge down the drive as Dr. Granville demanded, "What's that you were saying? Damn it, man, how did Bennett find out about Hamilton?"

"Someone must have stumbled on him. I could see from the gardens—a dozen or two men by the Mole, sorting themselves out into vehicles."

"Bennett must be wondering where I got to. I should be there when they bring him in, rather than wasting my time here." Granville was tense with worry.

"It wasn't a waste of time," Rutledge said, nodding to the constable under his tree as they turned out of the drive. "After all, this was the most likely place."

He drove fast, but with care on the wet roads. Air passing through the car brought a chill with it that cut through the drenched clothes clinging to his body, although the morning appeared to be warming up noticeably.

They reached the Mole as the last man was getting into a cart, dragging a canvas sack over his head to keep dry.

Bennett stood up in the wagon in which he was a passenger, thought better of clambering down again, and shouted across to Rutledge, "Where have you been?"

"To the house—"

But the inspector wasn't interested. He called, "There's been a landslip. To the west of here. A bad one, I'm told. We're on our way to see the extent of the damage." He motioned for Rutledge to follow, but the doctor objected angrily.

"A landslip, is it? Then put me down here," he said. "In an hour I'll have a surgery full of patients, and there's still Hamilton, if—when—you find him. You must tell Bennett what's happened. I can't take the time."

Rutledge paused to set the doctor down, and the man hurried off without a word, his umbrella bent to the wind, his feet sloshing through the rivulets of water running through the street. Then Rutledge put the car into gear again and hurried to catch up the tag end of the convoy heading west along the Devon road.

Hamish was vocal, reminding Rutledge of the alarums in the night.

"What the laddie saw. A man carrying anither man o'er his shoulder?"

"And heading in the opposite direction from the Hamilton house. Yes, I was just thinking about that. Before the rain came."

"Aye. No tracks."

"And no tracks the last time. A wily bastard, this one."

He followed the convoy along the road that led toward the Devon border, but it wasn't very long before they stopped and got out in the downpour, moving across a rising green headland that seemed to end in a jagged line across the horizon of the sea.

Bennett stood there, crutch digging deep into the wet earth. "The cottage is gone," he was saying. "And a good ten feet this side of it." He raised his voice to call peremptorily, "Damn it, Tatum, don't go any closer! There's no certainty it's finished falling, and we'd have no way of getting you out."

One of the townspeople stopped where he was, then gingerly backed away from the edge, nodding. "True," he said. "If it weren't for this infernal rain, we could have a better look from the water." There were cows grazing peacefully nearer the road, but none had ventured as far as the landslip. Seagulls were wheeling overhead, calling to one another and dipping out of sight to where the land had shifted and fallen. "A feast for the likes of them," Tatum went on.

The men were strung out in a rough line, staring at the sight. One of them turned to Rutledge and said, "It happens from time to time. In my grandda's day, three houses and a barn went over. That was a bad one."

"You said there was a cottage here?"

"If you could call it that. A tumbledown ruin, where no one cared to live. And you can see why, can't you? The last resident there was a brother to Mr. Reston. The black sheep in the family, you might say." He grinned. "He'll be glad enough that the cottage is gone now. People will finally forget it existed."

"Black sheep?" Rutledge asked, curious. There had been no mention of a brother. "Does he drink?"

The man shook his head. "Nothing so tame. A general reprobate. Wild for the ladies, if you could call them that. Gambled on whether a fly would land on his dinner. A petty thief and a troublemaker. When Freddy died, brother George must have fallen down on his knees in gratitude."

"What happened to him?"

The man frowned. "Odd, now that you mention it. He drowned on the strand, not a dozen yards from where they found Mr. Hamilton's body."

Bennett was calling to his men. "There's nothing we can do here after all. Might as well get out of the wet." He limped heavily toward the vehicle that had brought him out here, then veered as if the prospect of jolting back to town in a wagon wasn't a welcome one. "Seeing that you're here, Rutledge, I'll drive back with you. Save some time."

The man who had been talking with Rutledge quietly faded away, as if their conversation had never taken place. Rutledge nodded to him, but there was no return nod.

Rutledge had left the motor running, and as he climbed in and Bennett swung his muddy crutch into the rear seat, Hamish said, "'Ware!"

Turning the motorcar was a dicey proposition, for the ground was saturated and the tires sank deep. Rutledge gave the maneuver the attention it deserved while Bennett took out a handkerchief to dry his face.

"I saw Dr. Granville with you. One of the women having hysterics? Nan Weekes, most likely. Mrs. Hamilton doesn't appear to be the sort. But then you never know, especially if Mallory decided to make free with her."

Rutledge responded in a neutral voice, "Matthew Hamilton is missing."

Bennett swung around so that he could see Rutledge's face.

"Missing? What the *hell* are you talking about?"

"When Dr. Granville looked in on him this morning, he wasn't there."

"You're saying he came to his senses and just walked *out*?"

"We don't know. He wasn't there. I went at once to search the Hamilton house and grounds, but if he's at Casa Miranda, I can't find him. Unless he knows some way of concealing himself there. When I saw the gathering on the Mole, I assumed someone had sent for you, to tell you where to look. That this was a search party setting out."

Bennett swore, long and feelingly. "Why didn't Granville come to me, damn it? And what possessed the fool to leave? He'll take his death in this rain. That blow on the head must have unsettled his mind."

"Or someone was afraid he might regain his senses and remember more than was safe."

Bennett stared at him again. "You're saying he didn't walk away? That someone's got rid of him?"

"There was the Cornelius boy's nightmare. He saw something in the night. His mother told me it was a hunchback walking through the mist."

"Pshaw! That's nonsense."

"It might fit. If someone carried Matthew Hamilton over his shoulder."

"Then where in hell's name would he have taken him? And on foot? He's no lightweight, is Hamilton."

"A good question." Rutledge slowed as he reached the Mole. He didn't add that there were two motorcars to choose from at Casa Miranda, and a horse. Or that the constable had taken shelter under a tree, where in the heavier down pours, he could hear very little. "Do you want to get down here? I'd like to find a boat willing to take me around to the landslip. Before that I want to speak to Cornelius's son. In light of what's happened since last night."

"A boat in this weather? And what's there to see, I ask you? Don't be a fool, you're here to attend to Hamilton and his affairs, not to see the sights. Take me to Granville's surgery, if you will. A child's nightmare won't help us forward. There may be something Dr. Granville missed in his panic."

Rutledge stopped at the walk to Granville's surgery door and waited while Bennett got down. Bennett stood for a moment in the rain, as if torn between duties. "You're not coming?" he asked finally. "Are you insisting on going to the Cornelius house first?"

The last thing Rutledge wanted was Bennett's harsh impatience frightening an already frightened child. He compromised. "All right, I'll come here after I have a chat with young Jeremy." He glanced at the sky. The clouds had darkened again as another heavy squall approached. Not the best conditions for an open boat, as even Hamish was pointing out.

"If Hamilton is loose, he's in that house." Bennett shifted his umbrella against the shadow of more rain sweeping across behind them. "What I'm hoping is that Mallory was careless. If he was the one who took Hamilton away."

"I've told you, I searched the grounds and the house carefully."

"Not carefully enough, in my book. What better place to keep an eye on the man and his recovering memory than under your thumb? No one ever said Mallory was a fool."

"That's not something I want to contemplate," Rutledge replied. "What's even more worrying is if Hamilton went there under his own power, he could be out for revenge. Do you think he's that sort? You know him, I don't."

Bennett gave it a moment's thought. "If I were Mallory, if I didn't have the man myself, I'd be looking over my shoulder about now."

Then he was gone, making his way up the walk to the surgery door.

Hamish watched him go, saying, "It could be true."

Rutledge answered slowly, "He could also have been taken to that cottage that just fell into the sea. In which case, we might never see him again, or find his body."

"It's no' verra' likely. A verra' long way to carry a man's body withoot being seen."

Rutledge drew up in front of the Cornelius house. "I grant you. But if I were planning to do away with Matthew Hamilton, I'd have carried him as far as I could on foot, well away from Granville's surgery, and put him somewhere out of sight, until I could come back with some sort of transportation." It had been a risk, with the constable on duty. The horse, then, not a motorcar. But Jeremy hadn't seen a horse.

"Ye ken, Mallory's cottage is standing empty."

"There's that, as well."

When Rutledge presented himself at her door, Mrs. Cornelius was reluctant to let even an inspector from London interview her son this morning. Her manner was polite but firm, her expression cool and distant.

"He seems to have got over his fright, and I don't want to remind him."

"I shan't worry him about it," Rutledge said with a smile. "But I need to have a better feeling for what was out there— if anything. You say the nanny never saw whatever it was?"

"No one saw it but Jeremy. I expect he was half asleep and hardly knew how to describe what he witnessed, except in terms of monsters. I've told you, he's a child of immense imagination."

"And too young to tell anything but the exact truth," Rutledge reminded her. "I won't do him any harm. I promise you."

In the end he got his way, and the boy was brought down from the nursery to meet him. Well aware that his clothes were too wet to sit on the blue silk that covered the sitting room chairs, Rutledge pulled a wooden one away from the cherry desk under the windows and tried to make himself appear comfortable as he waited.

In the doorway Mrs. Cornelius stood aside and let her son precede her across the threshold.

A sturdy six-year-old, with intelligent dark eyes and a rather sensitive face, Rutledge thought as Jeremy walked into the sitting room. He was his father's son in build, and his mother's in looks. An only child, and not spoiled.

Hamish agreed. "No' a lad to imagine something sae grisly."

Rutledge greeted the boy and asked him to sit down for a moment. "Your mother tells me you enjoy looking out your window at night. Do you have an interest in the stars?"

Jeremy glanced at his mother, and then said, "I like the night. I see the fishermen going out, sometimes, and the stars when there's no moon." He smiled broadly. "Mrs. Ingram's cat digs up Mrs. Witherspoon's roses. *She* thinks it's the Harmon dog."

Rutledge laughed, pleased to find the boy so articulate. "I shan't tell her that."

"No. I like the cat. The dog is small and nips at my heels

when my mother takes me to visit Mrs. Harmon. She always smells of peppermint, but the dog is always in need of a bath."

His mother was about to admonish him, then thought better of it, standing guard at his back with her gaze fixed on Rutledge's face.

But it was Jeremy who was more perceptive. "Were you in the war, sir?"

"Yes, I was. In France."

"My uncle died of wounds at Gallipoli. I don't remember him very well. He was quite brave, my grandfather tells me."

"I'm sure he was," Rutledge answered.

"Were you brave too?"

Mrs. Cornelius said, "Jeremy."

But Rutledge, his throat tight, said, "I was given a medal." As if that was a measure of courage. "There were others who deserved it more." He coughed, then changed the direction of the conversation. "Tell me what you saw in the streets last night? Do you remember?"

The child nodded gravely, taking courage from his mother's presence. "I didn't like it," he said.

"Was it shaped like a bear?"

"There aren't any bears in Hampton Regis," the boy answered him scornfully. "And I've never been to the zoo in London. Have you?"

"Many times," Rutledge informed him. "My parents took me once. I particularly liked the giraffes. They have purple tongues."

Jeremy seemed enthralled with the idea. "Truly purple?"

"Truly. Now tell me about what you saw. If it wasn't a bear, what was it?"

"A man without a head," he said uneasily, moving closer to his mother. "I didn't like it."

"A big man, taller than I am?"

"I don't know."

"Wider than I am?"

"I couldn't tell. I didn't like it that he didn't have a head."

"I expect that's true. I wouldn't care for it myself."

Mrs. Cornelius was once more on the point of commenting, then fell silent again. But her eyes had grown anxious.

"You were quite a brave boy to tell your mother what you saw. I expect it was a fisherman with a heavy net over his shoulders. You weren't likely to see his head then, were you?"

The boy was suddenly still. "You think so?"

"It could be," Rutledge answered. "But I wasn't there, and I didn't see him."

Jeremy appeared to be replaying the scene in his mind. "But I don't think it was," he finally said. "He stumbled as he walked. As if he couldn't see."

"Was it two men, do you think? One with another over his shoulders? Carrying him because his friend couldn't walk far?"

The boy seemed to relax. "Yes, I hadn't thought of that." He smiled. "That was a nice thing to do, although I shouldn't like to be carried with my head hanging down. It would hurt after a while, wouldn't it?"

"Perhaps they didn't have far to go." Over the boy's head, his eyes met Mrs. Cornelius's.

And then Jeremy said, out of the blue, "I saw Mr. Harmon bring his son home that way one night. After he'd stayed late at The Merry Tinker. He was walking beside his father, and then didn't seem to be able to find his legs. They went in different directions. And his father put him across his shoulder for the rest of the way."

"Did Mr. Harmon have a head?"

"No. I couldn't see it for Lawrence."

"Well, there you are. You've been a very great help,

Jeremy. Your mother must be proud of you." Rutledge rose to leave.

"Yes, very proud," Mrs. Cornelius replied.

But Jeremy was still thinking about other matters, and he said as Rutledge reached the sitting room door, "It wasn't quite the same, you know, as Mr. Harmon. Somehow. I didn't like it."

On the street in front of the Cornelius house, Rutledge was met by an out-of-breath constable who nearly collided with him before he could slow his pace.

"Mr. Rutledge, sir!" He leaned one hand against the wing of the motorcar, fighting to get the words out. "Mr. Bennett says—come at once!"

Rutledge turned the crank and stepped behind the wheel. "What's happened?"

The constable shook his head. "I'm not to say, sir—only, come at once." He hauled himself into the passenger seat and pointed toward the Mole.

The sea had yielded its secret, then.

But as Rutledge reached the Mole and realized that no crowd was gathered there, the constable gestured east and added, "Dr. Granville's surgery."

"They've found Hamilton," Rutledge said to Hamish. "Alive or dead?"

He wasn't aware that he'd spoken the words aloud.

The constable stirred uneasily. "I don't know, sir. Truly."

It was a grim-faced Bennett who met him at the surgery. Leaving the constable to take up his station on the front walk, he ushered Rutledge down the passage to the door that led to the doctor's consulting room.

Granville was seated in a chair usually reserved for patients, looking drained and ill. There was a whiskey glass in one hand, but it was shaking with such force that the man couldn't even bring it to his lips.

Bennett, on Rutledge's heels, said, "Look behind the desk."

Rutledge went to the massive desk and leaned over it.

He had been prepared to see Hamilton lying there dead. But it wasn't Hamilton on the floor, just out of sight from the doorway. It was a woman, facedown, the hair on the back of her head matted with blood, her legs crumpled under her.

He knew her at once. Mrs. Granville.

Rutledge glanced at Bennett, then knelt to touch the side of her throat. The flesh was cool, and there was no pulse.

He straightened up and stepped away. Looking down at the body, he could picture her coming into the room and crossing to the desk, perhaps to leave a note for her husband. If there had been someone behind her, she hadn't feared him. Or perhaps if the room was dark, she hadn't even realized anyone was there. And as she reached the side of the desk, whoever it was had struck her hard enough to kill her. He noted that she was wearing a nightdress with a matching blue silk robe over it, her bare feet encased in incongruously plain woolly slippers. She hadn't expected to find a murderer here. A woman with no defenses, and no need to die, surely. A doctor's wife, used to tending patients, unprepared for violence.

He felt a wash of pity. She would not have cared to be seen by so many men while in her nightdress.

Hamish said, "She couldna' be mistaken for the doctor. Even in the dark."

She was a slight woman compared with Granville, and not nearly as tall.

Hamilton? Or perhaps she had thought it was he, standing there in the dark, asking her to help him. And she had stepped behind the desk to turn up the lamp on the far side. That would have sealed her fate.

Was it Stephen Mallory who had killed her because she

had caught him trying to carry Hamilton out into the night? What was it the doctor had told him earlier? The garden door had been ajar. But where was her husband, and why was she here in the surgery alone in the dead of night?

Unless she had answered a summons at the door because Dr. Granville wasn't at home. Yet the surgery doors were seldom locked—Rutledge had discovered that for himself, and anyone else could have done the same.

Rutledge turned back to the room and said, "Dr. Granville informed me that he'd already searched the surgery for Hamilton."

"So he had. But I expect he never thought to look behind the desk. It wasn't likely that Hamilton would be crouching back there, was it? Not with his injuries."

Rutledge turned to Granville. "Doctor?"

He roused himself with an effort. "No. I never—he couldn't have been behind there. My first thought was he'd come to his senses and dragged himself out of bed to find something for his pain. And so I'd gone through every room, expecting him to be lying in one of them, unconscious. He's a large man—I didn't think to look—*there*. Not over there. The cabinets behind the desk contain files. The bottom drawer I keep locked because it has certain drugs in it that I don't like to leave in the dispensary. Why should he hide over there? From me?" He got to his feet. "But then I saw that the garden door was ajar, and it occurred to me that he'd tried to reach his house."

"Why should your wife be in the surgery alone in the middle of the night? Surely you missed her at breakfast."

Granville wiped his hand across his mouth. "I wasn't here for breakfast. I had—" He broke off and ran from the room. They could hear him vomiting outside the garden door. After a moment he came back in, his face still pale, his hands fumbling with a handkerchief.

"I couldn't bear to touch her. I could see she was dead. I just sat here, and then somehow Bennett was here, and I made him look." He swallowed hard. "I'd been out with a case of congestive heart failure. William Joyner, that was. When I got back, I came directly to the surgery to look in on Hamilton. He was gone and I came for you. I didn't go to my house—I didn't want to disturb my—my wife. I saw no reason to worry her." With sudden ferocity, he twisted the handkerchief in his hands. "I'll kill Mallory for you. You needn't wait for the hangman."

14

They caught him as he lunged for the door, and Bennett swore as the doctor kicked out at his foot in his frantic effort to break free, cursing and fighting with the strength of fury.

It took them several minutes to settle him in the chair again, and this time Rutledge held the glass so that Granville could drink a little of the whiskey. Still, he managed to spill most of it down his shirt, and Bennett said testily, "It's not doing much good. Let it go."

Granville began to cry, his eyes red rimmed and unfocused. "I'm sorry," he said over and over again. "I'm sorry."

Rutledge wasn't certain whether he was apologizing to them or to his dead wife for somehow failing her.

They could hear the outside door opening and closing.

The constable came to the consulting room door and said, "It's the rector. Mr. Putnam. Shall I let him in, Inspector

Rutledge? I've turned away all the others as Inspector Bennett instructed, but I thought—"

"Yes, yes, bring him here. Warn him beforehand, will you?"

Rutledge went to the door as he heard Putnam coming down the passage with the constable, the two men speaking in subdued voices.

"Mr. Putnam? I think Dr. Granville has need of you, sir. And, Constable, where is the nearest doctor? Send someone for him, if you please. Directly. Take my motorcar. It will be faster. And lock the surgery door before you go. We don't want people walking in."

Putnam stepped into the room and went across to the doctor, kneeling by his chair. "This is shocking, I haven't quite— Will you not come with me to the house for a bit?" he asked gently. "I'll make you a pot of tea and you can leave these gentlemen to their duties."

Granville turned to face him, and at first Rutledge thought he was going to refuse to go with the rector. But then he stood up docilely and walked out of the room without looking back.

Bennett said as soon as he was out of sight, "Well, Rutledge, will you arrest that bastard now, or shall I?"

"Where's the proof that Mallory attacked Mrs. Granville? It could have been Hamilton."

Bennett stared at him in shocked silence, then found his tongue. *"Hamilton?"*

"Men with severe head wounds are sometimes muddled. If Mrs. Granville startled him in the dark, he might have thought she was whoever had attacked him in the first place."

"You're a fool if you believe that."

Rutledge was out of patience. "Stop thinking with your foot and your pride. We have a dead woman on our hands, and a missing man. Mallory has two witnesses at that house, remember. And we have no idea *when* Hamilton went missing. At least not yet."

"What was Mrs. Granville doing here at the surgery in the middle of the night, if she hadn't let Mallory in?"

"I don't know what brought her here. She could have seen a light and expected to find her husband in the surgery, not Mallory. She could have come to look in on Hamilton, and he woke up, dazed, confused, and afraid of the shadowy figure standing over his bed. When she turned away and went into Granville's office, he could have followed her. She could even have been on the point of turning up the lamp by the desk to see if her husband was asleep in his chair."

"Farradiddle. If it was Hamilton, what did he use for a weapon? There's none lying about that I can see."

It was useless. But Rutledge was irritated, and snapped, "A good barrister will bring up the possibility. We must be there before him."

Bennett would hear none of it. "You've done nothing since you got here but make excuses for that murderer. I told you from the start you'd come to protect him, not arrest him. It's plain as the nose on your face. Did he serve under you? Is that it?"

Rutledge started to reply but thought better of it. How was he to explain to Bennett that he was striving to be fair to Mallory because he had once hated the man. With a passion built of despair and aching resentment that strings pulled for one man had done nothing for so many others in greater need. Had done nothing, in fact, to save Hamish MacLeod and all those like him.

A tense silence between the two policemen lengthened.

Rutledge went to stand by the window, looking out at the rain forming puddles that became rivers through the back garden, any tracks of importance long since washed away.

Bennett sat cushioning his foot as best he could on a stool in front of his chair. The smell of whiskey was still strong in the room, from where Granville had spilled it. And Mrs. Granville's body was a forceful presence even though she was out of sight around the corner of the desk.

Restless with waiting, Rutledge used the next half hour to search the surgery for himself, with particular care given to the room where Hamilton had been lying. But there was no indication of a scuffle. The bedclothes, thrown back haphazardly, were the only sign of agitation on Hamilton's part—or haste on Mallory's. The Crown would be hard-pressed to say with any certainty what had happened. Adding to that, Hamilton's clothing and possessions were missing as well.

There was a brush of what appeared to be blood, only a thin streak, on the edge of the door, as if Hamilton had grasped it to steady himself—or Mallory had had difficulty hoisting Hamilton over his shoulder in the small space. And how could he have carried a dead weight out of the building and as far as the Mole?

Hamish said, "A barrow from the shed."

"Then where is it now? And why didn't Jeremy Cornelius see it? No, if it was Mallory, he came prepared to make Hamilton's disappearance as inconspicuous as possible. And so far he's succeeded."

But Hamish was not in the mood to agree. "What if the lad saw but one man, no' two?"

Hamilton himself, stooped in pain, his head covered to hide the bandaging. But what had possessed him to walk *away* from Casa Miranda? Unless he was too muddled to know what he was doing?

Rutledge went back to the doctor's office, but Bennett's unvoiced condemnation beat against him, and he felt as if he would suffocate if he stayed there. He had already looked in the closet where medicines and supplies were kept, searched the waiting room, the other examining rooms, scanned the shelves behind the doctor's desk, reached over it to pull open drawers and close them again, thumbed through shelves of files in another closet. Nothing appeared to be out of order. Nor had he found anything that might conceivably be the weapon that had killed Margaret Granville. All the same, for want of anything better to do, he returned to the waiting room.

Dr. Granville's medical bag stood forlornly where he must have set it down on his return from Joyner's house. A reminder that medicine was powerless against death.

Rutledge squatted beside it and opened the top. Inside there were boxes of pills and powders. He took out the nearest one. An emetic. The next he recognized as digitalis. A small notebook caught his eye, and he opened that to the page where a fountain pen had been clipped. Lines were scrawled there, dated today with the time given as four in the morning, describing treatment of one William Joyner whose heart was failing. Thumbing through earlier pages, he found that Granville kept careful records of patients he saw outside surgery hours. Joyner's name came up a dozen times, with a list of symptoms and medicines prescribed, treatment instituted.

He heard brisk footsteps in the passage. Setting the notebook back in the bag, Rutledge closed it and stood up. A youngish man with prematurely white hair stepped into the room. The constable following on his heels said only, "Dr. Hester, sir. From Middlebury."

"Thank you for coming." Rutledge introduced himself, and added, "This way." He led Hester to the office.

Hester nodded to Bennett, who said, "It's Dr. Granville's wife, sir, she's there behind the desk. I didn't like to ask him to touch her."

"Perfectly right."

Hester set his bag on the desktop and knelt beside the body, working efficiently and carefully in the small space.

"I daresay the cause of death will be skull fracture from the blow on the back of the head. She was probably unconscious before she hit the floor, and most likely dead shortly thereafter. Hard to tell until I've examined her in better lighting. She's been dead for several hours—the body is cool but rigor hasn't set in. As far as I can tell, she's not been interfered with in any way. I should think the body lies as it fell, moving very little after that. As I'm sure Dr. Granville is already aware, she probably knew nothing from the time she was struck. I can't say what instrument was used, but if there's nothing out of place here—" He gestured to the room at large. "Most likely the weapon was taken away by whoever did this."

"A cane?" Bennett asked. "We saw that the doctor has an assortment of canes and crutches in a closet. For all we know, one is missing."

"It would depend on the shape of the cane's head. I'd guess more round than angular. With sufficient force and room enough to bring one's full weight into play, a single blow in the right area of the skull could kill."

Rutledge said, "Most of them have a knob at the end for a better grip."

"Yes, that's the sort I keep on hand," Hester agreed. "It couldn't have done this. But that's not to say it's the only kind Granville has used." He glanced at the body. "Poor woman." It was the first time his professional manner slipped.

Rutledge saw in his mind's eye the rounded breast of the swan on Miss Esterley's cane. "Then it wouldn't have mattered whether the killer was a man or a woman, given the right weapon."

"Probably not." Hester got to his feet. "That's all I can give you here. You might have a look at those tongs by the hearth. Though I don't expect they were used. Unwieldy, I'd say."

Rutledge said, "I've examined them. No hair, no blood. Unless they were wiped clean."

Bennett looked around the room as Hester had done, hoping to see it through new eyes. The silver candlesticks. A pair of carved bookends in the shape of globes, Europe and Asia on one side, the Americas on the other. A paperweight in the form of a frog. A display of early airplane models in bottles, the tiny canvas bodies and thin wooden struts too delicate to survive use as a weapon, even if the glass didn't shatter.

Hester said, following his gaze, "Apparently one of Granville's cousins flew the damned things in France. And before he was killed, he made models of various types of craft for his parents. I expect no one wanted them in the house as a reminder. Either of you know what a knobkerrie is? Used in Africa for killing. Like a prehistoric club, actually, with a round knob at the end. Very efficient at caving in skulls. I've seen them. My grandfather spent some time in South Africa and up the western coast. He earned more as a doctor than as a prospector, and came home as poor as he left. Tells you something, doesn't it?"

And who else had been in South Africa? Certainly not Mallory. He could see the thought flit across Bennett's face. But Miss Esterley had grown up in Kenya.

"It doesn't serve to guess," Rutledge said finally. "If it's not here, we're wasting time. A simple hammer, brought with the killer? Who can say?" But that argued premeditation. And pointed to Mallory.

"Yes, possible." Hester took a deep breath. "All right, if you're finished here, help me get her to my motorcar. There's a proper canvas carrier, Bennett, if your constable will fetch it in. I'll have more to tell you when I know more."

* * *

When the body of Mrs. Granville had been removed, Rutledge went to the house where the rector was keeping the doctor company. Bennett stumped after him on his single crutch, trying to keep pace. The constable was once more set to guard the surgery, his young face already older in the watery noon light.

There was a fresh pot of tea waiting for them, and a plate of biscuits that Putnam had found somewhere, set out on a pretty floral plate.

Granville was sitting at the table, staring vacantly out at the rain, his mind clearly somewhere else. Bennett refused the offer of a chair and leaned against the wall with his teacup balanced in one hand. Rutledge found himself thinking that Mrs. Granville wouldn't have cared for people making free with her fine china, and would have worried about the cup in Bennett's fist.

Rutledge took his tea and drank a little of it to please Putnam, but then set it down and walked through the house, looking about him but touching nothing. On the first floor he found the bedrooms, and in what appeared to be Mrs. Granville's room the coverlet had been thrown back, as if she had expected to return to her bed.

From the window of her room she could look down on the rear of the surgery and the back door to the garden.

An interesting thought. Was that the way that Hamilton had left, either under his own power or over someone's shoulder? The door set ajar might also have been a diversion. Or Mrs. Granville could have left it open.

Nothing else was in disarray. But there was a light film of face powder spilled across the top of the dressing table although Mrs. Granville's hairbrush was placed next to her comb with tidy precision. Rutledge wondered if she was farsighted and failed to notice the powder there. Which would mean she could undoubtedly see as far as the surgery door.

Why had she risen from her bed and gone to the surgery?

Hamish said, "She thought she heard the doctor return. But he didna' come into the house. After a time, she went to find him."

"Because she feared Hamilton was worse and Granville might need her. Yes, it could be that."

He stood there in the middle of the room. It seemed cold, as if the living part of it had died with its owner.

The wrong place at the wrong time.

He went back down the stairs to find Bennett waiting for him in the hall.

"Well? I'm not up to walking about to no purpose."

"Nothing."

Bennett returned to the kitchen, but Putnam waylaid Rutledge in the passage.

"I came to the surgery this morning to speak to Hamilton, or at least sit with him for a time," he said in a low voice. "I never expected this!"

"None of us did. Least of all Granville. Damn it, I warned him to find someone to watch over Hamilton."

"And there might have been two dead, instead of one," Putnam replied quietly. "What's become of him? Hamilton. Granville told me he's nowhere to be found. That's hard to believe."

"God knows where he is. Where could he go under his own power? And if someone took him away, where is he now? Thrown into the sea from a headland, left to die where we haven't thought to look, carried far from here, and the body hidden?" Rutledge's own sense of failure was burning inside him, along with the fear that Mrs. Granville's death lay at his door. "Either way, taken or escaped, he could well be dead by now."

"I'd rather believe Mrs. Hamilton spirited him out of here."

"Mrs. Hamilton would have had no need to kill that poor woman."

"Yes, that's true. But someone else might have come, found Hamilton gone, and taken his frustration out on Mrs. Granville."

Rutledge looked at Putnam. "That's a very perceptive suggestion. But I've been to the house, and I can't convince myself he's there."

Hamish reminded him, "Ye didna' search the woman's room."

It was true. But to force his way in would have brought Mallory up the stairs, and what then? His instincts told him that Mrs. Hamilton had probably considered such a solution at some point, then failed to act on it. She'd have needed a motorcar, or the dogcart, and with either one, she risked Mallory storming out to stop her.

What did Felicity Hamilton really want? Or to put it another way, which of the two men tied to her emotionally did she love?

He deliberately changed the direction of the conversation. "You suggested in the nave of your church that I might wish to speak to a Miss Cole. Where do I find her?"

"I can't tell you that, I'm afraid. I only know of her because Matthew Hamilton spoke of her that one time. He described her as the most honorable and the most stubborn person he'd ever known. An odd compliment to pay a lady, you'd have thought. It stayed with me, what he'd said. I had the feeling it was very important to him, somehow."

The most honorable woman . . . In what sense? And Felicity Hamilton hadn't recognized the name.

"There's one other possibility," Rutledge continued. "There's a cottage just west of here where Reston's brother Freddy lived for some time."

Putnam's eyebrows flew up. "But that cottage was derelict. And if it went over with the landslip this morning, there will be nothing left but splintered wood."

"No one could have foreseen that, could they? And Freddy Reston drowned not far from where Hamilton was discovered on the strand."

Putnam clicked his tongue. "As a matter of fact, the finding was that he'd fallen asleep there drunk as a lord, and choked on his own vomit. It's the family that prefers to tell everyone he drowned."

"Freddy Reston's death could have given someone the idea of leaving Hamilton there by the tideline. And later it could also have occurred to someone that the cottage where Reston had lived stood empty. I'm not overly fond of coincidences."

"But surely you aren't suggesting that George Reston—and what reason could *he* have? That ridiculous clay figure is hardly grounds for murdering a man."

"For all any of us know," Rutledge told him, smiling ruefully, "Hamilton's relationship with Reston could have gone far beyond the original disagreement." He stopped himself from saying anything about Reston's past history of violence but did add, "George Reston is a man of temper. You've seen it, and so have I."

"Yes, alas, it's true. Still, a good man underneath."

Was that what he truly felt? Or was it only a priest's need to believe that no man could be wholly evil?

As Rutledge started to walk on, Putnam said, "You aren't going to be foolish enough to take a boat around to the slip in this weather, are you? You'll be lucky to reach the slip without swamping, much less be able to clamber about what's left of the cottage."

Rutledge stopped and said over his shoulder, "Yes, well, perhaps *someone* was lucky. The question is, who?"

"Would you mind if I asked Dr. Granville to come with me to the rectory? I don't care for the idea of leaving him here, with so many reminders of his wife everywhere he looks. He'll be better able to cope with them later."

Remembering the threat Granville had made against Mallory, Rutledge said, "By all means. I'd ask Bennett as well, if I were you."

Putnam smiled. "Indeed," he said, as if he had felt the tension between the two policemen.

Bennett, waiting for them in the kitchen, agreed at once to the suggestion, with the caveat that he didn't think Granville would leave his surgery.

But the persuasive rector was able to convince Dr. Granville to stay in the rectory for a few days, "away from here. Until you can come to grips with all that's happened."

Granville got to his feet, looking around as if he barely recognized his own kitchen. "It's raining," he said. "I'll need my coat. And my bag."

He was less pale now as the nausea faded, but his features were slack with exhaustion, and he had asked twice to Rutledge's knowledge what had become of his wife's body, as if he'd failed to take in the answer the first time.

Indeed, whatever was proposed to him was accepted without question, and Rutledge thought, "If we asked him to walk into the sea, he might well do it."

Rutledge found the doctor's coat and helped him into it, then handed him his hat.

At that point, the trained medical man came to the fore, and Granville said, frowning, "I have hours this morning. And Will Joyner is quite ill. I intended to look in on him again this afternoon."

"Your patients will be taken care of," Putnam said soothingly. "If there's anyone in dire need, like Joyner, we can send again for Dr. Hester. I'll ask Miss Trining to post a note on your door, and people can come to her to be sorted out. She's very trustworthy."

"Yes." Granville stood there as if unconvinced.

Bennett said, "Best go with him, sir. At least for the present."

When Putnam and Granville had left for the rectory, Bennett turned to Rutledge. "Well, then, what do you expect to do now? We've Hamilton missing and Mrs. Granville dead."

Rutledge considered taking the boat around the headland, and then dismissed it. The rain was heavier, although the wind, shifting to the south, was considerably warmer.

He said now, "Is there a gate from the back garden to the street behind the house?"

"In fact there is. Look, you can just glimpse it where the ash tree overhangs it." He led Rutledge to the window and pointed. "Ornamental, not meant to keep people out. The Granvilles had a little dog once, I expect that's why they put in the fence. You can also see that the distance from the surgery door to the gate is not that great."

"What's on the other side?"

"A lane used to bring horses and carriages round from the stables."

Rutledge stood looking out the window, his back half to Bennett. "Apparently Granville didn't see fit to lock his doors. Which tells me the gate wasn't locked either."

"I don't think most people lock up, even at night. Why should they?"

"But Granville knew Hamilton could still be in danger. He should have taken a few precautions." He remembered what Putnam had said—that there would have been two dead in the surgery, not one. Bennett ought to have posted a constable at the door, but he'd complained of being shorthanded.

"You can't blame him more than he's already blamed

himself. There was a nurse, set to come tonight. She was to sleep in the room next to Hamilton's." He shook his head. "She was a good woman, Mrs. Granville. You'd be hard-pressed to find anyone who disagreed with that."

The wrong place at the wrong time . . . Rutledge sighed.

"I'll drive you wherever you'd like to go. For the moment there's nothing more we can do here," he told Bennett. "And I should have put a call in to London an hour ago."

"I won't argue with that. My foot has all the imps of hell pounding it, ever since the doctor kicked it. Give me an hour to rest it, and I'll be waiting for you to come for me. You'll do well to get out of those wet clothes, while you can."

When he had rid himself of Bennett, instead of returning to the Duke of Monmouth, Rutledge made his way to Mallory's cottage outside of Hampton Regis.

It wasn't very hard to find, just down a short lane off the main road leading inland. There were no near neighbors.

If anyone had been inside since Mallory left in such haste, there was no sign of it. The rooms were tidy, the bed made with military precision, the kitchen clear of dirty dishes. But there was an empty whiskey bottle on the table by the best chair in the parlor, and a glass beside it with dregs in the bottom. The air still smelled faintly of a long night of drinking. As if Mallory had never gone to bed.

"Drowning his sorrows," Hamish said. "Ye ken, there's no witness to call him a liar."

It would be difficult to prove otherwise.

And this cottage was the perfect place to conceal Hamilton, alive, dead, or about to be killed. Rutledge had been too busy searching the house above the harbor to think of coming here. After that, Mrs. Granville's death had changed the course of the day.

If Bennett or one of his men had discovered Hamilton here, it would serve to condemn Mallory. By the same token, even the constable outside Casa Miranda would have to swear he hadn't seen anyone leave the house.

Hamish said, "It isna' sae perfect a place, then."

Not if the intent was to see Mallory hang.

Rutledge walked around the outside of the cottage, searching for tracks or indications that anyone had tried to use a shovel in the wet earth. It was only for thoroughness. He knew he'd find nothing.

He drove next to Miss Esterley's house. She owed Matthew Hamilton for the care given to her after her accident, and he might have felt he could turn to her.

Miss Esterley received him in the small parlor, concern on her face. "Gossip is rampant, Inspector. Mr. Hamilton missing, possibly dead. I'm not particularly happy, living here alone with murderers about."

"I can sympathize," he answered, taking the chair she indicated across from her. "But there's nothing I can tell you that will offer comfort."

"Which says," she told him bluntly, "you have no idea who is behind this madness."

"I was hoping," he said, keeping his voice neutral as he glanced toward the cane at her side, "that Matthew Hamilton might have felt he could turn to you in his time of need." The beautifully wrought silver swan seemed to mock him. The way the head was drawn back, the breast thrust forward under it. It was possible, he thought, but only just.

She was staring at him. "Are you suggesting that I'm *hiding* Matthew here, in my house?"

"I'm suggesting that if he asked you to help him leave Hampton Regis until he's recovered sufficiently to face his enemy, whoever it might be, you would at least entertain his request."

Her face was cold. "I haven't spoken to him for more than a week. And then only as we left the Sunday-morning service. I can't imagine why he would turn to me."

"He may have thought you were a friend."

That stopped her short. For a moment she looked away from him, her gaze finding the titles of books in a shelf along the wall under the windows. "I should have thought he would go straight to his wife." It was as if the admission cost her dearly.

"You know he couldn't. You know he wasn't a match for Stephen Mallory, not in his condition. If Mallory was the one who attacked him Monday morning, Hamilton would surely wait until he was well enough to challenge the man."

When Miss Esterley turned back to him, there were tears in her eyes. "The man I care about would have risked everything for her sake."

The shining knight to the rescue of the damsel in distress. He wondered if that was how she really saw Hamilton, or if it was her own disappointment speaking. The fact that he hadn't come to this house instead.

"Then you didn't know him well. It would have been foolhardy." It was said gently, without condemnation.

"You're wrong. I can tell you that if Matthew Hamilton was alive and in his right mind, his only thought would have been Felicity. No matter what the cost. And if he didn't go to Casa Miranda, to *her,* then he's dead."

The tears began to fall then, and she wiped them away angrily. "When I heard that Dr. Granville couldn't find him, my heart turned to stone. I refuse to believe he's dead, but in my heart I know he must be. Someone came back to stop him from telling what he knows. *Knew.*"

"Then why not kill him in his bed, there in the surgery. Why go to the trouble of removing him and taking the chance of being seen doing it?"

"For the very reason you're here. You don't know what has happened to him, and you'll likely never know." He handed her his handkerchief and she took it without thanking him, trying to staunch the humiliating flow. "I'm not in love with him, I never was. But I value—valued him—and I never believed I would lose him like this. I thought—I felt he would be there, a friend, for many years. And I was comforted by that belief."

Rutledge sat there, his mouth dry, unable to think of words of consolation. She had put the case for Hamilton's death very succinctly, and he knew that whatever she might say about Felicity and another woman's husband, she thought of herself as under Hamilton's protection too.

She went on relentlessly: "You don't know what it's like, living alone for the rest of your life, the man you were intending to marry dead on a battlefield you've never seen and will never visit. You don't know how he died, or when he died, or even why he died. Whether he was screaming in pain, or unconscious, or bleeding badly and left on the wire. You picture it in your mind, night after night, and try to reach out to him, to put an end to not knowing. Trying to tell yourself what you'd have said to him if you could have held him at the end. But there's nothing left. Only a polite letter from an officer, on the heels of the official notification. And after that silence and *emptiness*. As if he'd been swallowed up by the sea, and no one *knew*." She choked off the rest.

"I understand . . . ," he began.

But Susan Esterley said harshly, "No, you can't. You couldn't possibly."

Rutledge left soon afterward, and it wasn't until he was on the street, by the motorcar, that Hamish said, "She'd lie for him if he asked her to."

And Rutledge realized that she'd never answered his questions, except with a question of her own.

He swore as he remembered that he'd also planned to ask her about Miss Cole.

15

When Rutledge rang up London from the Duke of Monmouth Inn, it wasn't to speak to Gibson at the Yard.

His instinct warned him off, reminding him of the cold reception the last time he'd spoken to the sergeant. And he'd also be obliged to report the fact that Hamilton was missing and that there had been a second attack, this one ending in murder. Just now he needed time to think before Chief Superintendent Bowles summoned him in a blazing fury.

The call was to his sister.

Frances was surprised to hear from him. "I thought you'd been sent to Coventry," she said. "How is the weather along the south coast?"

"Wretched. But warmer. If the sun comes out, we'll have a taste of spring."

She laughed. "Then bring it back with you. London is as dreary as London can be."

"I need information about someone who was in the Foreign Office. He's retired now to England, but his last posting was to Malta. One Matthew Hamilton—"

He'd expected her to tell him that the name was familiar, but it would take several hours to track down whatever it was he wanted to learn. Instead she said, "But you must know him as well. He was at that party at Melinda Crawford's house. The one where you broke out in measles and had to be carried home. Mother was quite upset with you for making her miss a brilliant dinner."

"I don't remember much of that weekend." He'd been twelve and wretchedly sick. A long time ago . . . eighteen years?

"You played croquet with him. And won."

It was his turn to laugh. "That was *Matthew Hamilton*?"

"Of course it was."

"Good God. I thought him quite ancient. I expect he's only forty-eight, now."

"And still an attractive man, I must say. I saw photographs of him when he was at Versailles, they were in the newspapers for all of a week. He looked quite distinguished in that company of ancient men. Even as a girl I envied the women who played tennis with him. But I had my revenge, you know. He took me in to dinner, either because he felt sorry for me, abandoned and alone, or more likely, Melinda put him up to it. I was elated. My dinner companions were generally callow boys with spots, who either refused to speak to me or bored me to tears with their cricket exploits. I quite forgave you the measles." There was a pause. "Ian. Why are you asking about him? Please don't tell me he's dead."

"No. A person of interest in the inquiry that brought me here," he said, evading the question. "His wife is many years younger and can't tell me very much about his past."

"Has he killed someone?" Her voice was tight. "I refuse to believe he could *do* such a thing."

"The fact is, he's gone missing."

There was a silence on the other end of the line. Then Frances said, "All right, you'd rather not tell me more. So I won't pry. What do you want to know? Why he should have disappeared?"

"More to the point, has there been gossip about him, most especially about his career?"

"He wasn't very popular after expressing an opinion about the Peace Conference at Versailles. He'd been on the ambassador's staff in Turkey before the war, and as I remember, in Germany even earlier than that. The general view was that he should have been consulted but his position wasn't in accord with the intent of the French at the talks. Rather like that man Lawrence and his Arab connections, Matthew Hamilton had friends in Turkey and in Germany who were pushing for a different outcome. I daresay he was in the right, but no one cared to hear it. And so he chose to retire and return to England."

"Not under a cloud?"

"Not *precisely* a cloud. But some very important people were not pleased with him, and he knew very well what that would mean to his career. Or perhaps he was disillusioned. Or they threatened him with Paraguay. There are ways of getting even without actually sending him home in disgrace. I don't think he'd have cared for a South American posting, after Europe. And his interests lay there, of course."

"What interests?"

"He liked to poke about in the old ruins. A way to pass the time, at a guess, and if one lives somewhere long enough, it's natural to start to wonder what's outside one's window, so to speak. Remember Barton Wallace, who got caught up in those strange poles in Canada, and wrote about what the Indians were carving on them?"

Barton Wallace had been a friend of his father's, sent to

Vancouver to handle the Wallace family's Pacific trade for their firm. While there, he'd written a treatise on Indian totems, and it proved immensely popular.

"Yes, Wallace sent Mother a copy of it one Boxing Day."

"Well, I expect a man like Matthew Hamilton spent many of his holidays traveling to places he'd heard local people talking about, and word got out that he was there. It was rumored in the markets that he'd buy objects he liked without asking either provenance or source. Of course he couldn't dig himself, but thievery is rampant, and important, much less unknown, sites can't be guarded all the time. Such people sell real finds or competent fakes for whatever price they can ask. He sent Melinda Crawford the loveliest little marble figure of the god Pan, dancing. She was pleased, sure it was real, and put it in that curio cabinet of hers. When he left Turkey, there was some talk about his baggage being searched, but nothing came of it. And there have been other incidents where he was stopped by customs, but nothing of value was ever found. Part of it was probably no more than bloody-mindedness by the customs people, but once talk starts, it tends to cling."

Or, he thought, a well-placed bribe had done its work.

And the objects in the Hamilton drawing room hardly looked like replicas. Sometimes quality spoke to the eye, even when one didn't have the training or knowledge to back it up. A rare skill, a touch of elegance or excellence, that surely Hamilton had recognized too.

"There's luck as well," Hamish reminded him. But it didn't signify. There were too many pieces.

Frances was adding, "Add to that the fact that Matthew Hamilton seldom came home to England on leave. It isn't surprising that people jumped to the conclusion he had an ulterior motive for his travels."

"Was there a reason for staying away? Friends abroad, that sort of thing?"

He could picture her holding the receiver as one shoulder lifted in an expressive shrug.

"Ian, I don't know. I don't expect anyone does, except Matthew himself. I was only ten, my dear, I didn't *know* what secrets a young man would have."

"Would Melinda know? Did she stay in close touch with him?"

"You must ask her that."

There was another pause, and then she said, "Darling, is anything wrong? You sound—I don't know—rather *down*." She waited for him to answer, and then added, "You can't hide it. Not from me."

Which he should have thought of before he telephoned her, he told himself with a sigh.

"One of the people involved in the business that brought me here had served under me in France. For a short time. It brings back memories I'd rather not have raised."

"Yes, I understand that might be difficult. But you're going to be all right, aren't you?"

He made himself laugh, for her sake. "If I'm not, Bowles will have my liver."

She didn't press.

But he found himself thinking that it was easier to talk to Stephen Mallory about the war than to his own sister. It was something he hadn't expected, this isolation. At first he'd believed it was his own need, his own desperation, that locked the war in silence. A vain hope for time and peace in which to heal. Now he realized that somehow those who had served in France and elsewhere knew a world that couldn't be shared. How could he tell his sister—or even his father, if the elder Rutledge was still alive—what had been done on bloody ground far from home? It would be criminal to fill their minds with scenes that no one should have to remember. No one.

Frances was on the point of signing off when he thought of something he hadn't brought up.

"Do you know a Miss Cole who might have been a friend or relative of Hamilton's? Her name has come up here in connection with his, but no one seems to be able to tell me where to find her."

"Cole? Do you have a first name?"

"Sadly, no."

"It's not an uncommon name. A proverbial needle in the proverbial haystack. Surely Sergeant Gibson or someone at the Yard can locate her for you."

"They've got their hands full just now. And I don't have enough information about her yet to warrant taking up the Yard's time."

"They ought to be pleased with themselves at the moment. They've taken someone into custody for those wretched killings in Green Park. The newspapers are calling it masterly police work."

"*Who?* Did they say who it was?" he asked urgently.

"I don't think a name has been released yet."

Gentle God.

He could feel Hamish in the back of his mind, thundering like the guns in France. The walls of the telephone closet seemed to press in on him.

Was it Fields they'd taken into custody? Had Inspector Phipps come to suspect the same man, in his own roundabout fashion? Or had Constable Waddington, to shield himself from charges that he was courting while on duty, ignored Rutledge's instructions and reported Fields to the Yard?

He felt a strong sense of personal responsibility for dragging Fields into the search and told himself that Phipps had been thorough. It was Chief Superintendent Bowles, pressed by his own superiors to bring in the killer, who was not always reliable in drawing conclusions.

By the same token, what if someone else had been taken

into custody, in error? And the Yard knew nothing about Fields?

But Rutledge had been ordered off that case. In no uncertain terms. It had nothing to do with him now.

Aye, Hamish retorted, *duty before conscience. It's what got me shot.*

Frances was saying, "Ian? Are you still there? Ian?"

"Yes, just digesting the news. I'd been dealing with the Green Park inquiry, just before I was sent down here. If there's a name given, will you let me know?"

He told Frances how to reach him and then rang off.

He sat there for a moment, trying to reorder his thoughts.

Melinda Crawford's wide-ranging correspondence spanned continents, and if Hamilton had kept in touch with anyone in England during his years abroad, it might well have been with her. She had traveled most of her life and knew the world as few did. Her mind was razor sharp even in age, her wit was dry and entertaining, and her charm hadn't diminished with time. He himself had treasured her letters in France, reading them over and over because they took him away from the war for a little while.

Rutledge stood up and stepped into the passage, considering what to say to her. She would demand to know what his interest in Hamilton was. And she could spot a well-intentioned lie before he'd finished uttering it.

The respite from the cramped confines of the telephone closet was a relief, and he went as far as the front windows of the inn, flexing his shoulders. One glance at the sky showed him it was now much lighter, as though the worst of the squalls had passed. If he was going to risk taking a boat out to the landslip, he must do it while he could.

Melinda Crawford could wait. Miss Cole could wait. He had to know what was in the cottage that had gone down with the cliff face. If Hamilton was dead—and Rutledge was beginning to feel he was—then there were two murders to deal with. He set out briskly for the harbor, to look for the fisherman who had been cleaning his catch earlier. He'd gone, but another man was standing on the Mole, staring out at the sea.

Rutledge came to stand beside him and said, "It appears to be a little calmer out there."

The man turned. "Aye. I was thinking the same." He looked at Rutledge. "You're the man from London?"

"Yes. Rutledge."

The man nodded. "Perkins," he said in response, his weathered face deeply wrinkled from exposure to the sea and the sun. It was difficult to tell his age, but Rutledge put him down as close to fifty.

"Do you have a boat, Mr. Perkins?"

"That I do. You aren't of a mind to take her out, are you? I don't let my boat to any man."

"I was thinking of hiring you to row me out to where I could have a good look at the landslip this morning."

"It's a crazy thought. What for?"

"I'm sure it is. Nevertheless, I have a sound reason. We don't know if anyone was in that cottage when it went over. And Dr. Granville is missing one of his patients."

"He'd be a fool to take himself out to the cottage. It was derelict before, and will be matchwood now."

"A policeman can't write that in his report," Rutledge answered.

"It's Mr. Hamilton you're looking for?"

He nodded.

"It's not a thing he'd do. I don't know him well, mind you. But we've talked a time or two. He was used to the sea, serving as he did on that island. Malta. He'd take a boat out of that harbor, just to see it from the sea and then sail back through. He said it was built by knights who knew what they were about, and even the Turks couldn't take it by water."

"I understand the fortifications are formidable," Rutledge agreed. "Did you talk about anything else?"

"He said there were ruins there that were older than the Pyramids. I had a hard time believing it, but he said it was true. And I never knew him to be a liar."

"Will you take me out today? If it isn't safe, I won't press. But I need to see for myself that there's no one there."

"There'll be no one there now," Perkins said darkly.

Rutledge waited.

After several minutes of silence had passed, Perkins nodded. "You'll need rain gear, if you're to stay dry."

"Do you have any I could borrow?"

"You're a fair bit taller than me, but my son's things ought to fit. A little large, mind you, but they'll keep you dry. Do you have Wellingtons, then?"

It was a small boat, her name boldly painted on the prow—*Bella*—the mast useless in such variable winds, but two men could just manage her, pulling out from the Mole against the drag of the current, then making for a point under the headland from which they could feel the tug of the current back to the shore.

Even from there they could see the raw spill of the landslip, its heavy soil flowing like a river to the water, taking with it clumps of grass, young trees, and what appeared to be a chimney sticking up at an odd angle among a scatter of bricks.

It was a hard run to get closer, and Rutledge was sweating heavily inside his rain gear by the time they got there. But the waves hitting them at the wrong angle left the bottom of the boat awash and his sleeves wet to the wrist, water spilling down his head and under his collar and reaching as far as his back as he twisted and turned for a better view and called instructions to Perkins.

In due course they were within good range of the clumped and riddled earth. It looked out of place reaching into the sea, as if it still belonged to the high reaches of land above and had lost its way. The eddies about it were muddy, sucking at this foreign bit of land as if hungry, then coming back for more, larger chunks sinking as he watched.

The cottage was a ruin, beams and walls only so much lumber now, without form or structure. A cabinet peeked from under an edge of roof, and a small tin washbasin was caught on a rake, banging like a cheap bell against the handle. A table leg floated out to them, and then was pushed forlornly back again. A lumpy pillow lay like a dead bird against part of a door, as if it had been caught in the storm and taken shelter there.

Only part of the chimney, surprisingly intact, spoke of what the debris had once been.

"Rotted wood to start with. It won't last long out here," Perkins told him, shouting over the noisy waves lashing at the coastline. "This is as near as I can go. Or we'll be aground on what we can't see. And there's another squall on the horizon. Look there!"

Rutledge turned to see but calculated there was still time. "Is that ground firm enough for me to walk on? If it is, I need to go closer."

"What for? You can't tell floor from roof. And if there's any man in there, he's long since buried beneath whatever fell on top of him as the lot went over."

It was true. It would take men digging with shovels to find Matthew Hamilton's body in that morass. And even they couldn't do it before the water took it away for good.

But he had to be sure. There would be doubts, uncertainties. No body to allow the police to prove Matthew Hamilton was dead. Or that murder had been done.

Clever barristers and clever doubts, carefully placed.

Unless his bones washed ashore somewhere and were found, then identified. They couldn't wait for that.

Matthew Hamilton, victim and witness.

"Get me as close as you can, and hold her steady. I'll give it a try."

"Did living in London's fogs turn your wits?" Perkins asked sharply. "I'm not about to risk my boat on a fool's errand."

"Look at the water, man. It's clear just over there. If you can reach the foot of the cliff there, I can make it to that large rock, and then move across to firmer ground. Can you see where I'm pointing?"

Perkins growled deep in his throat, and Rutledge, startled at the similarity to the sound that Hamish made sometimes, turned quickly and almost swamped them.

"Here, you idiot, policeman or not, you'll watch what you're about," Perkins told him harshly.

In the end, Rutledge got his way, at a price, and Perkins did what he could to hold the boat steady enough for him to reach the boulder and then claw himself up on the flat surface. It was slick underfoot, and he thought, *I'll never make it back to the boat.*

Above him, the high rise of land loomed, and as he stepped across to the earth, he heard pebbles skittering down, like a warning that one false move could bring another twenty yards of solid ground down on his head, breaking up and burying him as it came crashing toward him.

But nothing happened, and he made the leap to the landslip, his feet sinking above the ankles in the soft, pliant earth. Laboring to bring one foot out and then another, he wallowed like a drunkard toward the first of the shards of lumber that littered the ground, many of the bits sticking straight out of the mud, others buried and only recognizable when his boots struck something solid underfoot.

It was a wild-goose chase, Hamish was telling him roundly. "And how ye'll manage to clamber back into yon boat again, God alone kens!"

But he was here now, and the only thing to do was go forward. Casting a glance back at the squall line, he wondered if Perkins would abandon him if it came to a choice between the boat and the stubborn fool who had brought them out here.

He struggled on, searching with his eyes, his hands busy keeping his balance. The footing was so treacherous he found a length of door framing and tried to use it as a cane, only to find that it sank too deep and nearly had him stumbling in its wake.

Sticks of furniture, a rusted pot, a vase—miraculously in one piece, the lilacs on its surface a small bit of color in the shambles—lay among the ruins. As Perkins had predicted, Rutledge could barely tell what room or what part of the structure lay where, the whole smashed to nothing. Like an iceberg, the debris went deep, only a portion of it showing on the surface where he walked.

He rescued the small vase and tucked it in a coat pocket, intending to take it back to Perkins as a souvenir. Bending over invited disaster again, and he slipped and fell, swearing, against a protruding beam and part of the chimney corner. For an instant, he could feel the earth under his body shift, and he thought, *This was not a very wise decision*, with a fatalism born of long practice.

Hamish was after him, urging him back to the boat, telling him to take the warning seriously.

After a moment of perfect stillness, he could sense that all movement had stopped, nothing more was going to happen, at least not now, and he shoved himself upright, testing his weight with extreme gentleness just where he stood. It was then that he saw something on the far side of the chimney, caught in what appeared to be the splat of a chair back.

With great care he shifted himself to one side, and then found a length of planking wide enough to use as a foot-bridge to the other side of the chimney, and then another added to that.

Walking on the slippery boards, he kept his gaze fixed to where his feet were set, and he didn't look up again until he'd come to the far end of his improvised bridge.

What he'd seen was there in front of him: a wad of bloody bandaging, the dark red already turned to a running pink in the rain. But bandaging it was. A doctor's work, he thought to himself.

He reached out for it, and in the nick of time stopped, remembering what he'd risked retrieving the vase. Move his weight a bare few inches more, and the plank behind him would dip like a board over a pool, sending him headlong and face-first into the smothering earth.

Just the fear of it made him shiver like a man in fever, but he caught himself and took a deep breath, shutting out the voice roaring now in his mind. He'd been buried alive once, in France. It didn't bear thinking of. And this time, there would be no body lying above him, giving him a precious pocket of air to keep him alive. Hamish's body—long since rotted to bones in the rains of the Somme Valley.

To one side he saw a rung from the broken chair or per-haps its brother, and carefully squatted down until he could retrieve it, though his feet slipped and nearly launched him where he most feared to go. Catching himself again, he used the muscles in his thighs to bring himself upright once more, and felt them burn with the effort.

He had himself under control now, and gingerly using the chair rung as a tool, he slowly brought the length of bandage toward him until he could grasp it safely and shove it inside his coat, water and all.

Matthew Hamilton had been here. Or had been brought here. But whether he'd gone over the cliff with the cottage or not, God alone knew. There was no way human agency could answer that.

Over the next five minutes, Rutledge thought he might not make it back to the *Bella* after all. It took enormous physical effort to reach the boat, climb up on the rock, and lower himself onto the thwart once more. By that time his thigh muscles quivered from fatigue in the cold air, alternately burning and tightening in spasms.

"You're a fair fool," the man shouted at him with resignation. "I'd not have brought you out, if I'd guessed. I should have left you there."

"A lucky fool," Rutledge replied with what little breath he could spare. In fact, it had taken far more than his share of luck to cross that unstable ground back to where Perkins was struggling to keep the *Bella* in the eddies off the rock.

The words were hardly out of his mouth when another five feet of earth came roaring down toward them, missing the wooden stern where he was sitting by no more than a few yards and sending them bouncing like a ball across the impact wave. For an instant he thought the swell would surely swamp them.

They'd taken on a dangerous amount of water, and Rutledge, who had been using an oar to shove off hard from the rock face, swung it inboard as quickly as he could to begin bailing like a madman in an effort to lighten the load they were carrying. But Perkins was nothing if not an experienced seaman, and he kept them afloat until the waves had subsided and there was only the sea itself to fight.

Then the long, hard pull to the Mole began, one eye to the weather, the other on their destination. Every time Rutledge looked up, Hampton Regis seemed to be no closer than it was before, while the squall line was bearing down on them faster than they could row. It was, he told himself, going to be a very near thing, and very possibly they'd lose the race.

But miraculously the rain held off until they had reached the street that ran along the harbor. Rutledge welcomed it then, to wash off the worst of the muddy earth that clung to him like a skin. He was glad to rid himself of his gear at the small house where Perkins lived and feel the cool air strike him as he walked back to the police station.

Perkins hadn't asked what he'd found but refused to accept the small vase Rutledge had given him along with the exorbitant sum owed him.

"That's an unlucky thing, that vase," he said.

"It survived," Rutledge pointed out. "That should make it lucky."

"I'm a superstitious man, Mr. Rutledge. I thank you for the thought, but I'm not happy with looking at that bit of clay and wondering why it was not crushed by what it endured." He looked up at Rutledge with sober eyes. "What the sea wants, it takes. In the end, it'ud pounded that thing to white dust and then washed it away as nothing. I don't want it to claim me in its place."

But why, Rutledge found himself thinking, if Hamilton had been on the sea so many times, had the sea waited until he'd returned to England to claim *him*?

What gods of clay or wood had he disturbed that came after him so great a distance?

The sea had nearly drowned Hamilton three days ago, but it had been cheated of its prey. Perhaps it hadn't forgotten.

Shaking off his black mood, Rutledge turned his mind to what he must tell Inspector Bennett.

16

The police station was a beehive of activity. Bennett was in a sober mood.

"I waited half an hour for you. Where the hell have you been?" he demanded, looking Rutledge over. "Crawling through a farmer's field, I'll be bound."

"Close enough. I've—"

Bennett interrupted him. "The Chief Constable was here. I don't know who told him what has happened—I'll wager you it was Miss Trining, damn her eyes—but he has given us twenty-four hours to find out where Hamilton is and who killed Mrs. Granville. He's not a man to be crossed, the Chief Constable. We've got one and twenty hours left."

"It's likely that Hamilton is dead. I went out to the land-slip. And this was caught on the back of a chair that had been splintered by the fall." He held out the wet bandage, and Bennett stared at it as if it could bite him.

"Good God!"

"I can't think of anyone else who might have left it there.

We must show it to Granville, to see if he recognizes his handiwork. Then we should have a talk with Mr. Reston."

"Reston couldn't have killed the doctor's wife, whatever you're suggesting. There's no sound reason for it."

"Unless she got in his way when he came for Hamilton."

"But why should he want to harm Hamilton? You won't make me believe it's because of some bits of clay on a shelf at the man's house. Mr. Reston may be a fanatic for religion, but that doesn't make him a murderer."

"There was a man in London he assaulted. Reston's victim didn't press charges, so there's no record of it. And he's got a violent nature."

"Still—" Bennett was already fitting his crutch under his shoulder and getting to his feet. "Have it your way then, but you'll be proved wrong. I won't walk there. I can't."

"I'll fetch my motorcar. Give me five minutes."

It was twenty minutes before he was back again, having taken the time to clean himself up. He carried his trousers down to the kitchen to be dried and pressed, asked for a length of oiled cloth for the bandages, and persuaded the young girl in the pantry to make him a sandwich from pickle, last night's beef, and a little cheese, though she protested that the luncheon ham would be ready in no more than a quarter of an hour.

Bennett came out and climbed into the passenger's side just as a strong beam of sunlight broke through the clouds and swept the rooftops and wet streets with a warm and brilliant light.

Bennett looked up at it and said, "We could do with a shift in the weather. I smell pickle."

Rutledge didn't answer. He put the motorcar into gear and drove to the Reston house.

Mr. Reston was at home, they were told by the maid, but was feeling a touch of dyspepsia.

"Please tell him Inspector Rutledge and Inspector Bennett are here on police business and require a word with him. We'll wait until he can join us."

She still appeared to be doubtful, and Rutledge could see that she was on the point of refusing them admittance. He stepped forward and she retreated a step. He moved into the entry.

"Where does Mr. Reston receive his business acquaintances? We'll wait for him there."

The maid reluctantly showed them to a small study where books on law and finance lined the shelves behind the broad, polished desk, and other calf-bound titles stood in orderly rows across the room, considerably older works on the Romans, the kingdom of Wessex, and the history of the southwest of England. On one of the spines the name RESTON was set out in gold lettering. Rutledge took it from the shelf and opened it.

The title was *Great Sermons for the Mind,* and the Reston who had written it was either the father or grandfather of the present owner. From what he could see the sermons were long and ponderous, their heavy Victorian righteousness apparent in their arguments for service and duty as a gentleman's responsibility to God and England and his less fortunate fellow men.

Rutledge turned pages at random, reading a line here and there. The strong Victorian voice spoke through words that stared up at him.

An upright man, whatever his calling, will address his business affairs with the same honesty he will show his family. To do other is to be guilty of a grievous fault that will lead him down the road to corrupt practices. . . .

God resides in the heart, and a cruel heart is godless,

a man to be feared for the harm he will do to others in his wickedness. . . .

Servants must be led to the path of godliness, and it is the duty of the head of every household to see to their training up in faith and to provide the guidance and example that will set their feet firmly on the way to God's grace. . . .

Children will obey their fathers in all things, and show—

He got no further. The door behind him opened, and George Reston stood there on the threshold.

"That is a very valuable book you're holding, Inspector Rutledge. I'll ask you to set it back carefully in its place."

Reston looked tired, or ill, as if he had had an unsettled digestion—or a long and arduous night. His face, paler than usual, was set in harsh lines, and he seemed to be holding to the door's frame to steady himself. Then he let it go and stepped into the room.

"I can't think why you are here. But I have been told of Mrs. Granville's death. It's a disgrace that with two policemen in my study, we are still no closer to learning why she was attacked."

Bennett opened his mouth, then closed it again. Rutledge thought he was biting his tongue.

He himself said, "I understand that the cottage that went over the cliff in this morning's downpour belonged to you."

Raising his brows in surprise, Reston answered, "Yes. Inspector Bennett could have confirmed that without disturbing me."

"And that your brother lived there for a time, before his—er—untimely death?"

"That's true as well. He was not a worldly man, my brother. I was forced to see to his welfare more than once. In the end,

I kept him in Hampton Regis under my eye. What does this have to do with the murder of Mrs. Granville, pray?"

"Has anyone else used this cottage since he drowned?"

Reston's mouth twitched at the last word. "Certainly not. Freddy lived there because he preferred to shame me. He could have been perfectly comfortable here with us, but he chose to make it appear that I was derelict in my duty to him. I let it go. He seemed to find the isolation to his liking and it calmed him." There was a sense of being wronged in his voice, the good brother taking the blame for the bad brother's ill treatment of himself.

Hamish, who had been quiet for some time, said, "Aye, a drunkard is no' a very easy man to deal with."

Two men, sharing the same blood, and as different as night and day. Had the writer of the sermons succeeded with one of the brothers and failed the other? Or had Reston been the one to drive his brother to drink? Rutledge found himself thinking that Reston was not a pleasant man to deal with, twisted in his belief that what he knew and what he had been taught set him above others. A man of limited intellect, perhaps, who had struggled where his brother might have soared and made his tormentor pay for it the rest of his life.

As if Reston had listened to Rutledge's judgment, he said forcibly, "He was the favorite, you know. My grandfather adored him. But he had no backbone, and he failed in life because of it. I did my best to protect and shield him, and I did my best to bring him around to his duty. No man can say that I didn't." He turned and glared at Bennett. "You will confirm that, if you please, Inspector."

"It's true," Bennett answered. "The whole of Hampton Regis can tell you as much."

Satisfied, Reston said, "And if you have finished with the subject of my brother—"

Rutledge said, "I went out to the landslip by sea. And in the ruins of the cottage I found a fresh bandage. It appears that Matthew Hamilton was either taken there or went there sometime in the early-morning hours. There is no other explanation for bandaging to be found there."

Reston seemed to fold in on himself, as if his stomach had failed him. He crossed the room and sat down behind the desk, his head in his hands. "I have had nothing to do with Matthew Hamilton's assault or his disappearance. Why must you drag my brother into this business?"

"Your brother drowned, Mr. Reston. Only a few yards from where Matthew Hamilton nearly died. The cottage is your property. Hamilton was in that cottage, if the bandages prove to be his. If you aren't responsible, tell me if anyone else had access to it, borrowed it, used it, or could have unlocked the door."

"The door was never locked. The cottage was falling *down,* what purpose would locking it serve? I daresay half the homeowners in Hampton Regis fail to lock their doors at night. We are not a violent place." He lifted his eyes to Rutledge's face, drawing on some inner strength that seemed to rise and sustain him. "I will not be badgered in this fashion. I have a solicitor who will speak to you on my behalf. Good day, Inspector."

Rutledge stood there for a moment, judging his man. "I am not accusing you of anything, Mr. Reston. But perhaps it would be wise to account for your hours last night between eleven o'clock and this morning at first light."

"I was at home in my bed, as a decent man should be." The words were spat out, anger barely controlled.

"And your wife can confirm that?"

"I will not have my wife dragged into a murder inquiry. She's delicate, and I'll not have her upset. You can accept my word, as a gentleman."

But that would not stand up in a courtroom. Rutledge let
it go. He had a feeling that Mrs. Reston might well tell him
whatever it was her husband wished, whether it was true or a
lie. *Delicate* might well be translated as browbeaten.

Bennett said, surprising Rutledge, "I have no choice but
to ask her, sir, if you will summon her. The Chief Constable
will insist. He was here earlier and made plain the fact that
he expected full cooperation with the police."

In the end, Reston sent for his wife, and after five or six
minutes she came into the room.

Henrietta Reston wasn't what Rutledge had expected. A
tall, slender woman with reddish gold hair that seemed to
shine in the dimness of the room and blue eyes that were
intense in a long, aristocratic face, she greeted her husband's
guests with courtesy and waited for an explanation.

Rutledge put the question to her, choosing his words carefully. "Mrs. Reston, as a matter of course we are asking
people where they were last night and into this morning,
from perhaps shortly before midnight until dawn. In the
hope that someone might have looked out a window and can
help us with our search for Mr. Hamilton."

Reston began to speak, then fell silent, waiting, his gaze
on his wife's face.

"My husband wasn't well in the night, Inspector. I read
for a little while, worried about him. But after a time, I fell
asleep and didn't wake up until the children came in to say
good morning. I don't remember looking out my window."

"And you cared for your husband in the night?"

She smiled. "We have separate bedrooms, Inspector. But
I could hear him moving about, pacing the floor between
visits to his dressing room, if that's what you want to know.
It was a very restless night for him."

She turned as she said the last words, her eyes going directly
to her husband. A message passed between them. But it wasn't,

Rutledge would have taken his oath, a message of collusion.

It was daring him to contradict her.

Outside, Bennett followed Rutledge down the walk to the motorcar. He said, as if continuing a conversation begun in the Reston house, "It's an odd marriage, if you want the truth. The money is hers. But he's built his empire, and he doesn't let her forget it."

It was the first time Bennett had been so honest about Reston, and Rutledge turned to look at him. "You're saying that there are strains on the marriage?"

"There was talk that she'd been in love with his brother first. I don't know the truth of that. The fact remains, she came of a better class. You can see it for yourself. Miss Trining has kept her tongue off Mrs. Reston. That will tell you which way the winds blow."

A better class, but no beauty. Except for her hair, which seemed to give life to her face.

Rutledge cranked the car, his thoughts straying from what Bennett was saying. Then he heard part of it and said abruptly, "Sorry, I missed that?" He stepped behind the wheel and turned to stare at Bennett.

"I said, she knew Mr. Hamilton from her childhood. Or so I was told. Not well, but their families moved in the same circles."

Was that what drove George Reston to fury? Jealousy, rather than a fanatical dislike for stone goddesses from foreign assignments that had kept Hamilton out of England most of his adult life?

And had the bane of his marriage without warning moved to the same village on the south coast of England, bringing back all that should have been buried and perhaps forgotten over the long years of exile?

"What was Mrs. Reston's maiden name?" Rutledge asked Bennett.

"Good God, how should I know? Reston married her long before he came here. You'll have to speak to the rector or Mrs. Trining, not me." He shifted his foot to ease it a little. "The Bennetts aren't on the same social rung as the Restons."

They went next to the rectory. Granville, Putnam told Rutledge quietly, had fallen into an uneasy sleep in one of the guest rooms. "If you could wait until a little time has passed before you question him?" he asked without much hope. "It would be a kindness."

But there was no time to be kind. And in the event, the doctor had heard voices and he came to the head of the stairs.

"I shouldn't have listened to you, Rector. I should have rested in a chair in your study. I kept dreaming that—that all was well." He began to descend the stairs, his face pale in the wan sunlight coming through the open door. "Mr. Bennett. Is there news?"

"Sadly, sir, no," Bennett told him. "Just that we need to have you confirm something for us." He turned to Rutledge, who brought out the oiled cloth and opened it so that Dr. Granville could see what it held. Putnam gasped and stepped aside to give his houseguest a better view.

He seemed shocked by the sight. "That's my work. Or as near as I can be sure. See how the pads are placed, to absorb bleeding? And then another over that in the opposite direction. Four such in a row. And more bandaging, to keep the pads from shifting as Hamilton moved his head. Which explains why this has held together." Professional pride had taken over. The truth hadn't yet dawned on him. "And notice here how I turn the end of the tape back on itself, to make it easier to find for changing without disturbing the patient." He looked up at the two policemen. "But where did you find this? At the Hamilton house? Why is it so wet? Does this mean—have you found Hamilton, then? I thought you said there was no news."

"This was in the cottage that went into the sea with the landslip. The cottage where Reston's brother lived until his death," Rutledge repeated for what seemed like the tenth time that morning.

"What was it doing there?" Granville was genuinely surprised. "You aren't trying to tell me that someone carried Hamilton out there? I can tell you as his doctor that he couldn't have walked that far on his own!"

"If he was in the cottage when it went over, then Hamilton is dead. But we can only confirm so far that he was there at some point. If you are quite sure about these?"

"Yes, yes, who else could these belong to? He's my only patient just now with a head injury. But none of this business makes any sense to me."

"Did Hamilton have visitors while he was in your surgery? Other than his wife?"

"Half Hampton Regis tried to get in to see him. I left strict instructions that he wasn't to be disturbed by anyone. My wife"—he cleared his throat—"my wife understood the seriousness of that."

"But anyone could have stepped in the garden door. Or come down the passage from the surgery door, if no one was about to stop him or her? Even at night?"

"Well, yes, but people aren't savages here, they asked after Hamilton but never pressed when we informed them that he was too ill to see anyone. I made it quite clear that his rest was essential to a full recovery." His voice was testy, as if Rutledge was questioning how he ran his surgery. "Look, are you trying to suggest that my wife neglected—"

"Not at all," Putnam cut in soothingly. "The man's asking if it could have happened quite by chance—no one around, and someone opening doors—"

Dr. Granville said curtly, "It's *possible*. It isn't likely. Even Miss Trining took no for an answer."

But in the back of the doctor's mind, Rutledge was certain, loomed the fact that he had failed to provide a nurse to stay with Hamilton and keep visitors away, both day and night.

And by not doing so, he might very well carry the guilt of his wife's death, whether he realized that yet or not. Down the years, when all was said and done, it might come back to haunt him.

Putnam, looking stricken, said only, "I think we should all have a little sherry. None of us has felt like eating any lunch, I daresay. It will do us good." And he left them there, walking into the rectory parlor to find the tray with decanter and glasses.

Bennett called after the rector that they had no time for sherry, thank you very much, and nodded to Dr. Granville as he took his leave. Rutledge noted as they closed the door behind them that Granville seemed to shrink inside himself, as if it had taken all the strength he possessed to keep up appearances.

Bennett was saying, "You were a little hard on him."

"He had to identify what I'd found. And it was important to know who might have slipped into that back room out of concern for Hamilton or even to scout in broad daylight how difficult it would be to come again at night. I'm beginning to think no one turned a lamp on. He or she may have had a shielded torch. Mrs. Granville must have been awake, waiting for her husband, and either an unguarded flash of light or some sound from the surgery attracted her attention. It was she who reached for the office lamp, and before she could light it, she had to be stopped. I'll wager you that's precisely what happened."

"Dr. Granville wouldn't have used a torch, he'd have felt

free to turn up the lamp. On the other hand, he might well have left a lamp burning, and it went out. And she came down to see why. Yes, that's bound to be what happened. But why take Hamilton away? Why not simply finish him there and be done with it?"

"Because without Hamilton, we can't clear up what took place by the sea on Monday. And without Hamilton we don't know what happened last night. If we'd been able to broaden our search for him before the cottage vanished, would we have found Hamilton there, dead of his wounds or exposure? Or only this bit of bandage to make us think he's still alive somewhere?"

"You make it far more complicated than it needs to be," Bennett complained as the motorcar began to roll. "Someone wanted Hamilton out of the way, and that someone also wants his wife. Add those facts together and we're back to where we were when you arrived. And in my view, if we don't arrest Mallory, we're derelict in our duty now."

"Where is the proof, other than walking into that house and holding Mrs. Hamilton at gunpoint? You can't support trial on that alone. You went out after him, Bennett, and put the wind up. He could very well be telling the truth, that he believed he would hang if you had your way. And he went to the one person who mattered to him, to tell her not to believe the police. Or turn it another way—he was desperately afraid that it was Felicity Hamilton who'd attacked her husband."

"You've taken his side. I say again, it was bound to happen. You were in the war, and that's a tie hard to break—"

"The war has precious little to do with this! I'd have gladly seen Stephen Mallory die in the trenches instead of—"

He stopped. But the words were spoken even if not finished. "*—instead of Hamish, who had no bishop uncle to pull him out before he broke. Who had had to go on fighting* *because he wasn't an officer, and men in the British Army did their duty to God and King, dying if need be without complaint. Instead of all the others I couldn't save, better men, better soldiers, who deserved a chance to live to see their children and their children's children."*

He tried desperately to cover his blunder, ending lamely even to his own ears, "—instead of being accused of murder today, and a dishonor to his uniform."

But Bennett said nothing, staring down the road, his face shadowed in the uncertain light inside the motorcar as the sun came and went. Something in his stillness was different now, as if a sudden thought had occurred to him. Or as if he'd read into Rutledge's short, sharp silence and unsuccessful recovery a revelation that shifted the relationship between the two men. Whether for better or worse, Rutledge was still too stunned to judge.

17

Bennett insisted that they go to Casa Miranda directly to speak to Mallory. "He'll be expecting us sooner or later. And I'd like to know how Mrs. Hamilton feels when she learns she could be a widow. That length of bandage is damning evidence that Hamilton's dead. And it just might shock her into her senses, make her see Mallory for what he is. But he won't let me in on my own. It's the two of us, then, together."

Rutledge paused at the intersection where he must make a choice, to rising land where the house stood or back toward the Mole and the police station.

Bennett was right; it was the next logical step in confirming what they feared.

But would it turn out the way the inspector was convinced it would?

Better to be there. To watch faces for himself. The question was, Would Mallory feel cornered and explode? Or would he simply give himself up, knowing that there was nothing more Hamilton could tell the police now? Had that been his reason for sending for Rutledge in the first place, gaining a little time until Hamilton died of his wounds without ever regaining consciousness? If so, he hadn't reckoned on Dr. Granville's medical skills.

Still, without Hamilton to testify against him, with no murder weapon found, with the constable on duty swearing Mallory hadn't left the Hamilton house last night, there was precious little evidence to hold him, even if Bennett succeeded in taking him into custody.

The entire complexion of the case had changed.

"He willna' give himsel' up," Hamish said. "You remember. He was a verra' stubborn man."

Stubborn—and sometimes impetuous, failing to look ahead at the consequences of his actions. He'd shown that impetuosity again in his flight from Inspector Bennett.

And now it could still drive him to suicide. Guilty or not guilty, it wouldn't matter if he believed he could exonerate himself in Felicity's eyes. A last grand gesture. Because the bubble of infatuation had burst, and it was unlikely, even if Mallory didn't stand trial, that Felicity would marry him now that she was free.

Rutledge considered postponing the confrontation until he'd made his call to Melinda Crawford. But what she could tell him about Matthew Hamilton had no bearing on what must be said to Stephen Mallory. And what would Bennett do while Rutledge was speaking with Melinda? Decide to storm the heights on his own?

"He willna' be put off," Hamish warned.

True enough. The die, as it were, was cast.

Rutledge pulled up the hill in a shower of the brightest light yet, although the wind was cool beneath the warmth of the sun. As he stepped out of the motorcar by the house door, he looked to the horizon. Where the squall line had been hours earlier, a long stretch of pale blue rain-washed sky was spreading.

Motioning for Bennett to stay where he was for the time being, Rutledge walked around the boot, trying to put words together to make their visit worthwhile. But he had condemned Mallory out of his own mouth, now, and it still jarred him. He hadn't meant it. He'd never wanted to see any of his men dead.

The knocker seemed to resound through his head as well as the house.

In due course, he heard Mallory call, "What's this visit in aid of, then? Was it Hamilton they'd found in the village?"

"No. But there appear to be new developments."

"You're not bringing Bennett in with you. I won't be outnumbered that easily."

"A truce then," Rutledge said quietly. "You don't want Mrs. Hamilton hearing what we will be shouting at you through the door."

Mallory swore. "Don't take me for a fool." But the words were more bravado, Rutledge thought, than anger.

"Unlock this damned door and listen to me. Then make up your mind."

The door, after a moment, swung slowly open, a small slit that showed Mallory's face in shadow.

"You know Hamilton went missing. We've found something to indicate where and possibly why. Bennett and I are here to put you in the picture. It is not going to be something Mrs. Hamilton will find comforting or reassuring."

Bennett, peering out of the car, moved his crutch to the front seat. Mallory said sharply, "Tell him to keep his distance."

Bennett stopped, his face flaring with anger. But he had

the sense to know that patience would gain him more in the end. Without a word, he simply set the crutch across his lap, the shoulder end out the far side window.

"Step out here for five minutes. I give you my word this is no trap. There isn't a sniper waiting with a rifle, there isn't a covey of policemen under cover in the garden. But Bennett is the local man, it's his problem as well as yours, and the sooner we sort it out, the better."

"He willna' come," Hamish said.

But in the end, Mallory, after a long look at Rutledge, stepped outside and behind him drew the door nearly shut. "Mrs. Hamilton is in the kitchen," he said grimly. "Looking at the larder." There was a wealth of information in the statement. Food was running low and his own attempts at cooking were a failure. What's more, Nan Weekes was still uncooperative.

Rutledge wondered what the maid would have to say when she was told that Hamilton was dead.

At a nod from Rutledge, Bennett heaved himself out of the motorcar, put his crutch under his arm, and hobbled forward.

For an instant the three men seemed to stand there like flies in amber, their positions determined by the strained relationships that separated them and made them antagonists, holding them in a pattern that had no beginning and no end.

Mallory broke the stiff silence. "Get on with it."

Rutledge said, "While I was here in the grounds earlier this morning, a house—or rather a cottage—out on the Devon road went over the cliff and into the sea in a subsidence."

"What does this have to do with Hamilton?"

"I mistakenly thought the activity I saw along the Mole meant that Bennett here had found him. Back to the cottage.

It was uninhabited, thank God, derelict in fact, and no one was hurt. But I went around by sea to have a look at what was left. It had to be done, in the event Hamilton had been inside and we could recover his body."

Mallory had been listening impassively, his face schooled to show no expression. Now he said, braced lines about his eyes, "Cut it short, man, was he there? Is he *dead*?"

"There was no hope of digging through the silt without grave risk to the searchers. But I found one of the man's bandages caught on a broken chair. Dr. Granville has confirmed that it's very likely the one covering Hamilton's head and face."

Mallory seemed to catch his breath on a word. And then he said, "You can't prove how it got there. Or why. And without a body, you can't be sure Hamilton is dead."

"The evidence is very strong now that he is."

"But how the hell—unless you were lying to me about his injuries—could he have walked out of the *surgery,* much less down the Devon road. How far is the cottage from here?"

"A goodly distance. A mile or so."

"Reston's cottage, was it? That's the only one—" He stopped, well aware that he might have said too much. Then he added, "Look, I live here, I've driven that road. There's a working farm just up the way, I've stopped there for eggs."

Bennett, watching him with intensity, said nothing.

Rutledge replied, "We'll be questioning the farmer and his family. Now that we have the evidence from the cottage."

"Well, I shouldn't have cared to walk out on a landslip. But I'm not surprised that you did it. What I find inexplicable is the fact that you can't put your hands on Hamilton. My God, he was my only *hope*." His face suddenly changed. "The problem now is who took him away, and that, my friend, should be proof I wasn't the one who attacked him in the first place!"

Bennett said, "By my way of thinking, if Hamilton had come to his senses in the middle of the night, he'd have dragged himself this far to find out what's amiss with his wife. And in all likelihood, he'd have shot you where you slept."

Mallory winced. But he retorted, "If he's lucid enough to walk this far, he'd have been lucid enough to remember I hadn't touched him. Why the hell wasn't someone sitting with him at night? No, don't answer that, I can guess what the good doctor said—that Hamilton was safe as houses where he was." His mouth turned down with the bitterness of experience. "Why do medical men assume that God gives them special dispensation? I've never met one who didn't think he could manage very well, thank you, in any crisis." Something made his head lift and his gaze sharpen. "Did I hear something out there? By the road?"

"There's a constable under the tree outside the wall. He's been here from the start. An—er—precaution."

"I don't intend to shoot anyone," Mallory told them irritably. "As long as no one tries to take the house by storm. Is that all you have to tell me?"

"There's another problem involving Hamilton's disappearance we haven't discussed. It appears that someone in the surgery in the dark either mistook Mrs. Granville for Hamilton or was seen by her while searching for him. She came to investigate, and whoever it was killed her."

"Gentle God!" Mallory exclaimed. "You can't lay *that* at my door."

"You have no witnesses to prove you were here all night. Not if Mrs. Hamilton was locked in her room and Nan Weekes was closed up belowstairs."

"*No.*" The word was explosive. "You're telling me that

I must compromise her reputation to prove I didn't do this murder. And besides, if you'll think about it, while I was out trolling half of Hampton Regis last night, what was to stop her from setting that blasted maid free and running to your constable out there for protection? Tell me that! Did he see *me* leave? Did *she* try to leave? You put him there, by God, he's your man. And I'm not up to shinnying down cliff faces into a stormy sea, much less clawing my way back."

"In her room, she couldn't hear you go."

"She's not a fool, either, Rutledge. If she'd had any inkling I was not in the house, she'd have screamed the place down. Probably for fear I'd gone back to the surgery to finish what I started. She may be my prisoner, but I'm hers as well. Did either of you stop to think about that? *She's kept me from going near her husband by seeing to it that I can't walk out this door.* And if I do, I've lost the only chance I have of seeing myself through this tangle to the other side."

Bennett, opening his mouth to speak, shut it again. And then, clearly against his better judgment, he said, "We've got off on the wrong foot, you and I, Mr. Mallory." He gestured with his crutch. "I'm paying for that as well as you. It would be simpler all round if we left this nasty business in Inspector Rutledge's capable hands. It's what he was sent here to do. Let him get to the bottom of these deaths. Before there's another. And in the long run, it will be easier on you and on Hampton Regis, not to speak of Mrs. Hamilton. She's suffered enough on her husband's account. She needs to consider how she wants to go about mourning him and marking his memory."

It was a reasonable speech, delivered in a reasonable voice. Only Bennett's eyes belied his calm, professional assessment of events: the local policeman pushed to admit that he'd been wrong at the start and offering a clear way out of a very difficult dilemma.

A desperate man might have believed it. A tired man might want to believe it. And Mallory was both. But he was also a man who'd spent time at the Front and was used to weighing up his chances. He might well see the hangman's noose at the end of his present road, but he'd crossed No Man's Land in the teeth of enemy fire, and he had felt death very close to him. It had left its mark in his courage.

He turned toward Bennett. "Yes, we did get off to a bad start, and I'm sorry for what happened to your foot, I'll tell you that frankly." His voice was also calm and reasonable, stating what he might actually believe and making it sound sincere, just as Bennett had tried to do. "But the damage is done as far as Mrs. Hamilton is concerned. I can't offer amends to her reputation even if I shoot myself. Hanging me would only make matters worse for her because it will all be dragged through the courtroom and the newspapers, raked up again for gossip and condemnation. And Matthew Hamilton dead is no good to my case. I needed him alive, whether you believe me or not. He could have saved me, he could have taken Felicity back, and I'd have left England. It would all have ended in the only possible *way*."

Mallory stopped. Then he said to Rutledge, "Your brief is still to find who has killed two people who didn't deserve to die. But make it soon. I don't think I can take much more of this."

He started to step back through the door and then paused with one foot on the threshold. "We've got no supplies. Let the rector bring us what we need. I won't shut him in with us. And he won't tell Felicity—Mrs. Hamilton—about her husband's death or Mrs. Granville's. She doesn't need to suffer any more than she has already."

Rutledge said to the closing door, "Mallory—"

There was silence behind the wooden paneling. But Rutledge had the most vivid image of Mallory standing there in the dimness on the other side, head bowed, hands over his face.

Climbing painfully into the motorcar, Bennett said, "I tried. No one can say I didn't try."

Rutledge took a deep breath. "It was admirably done. I'd hoped he would accept your offer. It was generous." But he found himself thinking that perhaps the visit of the Chief Constable had had a salutary effect on Bennett's determination to hang Mallory out of hand. It might still be there, but the policeman had triumphed over the broken bones in his foot when it was most needed.

But Hamish wasn't satisfied. He said, "Ye ken, he doesna' wish to go down in flames with you *or* the Lieutenant."

It was a chilling analogy. How many airplanes had they watched crash in flames over the Front? Even if the pilot got out, he seldom survived. But Bennett was determined to see that whatever the outcome for Rutledge or Mallory, he remained the local policeman in Hampton Regis.

The inspector was saying, "Did you believe him, then? That he's pinned in that house by Mrs. Hamilton's fears, and never set foot outside?"

"It could well be the truth. Certainly if Mrs. Hamilton woke in the night and realized that Mallory was nowhere to be found, her first thought must be that he'd used the cover of darkness to go down to Granville's surgery."

"There's no telling with women," Bennett said with a sigh. "She might have decided to cut her losses. Here's Hamilton dying, and her reputation damaged. She might well decide that her future was safer with Mallory than as a widow whose name was under a cloud. Husband murdered, gossip swirling about her wherever she went."

Rutledge tried to picture Mrs. Hamilton as a schemer. And

found to his surprise that while he couldn't put it beyond her to look to the future, all things considered, she might well be better off with her husband at the end of this ordeal. Just as Mallory had admitted. He also found it hard to believe that any feelings she might have had for Mallory would survive what the two of them were going through now.

But Bennett was right. There was no certainty with women. They saw their world in a very different light. They had to face condemnation of a different sort, the look in a man's eyes as he recalled a hint of scandal, the glance that passed around a circle of other women as she walked into a room. A hostess's hesitation in greeting her, an older woman's reluctance to present her to impressionable daughters. A whisper behind a fan, a man's hand slipping as they danced, as if testing her willingness.

And there was Nan Weekes, who would gladly add to rumors and speculation.

Rutledge dragged his thoughts back to Matthew Hamilton. Why had he been attacked in the first place? That was still the most urgent question. For once that had happened, Hamilton's death must have become a foregone conclusion, to prevent him from telling the police what he remembered. If Granville had failed to save Hamilton's life that first morning, Margaret Granville might still be alive. Or if he'd had the sense to put a guard on his patient, she might not have been killed. But it had all begun in the mist early on Monday morning. An opportunity seized? Or a victim stalked?

What secret was so important that an innocent woman's life had to be taken to protect it?

Rutledge delivered Inspector Bennett to the police station and then turned the motorcar in the direction of the surgery.

But after an hour of walking through the rooms, putting

himself into Hamilton's shoes and then into Mrs. Granville's, he was no closer to an answer.

It was while he was opening closets and searching through shelves that he did make one new discovery.

While the bedclothes in the room where Hamilton had lain were thrown back, as far as he, Rutledge, could determine, none of them had been taken away. Hamilton's clothing and all his personal belongings were missing, yes—whether put on his body or tied in a bundle. But now he noticed that blankets had been removed from the cupboard in the passage where they were stored for ready use. The evidence was so slim it wasn't surprising that he hadn't noticed it before. Like the sheets below them, the remaining half dozen blankets were folded perfectly and set squarely on their shelf. But the top one was skewed very slightly, as if by a hand disturbing them in the dark. Mrs. Granville would have left these as she had everything else, in perfect order. The doctor's wife carrying out every instruction with care and attention to detail.

Not proof, of course, and such as it was, it would have to be confirmed by Dr. Granville. But possibly an indication that Hamilton was still out of his head and needed to be hauled away like a sack of goods.

There had been sea mist and a rain. . . . To keep Hamilton dry was inconsequential surely, if the intent was to kill him anyway. No, trundled in a barrow or carried over the shoulder, it was prudent to shield him from sight.

What still struck Rutledge was the mind behind every move that the killer had made so far.

Meticulous planning and execution.

Nothing left to chance but Mrs. Granville's sudden appearance. And even that deterrent had been overcome.

Was Mallory capable of such planning? In the trenches he'd followed orders and carried them out with a soldier's

skill, but without passion or flair to spur on his men. Fore-
sight was deeply imbedded in most officers who had survived through to 1916 and the Somme. They learned. They
profited from the costly mistakes of others.

If positions had been reversed, Hamilton, the Foreign Service career officer, might have plotted Mallory's death and
seen it through with such precise skill. He'd dealt with the
Turks and the Germans, where every word and gesture had
been watched and scrutinized for its nuances. It was a hard
school and he'd survived in it.

Who had turned just such cunning against the man? And
why?

18

Rutledge went back to the inn for a late luncheon, eating quickly without speaking to anyone. He could feel the other diners regarding him surreptitiously, their ears cocked for his voice.

Bennett, nursing his foot, had all but dropped out of his usual haunts, growling in his cave like a wounded bear. And one didn't call on the policeman's wife, not socially, without a damned good excuse.

He on the other hand was a fish in a glass globe, Rutledge told himself wryly, living here at the Duke of Monmouth. The one man who could tell the inhabitants of Hampton Regis what had happened at the surgery this morning had to take his meal somewhere, and such a small town ran either to tearooms suitable for women or a pub or two where workmen could pick up their midday meal or stop by for a sandwich and a pint at the end of the day. He had seen the latter

tucked into back streets, with perhaps a small dining room
on the far side of the bar, and names like Fisherman's Rest
or The Plough and Share. Plain food, but filling and faster
service than the hotel. Nearer the Mole was The Drowned
Man, with a lurid sign of a corpse wrapped in seaweed lying
on the pub doorstep on one side and being handed a pint of
what appeared to be bitter, on the other.

It wouldn't have mattered today if the roast beef was
lightly burned, the potatoes dry, the beets hard, though he
had to admit the Duke of Monmouth had outdone itself in
the kitchen this morning. In fact, the meal was excellent,
and he was grateful that the cook hadn't been struck down
by Becky's mumps. Guests had come to overhear a brief exchange, like the one he'd had earlier with George Reston, or
a comment dropped into the silence as he was being served.
Those who'd misjudged their timing had had to linger over
their pudding or savory longer than was customary. Conversation had flagged noticeably as he walked into the dining
room and took his table at one corner of the room.

But he wasn't the friendly local man, someone who might
be hailed with "Good God, Bennett, are we all to be murdered in our beds? And was that the Chief Constable coming
out your door this morning? What's going on at the surgery?
My wife was turned away and the youngest with colic, mind
you. Is Mr. Hamilton dead? Was it his body Dr. Hester took
away?"

Word was out that there had been a death. It couldn't be
avoided. Dr. Granville's neighbors had seen enough to hurry
to a friend's home or a shop, passing on their eyewitness accounts. The question was, would any of them also remember
anything from the previous night that would be useful to
the police? He'd rousted one of Bennett's men from bed and
withdrawn the other from Casa Miranda for the day and set
them going door-to-door wherever windows looked out on

the surgery. It would be a matter of great good fortune if they came back with reliable reports.

He walked out, a subdued scraping of chairs behind him to follow his progress, and went directly to the telephone in its cramped closet.

There he put through the long-delayed call to Kent, prepared to wait patiently while it was answered at the other end and Melinda Crawford was summoned to the telephone.

Instead the maid informed him that Miss Crawford had gone to dine with friends and would be home at nine o'clock that evening. Was anything wrong? Miss Crawford would wish to know straightaway, rather than worry herself sick until she could reach him.

"You know how she is, Inspector," the voice at the other end of the line chided him. "I needn't remind you."

"Tell her it's a duty call, after I'd been swept by a strong sense of guilt," he said, smothering his disappointment at missing her.

"And not a minute too soon, as you well know! Good day, Inspector."

It had been Boxing Day when he last spoke to her. Nearly three months ago.

Hanging up the receiver, Rutledge was still standing in the shadows of the closet when he heard someone at Reception speak his name.

The desk clerk was saying, "He was in the dining room a short while ago, sir. Shall I see if he's still in the building?"

The male voice said breezily, "Don't bother. I'll be staying, if you have a large room with a sea view available."

"We have very few rooms with a sea view, sir. The Duke of Monmouth was a coaching inn in its day, and most of our guests were grateful to be spared the dampness of the Mole."

"A large room, then." After a moment, the man went on,

"I hear you've had a spot of trouble here. Cleared up, is it?"

The desk clerk answered with the caution of a local resident. "As to that, sir, you'll have to speak to Mr. Rutledge. If you'll just sign here, sir."

"Ah. Well, I shall require tea, if that's possible. I've had a long wet drive. At least the rain has stopped here. It's pouring farther to the east."

"I'll take you up, sir, and then have a word with the dining room staff."

"Just tea will do, and perhaps . . ." the new guest was saying as his voice faded in the distance.

Rutledge listened as the clerk led the way up the stairs, waiting for a moment longer until they'd turned into the first-floor passage and it was safe to step out of concealment.

He hadn't recognized the newcomer. But the name would be there in the hotel register. Walking quietly, he crossed to the desk and turned the heavy book his way.

R. G. H. Stratton was scrawled on the page.

Rutledge didn't know anyone by that name. Either at the Yard or in London.

He left the Duke of Monmouth and went out to his motorcar. Stratton, whatever his business was, could wait. Who was he? Not sent by Bowles, surely—Bowles preferred his chosen minions. But perhaps from the Home Office, following on the heels of a report from the Chief Constable that all was not well in Hampton Regis. The first of the firestorm.

Hamish said, "It'll no' be your inquiry for verra' long."

And Mallory would not care for that.

He drove again to Miss Esterley's house, and knocked at the door. She received him with concern writ large in her eyes. But her cane was nowhere in sight.

"I'm told that a body was removed from Dr. Granville's surgery this morning. I'm also told that it appeared to be too slight for a man's. I warned you earlier that Matthew was dead, if he hadn't gone to Casa Miranda and to Felicity. Was I right, after all?"

He followed her into the room where they had spoken before, and took the seat she offered him. "There has been a death. Yes. But it wasn't Hamilton's body that was brought out. It was Mrs. Granville's."

If he had slapped her hard across the face, she wouldn't have been more shocked. Blood rushed to her cheeks and she said, her voice not quite steady, "But—Mrs. *Granville*? I don't quite—"

"She was found behind her husband's desk this morning, dead of a blow to the head. Meanwhile, we haven't found Hamilton, alive or dead. But the only conclusion we can draw now is that he was killed as well. If not at the surgery, then elsewhere."

It was blunt, and he'd intended it to be, though Hamish growled at him for it. But if she had helped Hamilton to leave the surgery last night, he wanted her to know the cost. And where was her cane? He had seen it this morning.

Tears welled in her eyes, and to keep them from spilling down her cheeks, she gripped the arms of her chair until her knuckles were white. Whatever she might tell him about her relationship with Matthew Hamilton, on her side it went beyond simple friendship.

"I thought policemen," she said huskily, "were taught to break bad news as gently as possible."

"There is no gentle way to speak of murder."

After a moment she replied, "That's a frightful word. I don't like it. I can't believe anyone would wish to harm Mrs. Granville. What does she have to do with Matthew? She was always so eager to please. And she adored her husband. She'd have done anything he asked of her."

As an epitaph, it summed up the doctor's wife very well.

She had lived for her husband, and perhaps died in his place.

"We don't know the full story. But it appears she was there in the surgery when Hamilton went missing. That she either knew or saw something that she shouldn't have. And that knowledge was costly."

"Then Matthew couldn't possibly have left of his own accord. He'd have done his best to defend her. Why was she there, in the middle of the night? Had he been waking up? That's what everyone was hoping for. Was she sitting with him?"

"Dr. Granville had gone out to a patient and Mrs. Granville had retired for the night. Someone may have seen him leave, realized that Hamilton was alone, and took the chance that it would be safe to walk into the surgery. But something—a noise, a light, we don't know—must have disturbed her and she went to investigate. She couldn't have known there was an intruder. Either she thought her husband had returned home or she was afraid that Hamilton had come to his senses and was disoriented or in pain."

"Yes, yes, it would be just like her. I didn't know her well, but well enough to recognize her sense of duty." She smiled sadly. "She hadn't wanted to be a nurse, you know. She didn't have the stomach for it. She told me as much when Dr. Granville sent her round with flowers the day I was brought home from hospital. She worked with him simply because she liked to be close to him. How is he coping? He'll blame himself, you know. I don't want to think about what he must be feeling. I've known loss myself."

"Did you know Dr. Granville well, before your accident?"

"We met socially from time to time. He's a fine doctor, I can tell you that. I've never really cared for him as a person, I don't know why. That's ungrateful, I know, I have no business even saying such a thing. He spent hours with me after my accident and did everything he could to see that I walked again, and without a limp. I've told you. But he was—I don't know—always trying to impress me with all he'd done for me, as if he wanted me to know the full extent of the debt I owed him. And I did know it. But I didn't enjoy his company the way I enjoyed Matthew's," she ended ruefully. "I tried not to let him see how I felt. It would have been unkind. And he was married. There's that as well."

Hamilton had been married, but she seemed to view that differently.

After a moment she shook her head. "Somehow I'm not ready to believe Matthew is dead. I—it just seems so *ruthless,* to kill a helpless man, much less an innocent woman."

"When we've learned why Hamilton was attacked in the first place, we'll be able to answer that. The urgent question just now is why anyone would have wanted to take Matthew Hamilton away. The simplest solution is that he's dead now, before he can speak to the police."

He had told Mallory that Matthew had come to his senses briefly. Had that been an error in judgment?

"Well, it won't help Felicity in her predicament, of course. It won't help that man Mallory to prove he isn't guilty of assault. And even if Mr. Mallory struck Matthew down, it was still far short of murder in the eyes of the law. He should have given himself up."

Hamish was pointing out that she had shown less sympathy for Felicity's loss than she had for Dr. Granville's.

Rutledge said, "What do you know about Mallory? Could someone have killed Hamilton to revenge himself on Mallory? To make sure he was tried for murder and hanged?"

"I don't think I've met Mr. Mallory more than once or twice. I know very little about him, except for the whispers I've heard." She considered for a moment how to answer him. "I'm sure Inspector Bennett would love nothing better than to see the man in custody—the woman who does my washing gossips about the trial he's been to his wife over that injury to his foot—but you aren't suggesting he'd prefer to watch Mallory hang? That's rather far-fetched."

Rutledge smiled grimly. "And so we're back to the beginning, and why Hamilton was so severely beaten."

Miss Esterley regarded him with interest. "You are a devious man, aren't you?" she asked.

"If it wasn't Mallory who attacked him, then who found him walking that morning and quarreled with him? Who was disappointed in something he said? Who was afraid of something he might do? Who lashed out in such blind fury that before either of them quite realized what had happened, Hamilton was lying there bleeding and unconscious?"

She shivered, her gaze lifting to the windows, as if she could see beyond the walls and into the past. "You make it so—vivid. Personal."

"A beating *is* personal."

Miss Esterley answered slowly. "I don't know of anyone who was afraid of Matthew. After all, he'd only just come to live here, he hardly knew us, and most certainly couldn't know our family skeletons. As for disappointment, at a dinner party not a fortnight ago, I overheard Miss Trining tell him that she was very disappointed that he hadn't chosen to stand for Parliament. I'd never known him to express any interest in that direction—in fact, he seemed to be rather glad to be out of the public eye. And I most certainly can't picture Miss Trining taking a cane to him for refusing to consider a political future. But then Miss Trining sees duty in a different light from the rest of us. And as for someone being angry with him, we've come full circle again to Mr. Mallory."

"Was Miss Trining ambitious for herself? Or for Hampton Regis as the home of a sitting MP?"

"I don't believe it had anything to do with ambition on her part. It's more an abhorrence of wasted potential."

Hamish stirred, and Rutledge picked up the thought.

Wasted potential . . .

If Miss Trining had discovered Hamilton's penchant for dealing with grave robbers, she might have felt more than disappointment—she might have been furious with him for not being the man she'd believed he was.

But surely even if her temper had got the best of her on the strand, she would have owned up to her actions and taken full responsibility for them. Duty carried with it responsibility.

Before he left, Rutledge put one final question to Miss Esterley.

"Do you happen to know Mrs. Reston's maiden name?"

"Her maiden name? No, I don't believe I do. Is it important?"

"I've been told that she came from a very good family and might have known Hamilton in the years before he went abroad."

"Indeed? If that's true, I never heard anyone bring it up. And I'm sure it would have become known. When the Hamiltons arrived in Hampton Regis, everyone was scrambling for an introduction. Mrs. Reston would have been exceedingly popular, if she'd had any sort of connection. I've told you, I was the first to make his acquaintance, because of my accident. I know how quickly people suddenly discovered how very much they enjoyed *my* company." It was said wryly, even with a touch of bitterness.

But it was possible that Henrietta Reston had had her own reasons to keep the past in the past. And her relationship with Hamilton buried there.

* * *

It was not likely in a village the size of Hampton Regis that
Rutledge could avoid the newcomer, Stratton, for long if the
man set out in search of him. He had only to ask the desk clerk
for a description of the motorcar and he would soon track it
down. But as Rutledge left Miss Esterley, he was pleased not
to find Stratton leaning against the wing, waiting for him.

Rutledge went again to the rectory to assure himself that
Bennett had spoken to Mr. Putnam about the larder at Casa
Miranda.

Bennett had sent someone round, Putnam told him in a
low voice. And he was to be driven up to the Hamiltons'
door in a greengrocer's cart at a quarter past three.

"Dr. Granville is asleep finally, and I hesitated to leave
him alone just now. But I'll only be there long enough to
help hand in the choices that Mrs. Bennett is making. I can
only hope they're to Mrs. Hamilton's liking."

Rutledge smiled in spite of himself. "Quite."

"That's a volatile situation, you know, with Mr. Mallory.
I have prayed to find a way to resolve it. I'm sure he wants
to find a resolution as well. But so far there's been no clear
answer."

"There will be none, until we discover who tried to kill
Hamilton."

"Yes, sadly, it's for the law, isn't it, to bring us safely
through. I can only do my best to keep peace where it is
needed most. And that's here for the moment."

"Thank you for agreeing to help."

"Not at all. You will keep me informed, won't you? I can't
be everywhere, and of late I seem to have been in all the
wrong places." It was said ruefully but with conviction. "I
should have foreseen something. If I had known my flock as
I so often pride myself I do, I should have sensed the injuries
that were driving people to desperate measures. Whatever it
was that has led us to this."

"It isn't your failure, Rector. Murder is a private matter. It's when a man or woman has no other resources available that he or she turns to a last act of violence. Would that a priest *could* do our work for us at the Yard."

"Small comfort, Mr. Rutledge, when it is one of your own who has been maimed and now murdered. I lie awake with that knowledge on my soul, and tell myself that somewhere I shall find that slim gleam of understanding I need to go forward."

Alarmed, Rutledge said, "You'll stay out of this, Mr. Putnam. Any knowledge you feel you possess, you must bring to me. Do I have your word on that? This is a cold-blooded killer, not a lost sheep from St. Luke's flock who can be brought back into the fold with a prayer for guidance."

Putnam smiled. "I'm not as brave as that. You needn't fear. I'm no Becket, challenging kings or murderers. But I ought to be clever enough to understand my own congregation, don't you think?"

With that he shut the door softly and left Rutledge standing on the rectory steps.

Miss Trining was not pleased with Rutledge and made no bones about it.

"I summoned the Chief Constable," she said, sitting in the tall-backed chair in a parlor that was as grand as a drawing room, brocade and polished wood and floors that shimmered beneath the feet of elegant furnishings older than the house itself, possibly the dowry of an ancestress. "I felt it my duty to express my belief that events had got out of control. Inspector Bennett is all well and good, but his abilities are limited. And I doubt you have the experience to guide him."

In the place of honor over the mantel hung a portrait of a Victorian gentleman, soberly dressed in black and standing in a pose reminiscent of paintings of the late Prince Albert designed to grace shops bearing the seal *By Appointment.* . . .

Hamish had no difficulty with the family likeness. "The MacQueens bred true as well," he commented.

"I appreciate your strong sense of duty, Miss Trining. It becomes your role in Hampton Regis." The words rolled off Rutledge's tongue effortlessly. He had dealt with busybodies before.

"What *is* going on?" she demanded. "I particularly asked the Chief Constable to come here and tell me who is dead. It can't be Matthew Hamilton, I refuse to believe it. But if it isn't, why is the surgery shut tight and guarded by Constable Coxe?"

"Miss Weekes's cousin, I believe?"

"Yes."

Not the young constable who had fetched Dr. Hester from Middlebury, but an older man with grim eyes. Rutledge had taken a hard look at him, thinking to himself that if anything happened to Nan Weekes, Coxe would be difficult to manage. Assuming the pair were as close as she had tried to make him believe they were.

"The truth is, Miss Trining, that Mr. Hamilton is no longer in the surgery. At some point in the night, he either was helped to leave it or was carried away."

"By whom, pray?" Her anger was apparent. "Was it that foolish wife of his? It was my *clear* understanding that he shouldn't be moved—I'd even suggested that he be brought here where he could be more comfortable, and Dr. Granville was set against it."

"It was done without Dr. Granville's knowledge or consent."

"How like her. Then I was quite right to have brought this

matter to the Chief Constable's attention. Specialists should have been brought in at once for consultation. Indeed, I'd pointed that out to Dr. Granville myself. I must tell you, the man is arrogant about his skill at times. But then he doesn't come from a refined background. He was adopted by the Granvilles, you know. A promising boy who showed an early aptitude for medicine and repaid his new family poorly for their kindness. Why else should he be looking after farmers and shopgirls here in Hampton Regis when his foster father is in Harley Street?"

Wasted potential.

"Unkindness?" he asked, with just the right level of curiosity to elicit information from her rather than the sharp edge of her tongue.

"I'm told there was a young woman whom he met shortly after he set up practice. Her father was a nabob, made his money in South Africa, you know, friend of Rhodes and so on. When he discovered that his daughter's suitor was merely fostered and not a Granville by blood, he rather publicly put an end to the affair. Accused him of playing with her affections, in fact. The foster father, accepting the nabob's version of the situation, refused to have any more to do with our Dr. Granville. Guilty or not, it finished him in London society, and of course he had to leave."

"That doesn't appear to me to reflect poorly on Dr. Granville. Rather, on his foster father."

"Mr. Rutledge, it is ingratitude we are speaking of," she told him in her severest tone. "Ingratitude for putting his benefactor in such an untenable social position. A man of his upbringing should have risen above the class in which he was born. And he failed to do that. The medical profession must be seen to be above reproach. That is why doctors are accepted in Society."

He wasn't in the mood to challenge her views. He said,

"He married Margaret Granville after leaving London?"

"Yes. Entirely too timid to be a doctor's wife, but I must say she's shown herself to be a devoted assistant. Her father was a country vicar, no money at all, but her mother came of good family and left her a comfortable inheritance." She glared at Rutledge. "You have intentionally diverted me from what Mrs. Hamilton saw fit to do in regard to her husband's care. I find it appalling, but I will be charitable and put the greatest blame on the man with whom she is presently consorting."

"Mrs. Hamilton as far as we can determine never left her house last night. And I don't think she could have removed her husband without help."

"Then the two of them are in it together. Just as I said. Mallory and Matthew's wife."

"We've searched the house and grounds. We've had to accept the possibility that Hamilton is very likely dead."

She leaned forward in her chair. "He can't be dead!" The shock was real and it took her a moment to recover. "I refuse to believe you."

"We can't find him, Miss Trining. The fact is, someone has gone to a great deal of trouble to be sure that we don't have his body."

"Was it that man Mallory, finishing what he'd started? Why did you not put a guard on Mr. Hamilton? It's negligence, Inspector, sheer, blind *negligence*. What excuse does Dr. Granville put forward for this turn of events? I'd like to hear it." She was furiously angry, beside herself with it. But Rutledge found himself wondering if she was afraid—afraid that he was tricking her.

"Dr. Granville has no excuses to offer. His wife was killed last night, presumably as she came to the surgery in her nightdress to see why someone was there at such a late hour."

Miss Trining stared at him. After a moment she demanded, "And where was the doctor, pray?"

"He was attending a case of congestive heart failure."

She digested that, nodding. "Will Joyner, I expect. His daughter is without doubt the worst cook in Hampton Regis. What she feeds him I shudder to think, but it has done him no good. I've been there when Dr. Granville gives her instructions, and never fail to wonder at her stupidity. I shall have to offer to bring Dr. Granville here. He can't wish to stay in that house tonight."

"Mr. Putnam has taken him to the rectory."

"And quite right. Mr. Putnam has a very acute sense of what's best. I shall send them their dinner. At least they'll have no worries there." She shook her head. "I find it hard to take in. I spoke to Margaret Granville only yesterday, we were planning the spring gala at the church. She was to make the table decorations for us to sell. And I shall have to find another volunteer for that."

Noblesse oblige.

The Miss Trinings of this world coped. It was their duty.

She couldn't have removed Hamilton alone. And Rutledge couldn't quite see her as a coconspirator with anyone else in Hampton Regis.

He could safely strike her off his list of suspects.

19

Rutledge took a quarter of an hour to search out the man Joyner, the patient with congestive heart failure, and found him resting quietly in his bed, watched over by an anxious woman in her thirties. She looked tired, eyes red-rimmed from lack of sleep and from worry.

"He's only just drifted off, Inspector," she told him on the doorstep of the small house on the road east, a mile beyond the churchyard. "Doctor says rest is what he needs."

"I shouldn't like to disturb him, Miss Joyner. Dr. Granville was here in the night, you say?"

"Yes, he's good about that. I send the neighbor's boy along, if Dad takes a turn. He's pining for Mother, that's what it is, but I don't want to lose him. It's his pension pays for this cottage, after all."

Practical, the way the poor so often had to be.

Curiosity got the better of her. "What's this about, Inspector? Mr. Bennett never comes to look in on us. Even when Dad had the influenza and nearly died."

"Dr. Granville lost his wife in the night. We're trying to pin down the time of her death."

"Oh, the poor man! I shan't tell Dad for a bit, it will upset him no end. And I asked after her, I remember I did. Doctor said she was in her bed and asleep, as I ought to be."

"What time was Dr. Granville here?"

"I sent for him soon after one o'clock, it seems to me. And he sat with Dad until he was quiet. Five or six, it must have been by that time. I heard the neighbor's rooster start crowing."

"Thank you, Miss Joyner. I won't keep you any longer."

She said, "You'll tell Doctor how sorry we are. I'd hate to think of him being here when his wife was so ill and needed him. Makes me want to cry."

"There was nothing he could have done," he assured her, and left, before the next question was asked: how Mrs. Granville had died.

Hamish said, "It wasna' necessary to come here."

But Bowles would ask for such minute attention to detail. It would balance what London would see as his unnecessary venture out to the landslip. Even if it had produced that tantalizing bit of bandage.

It also established that Granville had come east, not west, when he went out on the Joyner call. He wouldn't have been a witness to whatever had been done on the road to Devon.

Worst luck. It would have helped to corroborate the story that young Jeremy Cornelius had told.

Mr. Putnam, leaving a note for Dr. Granville on the hall table, collected his coat and was standing in the rectory drive when the greengrocer pulled up with his cart.

The horse, an old hand at the game, stopped as soon as Putnam approached, waited for him to clamber up to the high seat beside Mr. Tavers, and then walked on.

Circling the drive to the gates in the low wall, Tavers said, "I'm not setting foot in that house. I'm not finding myself shut up there with a revolver at my head. Not good for business."

Putnam said, his voice pacific, "You won't be in any danger. Mr. Mallory isn't a madman, he's just frightened that what happened to Mr. Hamilton is going to be laid at his door, simply because he had had a quarrel with Mr. Hamilton. Well, not precisely a quarrel. A difference."

"But Hamilton's gone missing. And Mrs. Granville is dead. What did he have to do with *that* nasty business?"

"I don't think Mr. Rutledge or Mr. Bennett has come to a conclusion about that. Not yet."

"Mrs. Bennett has an opinion, and it isn't in Mallory's favor, I can tell you that."

"Yes, well, I'm sure she's worried for her husband. He blames Mr. Mallory for the injury to his foot."

"My point exactly. A volatile temper, that's what Mr. Mallory has, and it got the better of him this time."

"Have you ever seen him lose his temper?"

"When he first came to Hampton Regis, Mrs. Tavers noticed how edgy he was, and uncertain in his moods. She said to me he was not one she'd like to meet along a dark road in the middle of the night."

"I understand Mallory had a very rough time in the war."

"And so did my son Howard, the youngest. But he's not going about bashing in heads and keeping another man's wife against her will, is he?"

With a sigh, Putnam said, "Don't worry, man, I shall take everything inside the house. You need only set the parcels by the door." Changing the subject, he asked, "Have you been considering one of these new lorries for your business?"

"Not as long as Fred here is still pulling his weight," Tavers retorted.

It was a tense greengrocer who drew up in front of Casa Miranda and halted his horse to let Putnam step down.

Putnam tapped at the door and waited, wondering what his reception would be.

But Mallory, casting a swift glance outside, said, "Good afternoon, Mr. Putnam. Is there any news about Mr. Hamilton?"

"Sadly, I haven't any. I wish I had."

Mallory swallowed his disappointment. "Thank you for rescuing us from starvation. If you'll just bring the parcels to me, I'll carry them the rest of the way."

"Of course."

Tavers stepped down, turned his back on Mallory, and began to pull out a box of goods. Putnam hurried to help him and lifted the first box with a grunt. He ferried it to the man waiting in the doorway and went back for the second. When he had transferred the fifth box, and Tavers went back to his seat on the cart, Putnam approached Mallory diffidently.

"I shan't presume on a mission of mercy," he said quietly. "But I can offer my services for what they are worth."

Mallory said, "I wish you would pray for us, Rector. We're tired and dispirited. And Nan Weekes has made the worst of this business. I hadn't counted on that. I thought she'd do more to comfort her mistress."

"Would you like me to speak to her. She may be frightened."

Mallory gave a short bark that wasn't amusement. "Yes, and while I guard the door, what then?"

Putnam said with asperity, "I do not represent the police, Mr. Mallory. My duty is to God. If you ask me to help you, I would be here as his representative, and no one else's."

Mallory wiped a hand over his face. "I'm sorry, Rector. Yes, if you would have a word with Miss Weekes, I would be

grateful. It would make life within this house a little less—"
He shrugged. "I'm no match for two angry women." Then
as Putnam seemed to take a step forward, Mallory said, "I
haven't told either of them about Hamilton. Or about Mrs.
Granville. It was unnecessarily cruel, to worry Mrs. Hamilton when there's nothing she can do. You'll respect that,
won't you?"

"I understand. I'll just ask Mr. Tavers to wait." In a
moment he was back. He passed Mallory at the door and
made his way into the hall, wondering if he would encounter Mrs. Hamilton on his way belowstairs. But she was not
waiting for him. He found the room where Nan Weekes
had been incarcerated and saw that the key was in the door.
Turning it, he stepped inside.

The woman standing with braced shoulders where she
could face whoever came into the room, raised her eyebrows
as she recognized the priest.

"You've come to tell me it's over," she said flatly. "Did he
kill her and then himself? It's what I've been expecting, but
I've heard no gunshots."

"Nan, nothing has changed. I've come because Mr. Mallory feels you need the little comfort I can offer. It's been a
trying few days."

"Trying." She seemed to spit the word at him. "It's not
what I'd use, not trying. They're tormenting each other and
tormenting me. I blame both of them, her for giving him
false hope, and him for not seeing that he wasn't wanted
here."

"You think that's what has happened?" Putnam asked.

Nan Weekes said, "A decent woman doesn't find herself
pursued by a man she turned down. A decent man takes
his dismissal. But my cousin has seen him watching this
house of a night, from across the way. And she looks out
that window toward him, in the morning. I've seen her when

I go to bring down the ashes, and if I've seen her, so has Mr. Hamilton." She turned away, as if she preferred not to face him for the next question. "No one tells me how Mr. Hamilton is faring, after that beating. I'm not to speak of it, she says. It's too painful, she says. And who else could have given it to him, I ask you, but that Mr. Mallory? Is he dead? Is that why you've come, to offer comfort to the widow?"

"No. I don't know how Mr. Hamilton is faring, Nan. I haven't been to see him, you see. For several days he wasn't allowed to have visitors, he was too ill."

He had kept to the letter of his promise, Putnam thought. But not the spirit of it. With a sigh, he said, "Could you bring yourself to help Mrs. Hamilton through this ordeal? You may not approve of her actions, but you cannot judge what's in her heart, you must leave that to God. For now, your strength and your willingness to be a witness to her ability to steer Mr. Mallory toward a peaceful end is your first duty to Mr. Hamilton. Will you keep that in mind? Will you stay here, make no trouble for either of them, and do what you can to help us while Mr. Rutledge is trying to bring Mr. Mallory to his senses?"

She said, "If you say so, Rector. But it was Mrs. Hamilton who gave him that revolver. And if anything happens to me, you must tell my cousin that I told you as much. He's one of Mr. Bennett's men, he'll see things set to rights."

"I think you must be mistaken—"

"That I'm not, Rector. I was there on the stairs, wasn't I? It's Mr. Hamilton's revolver from his foreign service that Mr. Mallory has, and I've been praying since I was shut up in here that he would turn it on himself and be done with it. It would be her punishment, wouldn't it? And very fitting."

Putnam stood there, rooted to the spot for an instant longer. Finally he said, "Nan, you're no better than they are, when you say such things."

"That's as may be. Will you give Mrs. Granville a message from me, if you please? I've got her best sheets at my house, to iron them properly. They'd have been back by now if I weren't shut away here. If she needs them, she can go and fetch them. I'll understand."

The rector replied slowly. "I expect to see Dr. Granville shortly. I'll make a point of passing this information on."

She laughed, without humor. "He wouldn't know the best sheets from the everyday ones. No, it's Mrs. Granville you must tell. I wouldn't want her to think I'd mislaid them."

He asked her, tentatively, if she would like to pray with him before he left, and she bowed her head stiffly while he did, drawing on his training to sustain him. But he saw that his hands were shaking as he locked her door again. And he wondered if Nan had noticed it as well.

Rutledge was driving back into Hampton Regis from Miss Trining's house when he saw George Reston and two other men walk into a row of offices just up from the Mole. They appeared to be in earnest conversation, and the younger of the three carried a sheaf of papers in his hand.

He passed them without showing any interest in them. But when they had gone inside, he turned the next corner and drew up in front of Reston's home.

The maid informed him that Mrs. Reston would receive him, and he followed her down the passage to a small room that was warm from the fire on the hearth and bright with lamplight.

"I was glad to see that Mr. Reston is feeling better," he said. "He appeared to be with business associates just now, near the Mole."

"He didn't want to keep to that appointment, but he had no choice." She regarded him coolly. "It had been arranged several days ago and one of the men has to return to Winchester tonight. Why have you come back, Mr. Rutledge?"

"First, I should like to ask you if your maiden name was Cole."

"It was not. My father was Edward Farrington, we lived in London and Sussex. I don't see that that has anything to do with your business here in Hampton Regis."

He tried to place the name. Something to do with law or finance, he thought. Certainly a firm connected with some of the best families in the country. Mrs. Reston had indeed come down in the world, and it was there in her face as she watched him search his memory. But he was careful not to let her see his conclusion.

"And your second reason?"

"Because I think you must know more about Matthew Hamilton than your husband is aware of, Mrs. Reston. And I didn't feel I should say as much in his presence."

"Our parents traveled in the same circles, we met a time or two, but it was not an event I remember with great fondness, if that's what you are asking me. He was just one of many people invited to the same house parties and weekends in the country. I enjoyed them. One did then, before the war. It was a very pleasant way of life. I miss that, I think a good many people must. It was a golden time. By the time I married George, Matthew Hamilton was abroad. I don't think he recognized me when we were introduced here in Hampton Regis at Miss Trining's dinner party. I didn't press the memory."

"But your husband, if I'm not mistaken, is very certain you do remember Matthew Hamilton, and with some warmth."

"Call it a matter of revenge, Inspector. It didn't drive my husband to attack Mr. Hamilton when he was out walking Monday last. And it hasn't driven him to do anything drastic now."

"You can't be sure of that. Revenge is sometimes bloody and swift."

"My husband bought me, Mr. Rutledge. Like goods in a shop. Or so he feels. I've seen it in his eyes when he looks at me. He wanted to improve his position socially, and my father needed money rather badly. It was an arranged marriage. Two years later, my uncle died and my father had all the money he could ever wish for. And I had George Reston for my husband. There was no respite for me. But I have finally brought him around to my way of thinking—I have created a past I never had. Embroidering my relationship with Matthew Hamilton into something more than the brief acquaintance it actually was. And George can't afford the scandal of divorce. We manage together very nicely at the moment. And I shall deny I told you a word of this, if you meddle."

"You believe he couldn't have beaten Hamilton nearly to death. But I've been informed he attacked another man in London, nearly as severely."

"I know my husband. He wouldn't have touched Hamilton. And as Mr. Hamilton has no way of knowing the role he's played in my life, he's not likely to give George any satisfaction."

"Matthew Hamilton is probably dead, Mrs. Reston. And you can't be sure that your fantasy hasn't driven your husband to murder. After all, the last indication we have of Hamilton's whereabouts was in that cottage that went over in the landslip."

"I remind you that anyone could have found a way inside. It was known to be abandoned. We had no reason to lock it or board it up. There was nothing inside of any value."

Except, Hamish roused himself to point out, a small vase painted with lilacs.

"Was the man your husband attacked in London another

of your fantasy love affairs?" Rutledge's voice was harsh, and he meant it to be.

Stung, she said, "That was a matter of business, Mr. Rutledge. I knew nothing about it until George told me that he was taking a position here, in Hampton Regis, and why. His partner, fool that he was, had been using client funds improperly, and George lost his temper when he found out. I never liked the man, I felt he was responsible for our leaving London, and I am sure that he deserved what he got after badgering my husband publicly to help him make restitution in time."

"You seem to have a very callous disregard for human suffering, Mrs. Reston."

"Yes. I was taught by masters. No one ever stepped forward to protect me, Inspector. I wonder why I should feel any driving sense of duty to protect anyone else. Let me tell you something about love. It can be very cruel and very greedy. I've had done with it. And that has given me a freedom that I cherish."

Rutledge, walking through the inn doors, saw someone rising from a chair set to one side of the Reception desk.

It was Stratton, striding forward with his hand proffered.

"I say, Inspector Rutledge? Robert Stratton, Foreign Office. Is there somewhere we can talk privately?"

Rutledge led him to a sitting room beyond the stairs and closed the door behind them.

"I've been sent down with a watching brief. Mr. Hamilton is one of ours, and naturally we feel some concern for his welfare."

"Mr. Hamilton, as I understand it, has retired."

"As indeed he has. But he's suffered rather severe injuries and his wife is under duress. I'm here to act on his behalf in any way that's useful. For instance, to see that he receives adequate medical attention and is moved to hospital if the local man isn't up to the task."

"I have no doubt that Dr. Granville is a good doctor. The problem is, Mr. Stratton, that we seem to have mislaid Mr. Hamilton. He was not in the surgery this morning when Dr. Granville returned from an emergency."

Stratton frowned. "I don't quite understand."

Rutledge took off his overcoat and sat down. "I'm at a loss myself. How did the Foreign Office learn about events in Hampton Regis? I wasn't aware that the attack on Mr. Hamilton had received widespread attention."

"An ear to the ground—"

"I'm a policeman, Mr. Stratton. I'm afraid that won't do." Rutledge waited grimly. "Who contacted the Foreign Office? And who sent you to Hampton Regis? I'd like to clear this with the Yard before I give you any more information. For all I know, you're the man who attacked Mr. Hamilton while he walked by the sea four days ago. If you've lost him, so have we. And I'd like to know why."

Stratton took the chair on the other side of the small table at Rutledge's elbow. Looking up at the painting above the hearth showing the Duke of Monmouth standing on a battlefield, banners flying and men dying at his feet, he said, "That's an abominable work. It didn't happen that way."

"The hotel is named for him. It's to their advantage to show him as an heroic figure. I'm still waiting."

"I was a friend of Matthew Hamilton's at one time. I hope I still am. The problem is, we've wondered, some of us, if he's writing his memoir. When the Chief Constable dropped a word in the right ear that Matthew was in serious condition and unconscious, we wondered if we might find ourselves with a posthumous publication. Disappointed men sometimes use the pen when the sword has failed them."

"And you are here to ferret it out if anything should happen to him?"

"I'm not from the Foreign Office. That is, I am, but not officially. I came as a friend. He'll do himself no good, raking up things best forgotten. The newspapers will make much of it, then lose interest. But by that time the harm will have been done. He, er, kept diaries. We do know that. We don't know what was in them."

Rutledge asked, "Did that have anything to do with the customs inspections he endured from time to time?"

Surprised, Stratton recovered quickly. "I daresay he invited them with his rather cavalier approach to other people's property."

"If something was sold on the open market, it was hardly appropriated by Mr. Hamilton. He simply bought the object. As I understand it."

"All very true. But of course when a man has a reputation for buying without asking questions, he encourages tomb and site thievery. It's simply not done. Still, a handful of rare statuary is not my interest. I've seen his collection and wouldn't give it house room. We could never understand why Hamilton chose to live in Hampton Regis rather than London. The only answer was that he found it the perfect place to work. Quiet, out of the way, attracting no attention other than the social aspirations of his neighbors. A perfect place."

"Did it occur to no one that he might like that house above the sea, that he chose a quiet place for the first years of his marriage, to give it time to flourish?"

"Of course it occurred to us, we're not fools," Stratton retorted irritably. "But it was unlike him. There was no connection in his past to this part of England. His wife wasn't from this vicinity. Hampton Regis is a very long way from London, not so much as the crow flies, you understand, but

in the kind of life everyone expected Hamilton to lead. It
aroused our—suspicions."

"It might well send them soaring to learn that Matthew Hamilton has vanished." Rutledge got to his feet and
lifted his coat from the back of the chair. "What's more,
a woman was murdered at the same time and in the same
place. If Mr. Hamilton has been writing an account of his
career, it has upset more than his friends, it's unleashed an
enemy."

Stratton was still standing there, stunned, as Rutledge
walked out of the room.

It was half past nine before Rutledge again shut himself
inside the telephone closet and put in his second call to the
home of Melinda Crawford.

Her voice was strong as it came over the line, and Rutledge smiled to hear it.

"Well, Ian, what have you got to say for yourself, neglect-
ing an old woman until she's left to wonder if you are alive
or dead—and on the brink of not caring either way!"

Melinda Crawford, a child in 1857's bloody mutiny of
native troops in India, had survived that and cholera to
marry, lost her husband when she was in middle age, and set
about traveling as an antidote to grief. Returning to England
in what most would have considered their final years, she set
up a home in Kent and soon acquired a large and interesting circle of friends. If she was still waiting to die, no one
suspected it.

"Mea culpa," he said. "Blame the Yard, if you like. It's
half their doing. I'd asked for leave to visit you, and they
wouldn't hear of it." It was the truth. But he made it sound
like a lie.

"A likely story." She waited on the other end, knowing
him too well.

"It's about Matthew Hamilton—do you remember him?"

"Of course I do. Are you breaking bad news, Ian? It's late and I shan't sleep a wink tonight."

"The truth is, I'm calling to ask if you knew one of his friends, a Miss Cole."

"Ah. Miss Cole. How did you come to know about her?"

20

Nothing that Melinda Crawford said or did surprised Ian Rutledge—he had grown used to her ability to leap ahead of a conversation or catch at a single word or phrase and divine what the speaker wished most to avoid.

Her question now was heavy with shadings. As if by asking him point-blank, she could somehow deflect his curiosity.

Rutledge said, "For a start, who is she, and where does she live?"

"She's a young woman Hamilton knew many years ago. Why don't you ask him about her?"

"I can't lay hands on him at the moment. You'll have to do."

"I expect she lives where she always has, in Exeter. With an aunt, although the elder Miss Cole may have died long since. In that case, your guess is as good as mine."

Exeter was not that far from Hampton Regis—in fact, along the west road to Devon.

"How did Hamilton come to know her?"

"As so many people came to know each other before the war. As you met Jean, at a weekend party. There were a goodly number of young men and women there—the host's son had just come down from university and there was tennis, boating on a small lake, dancing on the terrace, even croquet. Quite tame by modern standards, no doubt. Terribly Edwardian."

He smiled. She was deliberately trying to distract him.

"And why did our Miss Cole and Matthew Hamilton even recall each other long after this uneventful weekend party was a memory?"

"You must ask him that. I recollect a lovely girl, very well mannered and quite pretty."

"And so they became friends?" he urged.

"I expect Matthew thought he'd fallen in love with her. But nothing came of it."

"In what sense? That they were unable to make a match of it? That she wasn't in love with him? Or it was no more than a summer's romance?"

"She went back to Exeter with her family, and Matthew found himself offered a position in the Foreign Service."

"And who was behind that offer? Was it you? To get him clear of her clutches?"

He could almost hear her snort down the line. "You'll not put words into my mouth, young man. It's rude," she said tartly.

"I offer my sincerest apologies. Melinda, why should he describe her as the most completely honest person he knows?"

"I'm delighted to hear you at last use the present tense with Hamilton. I was afraid he was dead."

Rutledge swore under his breath. "Will you at least tell me how to reach Miss Cole?"

"I truly don't know. We never corresponded. You're a policeman, Ian, you'll find her if that's what you wish to do. Exeter isn't that large, as I remember."

And with a brisk good night Melinda Crawford was gone, the line echoing emptily behind her last words.

He sat there with the receiver in his hand, until the operator spoke in his ear, rousing him from his thoughts. He gave her the number for Scotland Yard.

In fact it was time and past for him to confer with the Yard. Indeed, he found that Bowles had left a message with the switchboard for any telephone call from Hampton Regis to be put through at once.

Rutledge considered that as he was waiting for Bowles to pick up at his end. *Not from Rutledge—from Hampton Regis.*

Hamish said, his voice seeming to echo hollowly in the small closet, "No' a good sign." He had been quiet for some time, and Rutledge jumped at the sound so close to his head that he could have sworn he felt Hamish's breath on his ear.

But Bowles was speaking now and he needed all his wits about him. "Rutledge? I'd expected to hear from you sooner."

"Yes, sir. We're shorthanded and I wanted to be the one to break the news of Mrs. Granville's death in certain quarters."

"Good. And as for shorthanded, the Chief Constable is arranging for more men, at Inspector Bennett's request. Didn't he tell you?"

"I haven't been to the station since midmorning."

"Time you did. These men will be called in from outlying towns, and Bennett is arranging accommodation for them. Expect them tomorrow morning, no later than six-thirty. Bennett tells me that's time enough."

"We should establish a watch along the coast as well, anywhere a body might wash ashore."

"Yes, I've heard your theory that Hamilton went over with the landslip. Early days yet, Rutledge, early days. It could be what you're meant to think. However, the Chief Constable has spoken to his counterparts west of you, and a watch is well in hand. I expect you to cooperate with Bennett, man, not run your own show."

"I understand, sir," Rutledge answered, offering no excuses. But he could feel Hamish bristling at his back.

Bloody-minded Bowles. It was another of the appellations attached to the chief superintendent's name. Men in the ranks preferred Old Bowels.

"We don't mislay important men, Rutledge. Find Hamilton, or find his body. And the doctor's wife, for God's sake—that's two murders, if Hamilton is dead. And I don't want to be hearing of another."

"I understand," Rutledge said for the second time. "This killer leaves very little trace of his passage. He's clever and he's quiet. It's not easy to find his tracks." He regretted it before the words were out of his mouth. A fatal weakness, apologizing, making excuses. It was how Bowles would view his explanation.

"Then you'll just have to be cleverer, won't you? I'll expect a further report by noon tomorrow. And I suggest for now that you and Bennett decide between you how these extra men are to be deployed. I shan't care to hear you've wasted your resources."

Bowles rung off before Rutledge could ask him about the Green Park murders and the name of the man Phipps had brought in.

He swore, but it brought him no satisfaction. As he opened the door to the little room, Hamish reminded him, "You havena' been completely honest with yon inspector."

He *had* kept information from Bennett. But for very sound reasons. Or so he had told himself. And he was not about to

drag Miss Cole into the equation until he knew more about
her. *Honest* was the way Putnam had described her—it was
how Hamilton had portrayed her to the rector. But could
there be bitterness as well?

He considered that possibility and then discarded it.
Surely too much time had passed for that.

It must have been years since Hamilton and Miss Cole
had met. For all Rutledge knew—or even Hamilton, for that
matter!—she had long since married happily, borne children, and was now a middle-aged woman with no other interest than her family. And Matthew Hamilton was a name
she read in the newspapers from time to time, and recalled
over the breakfast table how she'd won at tennis with him in
doubles, and whether or not he was a good dancer.

But something there was. Melinda Crawford had done
her best to discourage him from finding the woman. And
that had been an error in judgment on her part. It had served
only to fan his interest.

Hamish said, "If she'd made a promise, she'd ha' kept it.
And no' told you why she couldna' speak of it."

Rutledge listened to the voice in his head and came to the
conclusion that Hamish had read Melinda Crawford better
than he had.

It was an unsettling thought.

Late as it was, Rutledge went straight to the police station,
found that Bennett had already gone home for his dinner,
and ran him to earth there.

Mrs. Bennett had just set out their tea. A plump woman
with a round face, she looked Welsh. And the soft rhythm
of her speech confirmed it. "I'll just see if Mr. Bennett is
available, sir," she told him, and left Rutledge waiting on
the doorstep.

When she led him back to the sitting room, there was a
second cup for him on the tray by the hearth. A good fire

had warmed the atmosphere, but his greeting from Bennett was cold, with an underlying wariness.

Mrs. Bennett did her duty as hostess, then discreetly left them alone. As Rutledge looked down at his cup, he saw that it had been painted with a scene of a Welsh castle. Harlech, most certainly, and there was Beaumaris on the cake stand. More of the same souvenirs took pride of place in the glass-faced cabinet between the two windows, and a watercolor print of Snowdon at sunset hung above the hearth.

"If you are expecting me to leave the house tonight, you've got another think coming."

"I've just spoken to Bowles. I'm here to discuss how we'll use these men the Chief Constable is sending us tomorrow."

"They're at your beck and call. My men are tired and they have their regular duties to perform. We can't keep running them morning and night."

"I agree. Any word from the constables questioning Dr. Granville's neighbors?"

"None of importance. A dog barking, but no idea what time that was. A child up with the croup—Betsy Drews is her name, and her mother did see Dr. Granville leave. He had a small boy with him, and Mrs. Drews recognized him as Jimmy Allen, the one Miss Joyner sends along at time of need. Mrs. Drews was worried that Betsy might take a turn for the worse while Granville was out on the call, but she finally got her daughter to sleep without any more trouble, and that was the end of that. The dairyman saw him coming home. The times match what Granville himself told us."

"Yes, I called on Miss Joyner myself, earlier. It appears that whoever came to the surgery after Granville left had a good three hours clear in which to work. More than enough time."

Bennett offered him the small plate of sandwiches and another with slices of lemon cake with poppy seeds. Rut-

ledge suspected that they weren't prepared for a guest and
declined with thanks. Bennett didn't press him.

"We have to keep in mind that Hamilton could have attacked Mrs. Granville," Bennett continued. "In his muddled
state, he might not have understood what he was doing.
And if she startled him, he'd leap first and think second. He
might have killed himself later out of shame. It may be that
whoever helped him didn't even know about the killing."

It was a change in viewpoint that caught Rutledge off
guard. Was this a result of Bennett's conversations with the
Chief Constable? Or had he realized that it was going to be
difficult to prove that Mallory had slipped into the surgery
and removed Hamilton? It was hard to tell.

He didn't need Hamish's soft "'Ware!" to warn him to
watch his step.

He said, "True enough. But his wife was still under duress
at Casa Miranda. Wouldn't he have felt his life better spent
tackling Mallory?"

"We can't be sure, can we, what Hamilton knew or didn't
know. Or even if he was capable of reasoning. As I see it,
after attacking Mrs. Granville, he might have felt he served
his wife better by killing himself."

Rutledge had a sudden, sharp image of himself standing
beside that bandaged body discussing events with Dr. Granville. And beside them, Hamilton lay in a stupor, apparently
unable to hear or to speak. And later Bennett and Granville
between them had tried to rouse him as Rutledge had done
so briefly. Could Hamilton have absorbed snippets of those
conversations, and twisted them into something far less ac-
ceptable—that his wife was in league with Mallory? If that
was true, he'd want to take himself as far away from them
as he could, until he was well. Attacking Mrs. Granville by
mistake would have shaken him badly.

Had he mistaken her for Felicity, in the dark?

Only Dr. Granville could tell Rutledge if this was possible. But he'd seen men on the battlefield with head wounds. One had walked in stumbling circles, screaming. And another had sat with his back against the trench wall talking to his mother, begging her not to lock him in a dark room, unaware that the blackness surrounding him had nothing to do with childhood fears.

He finished his tea and set the cup on the tray. "I've also been told that there's a watch along the coast, in the event Hamilton is washed ashore."

"Currents are tricky in this part of the world. He may be washed out to sea, then brought in again to the west of us. There's rocks in Cornwall that trap corpses. But what he'll look like by that time, that's another question. We may never discover the true cause of his death."

Rutledge left, thanking Mrs. Bennett as she led him to the door. Walking out to the motorcar, he couldn't be sure whether Bennett's failure to tell him all that the Chief Constable was offering had to do with an interloper on his patch—or a very clear recognition that this was Bennett's opportunity to show himself a competent and resourceful policeman in his own right. He rather thought that the complacent Bennett had come to the conclusion that with the Chief Constable looking over his shoulder, it behooved him to change his ways. An awakening.

Rutledge went next to the rectory, more than a little worried about Putnam after their last conversation. The rector assured him that food had been delivered without incident. There was the rich scent of frying ham wafting through the door, and Rutledge thought he smelled potatoes and cabbage as well.

"And I spoke with Nan Weekes," Putnam was saying. "For her own sake, I encouraged her to be less intransigent and more cooperative. The stressful conditions in that house are very worrying to me, and no doubt to you as well."

"And I don't see a swift resolution," Rutledge admitted. "Thank you, Rector."

"Would I could do more," he said with a sigh, and closed the door.

Rutledge drove on to Casa Miranda, and found the odors there less appetizing. Someone had burned the meat, acrid smoke greeting him when Mallory finally admitted him to the house.

"I won't be alive to be hanged," he said with grim gallows humor. "I'll starve or be poisoned first. What do you want now?"

"I need to look through Hamilton's papers. There's the possibility that something he'd done abroad has come back to haunt him."

"Those confounded statues ought to haunt the man. I'm tired of staring at them. Felicity—Mrs. Hamilton—must give you permission."

Mrs. Hamilton, when she came to the study where he'd been left to wait, had a smudge of flour on her nose and an air of hurt resignation. She said to Rutledge, "I don't know that I should give you leave to go through Matthew's desk. I don't see why we can't wait until he's awake."

Mallory had left the two of them together, withdrawing quietly. Rutledge wondered if he were in the kitchen trying to resurrect his dinner.

"We have no other leads, Mrs. Hamilton. Half the village is convinced that Mallory here attacked your husband. The other half holds every opinion gossip can think up, from some past deed following him here from abroad to a boatman telling me that the sea claims its own in time. As if the Mediterranean pursued him to England." He tried to keep his voice light, but she wasn't diverted from her concern.

"Well, it's none of anyone's business, is it?" she said with asperity.

"London has only so much patience. If they recall me, the next man may not be as willing as I am to search for answers in the past."

"Oh, very well. The key to the desk is in the lock. But I beg you to put everything back where you found it. I shan't care to have Matthew unhappy with me." She crossed to the desk and took the key, holding on to it, as if hoping he might still change his mind about the need for it.

"I'll be very careful," he promised.

She sighed, passing it to him. "Inspector Bennett will grow old with gout. Mrs. Bennett's menu choices would feed ditchdiggers, and I was never fond of parsnips. But you may thank her for her thoughtfulness. I'm learning to be grateful for small things, like warm bathwater and my clothes in order in my closet. No one can make tea the way—" She broke off, looked away from him, and then said, "Will you please tell me how Matthew is feeling? I dreamed last night I was burying him and I couldn't find his best suit. It was frightful, searching everywhere, and the coffin ready and the mourners in the drive. I woke myself up crying."

"It's been extraordinarily difficult for you, Mrs. Hamilton. But your husband would admire your courage, if he were here to see it. A day or two more, perhaps, and we may have some relief for you."

"It wasn't Stephen who attacked him. I can tell you that now. He doesn't have it in him to do such a thing."

"I'm sure we'll have the truth in time."

"Yes, but you don't understand. It's like being married, shut in here together with no one else to talk to. We fight over the smallest things, we storm out of the room in a nervous fury, and then come back again because there's nowhere to go. And Nan bangs on the ceiling until I'm heartily sick of it. I just want Matthew back again, and everything the way it was."

"How does Mallory feel about it?"

She smiled, her face coming to life for the first time in days. "He will probably be very happy to see the last of me. He was annoyed with me when I burned the potatoes, but that was only because I'd burned my finger as well and had gone to dip it in vinegar and soda. And he said, 'Felicity, I have money, I would have provided you with everything in life that Matthew has, and treasured you for yourself. But you had told me all those years ago when we were in love that you could *cook*.' And I was just as annoyed, and I said, 'Of course I can cook, it's only that I've had very little practice.' I burst into tears and he said, 'I'll go fetch Nan.' But I didn't want to be shown up by her, she'd never let me forget it, and she'd find a way to tell Matthew as well. So I told him that if he did, I'd leave here when he slept and never come back again."

From her expression Rutledge could see that she believed she had won the skirmish and she felt better after proving her self-reliance. But it was also clear to him that whatever feelings these two people had kept hidden away for the other, time and closeness had diminished them.

"It's like being married," she had put it, like an elopement gone wrong. Living in a garret on slim resources and without public acceptance, and trying to pretend that love was enough.

He felt pity for her, but there was no hope he could offer her. And to tell her that Matthew was very likely dead and their circumstances here at Casa Miranda had taken a dreadful turn, would be cruel. How would she cope, if in the end, she knew Mallory would be taken away to be tried and hanged for two murders?

She seemed to sense his change of mood and said sharply,

"Are you keeping something from me, Inspector? Have you told Stephen more than you've told me?"

He'd lost sight of the fact that women often read minds or at the very least were sensitive to shifts in emotion.

"I was thinking," he told her, "that Matthew Hamilton is a very lucky man."

She blushed, her eyes filling with shining tears.

"When I have him safe again, I'll never let him go. You can tell him that for me."

And she was gone, leaving him with the key to the desk in his hand.

Rutledge waited, almost certain Felicity Hamilton would have second thoughts and come back to ask him to leave. When she didn't, he crossed the room, unlocked the top drawer, and began his search.

There were accounts, letters to a man of business, receipts for payments made to firms shipping his household goods from Malta, and other papers relating to Hamilton's affairs.

Under them there was a photograph of a cream stone house on a narrow street, its facade plain, but the intricacies of the lacing around the oriel windows were very old and created by a mason with expert hands. Rutledge stood there looking at it, and then turned it to the reverse side. It said, "My house in Malta, Casa Miranda, near a shaded square where I often take my tea. The cream cakes are better than any I've tasted anywhere else." It was as if he had expected to send the photograph to someone and had described it for him or her. The sort of thing a friend might include in a letter to Melinda Crawford.

Rutledge shut that drawer and went to the next. He found more accounts for the Malta house and those from another one in Istanbul. There were letters to and from a man of business, and a name caught Rutledge's eye as he was setting them back in the folder he'd opened. "I shall want

George Reston's assurance that all is well again, and afterward I shall move my business to the firm in Leadenhall Street, London." There followed the direction of a firm that Rutledge recognized as old and well-established: McAudle, Harris, & Sons.

And why should George Reston have to give his assurance that all was well again?

Rutledge went back to the correspondence and read it more thoroughly. The letter was dated shortly after Hamilton had returned to England.

George Reston's London partner—a man by the name of Thurston Caldwell—had been borrowing from Matthew Hamilton's funds for his own purposes. On a small scale at first, and then with increasing assurance as his client had remained abroad.

If such a breach of trust had been made public, it could have ruined Reston as well as Caldwell, and probably led to prosecution.

Hadn't Mrs. Reston said something about misappropriated funds, and the partner deserving what he got, when Reston lost his temper in public and attacked the man?

Small wonder, then!

Rutledge realized suddenly that she had chosen the perfect instrument for her revenge on her husband. Not just someone she had known as a girl, but a man who had been defrauded by Reston's London partner. A double-edged sword that had descended with all the force of long-dreamed-of vengeance behind it.

And had Reston, twisting and writhing like a puppet in a tempest, turned not on his tormentor but on a man completely unaware of his role in the failure of a marriage?

21

Rutledge went on searching through the drawers of the desk and then in the bookshelves that stood across from it. Volumes of history and travel, some of them in French or German or Latin, had been lined up by date and subject, according to a master plan. He could follow it clearly, as if Hamilton had had time on his hands to devise a careful cataloging of his library—or could afford to hire a scholar to do it for him.

And would there be room here for diaries as well? He thought, rather, that there would be.

It took him half an hour to locate them, a set of exquisitely bound volumes in tooled cordovan leather, gold leaf on the edges of the pages, and scrollwork on the binding, but no titles. At first he'd expected the set to be a collection of verse or Latin authors or even, thinking of Reston's library, biblical references. When he opened the first of the slim works, he discovered that each covered a year of Matthew

Hamilton's life from the time he took up his career to—so it appeared—the last entry on the night before he left Malta:

The Knights and I part company finally. I have followed them from Acre to Rhodes to Malta, not with intent but because they were before me on the road. But I have come to a newfound respect for men who lived and labored in the heat of the Roman Sea, and I understand their fascination with the harsh light of noon and the soft light of dawn and the long rays of afternoon. I have stood on the ramparts as they must have done, waiting for moonrise, and I have found a measure of peace. If these walls are haunted—and it is likely that they are, given the blood spilt here—these shades have been kind to another traveler, passing unseen behind me or standing at a distance, watchful until I go. I wonder what my life would have been if I hadn't come here or to any of the other places I have lived in my exile. I wonder how I share fare in England. But it doesn't matter. I have left a part of me wherever I have lain my head, including my youth. What remains will be satisfied to go home.

It was a poignant farewell. And there were equally poetic entries over the years, as the writer sat in a café and sipped coffee or finished a last glass of wine before going to bed. The rest was a meticulous account of a busy life and a devotion to duty that spoke of loneliness as well as dedication. Names, dates, times, places, matters up for discussion, resolution arrived at for every meeting and official function. Brief but incisive comments on people everywhere, from donkey men on Santorini to political appointees in the courts of the Kaiser and the viziers of Turkey. Cameos, perceptive and devastatingly honest, of visiting dignitaries and other diplomats serving their countries. And amusing sketches of the Englishmen he encountered or who had served with him in this or that capital. During the war years, there was a list of names, framed in black ink, of friends who had fallen.

Rutledge closed the last volume and put it back on the top shelf where he had found it.

A man could reconstruct his entire professional life from such a detailed account of twenty-odd years abroad. As an aide-mémoire the diaries were priceless.

Whether Matthew Hamilton had intended to use them in such a way, Rutledge had no idea. But there was enough privy information in them to ruin more than one career. Or to provide a rich vein of blackmail material for an unscrupulous reader. And Hamilton had not spared himself on the pages, either.

Robert Stratton had every reason to fear the existence of the diaries. Whether he had ever confronted Hamilton about them, on the strand here in Hampton Regis or in the narrow, dirty streets of Istanbul, or bribed ill-paid customs officials to find and confiscate them at port cities, it was certain that the Foreign Office knew nothing of Stratton's presence in Hampton Regis today.

The door opened, and Rutledge looked up, expecting to see Mrs. Hamilton on the threshold. But it was Mallory who stepped into the room. "You should go. I've been patient long enough."

"I was just coming to find you. What do you know about Hamilton's financial dealings?"

"Precious little." He closed the door. "Should I be interested in them? Is there something that will hurt Felicity?"

"Not that I can see. But there was some trouble early on, when Hamilton returned to England. Does Mrs. Hamilton know the details of how his money was managed when he was abroad?"

"I've heard her remark, since I've been here, that his financial advisers don't care for her. She suspects there was some trouble over resuming control of his money, and although it's settled now, the man couldn't be counted on to do her any favors. She seems to think the man blames her for enticing Hamilton back to England and cutting short his career. In all likelihood, he may believe that if Hamilton hadn't married, he'd have gone abroad again."

"But Hamilton didn't know Felicity before he came back here, did he?"

"Of course not. It was my misfortune that he met her at a dinner party in London, while I was still in hospital. But that wouldn't matter to a man like Caldwell, caught with his hand in the till—it was easier to point the finger of blame at a new wife."

"Were there discrepancies in the accounts, do you think?"

"Hamilton's not one to be gulled. I expect there was a swift rearrangement of funds to cover any difference in sums. Otherwise, the police would have been brought in. Are you telling me that Hamilton's banker has been stalking him?"

"I'm only saying that there may be another motive besides an affair with his wife."

"*I never—*"

Rutledge cut him short. "I'm not accusing you. I'm telling you that it's very likely that a good case could be made on your behalf, bringing up the issue of embezzled money versus your past relationship with Mrs. Hamilton."

Mallory took a deep breath. "All right. Thank you. But it isn't Hamilton's man of business here in Casa Miranda with her. Bennett won't give a curse in hell for him. And where is Hamilton, come to that? I've had a rough day of it, keeping what I know from *her*. Is he dead? Rutledge, damn it, tell me!"

"I don't know any more now than I did this morning."

"God help us. I thought Scotland Yard could walk us through this maze and bring us safely out the other side."

"Scotland Yard," Rutledge told him with an edge to his voice, "is only as good as the information given it. And so far, that's been precious little."

Rutledge was very tired when he reached the inn. Hamish, hammering at him, was a dull ache that wouldn't leave him, a reminder that he had failed Mrs. Granville as well as Matthew Hamilton.

He stretched out on his bed in the dark and, hands behind his head, stared up at the ceiling. There was one more thing he had to do this night, and he wasn't sure where to begin.

Would Miss Cole be expecting a policeman at her door? Not unless she'd learned of events in Hampton Regis. And that was unlikely—the newspapers still hadn't got wind of the assault on Hamilton or the murder of the doctor's wife. It would be left to him to break bad news.

Or would she feel only a sadness for an old acquaintance? Rutledge hadn't seen any mention in Hamilton's diaries of Miss Cole or even of a married woman who might be her in later years. He hadn't read them line for line, of course, but enough to have a very good feeling for what they contained. Indeed, Hamilton had seldom written about England, except for the occasional reference to a personal letter from a friend. Rutledge had come across Melinda Crawford's name here and there, most often in connection with something Hamilton had seen or done or found that he knew she would enjoy hearing about in a letter. Whether Hamilton had actually written to her Rutledge didn't know. He'd have to ask Melinda Crawford that. Hamilton might simply not have had time to keep up a lively correspondence, much as he might have wished to. Yet he'd spoken of Miss Cole to the rector.

After twenty years.

On the other hand, there was the photograph of the house on a quiet street in Malta, identified and ready to send. But clearly never put in its envelope. As if second thoughts had entered into the urge to keep a friendship alive, and in the end Hamilton had broken himself of the habit of following through on these small courtesies that would have left doors in England ajar.

And then he had come home and fallen desperately in love with a young woman. To recapture his lost youth? Or because in her eyes his years abroad were merely a romantic past, and she had no experience on which to judge the dangers and hardships and emptiness of a world where politics and protocol and too many secrets circumscribed everyday life.

Rutledge closed his eyes, trying to define what the relationship between Miss Cole and Matthew Hamilton had been. Instead he saw Jean's face against his eyelids, and then Mallory, his uniform filthy, his face blistered from an early-morning gas attack, sitting with his back to the trench wall and weeping for his dead. But Hamish hadn't wept, he had moved quietly among his remaining men, touching a shoulder here, saying a word there, bending over a soldier who was shaking and offering him a cigarette to steady him, binding up a wound that didn't merit the journey back to an aid station. Then he had turned away and rested the splayed fingers of one hand against the earthen wall of the trench, his head coming down to touch them as he slept where he stood. For a mercy the guns were silent and for a few precious minutes the peace lasted.

Rutledge had watched from a distance. There had been nothing he could do, nothing he could say. And so he had turned his gaze back to the wire and the last lingering feathers of color in the clouds, a pink already shading to lavender and gray as night came on.

In a war mourning had to be done privately. There was never any time for more than a snatched thought, a swift prayer, a curse at what Fate had dealt men too young to die. No ceremony, no flags, no fanfare or trumpets. They were all too busy striving to live one more bloody day.

Hamish was saying, "I do na' ken why ye're driving sae far. She couldna' ha' come for him. How would he summon her? Wi' no telephone in the surgery? And she canna' have killed the doctor's wife for his sake."

Rutledge was driving west, toward the city of Exeter. The road followed the sea for a time and then turned away, miles sweeping under his wheels, and a soft wind blowing that smelled, he thought, of plowed earth.

He responded, "It isn't the surgery I'm thinking about. We can't be sure she hadn't had news of him over the years, even if he'd failed to write. For that matter, now that he's back in England, she could have wanted to see him again. And the meeting on the strand was not what she'd expected. She could have walked away, and then turned back to strike him down."

"Oh, aye, and what of yon doctor's wife?"

Rutledge frowned. "There's the rub. Solve the riddle of the attack by the harbor, and that solution doesn't fit the murder at the surgery. Explain what might have occurred in the surgery, and it doesn't clear up what happened by the sea. It's as if we've got two separate crimes, for two entirely different reasons. If Hamilton isn't dead, it's very possible he killed Mrs. Granville by mistake."

Why risk removing Hamilton, when he could have been

smothered where he lay with a pillow? If Hamilton had left the surgery of his own volition, why didn't he go back to Casa Miranda? And even if Hamilton had inadvertently killed Mrs. Granville, he couldn't have attacked himself on the strand. Stephen Mallory could have tried to kill Hamilton the first time and succeeded the second time. But George Reston had nearly as strong a motive as Mallory. And in his eyes, if no one ever discovered what had become of Hamilton now, it might seem a fitting torment for Henrietta Reston to live with.

They were soon on the outskirts of Exeter, and Rutledge cut his speed.

It was a cloth manufacturing town from Norman times and a trading center that had brought it wealth and sometimes unwelcome attention. William the Conqueror had laid siege to it in person. It sat by the Exe River, and Francis Drake had supped with Walter Raleigh in Mol's Coffee House here.

The cathedral's Norman towers were wreathed in clouds as Rutledge came through the city, and the street lamps cast a watery light across its medieval west front. The motorcar's rain-washed windscreen gave the sculptures a flickering, shadowy life of their own, and Rutledge, glancing up at them, could have sworn they moved.

It was a measure of how tired he was.

He found the police station and asked an overweight sergeant on duty where he could find a Miss Cole who lived with her aunt. The sergeant replied irascibly that until he knew the business of the man in front of him, such information wouldn't be given out.

Rutledge introduced himself and received a long stare in return as the sergeant wondered aloud what had brought a Scotland Yard inspector to this part of the West Country.

"A personal matter," Rutledge informed him and waited.

"Indeed, sir. I'll just call Constable Mercer, and he'll take you there. Though it's late to be paying a social call."

"I've had a long drive, Sergeant."

"Indeed, sir." He summoned the young constable, and while they waited for him, the sergeant said, "The house isn't far, sir, it's a tall one set back from the road, just past the turning where you came into town. Ah, Constable, Mr. Rutledge here is from London, Scotland Yard. Could you show him Miss Miranda's house and let them know it's all right to open the door to him."

Miranda Cole. *Casa Miranda . . . the house of Miranda*.

Rutledge caught himself in time, on the point of saying it aloud.

With Constable Mercer seated stiffly beside him, Rutledge drove back to the way he'd come. He soon picked out the iron gates to Tall Trees, which Mercer had told him to watch for, and then three houses to the east of that, saw a small Georgian dwelling with pillars to its portico and a wing to one side.

With the constable in tow, Rutledge went to the door and knocked. It was several minutes before an elderly maid answered his summons, her gaze moving from him to the constable with some alarm.

"Good evening, missus," Mercer began. "This is Inspector Rutledge from Scotland Yard, to see Miss Miranda. I was asked to bring him here, so you wouldn't be worrying about strangers at the door at this hour."

Her gaze returned to Rutledge, sweeping over him as if he'd brought trouble with him. "I should hope it could wait until morning. Miss Cole and Miss Miranda have retired."

"I'm sure Miss Miranda Cole will see me. Tell her I'm here about Matthew Hamilton."

The maid's mouth tightened. "I'll ask her."

They stood there for what seemed like five minutes. Finally the maid returned and said to Mercer, "There's a cup of tea for you in the kitchen, Constable. Mr. Rutledge, if you'll come with me."

She ushered him into a room at the back of the house, the curtains drawn against the night and lamps burning on tables by the window and by the hearth. A fair-haired woman stood by a chair across the room, her face showing no interest in him or his business.

The colors of the room were faded, as if no one had given a thought to decorating for many years—the rose paper on the wall now more ashes of roses, and the carpet, in a style more French than English, seemed to have lost interest in life. Yet the room was spotlessly clean, as if to assure godliness if not beauty.

"Miss Cole?" It was a courtesy. She must be the woman he was seeking, the age was right, and something in her face, a strength, a poise, seemed to match the man that Matthew Hamilton had become.

"Yes. I understand you are here about Matthew Hamilton. I've been told he's returned to England, but he has yet to call on me."

"I'm afraid he's missing, Miss Cole. We've been contacting everyone who may have information about him. In the hope that we'll be able to find him quickly. You'll understand when I tell you that he's been under a doctor's care for several days, and there is some anxiety about his health."

"That doesn't sound like the Matthew Hamilton I remember. He was always a sensible and practical man. Nevertheless, I'm sorry to tell you that you've wasted your trip. He isn't staying with me."

He had the feeling she was fencing with him, choosing her words to discourage him.

"Miss Cole, Matthew Hamilton is in trouble, and I'd thought he might have turned to you for help."

"What kind of trouble? The Matthew Hamilton I remember was not likely to be of interest to the police."

"When did you last see him, Miss Cole?"

Across the room the woman stirred and then was still again. "I'm blind, Inspector. I have been for many years. The last time I met Mr. Hamilton, he was young and so was I. We parted on good terms, and agreed to go our separate ways. He's not likely to call on me now, and I would be as surprised to see him at my door as I am to see you there. Good day, Inspector. Dedham will see you out."

Blind . . .

So that was what Melinda Crawford had not wanted to bring into their conversation.

He realized that there was nothing more to say, nothing to do but leave. A blind woman couldn't have attacked anyone, not in the way that Hamilton had been injured. And she couldn't have come for him, even if he'd been able to contact her. Or tried to kill him in Dr. Granville's surgery. Yet she must have been a greater part of Hamilton's life than even she knew. Or Felicity . . .

But would she give him sanctuary?

Rutledge spoke into the silence, his voice reaching her across the room, forcing her to listen.

"I don't believe that the fact that you're blind entered into his friendship with you. He has named two houses that I know of for you—Casa Miranda in Malta and again here in England. There may have been others. It was a reminder to him that he'd known you and it tells me as well that if you had turned to him for help, he wouldn't have refused you. We had hoped he might trust you to safeguard *him*."

"He wouldn't refuse anyone coming to him in trouble. It's his nature to be kind. And I have not needed his help through the years. If you are interested in why his house should bear my name, you must ask him. As for our friendship, you know nothing at all about that."

"I can't ask him. He was attacked and badly beaten by someone who left him to die alone, in great pain. I'm charged with finding that person."

"I thought you said he was missing."

"He is. He left his bed in the doctor's surgery sometime during the night. We don't know how, or why. Whether he had help or walked out under his own power. But in the morning we found his room empty, and the body of the doctor's wife lying in the next room, murdered."

She stirred again, this time her attention riveted on his face. "Murdered, you say? But that's—that's appalling. Mr. Rutledge, are you trying to frighten me?"

"Not at all. I've come to warn you." His voice was earnest. "If Matthew Hamilton reached you under his own power, we need to know what he remembers about the attack on him. And why he left the surgery. And why Mrs. Granville was killed. It's possible that he attacked her in the dark, not knowing who she was until it was too late. If that's the case, you may also be in danger."

He wanted to add that she was defenseless and her house isolated, but he thought she was clever enough to understand that for herself.

"Nonsense. And it doesn't signify anyway. I've told you that he's not here."

"His wife is being held prisoner against her will. If Hamilton had nothing to hide, why didn't he go to her and try to help her escape? If he loved her, why didn't he move heaven and earth to free her? Even at risk to himself."

She put up a hand to stop him. "You are a very pitiless man, Mr. Rutledge. You have frightened me for your own ends. I won't hear any more of this."

Without appearing to be using her hands, she let her fingers lightly touch pieces of furniture in her path, walking toward the door from memory. Before he could stop her she had gone through it and called to her maid.

He didn't try to follow her. Hamish was already telling him that he had overstepped his bounds.

And what would Frances or Melinda Crawford have to say about his conduct here?

But a policeman was charged with sifting facts and probing truths. Even those secrets innocent people tried to hide from him. If Hamilton had remembered his relationship with her for twenty years, Rutledge found it hard to believe that Miranda Cole cared so little for him. Unless their romance had been one-sided from the start.

Unrequited love? Or what might have been?

He turned and walked back the way he had come, through the door and out to the motorcar. Someone slammed the heavy door behind him. He thought perhaps it was the maid. After a few minutes, Constable Mercer came hurrying around the corner of the house, murmuring "Sorry, sir!" as he stepped into the motorcar.

For a moment Rutledge ignored him, standing there looking up at the house. It was impossible for Hamilton to have come this far, in his condition. And it would be impossible for a blind woman to go to Hampton Regis and bring him here. Neither her maid nor the elderly aunt he hadn't met would have been able to lift a man of that height and weight.

A wild-goose chase. But he thought, if it wasn't Miranda Cole, and it wasn't Miss Esterley who had spirited Matthew Hamilton to safety, who was responsible for what had happened to the man?

And the question brought him again to George Reston. Or Robert Stratton.

Rutledge took Constable Mercer back to Exeter and then faced the long drive back to Hampton Regis.

"Circles within circles," he found himself saying to Hamish as they shared the darkness behind the powerful glow of the headlamps.

"She called you a liar."

And a man without pity.

But why would a man like Hamilton name his home for a woman he'd not seen for many years? Sentiment was unlikely. Guilt, then, a reminder of what he'd done when he was young and felt ashamed of, in later life? Guilt was a strong emotion, it drove people into paths that they hadn't intended to take. He understood it, in his own case, though Dr. Fleming had first pointed it out to him.

"You survived the war and can't forgive yourself for surviving, when others died or were maimed. Until you do learn to forgive yourself, you'll never be completely whole."

"I don't need to be whole," he'd responded. *"Only to function to the best of my ability. I want to return to the Yard."* May of last year, he'd said those words to the man who'd brought him so far, and could take him no further on his journey back to sanity. He still had an appallingly long way to go.

"Yes, well, it could be a good thing or a bad thing, Ian, to go back. Only you can know which."

"It isn't a question of good or bad, it's a matter of working twelve hours in a day until I'm too tired to think. Here, in hospital, I do nothing but think."

"Are you trying to leave here to escape me and look for your own way out?" Fleming had asked bluntly.

"Self-slaughter? I can kill myself here just as easily. Well, not as easily as pulling a trigger, but it can be done. You know that."

"Yes." Fleming had sat there, watching him. *"All right*

then, let's see what happens. Your people at the Yard want you back. Let's give it a month and find out whether you are healed sufficiently to face what's in your head."

And it had been a terrifying month, that June. A month without mercy. But he'd survived that and nine more. It was March of 1920, and he was still alive.

Whether the struggle had been worth it, he didn't know. He couldn't stand aside and be objective. Not where Hamish was concerned.

By the time Rutledge reached Hampton Regis, he was too stiff and too drained to seek his bed.

Instead he stopped the car some distance past the Mole and for an hour walked along the strand, pacing back and forth, listening to the roar of the waves coming in, feeling the crunch of his heels on the wet shingle, and remembering how he'd nearly been sucked into the mud of the landslip. Was it only just that morning?

And what the bloody hell was he to do about Matthew Hamilton?

By the time he had turned for the Mole, he startled a fisherman coming down to the boats tied up there.

The man swerved, then swore. It was Perkins, who'd taken him out to the landslip. "Damned if you didn't turn my heart over in my chest, Mr. Rutledge! I thought for certain the sea had given up Matthew Hamilton."

22

Rutledge was up early, waiting at the police station when the extra men came in from outlying towns, arriving on their bicycles.

He set four of them to work on the west road, knocking on the doors of farmers and householders on either side of the Reston cottage. Two more finished canvassing the shops and businesses along the Mole for anyone who had seen Matthew Hamilton walk down to the strand on the morning he was attacked. And one of Bennett's men was to finish the last of the names on a list of Dr. Granville's neighbors.

That left one man to return to guarding the house on the hill.

When that had been done, Rutledge set up a room for himself in the back of the station, using what had been storage space until 1914, when it was enlarged to stockpile gear for rescuing men washed ashore in U-boat attacks.

It was a bare room, painted an ugly brown, no windows, and a deal table for his desk. But it gave the newcomers ready access to him, and it kept them out of Bennett's way.

He was just sitting down gingerly in the chair someone had brought him, testing it for a wobble on the uneven flooring, when the outer door of the station was flung open and someone shouted his name.

Rutledge came on the run and found himself face-to-face with the young constable who had been at the surgery with Bennett the previous morning. He was out of breath and in some agitation.

"They're shouting for you at the house, sir," Jordan blurted out. "I don't know what it's all about, but I could hear him, that Mr. Mallory, sir, yelling for me to pay attention, damn it—begging your pardon, sir—and finally I stepped out to the gate to see what the uproar was. I'm to bring you back with me, sir."

"My motorcar is around the corner. Come along."

Bennett had peered out of his office to listen. "Here!" he said, reaching for his crutch. "Wait, I'm coming as well."

Rutledge had the engine cranked and was behind the wheel when Bennett caught them up. He got in, careful of his foot, and had barely slammed the door when Rutledge was moving.

It was no distance to the house, but to Rutledge the road seemed cluttered with marketgoers and lorries passing through to the west. He threaded his way among them, reached the turning up the hill and gunned the motorcar into a leap forward.

Hamish, in the back of his mind, was a low, familiar rumble, like the guns in France.

They reached the front door of the house, and Rutledge said to the constable, "Take up your station again. I'll call if I need you."

Jordan hurried down to the gates as Bennett, already out, pounded on the front door.

It was opened by Mallory, his face pale and so lined with worry that he seemed to have aged overnight.

"I sent for Rutledge," he snapped at Bennett.

"It makes no difference. What's happened? Did Hamilton show up in the night?"

They hadn't speculated in the short ride from the police station, but it had been in all their minds. Rutledge waited for Mallory to answer.

"He was here. There's no other explanation. And he's killed Nan Weekes!"

They stood there staring at him, their faces blank with astonishment.

Rutledge, the first to recover, said, "How did he get in?"

"I don't know. I've only just found her. If you'll give me your word that I'm safe with you in the house, I'll let you both inside. If not, it's Rutledge only." He moved slightly, and they could see the revolver in his right hand, half hidden by the doorjamb.

"Where's Mrs. Hamilton?"

"In her room. She's going to need something. I've never seen her so distraught."

"That can wait. All right, then. My word," Bennett told him.

"And mine," Rutledge assured him.

The door opened wider and Mallory let them pass by him. He nodded to the door behind the staircase that led down to the kitchen passages. "That way."

They walked briskly down to the kitchen, and to the small room that had been the maid's prison.

Hamish, behind him, seemed to be telling him something, but Rutledge couldn't make out the words for the thunder in his head.

She was in her bed, one arm dangling over the edge, the other flung awkwardly above her head. A pillow lay on the floor.

"Suffocated," Bennett said, bending over her. "We'll need the doctor to come and have a look."

Rutledge, at his shoulder, remembered Chief Superintendent Bowles's voice on the telephone: *"That's two murders . . . and I don't want to be hearing of another."*

"Have you touched her?" he asked Mallory, who was waiting by the door, leaving the room to them.

"I called to her. When she didn't wake up, I came in and snatched up the pillow, thinking she was playing at something. Pretending to be ill. She's dead, I know the dead when I see them. You don't need Granville to tell you."

"Was the door to this room locked?"

"Yes. But the key's on the outside. Anyone could have used it and still locked it behind him."

"When did you last see her?"

"About eleven o'clock last night. I came to ask if she needed anything before I went to—where I spend the night. As I always asked, mind you. She was not feeling well, she said. Dinner hadn't agreed with her. I told her, it's the best we can do. But she thought the meat had gone off. She said the butcher hadn't given us the best cut."

Bennett, straightening up, turned to look at him. "My wife ordered that food. She'd not have sent bad beef."

Mallory said wearily, "I don't know whether it was good or bad. I was very tired, I told her we'd deal with it in the morning. And in my view, she'd eaten enough for two, it was probably nothing more than indigestion. I think I may have said as much, and she called me callous. I told her that if she'd agreed to cook it for us, we'd have all been better served."

"So you were quarreling?" Rutledge asked.

"Not quarreling, it was no more than the long-running tongue-lashing we were greeted with, morning and night. But she surprised me then, telling me that she'd spoken to the rector while he was here, and if I'd call her in the morning, she'd be willing to prepare breakfast. I told her I'd have to watch her like a hawk and wasn't sure if it was worth the trouble. And she answered that as long as Mrs. Hamilton was here, she wasn't leaving."

"That was an about-face," Rutledge commented.

"Yes. I didn't know if it was a trick or not. I didn't care. I said I'd consider it, and I made sure she had water for the night. And then I shut the door and turned the key."

"And she didn't pound on the door or scream or cause any other disruption during the night?"

"If she did, I didn't hear it. We've learned to shut it out, actually."

"Has Mrs. Hamilton seen her?"

"To my sorrow, yes. She heard me shouting for the constable out there. And she came at once to ask what was wrong. Before I could stop her, she'd run down here. I heard her scream, and then she was up the back stairs into her room and wouldn't open her door." It was there in his eyes. *She thinks I've done this.*

"We'll need to speak to her in good time," Rutledge told him. "If it was Hamilton, how did he get in?"

"It wasn't I. And it wasn't Felicity. Who else could it have been?"

"Let's have a look at the doors and windows, then," Bennett said. "If Hamilton got this far and killed the maid, why didn't he hunt you down as well?"

"Because he couldn't find me, I expect. I've told you, I have found a way to sleep. He may know the house better than I do, but I wasn't where he looked."

"And you heard nothing in the night?" Rutledge persisted.

"Nothing." It was curt.

"Did Mrs. Hamilton hear anything?"

"She says she didn't. I asked her."

They moved away from the bed, came to the door, and passed through as Mallory backed away.

It would have been easy, then, to overpower him, word given or not. Two men against one. But he still held the revolver, and in the passage outside the servants' hall door, any shots fired would ricochet, even if they missed their intended target.

They made the rounds of the house. None of the doors had been built to keep murderers out. Their locks were old, heavy, the bolts fitting into worn wood. But nothing was broken, and the windows were properly latched.

Rutledge said thoughtfully, "Hamilton's keys went missing with him."

"So they did," Bennett answered.

Whoever had taken Hamilton had freedom of the house.

Rutledge interviewed Mrs. Hamilton alone. It took some time to convince her to unlock her door, but when she finally opened it, her face tear-streaked and so pale he thought perhaps she'd been sick, she held on to the frame as if to a lifeline.

"Will you come downstairs and be comfortable?" he asked her gently. "We've made tea. It will warm you a little."

But she shook her head. "I said to him—to Stephen—that I hated her and wanted her dead. Not two days ago. I never thought he would *kill* her . . ." Her voice trailed off into tears.

And Rutledge remembered that she hadn't been told that Hamilton wasn't in the surgery, under Dr. Granville's eye.

"He was upset when dinner turned out so badly. I didn't mean for him to take me literally, I was just torn about Matthew and worried—but it's no less my fault, is it? I should have been braver, I should have borne with all the trouble and said nothing."

She began to cry. "I didn't truly want her to die. But I'm to blame, I'll have to be judged along with him. He wouldn't be here if it weren't for me, and I'm so frightened, I think my heart is going to *break*."

It took him several minutes to calm her enough to tell her about Hamilton. He left out any reference to Mrs. Granville, and he said nothing about the Reston cottage.

It was cold comfort.

"Oh, my God, are you telling me that it could have been Matthew? That he thought—but surely, he'd have realized that wasn't Stephen down there? That it must be Nan. Or—or *me*."

"We don't know. We don't know what state of mind he's in. We don't know if he could have survived in the cold rain yesterday morning. Please, you must tell me anything you can that will help us find him. It's urgent, Mrs. Hamilton—you must tell me whatever you know, however impossible it may sound."

But she was beyond thinking, and in the end, he brought her tea, told her he would be in the house for another hour or so, and prepared to shut her door.

"Is she—is Nan still downstairs?" She shivered. "I shan't be able to swallow a bite of food now. I'm so *frightened*."

"She must be taken away now, to her family. You needn't know, you needn't watch."

"I must talk to her cousin. I want to tell him that it wasn't intended, that we were just upset."

"Let me speak to him on your behalf. I think it might be better just now. Would you care to have us ask for Mr Putnam? He can offer you comfort."

She shook her head. "I can't pray. I'm to blame."

"I don't think Mr. Putnam cares about any of that."

But she shut her door without answering.

"She didna' know," Hamish said as Rutledge went down the stairs. "It wasna' her doing."

"Not directly," Rutledge replied.

Bennett went out to his constable and sent for Dr. Hester.

He came at length, but before he could reach the house, Nan Weekes's cousin arrived, in a fury that was loud and uncontrolled.

"Where is she, then?" Constable Coxe roared from the drive. "And where's the bastard who's been hiding behind her skirts? I'll see him hang, that I will. Come out, you bloody coward and talk to me. Tell me how a poor woman died doing her duty."

Rutledge, on his way to speak to Coxe, had first to deal with Mallory. His face red with a mixture of feelings, his eyes wild, he was about to confront the man outside, his pent-up emotions badly in need of an outlet. "I'm not standing for this, he has no *right*—"

"No, don't be a fool, Mallory. He wants to draw you out there. Are you ready to leave this house and face being locked up in the station?"

"Little good it's doing me to stay here. Nothing has gone as I'd expected, I ought to step into the garden and end it. But that's an admission of guilt, and I won't make it. I tell you, whether you want to hear it or not, Matthew Hamilton is alive and on a rampage. It's the only logical explanation. I'm certain he meant to kill Felicity when he killed Mrs. Granville. And when he got it wrong, he came here looking for her. He thinks—God knows what he thinks. But he found that poor woman instead. What will he do when he realizes this is his second mistake?"

"Why would Hamilton want to kill his wife, and not you? Are you saying he believes *she* attacked him on the strand?"

"Use your wits, Rutledge. The Hamilton's man of business isn't likely to be here in Hampton Regis after Felicity. If he's the one who finished Hamilton, he knows his client is dead, and is back in London busily covering his tracks. He doesn't need to muddy the waters by killing Felicity. He's hoping I'll do it for him." The shouting beyond the door was growing more abusive. "All right, go out and shut up that fool before I'm tempted to shoot him. They can only hang me *once*." He moved out of Rutledge's way.

Rutledge opened the door and stepped out.

Coxe was a burly man, his face lined with years in the sun and his eyes, used to staring out to sea, hooded under heavy lids.

"Mallory isn't coming out, Coxe. You might as well stop making a spectacle of your grief and go home. We'll bring your cousin to you as soon as may be. She'll need you then."

"You can't protect him, Rutledge. I didn't believe Inspector Bennett when he told us you were, but I believe it now. That man in there is a murderer. Give him up and let him face charges."

"We have no proof that he's killed anyone."

"He's locked in a house with two women, and one of them is dead. It doesn't take a London policeman to know what must have happened. When she wouldn't let him have his way with her, he killed her to shut her up."

"She was smothered in her sleep, not interfered with. Go home. Or I'll have you locked in the police station and forget where I put the key."

Coxe examined Rutledge, looking him up and down without insolence but with judgment.

"I'm not afraid of Scotland Yard. This is my flesh and blood, lying there dead."

Rutledge said nothing, standing between Coxe and the

house with the authority of a man used to command. It was a presence that had served him well in the trenches. He had learned it over the years, dealing with everything from drunken men outside pubs to riotous fans at football matches. One man, unarmed, several stone lighter than the heavy-shouldered, angry constable in front of him, wrapped in the certainty that he would be obeyed.

Coxe tried to stare him down and failed. In the end, suddenly mindful of his own career, he blustered, "I didn't say good-bye. I sent her to work that day, telling her I'd not eat what she spoke of making for our dinner. I told her I was tired of a pasty made from what was left of Sunday's roast. That I worked hard and didn't need to cut corners to save for my old age."

He wiped his mouth with the back of his hand. "I spoke out of turn. And I never had the chance to make amends. She's dead, and there's an end to it. But not for me. He took that from me, that bastard behind the door listening to me."

Rutledge waited.

"All right, I'm going. I owe no apology to the house, save to Mrs. Hamilton. I'll pray for her. Odds are, she'll be dead in another day or two."

And with that he turned on his heel and walked away.

Rutledge saw him out of sight.

Not five minutes later, Dr. Hester arrived and, following instructions, brought Mr. Putnam with him. The rector was shown up to Mrs. Hamilton's room and Bennett went to find the constable who had been on night duty at the house. Rutledge took Hester to the servants' hall.

He examined Nan Weekes, and said, "Very likely smothered as she slept. Taken by surprise, she didn't have much chance to fight her murderer off. A knee already on her chest, a determination to see it through. That's what it took."

He lifted the maid's hands one at a time. "See, she grazed

her knuckles against the wall there. But her nails are clean. He'd have been wearing a coat, long sleeves, something that protected him."

"A man or a woman, do you think?"

"It would depend on the killer's state of mind, I should think. A timid man might fail where a resolute woman succeeded. Hatred breeds strength, oftentimes."

Hester looked around the room, bare and yet somehow holding on to the anger and fear trapped with the woman confined here. "She couldn't have run, even if she had been awake; there was nowhere to go. But he didn't give her a chance to escape. He must have been very quiet, coming through that door. Dark as it was, she never saw his face, even if the pillow had slipped." He turned over the pillow on the floor. "It's one of the feather pillows from an upstairs bedroom, I should think. Servants don't often sleep that comfortably. Fairly new too, and therefore better able to do the job."

"I'm told that bedding was brought down from one of the guest rooms."

"Yes, that fits. Well, that's all I can tell you. Sorry."

"Mrs. Hamilton is in the house, and in distress. Will you leave something to help her through this?"

"I'll see her, if you like. As for Miss Weekes, shall I take her back with me?"

"If you would."

"Yes. I'm getting quite a collection of Dr. Granville's patients." Dark wit from one professional to another. "But I daresay he won't feel up to returning to his surgery for a few days yet. Not until after his wife's funeral." He closed up his case. "Whose hand is behind this, do you know? It's not a very safe thing, to have whoever it is loose on Hampton Regis. But he failed with Hamilton, so I'm told. First try at any rate. I wonder what this poor woman did to make herself a target?"

"As far as we know, nothing. Mistaken identity?"

Hester turned to look at Rutledge. He was quick, his mind already leaping ahead. "Really? If you're telling me that first Mrs. Granville and then Miss Weekes were killed because someone thought they were Felicity Hamilton, then I'd see to it that that policeman spent the night outside her door, not under that tree by the road."

Bennett joined them then, with word that the constable had seen no one come or go from the house during the night. Hester gave him an abbreviated account of his preliminary examination. Then he prepared to move the body.

Looking down at the woman, Bennett said to Rutledge, "My money is still on Mallory. Hamilton's dead, a scapegoat. Problem is, how are we going to prove any of it? You were saying before we have a clever bastard on our hands. But even clever bastards make mistakes. Let's hope nobody else dies before he makes one."

Putnam spent some time with Mallory, and then went back a second time to knock on Felicity Hamilton's door. When she answered, his heart went out to her.

"My dear child!" he said and held her as she cried on his shoulder.

It seemed to ease her a little, although he could see that she was frightened and feeling the onslaught of responsibility for all that had taken place since her husband had been carried into Granville's surgery.

He sat with her, brought her tea and a sandwich he'd managed to put together in the kitchen, careful to avoid the room where Nan Weekes had died.

But he had gone in to the maid before her body was removed, giving her the comfort of the church, wishing that she had heeded his encouragement to cooperate and had

died without such resentment on her conscience. He tried
to keep himself from dwelling on the question of which of
the household would be blamed for her death. Mallory most
likely, although it was even possible that Felicity might have
been tempted to rid them of such an angry presence. He
hoped Rutledge wouldn't look in that direction. He himself
felt none of the animosity toward Mallory that others had
expressed, seeing only a wounded soul. But he grieved for
the maid, in his own way.

After Felicity Hamilton had eaten, Putnam offered to
come and chaperone her, now that Nan was dead.

But she shook her head. "I must see it through," she told
him. "I was the cause of so much of the trouble here. I must
somehow make restitution."

"You shouldn't concern yourself with that. Leave it to Mr.
Rutledge, my dear."

"Where is Matthew, Mr. Putnam? No one will talk to me
about him. And I know what the police must be thinking.
If it wasn't Stephen who killed her, then it was Matthew,
trying to find Stephen and stumbling on Nan instead. But
she wouldn't have given him away, you know, even if he'd
decided to slaughter half of Hampton Regis."

"Is that what you believe must have happened? That he
managed to make his way here?"

She rubbed her temples, as if her head throbbed. "Either
I'm married to a murderer or locked in this house with one.
And I don't want to think about that. Stephen was as tired
as I was of Nan's tantrums, he could have killed her out of
sheer despair. But not in cold blood, not in her sleep. Matthew could have decided that it was Stephen who was on the
strand with him and wanted revenge. But why harm Nan?
She liked Matthew, and he was wonderful with her, keeping her jolly when I couldn't. She didn't like me very much.
And now either way I've got her killed." Felicity turned to
look out the window. "If Matthew came searching for his

revolver and couldn't find it because I'd given it to Stephen, Nan could have told him. She *knew*."

Putnam didn't put what was on his mind into words. That Nan, in that back passage, would have raised the alarm if someone had crept in. And it might have been all the warning Stephen Mallory and that revolver of his needed.

He was ashamed of the thought as soon as it had formed.

But almost at the same time that Putnam was considering the possibility, Bennett brought it up to Mallory.

"All right, let's assume for the sake of argument that this is Mr. Hamilton's work. In for a penny and all that. If he's going to be hanged for Mrs. Granville, what's one more corpse? And if he wanted you badly enough, he might feel that the maid was a fair exchange for the opportunity. Only, he discovered you had his revolver. Oh, don't be a fool, Mallory, it must have been his, you weren't in possession of one when you ran me down."

"I can't see why Hamilton had to hurt her," Mallory said, rubbing his face with his hands, as if to scrub away his fatigue. "At least if he's in his right mind. If he'd come to the bed and put a hand over her mouth, she'd have listened to him and done whatever he asked. Mrs. Hamilton tells me she thought he walked on water."

Rutledge, the devil's advocate, said, "In the dark, how could he know it was Nan? Or even that she was here? Besides, if he'd touched her, she'd have screamed bloody murder before he could convince her who he was. Her first thought would have been that you were in the room with her, Mallory. What I want to know is, if Hamilton is alive, if he didn't go into the sea with that cottage, where was he concealed, all day yesterday when we were searching everywhere for him?"

"In the Granvillle house?" Bennett asked, hazarding a

guess. "We never actually searched it, only the surgery. And after Granville went to the rectory, it stood empty. Or there's the church. Putnam is half daft, he wouldn't have noticed Hamilton if he'd hidden himself beneath one of those wretched choir stalls. Besides, he was occupied all the day with Dr. Granville. I doubt he set foot in the church."

"Then why did we find bandages in the ruin of the cottage?" Rutledge reminded him. "You can't convince me they belonged to anyone else but Hamilton. If he had the strength to make it as far as the cottage, I don't think he could have walked all the way back into Hampton Regis."

"How do you know it was Hamilton who left that bandage out there?" Mallory interjected. "Someone could have done it for him, to throw you off his scent. Then the question becomes, who would help him, knowing he'd killed Mrs. Granville and now Nan Weekes?"

Hamish said only, *Mrs. Reston.*

Rutledge took a deep breath. "It all comes down to the fact that if Hamilton's dead, whoever killed him is still out there. Which brings us to the next problem. Why isn't he satisfied now?"

Mallory's tiredness dropped from him. "I hope you aren't suggesting that he's after Felicity? In God's name, *why*? And why kill me? I'm the one who will hang, for Hamilton, for Mrs. Granville, and now for Nan. Kill me and the police will know I'm not guilty of any of this." He looked from Bennett to Rutledge. "What worries me most is that Hamilton is on the loose and half demented. And if that's the case, he's a very dangerous man. I can tell you I'm not looking forward to nightfall, if that's the case."

"What about his injuries?" Bennett said. "And who was it attacked him on the strand?"

"He might not have been as badly injured as Dr. Granville thought," Rutledge said, slowly. "But there's someone who might have struck Hamilton down by the Mole, who might have come back to get rid of him after learning he wasn't dead, and who could have a very good reason for wanting to get into this house."

He told them about Stratton and the diaries.

But Bennett shook his head. "I can see this Stratton arguing with Mr. Hamilton Monday morning, and anger getting the best of him then. I don't see him killing two other people over a book that's not been written. And how did he get in and out of Hampton Regis that day without anyone seeing him? I don't think that's possible." He turned back to Mallory. "As for tonight, there's the safety of the station for you, Mr. Mallory," Bennett offered. "Safe as houses. And as for Mrs. Hamilton, we'll put her up in my spare bedroom until this is finished. No one will touch her there."

Mallory shook his head. "I've told you from the start, to turn myself in is an admission of guilt."

"You're helping us with our inquiries," Bennett pointed out.

"And Hamilton, if that's who is behind these killings, vanishes abroad and I'm left holding the bag. I've got the revolver. I don't want to kill him, but I can damned well knock him down. I'm a decent enough shot for that."

"Here, there's going to be no gunfire in this house, tonight or any other time," Bennett corrected him.

"Yes, well, we'll see what the night brings."

"Let Putnam take Felicity with him. I'll stay in her place and together we'll keep watch," Rutledge said to stop their bickering.

"She's no safer in that rambling warren of rooms in the rectory than she is here. Can you picture Putnam defending her? No, she'll remain in the house, even if I have to sleep across her threshold."

"Think about it," Rutledge urged him. "You're out on

your feet, man. And you've got my word that I won't take any steps against you. But another pair of eyes and ears could be very welcome at three o'clock in the morning. The wind is rising out there. You'll be wishing by then that you'd agreed."

"I'm armed, and Hamilton isn't," Mallory retorted, stung by Rutledge's suggestion.

"Yes, but remember that old children's riddle about transporting geese from one side of the river to another, while making certain the fox isn't left with the flock on either bank? If I'm here and it comes to shooting anyone, I'll be your witness. Otherwise it's your word against a dead man's. A man you're already accused of beating until he was unconscious."

It was unarguable. And Rutledge could see that Mallory was torn. In the end, he went up the stairs to speak to Mrs. Hamilton and the rector.

When he returned, he said only, "She wants you to stay. The rector offered, but I'd as soon have another soldier at my back tonight. Now if you've finished here, I'll thank you to be on your way."

"I'll be here before dark," Rutledge told him. "You can search my case for a weapon, but there won't be one."

23

Rutledge had given his word, but he made his plans with the care of a seasoned campaigner.

He set his men to guard the house, concealing them well out of sight. One stood in his room at the Duke of Monmouth, field glasses at the ready. Two others watched the roads to the headlands on either side of the Mole. And one was in the church tower, with its sweeping view of the town. They went early to their positions, armed with hot tea in thermoses and sandwiches put up by Mrs. Bennett. Constable Jordan was relieved in due course by his usual replacement. And another man kept an eye on Constable Coxe, as a precaution. Rutledge had also asked one of the men sent from another village to observe the Reston house, placing him where he could see it clearly, in the Cornelius family attic.

Mrs. Cornelius, a little anxious, had not wished to have a policeman spending the night in her attic, but Rutledge had assured her that it was to watch the same route that her son's monster had taken two nights before. Not precisely the whole truth, unless the headless man had been Reston himself, but it served to allay her suspicions. He didn't want gossip flying about the town before morning.

"But why should he come again? I'd nearly convinced myself it was Jeremy's imagination, Mr. Rutledge, though I was reluctant to believe it at the time."

"Your son's imagination made a monster out of an ordinary event. What I'd like to discover is what he actually saw. It will clear up any remaining questions I might have now."

"I must say, I've not really recovered from the news that Mrs. Granville is dead. And now poor Nan Weekes. We've never had anything of this sort happen in Hampton Regis before. And you're quite sure that you aren't trying to comfort me by telling me my family is in no danger?"

"If I thought you were, Mrs. Cornelius, the constable would be guarding your door, not standing at an attic window."

Later, Mr. Putnam, concerned for the safety of everyone involved, asked Rutledge if it was wise to lay a trap with human beings as bait.

"Do you know of another way to catch this killer? He's cold-blooded, he's clever, and he's not about to offer himself up to us without a fight," Rutledge pointed out.

"Yes, well, you know where to find Dr. Granville if there's any trouble."

"Pray that it doesn't come to that."

Before leaving the station to pack a small case with what he needed, Rutledge spent an hour reading the reports of his men from the day's monotonous rounds of questioning. He paid particular attention to the reports from the road where the cottage had stood. The only small flutter of excitement there had been a fox in the henhouse of the small farm where Mallory sometimes bought eggs.

A waste of time, Bennett told him. "But then, most police work comes to nothing. It has to be done, and we do it, else we're slack. Mountains of paper and ink for one small grain of truth."

Rutledge thought of all Inspector Phipps's preparations to guard Green Park in London and a man who had watched them with interest from a nearby street lamp.

He had reported Nan Weekes's death to Chief Superintendent Bowles.

"It's to stop there, Rutledge, do you hear me? I'll not be greeted in the morning with more bad news. And heed me on this as well. If Hamilton isn't right in his mind, you're not to let Bennett clap him up in Hampton Regis. We'll bring him to London and sort it out."

"Yes, I've thought about that possibility."

"Then see that it's done. I'm not best pleased with this trap you're so keen to lay. On the other hand, if there's no other possible way to lure a killer into the open, then we've not got much choice. But I'll thank you not to let that fool Mallory start shooting before we know what we're about."

Stratton was waiting for him by Reception, stepping out of the lounge with a glass of sherry in his hand.

"Well met, Rutledge. Can I offer you anything?"

"Thanks, but I'm still on duty."

"A long day," Stratton agreed. "There's been another killing, they tell me. This time a maid working for Hamilton. And Matthew's still missing."

"We hope to have someone in custody shortly. Which reminds me, Stratton, where were you last night? Not wandering about Casa Miranda looking for diaries, by any chance."

"God, no. I understand that the man who is holding Mrs. Hamilton a prisoner in her own house is an ex-officer armed to the teeth. I'm not that brave, I can tell you. What I'd like to know is if you found anything there."

"How did you know I was at the house last evening?"

"Opening doors in a busy inn can lead to unpleasant surprises, but I found a room where the windows do look out toward the Hamilton house. Yours, in fact. And I saw you go there while I was surveying my options."

"In future, I'd consider spending my evenings with the drapes drawn, if I were you," Rutledge said pleasantly. "It would be wise."

Stratton's eyebrows rose. "Expecting more trouble, are you?"

"No. Just a friendly warning that people who meddle with a policeman going about his duties often come to grief."

"You haven't answered my question about the diaries. Do they exist, do you think?"

"If they do, they belong to Matthew Hamilton. If he's dead, they belong to his estate. Neither you nor I have any right to them."

"Do you think it fair for one man to hold the fate of many in his hands while he decides what to do with information he should have been sensible enough not to collect in the first place?"

"The peccadilloes were not his, Stratton, they were yours, whatever it is you're living to regret now. You should have thought of that in good time."

Stratton grimaced. "I can only plead youth."

"Then you'd better pray that Matthew Hamilton has learned discretion as he aged. Or that his wife doesn't wish to memorialize him—assuming he's dead now—by publishing his life's history."

He turned to walk away. But Stratton said, "Gaming debts are not a disgrace. It's just that I'd rather not have my fondness for playing the odds publicly acknowledged."

In the reference to Stratton that Rutledge had seen, it wasn't gaming debts that had been mentioned. But he didn't stop, moving on toward the stairs.

"Then you've nothing to fear, have you?" he replied over his shoulder.

But he found himself agreeing with Hamish that Stratton was a very clever man, and so was the murderer he would soon be waiting for.

Twenty minutes later, Rutledge went to the inn's kitchen and begged a box of sandwiches from the staff, with apples from a silver bowl in the dining room. Then he made certain that his torch was ready for use and added to the case the extra pair of field glasses that Bennett had found for him. Finally he dressed in dark clothing that was serviceable and warm.

Hamish was not best pleased. "Yon Mallory has told you—he killed you once before."

"That was just a game his doctor played. It has no bearing on the present situation."

"Oh, aye? Does the *lieutenant* ken it was a game?"

"He won't shoot me."

"I wouldna' turn my back on him in the dark."

It was nearly four o'clock when Rutledge walked up the hill to Casa Miranda. His motorcar stood in the yard at the inn, where he'd left it each night of his stay.

As a ruse, it wasn't very successful, Hamish had pointed out. "No' if Stratton is watching fra' a window."

"He'll find a constable in my room tonight, if he ventures in there again. What's more, I left orders for the constable to lock himself in, as an added precaution."

He spoke to the man on duty under the swaying limbs of the evergreen, remarking on the wind's force.

"I'd not like to be out on the water this evening," the constable replied. "But I should be warm enough."

"Stay in plain sight after dark."

"Yes, sir, I'll do that."

Rutledge went on to the door and knocked. Mallory answered quickly, smelling of whiskey.

"You're a fool to drink tonight," he said shortly.

"I'm not drinking. It was one glass, and I downed it with a sandwich. The house is cold. I built a fire in Felicity's bedroom, and one in the back sitting room, to make it appear to be occupied. What's in the case?"

Rutledge let him paw through it.

"And you're not armed?"

He opened his coat and gave Mallory time to inspect him as he turned in front of him.

"All right, then. I accept your word."

"There are more sandwiches in the bag. Fruit. I'm not sure anyone is in the mood to prepare dinner."

"When do you think he'll come? If he does."

"Late. When we're tired and not as alert."

"Yes, that's what I'd told myself." A gust of wind shook the windows overlooking the sea. "Damned wind. And this house creaks like all the imps of hell are loose in it. Felicity is waiting. She's not taken the powder that the doctor gave her. Hester, I mean. She wanted to see you were here first."

They went up the stairs, and Rutledge could hear their footsteps echo through the silent house.

Felicity Hamilton unlocked her door at the sound of Rutledge's voice.

He stepped into the room, feeling the warmth of the fire, and said, "Not to alarm you, just a precaution. Are you certain no one can reach your windows from the outside? If not, we'll find a more suitable room."

"I prefer to stay here. But I looked, before the light went. I'd thought about that too."

He showed her the sandwiches, pointing out that there

was a variety, chicken and ham and cheese with pickles. "And here's enough tea to see us through the night. Is there anything else you require? Water for your powder?"

"I have water, Stephen saw to that. I'm not sure I want to be asleep if there's any trouble."

"We're on the other side of the door."

He went out. Mallory was dragging comfortable chairs from other bedrooms, with pillows and blankets and a pair of heavy quilts. "It will be drafty," he said in explanation, then added a decanter of whiskey to their makeshift night camp. "As a blind for shooting lion, I think the lion has the advantage."

"A lion can smell us before we see him. A man can't. What about the back stairs?" Rutledge asked. "He could come from there rather than the main staircase."

"I've got a chair braced against that door. If he tries the knob, we'll hear him. If he intends to reach us, he'll have to use the other stairs."

While Mallory was collecting matches and lamps, Rutledge double-checked the servants' door to the back stairs. It was solidly braced, and anyone attempting to come through would find himself making a considerable racket.

They settled down in the silent house, listening to the wind outside, and prepared to wait. Mallory brought out a small portable chess game, but they were evenly matched and it palled after a time.

Mallory said, "I'll wager he doesn't come. It will all be to do over again tomorrow night. You have to remember, he's been badly hurt. He may need a night's sleep before he can make the effort a second time."

"There's that," Rutledge agreed. "Still, I don't want to run the risk."

"Nor I."

Felicity Hamilton called through the door, "Is anything wrong?"

"We're just passing the time. Don't worry. If you want to sleep at all, between now and midnight might be best," Mallory replied.

"Yes. I don't want to turn off my lamp. But should I?"

"The drapes are drawn. Be certain they're tightly closed. It should be all right then."

"I could set it on the floor on this side of my bed."

"Too great a risk of fire."

"Yes." It was a forlorn affirmative, and there was silence again from her room.

"I pray to God she sleeps," Mallory said grimly. He poured a little whiskey into a fresh cup of tea. "I can't count the times I wished for Dutch comfort in the trenches. If only to keep out the wet and the cold."

"I don't want to talk about the war," Rutledge told him shortly. "We can't afford to be distracted."

"But it's there, isn't it, in the back of your mind? Mine as well. Will it ever go away, do you think?"

"If God is kind," Rutledge answered, and pulled a blanket across his shoulders against the cold that was inside as well as out.

Sometime close to midnight, Mallory said in the darkness, "Do you ever dream—I mean, *dream*?"

His voice, like Hamish's sometimes, came out of nowhere. They had turned down the lamps and set them inside the nearest room, to preserve their night sight.

Rutledge finally answered him: "No."

"You're lying."

"I've told you, I don't want to discuss the war."

"I have to talk about it. It's the only way I stay sane."

"Not to me, you don't."

"Tell me about Hamish and the rest of the men I knew. How they died."

"No!"

"I need to hear it."

"I need to forget."

There was a long stretch of silence, then Mallory asked, "If I didn't attack Hamilton, who did?"

"A good question. What I'm wondering now is if we've got two separate problems. The initial attack—and what it might have set in motion."

"Yes. Like running over Bennett's foot. It wasn't intentional, but I did it, and I'm paying for it. What I don't understand is, why Hamilton, in the first place? If you'd asked me, I'd have said he's the last man to find himself in trouble in Hampton Regis."

Rutledge's chair creaked as he tried for a more comfortable position. "Which explains why Bennett came to question you at the start. There's been gossip, Mallory. You should have considered that, for her sake if not your own."

A sigh answered him. And then, "Yes, well, you haven't been in love. You don't know what it's like to pin your hopes on someone throughout that bloody war, and then discover that she's learned to love someone else."

But he did. And it was none of Mallory's business.

"Did you expect her to wait for you? That was where you went wrong."

"I had hoped she would. But I left her free to make that choice."

"And she made it. You failed her by not accepting it and walking away."

"When I was released from hospital, my doctor made me swear I wouldn't come to Hampton Regis. But then I thought, what harm can it do, to live near her? And soon it was, what harm can it do to see her? I convinced myself I'd been extraordinarily careful, that no one would guess how I felt."

"In a village the size of Hampton Regis? Where you can't cross the road without being seen?"

"If Hampton Regis is a hotbed of gossip and general nosiness," Mallory demanded with some heat behind the words, "why hasn't someone come forward to give you the information you need about Matthew Hamilton's disappearance?"

Felicity Hamilton's voice came through the door panel. "What is it, what has happened?"

"My apologies, Mrs. Hamilton," Rutledge said at once. "Mallory and I were engaged in an argument over how gossip works. We didn't intend to disturb you."

Mallory said in a lower tone, "You haven't answered me."

"I don't know why we haven't got what we need. It was late at night. Most decent people are in their beds. The pubs are closed. The milk wagon hasn't gone round. The fishermen haven't gone out—"

He broke off. From a room downstairs had come the sound of someone or something scratching at a window.

"Stay here. Don't leave Mrs. Hamilton, whatever happens. And for God's sake, don't shoot me as I come back up the stairs," Rutledge told him.

But when he finally located the source, it was a limb blowing back and forth across the glass panes of a drawing room window as the slender trunk of an ornamental fruit tree just outside dipped and swayed in the wind.

He stood there, looking out at the blustery night, and thought, *He's not coming. Not on a night like this. He needs his ears as much as we need ours.*

Hamish answered him in the darkness, "I wouldna' go back up the stairs."

"I don't have much choice. Mallory will come down here if I don't return."

He wondered how his watchers were faring. But there was no method of communicating with them. A field telephone would have been useful tonight, he told himself, turning away from the window.

He went to the hall and called up the stairs, "It's Rutledge. Nothing but the wind."

Mallory's voice surprised him, rolling down from the head of the steps, invisible in the well of darkness there.

"I was beginning to worry. You're a perfect target, you know. Against the panels of the door. I'd keep that in mind if I were you."

Rutledge took the steps two at a time. "Thanks for the warning," he said, and passing Mallory, nearly invisible except for the sound of his breathing, he felt a distinct shiver run down his spine.

Rutledge had lost track of the time. Eternity, he thought, must be like this. A world where there was no mark for day or night, or for sunrise or sunset, just an endless expanding infinity. He wondered what the rector would make of that.

The crash, when it came, seemed to shake the foundations of the house. Later, thinking about it more clearly, he told himself it had done no such thing.

Felicity Hamilton cried out, and came at once to the door, fumbling with the lock.

"No, stay where you are," Mallory murmured in her direction. "Rutledge, where did it come from, that noise?"

"I couldn't tell. The back of the house, I think."

She had the door open, standing there outlined in the dim glow of her shaded lamp, fully clothed and clutching a shawl around her shoulders. "Don't leave me!" she begged. "I won't stay here by myself."

"Felicity, for God's sake—"

"No, if you go, I'm going too. I won't be cornered like this."

Rutledge said, "We've got a choice. Stay and wait, or go and investigate."

They listened, holding their breath as they did. But there was no other sound from below.

"If he's in the house, he could be anywhere," Rutledge said softly. "We could walk straight into him before we knew he was there."

"He must be searching rooms. One at a time. It sounded as if he'd knocked over something."

"It was more like a window breaking—glass falling," Rutledge said.

"I think it must have been the dining room," Felicity whispered. "It was in the back, at least. I know how this house creaks in the wind, like a ship at sea. It wasn't like that."

"Which bedroom is over the dining room?" Rutledge asked her.

"The guest room, second door beyond the stairs. On your right."

"I'll go and have a look," he said, but Mallory stopped him.

"We shouldn't separate. That was the bargain."

"I went down alone before."

"That was different, damn it. It was suspicious, but not threatening."

They were on their feet, standing together in the dim light. Mallory turned to Felicity. "If you must stay here, shut that door. I can't see with your light in my eyes."

She did as he asked, and the passage was dark again. Rutledge nearly jumped out of his skin as her hand brushed the back of his shoulder, so certain it was Hamish that he nearly cried out. But she was just moving nearer, he could smell the scent she wore as she clutched at Mallory's arm, the paleness of her shawl picking her out as his eyes adjusted again to the lack of light.

"You won't shoot him, promise me you won't. If it's Matthew, we don't want to hurt him," she was whispering importunately.

"Shhh." Mallory leaned forward, as if to help his ears penetrate the shadows that lay between them and the top of the stairs.

But nothing came up the stairs, neither a figment of their imaginations nor a shambling wounded man half out of his mind.

Rutledge thought, standing there, *It's easy to believe in monsters in the dark.* Young Jeremy was not alone.

And Hamish, whose ears had always been the sharpest, said, "He isna' coming."

Rutledge replied silently, "You can't be sure. The stairs are carpeted."

"He's no' coming. It's a game."

And although they stood there for another quarter of an hour, pinned where they were by the tension of not knowing, Hamish proved to be right.

In the end, the three of them ventured down the stairs as the first gray threads of light broke over the horizon and the head of the staircase loomed ghostly in front of them. It didn't take them long to find what they had heard. A long black length of tree limb had been driven through the panes of the dining room window, protruding like a battered and obscene spear above the shattered bits of glass scattered on the polished floor below it.

Rutledge went outside then, but beneath the window the thick matting of leaves blown against the foundations masked any sign of footprints.

He could see the tree where the limb had come from. Three had broken off, one of them driven deep into the soil, another leaning crookedly against the foundations, and the third thrust through the window.

But what he couldn't determine, in spite of carefully

searching for any sign that might confirm it, was whether that one branch had had the help of a human agency to ram it through the glass. He could have done it, tall as he was, and actually reached up to pull it out as Mallory shoved it toward him and then went for something to patch the hole.

He remembered what Hamish had said, that someone was toying with them. That someone had known the house was a trap and played with their nerves.

He hadn't spoken to his watchers. And they might well tell him a different tale.

24

Felicity insisted that she would make breakfast for him before he left the house. Rutledge wasn't certain whether it was because she wanted to keep him there until daylight had swept away the shadows of the night, or because she was afraid to be alone with Mallory any longer than was necessary.

And so the three of them sat in the dining room, chilled as it was after a night of wind pouring through broken glass. Mallory had patched it with a length of wood he'd found somewhere, but when the wind blew from the sea, it whistled incessantly. A reminder of their fears.

She had cooked rashers of bacon and boiled eggs to go with them, made toast without burning it, and found a pot of jam that tasted of summer. Rutledge had made the tea, reminded of a kitchen in Westmorland, the warmest room of the house and the busiest.

Hamish retorted that Rutledge had been a stranger there as well as here.

"Nan didn't make that," she said, setting the jam on the table between the two men. "It was a gift from Miss Esterley. She thought we might enjoy it. Matthew was saving it for some reason. I don't quite know why. At least that's what Nan told me when I asked what had become of it. I wrote a note to thank Miss Esterley, all the same."

"How many days a week did your maid come here?"

"Three days. On Tuesday she went to Mrs. Granville, and on Thursday and Saturday she went to the Restons. She told me only last month that if I could do without her one of my afternoons, she'd go to the rectory. The elderly woman who has been housekeeper to Mr. Putnam is considering moving away to live with her daughter."

"Miss Esterley has her own maid, I think?"

"Yes, that's true."

"Was Nan much of a gossip?"

"She never gossiped with me. Whether she gossiped about me I don't know. Must we talk about her? It makes me ill, just thinking about her. How do you work as a policeman, Mr. Rutledge? I couldn't bring myself to do what you do."

"Someone must keep order," he answered lightly. "It's what makes life possible for everyone else."

"I hadn't thought about it in that light. Matthew said once that he could measure a country's future by the honesty of its police force." Her face clouded. "Where is he, Mr. Rutledge, and why is he doing such things to us?"

"We don't know that he is."

"We've assumed that he is. I was so frightened last night. I hardly slept."

"And it's to do again tonight," Mallory reminded her. "Unless he's found today."

"I wish I knew what had happened to him when he went

walking that day. I've wished so many times I'd begged him to stay home with me. But there was no way of knowing, was there, that it would be different that morning. Do you think he's ever going to be—in good health again?" she ended, trying to find the word she wanted and failing.

"Dr. Granville felt he would recover physically. Bones knit and bruises fade. We can only hope that his mind will heal too," Rutledge answered.

"But why would he kill Nan? It makes no sense," Felicity said.

Mallory put in, "It makes as much sense as killing—" He broke off, appalled at what he'd nearly said.

Felicity Hamilton was sharp, in her own way. She stared at him, then asked, "Who? Who else is dead?"

Mallory tried to recover. "It makes as much sense as killing me," he ended.

"No, that's not what you were going to say. Mr. Rutledge? Has everyone been lying to me? *Who else is dead?*" When he was slow to answer, she said accusingly, "I knew you were all keeping something from me. I knew there was something more to Matthew vanishing like that. *What has he done?*"

"It was Mrs. Granville," Rutledge finally told her. "She was found in the surgery, the only reasonable explanation being that she saw lights and went to investigate. We don't know for a fact that Hamilton touched her."

"So that's why it was Dr. Hester, yesterday, and not Dr. Granville—" As the enormity of what she had just heard registered, she turned on Mallory with such anguish that he flinched. "What have we done to him, Stephen? Between us, what have we *done*!"

And she was gone, leaving Mallory sitting there like a man turned to stone.

Rutledge went upstairs later and tapped on the door. "Mrs. Hamilton?"

But she wouldn't answer him. He tried again, and then said through the panels, "Do you want to leave with me, Mrs. Hamilton? I've spoken to Mallory. He tells me that you're free to go, if you wish."

He listened to the silence on the other side, concerned about her.

Hamish said, "She willna' heed you. Open the door."

Rutledge hesitated, unwilling to test the door. If it was locked, he couldn't in good conscience knock it down. If it was unlocked, he would be violating her only sanctuary now in this house.

Hamish persisted, and finally he put his hand to the knob.

She was lying on the bed as she had been once before, her back to him, her hair falling in a tumble across the pillow. Asleep or pretending to be.

This time, there was a difference. Beside the bed, on its side and half empty, was the decanter of whiskey that Mallory had kept in the passage last night. Rutledge was certain he'd put it back where he found it this morning, along with the bedding and the chairs they'd used. But Mrs. Hamilton had found it. She had also emptied the box of powders Dr. Hester had left for her, taking them all at once with the whiskey.

Rutledge shouted for Mallory, and then was too busy to wait for him. She was breathing heavily, but he thought that could be only the whiskey and the fatigue of the long night as much as the sedative starting its deadly work. He picked her up in his arms and started for the stairs.

Mallory met him halfway and said only, "God in heaven."

They got her to the kitchen and stretched her out on the worn table there, covering her with one of the blankets that had been in Nan's room. Without ceremony, Rutledge thrust her fingers into the back of her throat, and as she retched, he pulled her head over the edge of the table.

She vomited only a little, and he tried again, this time more successfully.

"Strong tea, as strong as you can make it," he told Mallory. "And then send the constable on duty for Dr. Granville."

When nothing else worked, he got hot water from their breakfast tea and salt from the worktable down her throat, and the combination brought up the rest of the contents of her stomach.

She lay there, moaning in discomfort, but he held her head again and made her swallow the tea, though her throat was sore and she could hardly keep it down.

It was rough-and-ready treatment, without medical advice, but he had dealt with drunks, and what mattered was ridding her as fast as possible of what she'd swallowed.

There was no way to know if the powders would have killed her. Or if the whiskey mixed with them was a deadly brew. He had acted first and worried later.

By the time the rector and Dr. Granville had arrived, she was lying on the floor, wrapped in blankets with a bottle of hot water at her feet. Tears ran down her cheeks, and her hair on the pillow was dark with vomit and water and sweat. The kitchen was sour with the smell of sickness.

Dr. Granville, kneeling on the floor to examine her, said, "You seem to have got most of it in time. What was the sedative, do you know?"

"I don't know." Rutledge turned to Putnam. "What's left is lying on the floor of her bedroom. Will you bring them down?"

Mallory said, "I'll see to it," and was gone before Rutledge could stop him.

Granville did what he could to make Felicity Hamilton

more comfortable, speaking gently to her, bathing her face
and hands to cleanse them of the smell of sickness, and
promising to send some broth by Putnam, to give her a little
strength. She responded, smiling wanly at him and clinging
to his hand. It was as if such small kindnesses touched her
deeply.

He said, lifting her shoulders to offer her a sip of water,
"It will all seem like a nightmare, you know, when this has
passed. Something you remember sometimes, but without
the power to frighten you anymore."

She answered, "It was a stupid thing, to take the powders
all at once. But I was so tired and I didn't know who to trust,
what to believe. I wanted it all to be over with, I wanted
to sleep forever, without having to think about anything
again."

"If Mallory will allow it, I'll look in on you a little later.
To make sure you're feeling better."

Rutledge, suddenly aware that Mallory hadn't come back,
turned and ran out of the kitchen, heading for the stairs.

He found the man sitting disconsolately on her bed, the
revolver between his hands.

Rutledge said harshly, "Kill yourself here, and you might
as well kill her. The effect will be the same."

"I know. I've thought of that. I'm just out of solutions,
Rutledge. I might as well give myself up to Bennett and let
it be over. Granville can take her back to the rectory with
him and find a woman to sit with her until her mother can
get here. She's never liked her mother. It will be the last
thing she wants to happen. But we've come to the end of the
road."

Rutledge bent to collect the scattered papers that had held
the sedative. "You're a fool, Mallory, for getting yourself
into this scrape and for dragging her with you. But I'm
damned if you're going out with a whimper, as you did in

France. Get yourself cleaned up and come downstairs. This isn't over, and you'll play the role you laid out for yourself."

"I'm too tired to care."

"Then care about her, for God's sake."

Rutledge turned on his heel and left. He was halfway down the staircase when he heard Mallory shut Mrs. Hamilton's bedroom door and walk heavily down the hall to the bath.

He gave Granville the papers the sedative had been folded into, and the doctor sniffed them before balling them up and tossing them away. "Mild enough. And probably not enough to kill her. But you did the right thing, though I doubt she'll thank you for it."

"She was frightened by the maid's murder, and last night was not the best time to sleep well."

"Yes, there were trees down on some of the farms. The Joyners lost an apple tree, and their neighbors had a large trunk come through their roof. They told Miss Joyner it sounded like the crack of doom. One of the roads was blocked as well."

"You were out there?"

"The old man was having trouble breathing again. I doubt he'll see the spring, but then he's of strong stock. He may surprise me yet." He stretched his back. "We ought to get her to bed. What shape is it in?"

"It's ready for her. I was just up there."

"Good."

With Putnam going before them to manage the doors, they got her up the stairs and into her room. Rutledge saw that Mallory had taken away with him the decanter and the small bedside carpet where it had rolled and spilled. Dr. Granville tucked her in with surprising gentleness, and said, "I'll have no more foolishness from you, my dear. You'll see this through for your husband's sake."

"Thank you, Dr. Granville. I'm so sorry—after all you've been through." It was the closest she could come to apologizing for what her husband might have done. She lay there, eyes overly large in her pale face, overcome by drowsiness after her ordeal. Putnam took her hand, and in the other she clutched the handkerchief he'd found for her. Tears seemed very near the surface. "It's been very trying for all of us."

"Sleep if you can. I'll send along the broth, and if you drink that, it will strengthen you." He turned to Rutledge, standing by the door. "We should have a woman come and sit with her. Do you think that's possible?"

"Miss Esterley might agree," he said. "Someone who won't gossip."

Mr. Putnam looked up and said, "Shall I go and see?"

"Dr. Granville will see to it, Rector. You're needed here at the moment."

"Don't leave me," Felicity Hamilton asked. "Not until I'm asleep."

"Yes, by all means. If it's a comfort to you, my dear, I'll gladly stay."

Rutledge accompanied Dr. Granville to the door. "Thank you for coming. There was no time to send for Dr. Hester."

"I understand. It's the least I could do, after the debacle with her husband. There's still no news of him?"

"None."

"He's dead, then. In that cottage. There aren't that many places for a man to hide in Hampton Regis, when everyone is on the lookout for him."

"I still find it difficult to believe he could have walked away under his own power. What's your opinion?"

Granville gave his question serious consideration. "Anything is possible, medically speaking. But that means he must have killed Margaret. And I refuse to believe it. Someone took him away, and that someone had already done his best once before to see Hamilton into his grave."

"You know the people here. Can you tell me who might have started this by attacking Hamilton in the first place?"

Granville shrugged. "Your best suspect is Stephen Mallory. But then someone else could have decided to finish his work for him. Get him to confess to what happened out there by the water, and clear that up. Then you can begin to think about Margaret's death. And Nan's."

"I've asked myself again and again why these two women needed to die. There's no clear answer."

"Nan worked for a number of people over the years, Rutledge. You can't be sure what secrets she took with her when she was killed."

"But the house was locked."

Granville raised his eyebrows. "What difference does that make? Hamilton isn't the only person to have lived in Casa Miranda, you know. And I doubt he thought to change the locks. There must be other keys floating about. For that matter, you could probably collect half a hundred from other houses of the same age, and find that some of them fit. Ask the rector to test his."

When Granville had gone and before Mallory had presented himself again, Rutledge tapped lightly on the door to Mrs. Hamilton's room.

"Sorry to disturb you, Mr. Putnam. I should like to borrow your keys for a little while. Do you mind?"

Putnam, his eyes on Rutledge's face, said, "Ah, I haven't given Dr. Granville one, have I? My mistake. Thank you, Inspector." He brought them to the door. "It's rather an unconventional collection, I'm afraid. I never think to take off one when I add another. Those to this side of the longest one are to the church. The others are the rectory keys. I can't tell you where one or two of them came from. My predecessor, very likely."

He passed them to Rutledge.

"You aren't leaving, are you, Inspector?" Felicity asked anxiously.

"Not for a while," he reassured her.

And then he set about trying the rector's keys on the locks of Casa Miranda.

The trouble, he thought, was that there were too many doors. The main entrance facing the drive possessed a newer lock, and none of Putnam's fit it. There was a door to the back garden, another down a short passage where Mrs. Hamilton or her predecessors had cut and potted plants for the house, several ways into the kitchen area, and a door leading directly into the servants' quarters, where they could come and go without walking through the kitchen. The cellar door boasted a padlock.

He found, working methodically through the handful of keys, that while several of them raised his hopes at first, only two of them actually fit into a lock well enough to reach the tumblers. Both turned stiffly at first, but after a little effort on his part, he heard the tumblers fall into place.

He now had two keys that unlocked two house doors: one that led to the servants' belowstairs quarters and the other to the door where tradesmen brought their goods and supplies. Holding them up to the light, edge to edge, he could see that they were identical.

Dr. Granville had been right. It wasn't only Matthew Hamilton who could enter the house at will but anyone in Hampton Regis who possessed a key of the same shape.

Rutledge returned the keys to Putnam, told Mallory that he would be back within the hour, and left the property, walking quickly in the direction of the police station.

His watchers had left their reports on the table that served as his desk.

Rutledge thumbed through them quickly and found that

the man in the church tower had seen very little. "The way
the trees were tossing about," he'd scrawled in pencil, "it
was nearly impossible to be sure what was shadow, what
was dog, and what was not. I saw the constable on watch
a time or two, and that was all I could identify with any
certainty."

There had been no trees to speak of between the man in
the Cornelius attic and the Mole. He reported no activity
until two fishermen went down to look at the sea and walked
back again ten minutes later. Mr. Reston was not seen leaving his house.

Nor had Constable Coxe.

The constable in Rutledge's room at the inn swore he'd
seen someone moving about in the shadows, "But not clear
enough to be sure who it was. He didn't walk up the drive to
the door, I made certain of that. But where he went I can't
say. The constable paced about a bit, and he might have had
a clearer look."

The constable declared he'd seen no one.

Hamish said, "It could ha' been Stratton, poking about."

"Yes, I think it very likely was."

No one had made an attempt to climb up from the sea,
and no one had gone to the other cliff, where Mallory had
watched the lights of the Hamilton house from his motorcar.

"A night's sleep lost for verra' little."

Rutledge could feel the tiredness across his own shoulders. "I wonder if Stratton made free with the hotel keys."

"It doesna' signify. They do na' look the same."

It was a good point. The key to his own room was newer
in style and shape. But what about those to the kitchens and
the service entrance? He made a mental note to look.

He tossed the reports aside. No one had come to Casa Miranda after all. In all likelihood the branch had driven itself

through the fragile old glass of the dining room windows.

And his men were sleeping now after a long cold night.

He got up and walked to the door of the police station. The wind had dropped with the dawn, leaving twigs and bits of straw, scraps of paper and any other debris not nailed down scattered on lawns and pavement. The lid from a dustbin had been wedged tightly into a clump of bare-limbed lilac, and someone's hat was caught on a branch of a tree by the nearest house.

Hamish was telling him that a good officer could have put that wind to use last night, infiltrating half a dozen men through enemy lines. "Crawling on their bellies, they'd no' make a silhouette against the sky."

"But Hamilton wasn't in the army," he said. "And so he didn't come. Or whoever it is, with a fierce design on everyone around Hamilton."

He went for a walk, climbing the headland across the sea from the house. It wasn't terribly high, but it gave a good view of Casa Miranda. He could see the marks left in the damp soil by a motorcar's tires. Mallory, then, and his obsession with Felicity Hamilton.

Out to sea, Rutledge could just pick out a steamer passing on the horizon, black smoke marking its progress along the rim of the sky. Nearer in, a fishing boat bobbed, for the current was running fast.

His thoughts kept returning to the events of the night.

We were prepared for a frontal assault, he reminded himself. *And too many people knew that. So the killer never came. The bough through the windowpane notwithstanding.*

"If I had it to do over again," he told Hamish, unaware that he was speaking aloud, "I'd spread my forces better. I'd see that the lure was more enticing. And I'd watch the lamppost."

"There willna' be anither time. Have ye no' thought it

was the man's defense of the Germans that unsettled some- one who lost a son or brother or lover in the war? Ye ken, the Kaiser is in Holland and untouchable, but his advocate is here in Hampton Regis. But two wrongly dead is a verra' high price for revenge. It's over, and yc're no closer to the killer than before."

Rutledge turned from the view, feeling the damp biting through him, though the sun was making a yeoman's effort to warm his shoulders.

"The killer may think it is finished. He doesn't know me."

There was a shop near the police station, and Rutledge walked toward it, thinking about a hot cup of tea. He had drunk only half of it when one of Bennett's men came to fetch him.

There had been a telephone call for him from Exeter. Someone from the hotel had brought the message to the police station.

25

Rutledge decided, as he paid his account at the teashop, to return the Exeter telephone call from the Duke of Monmouth. He could count on more privacy there.

Constable Jordan, not to be put off, said, "Inspector Bennett would like to know, sir, if this is to do with Mr. Hamilton."

"Tell Inspector Bennett that I've found a woman who knew Hamilton as a young man. She may have remembered something useful. When I spoke to her last, she wasn't very encouraging. But she's had a little time to think about it."

"Yes, sir. Something in his past, then. Inspector Bennett asks you keep him informed, sir."

Bennett had been curt about Felicity Hamilton's attempt at suicide, describing it as nervous theatrics. "I'd send Mrs. Bennett along if it weren't for putting another pawn in Mallory's hands. It's better for that whole house of cards to come tumbling down. And it will, mark my words. If not today, by tomorrow." There had been satisfaction in his certainty, as if this had been his plan from the start.

Rutledge nodded and walked briskly on. Halfway to the Duke of Monmouth, he encountered Dr. Granville coming toward him.

"I was just coming to find you, Rutledge. Miss Esterley has agreed to consider staying the night. It was the best I could do. But I was able to arrange a thermos of broth for Mrs. Hamilton, and I'm taking it up when it's ready. Unless you're going back yourself? The Duke of Monmouth kitchen is preparing it now."

"I'll see to it. Thanks."

"If you need me, I'll be at the undertaker's. After that, you'll find me at the rectory. No later than one or half past, I should think." He walked on, his shoulders braced for the ordeal ahead.

Rutledge looked after him, not envying him. On impulse, he called after Granville, "Would you rather wait until I can spell Mr. Putnam?"

Granville turned. "I don't know that his company would make it any easier. But I'll need to confer with him about the service. Let him stay with Mrs. Hamilton as long as she needs him."

Rutledge reached the inn and shut himself into the telephone closet. He put through the call to Exeter and found himself speaking to an Inspector Cubbins.

"I'm calling on behalf of a Miss Miranda Cole," Cubbins told him, curiosity thick in his Devon voice. "She has asked me to tell you she regrets her stubbornness yesterday. If you could find it in yourself to forgive her, she'll speak with you again this afternoon."

It was not the message Rutledge had expected from her. As the silence lengthened, Cubbins asked, "Is this by any stretch of my imagination something to do with what's going on there in Hampton Regis? If it is, I'd like to hear about it. I'm told one of my constables took you to the Cole house in the evening when I was off duty."

"'Ware!" Hamish warned.

Rutledge, brought up short, said, "I called on her, yes, to see if she could give me any information about Matthew Hamilton's early years in England. She knew him then but hasn't seen or as far as I know heard from him since that time. I thought, a formality. Who brought you the message? Is there anything wrong?"

"Should there be?"

"All was well when I left her."

"Then it's well now. Her maid, Miss Dedham, came in not half an hour ago. She refused to wait, just delivered a note from her mistress and went back to the house. But she seemed perfectly composed." There was a pause. "How did you come to hear about Miss Cole?"

"A woman in Kent told me Miss Cole had moved in the same circles as Hamilton and his family. It was a shorter drive to Exeter."

"So it is." Rutledge could hear fingers tapping on the man's desk. "You'll come and fetch me if there's more than a formality involved, won't you? I'd like to think we look after our own."

He took a chance. "If you've nothing better to do, meet me there."

"We don't have murderers running about undetected, but I've got a pleasing sufficiency on my plate at the moment. No, I leave it to your good judgment, Rutledge. You know where to find me."

And he rang off.

Rutledge went to the dining room for Mrs. Hamilton's broth and discovered that luncheon would be served in fifteen minutes. He used the time to dress for his coming meeting with Miss Cole and then ate his meal in his usual corner.

He dropped the thermos of broth at the door of Casa Miranda.

Mallory, accepting it, said, "She probably won't touch it, now that I have."

"She isn't expecting you to poison her."

"You'd think she was, refusing to let me come near her."

"Leave her alone, Mallory, and set your own house in order."

With that he turned on his heel and strode back to the motorcar.

"Where will you be, if we need you?" Mallory called to him.

"Not far away."

"I saw you on the headland over there. Did you find anything?"

"Only the marks of your tires," Rutledge retorted as he let out the clutch. "So much for secrecy and discretion."

At the end of the drive, he turned to the west, soon leaving Hampton Regis behind.

It must have been market day somewhere, Rutledge decided, driving through the second herd of cows moving placidly along the road ahead of him. He caught up with another cart shortly afterward, laden with chickens in wicker baskets. They squawked in alarm as the motorcar passed by.

But he made steady time in spite of the traffic, and it was only a little after afternoon tea that he found himself pulling into the drive at the house where Miranda Cole lived with her aunt.

Dedham answered his knocks, her face drawn as if she hadn't slept well. "She's expecting you. Don't upset her any more than you already have."

"I never intended to upset your mistress."

She opened the door to the sitting room, ushered him in, and shut it almost on his heels with a snap that told him her opinion of him.

Miss Cole was sitting in the sunlight that poured through the window beside her. He thought at first that she'd been crying, and then realized that her eyes were red-rimmed from lack of sleep.

It had been a long night in this house as well as the one named for this woman in Hampton Regis.

"Sit down, Inspector. I have had my tea. You'll find the pot is still warm, if you care for a cup."

"Thank you, no."

"Then please tell me, from the beginning, what you know about Matthew Hamilton and everything that happened to him in the last week."

Rutledge began with Mallory's decision after leaving hospital to live outside Hampton Regis, and his inability to stop himself from seeing Felicity, one way or another.

"Is she pretty, the woman Matthew married? Felicity." She seemed to taste the name, as if it could present her with an image of his wife.

"I would call her pretty. She has a vivacity that must be attractive in happier circumstances. And a certain vulnerability."

He went through the morning that Matthew Hamilton had walked along the water, and how he had been found. Watching her—for she couldn't see him and he kept his gaze steady, reading each expression that flitted across what she must have supposed to be a still face—he thought, *She wasn't blind from birth. Her eyes follow me when I move. There must be some sense of light and dark, or perhaps a range of shadows.*

But she couldn't distinguish, for instance, the shabbiness

of her surroundings. How the colors had faded, and how alive she looked among them, her fair hair and the dark blue sweater and string of fine pearls setting her apart, as if she'd wandered here by mistake.

She lifted her hand to her face as he described Hamilton's injuries, and said, "He must have been in great pain."

"The doctor took every care of him," he assured her.

As he told her about Mallory's race to speak to Felicity, and the subsequent decision to hold her against her will until Rutledge arrived from London, she said, "You know this man, don't you? From the war, was it? I can hear the difference in your voice as you describe him."

He hadn't been aware that he was betraying himself as well.

Hamish, his own voice soft in Rutledge's ear, said, "She has lived wi' blindness a verra' long time."

"We served in France together," he conceded, and left it at that.

The rest of the story unwound like wire from a spool, tangled sometimes because she didn't know all the players. And at other times, she would interject a question or comment that was remarkably astute.

She was interested in Miss Esterley, who had become friends with Hamilton after her accident. "He had a way of making it seem that you had his entire attention," she commented, her first personal remark. "It isn't surprising that someone alone at such a trying time might feel comforted."

"I've not had the good fortune to know him at his best," Rutledge said. "But yes, he was kind to her, and it was valued."

When he reached his account of Hamilton's disappearance, she was tense in her chair, her hands tightening and her body braced.

But she stirred as he once more described Mrs. Granville's death, almost as if she were hearing it for the first time.

The sun had gone in, and darkness was coming down. She said, as if to gain a little time, "Could you light the lamps, please, Inspector Rutledge? And hand me my shawl? It should be there on the table by the door where you came into the room."

He saw to the lamps and found the shawl where she'd told him to look. By the time he'd returned to his seat, she had herself under control again.

Nan Weekes's death shook her to the core.

"How did anyone get into the house? Surely it must have been this man Mallory. What has become of Matthew's keys? Have you thought to look for them?"

"His clothing was taken from the surgery the night he disappeared. If he's alive, he must have the keys as well. Another reason why it's imperative to know who may have them if he doesn't."

"But I don't understand. If he was attacked, then he's a *victim*."

"Of the assault, yes."

"I think your Inspector Bennett may be right, that this Lieutenant Mallory is behind everything that's happened. Mrs. Granville's death and the maid's death," she said, grasping for straws to build her case. "And Matthew has been made to look like the scapegoat."

"I'm beginning to think Mallory was intended to take the blame. For that death and Mrs. Granville's."

"Well, there you are, then. Matthew had nothing to do with it."

"Then where is he? Why hasn't he come forward? And who besides Hamilton cares whether Mallory is hanged or not?"

"Surely there are other suspects?"

"A very short list. Perhaps you're willing to help me add to it. Or take one away by telling me Hamilton is dead."

She shivered. "Believe me, I wish I could help you."

"Mallory may be innocent. If he is, he's already suffered more than enough. There's that to consider as well." He waited. "I've come because Inspector Cubbins tells me you have something to say to me. I hope it's true. Or I've wasted my time."

She sat there for a time, a frown on her face, her eyes downcast. Finally she picked up the bell at her elbow and rang it.

Dedham came to the door, clearly expecting to see Rutledge off the premises. Instead Miss Cole said, "Could you bring us fresh tea, please, Dedham? I think we rather need it."

She added as the door closed again, "You place me in a very awkward situation, Inspector Rutledge. But I can tell you frankly that Matthew Hamilton, when I knew him, was incapable of killing anyone. A good man, a fair man, a caring man. I don't want to believe that he's changed since then." She looked toward the window, where the light had all but faded. But it was another light she searched for. "I've never been connected to murder before. It's unspeakably frightful."

"None of us can say with certainty that we won't kill, if driven to it. I have killed men in the war. They were no better and no worse than I was. But because of the uniform they wore, they had to die in my place. And because of the uniform my own men wore, I had to send them out to shoot strangers."

"Yes, that's what happens in war, people are killed. It isn't personal, is it? Like this."

"When you watch the living force go out of a man's face as you fire your weapon into his unprotected body, it is very personal," he told her grimly.

That gave her pause. "I begin to see. I'm sorry."

The tea came soon afterward, and Dedham had added sandwiches to it, and cakes iced in pale green, as if intended for a celebration that hadn't taken place.

Rutledge poured, so that the maid could be dismissed. Miss Cole took her cup, drank deeply as if the tea were a lifeline, and then set it aside.

"If Matthew Hamilton is dead, you'll have no answers in the end," she warned him.

"I can't help but pray that he's still alive. We need to close this case. It has done great damage to too many people. Dr. Granville, the maid's cousin. Mrs. Hamilton and even Stephen Mallory. Others have been dragged into it as well. It would be unkind to let them all go on suffering."

"But what will you do, if you find him? Carry him off in custody, like a common felon while you sort this out?"

"Hardly that, unless we caught him with a weapon in his hand, trying to kill someone. My first question would have been, 'What happened on your last walk?' And my second, 'What happened in that surgery?'"

"If he can't tell you, what then?"

Rutledge set his own cup aside. He answered her honestly, weariness infusing the words with what sounded very like despair. "I don't know."

She closed her eyes and leaned her head against the back of the chair.

"Do you believe me, that he was incapable of murder, when I knew him all those years ago?"

He took a chance, over Hamish's fierce objections.

"I'll try, once you've told me why it was you wouldn't marry him."

Her eyes flew open, her head coming up with a snap. *"You have no right!"*

"There are two people dead, Miss Cole. Women who never harmed anyone to my knowledge. But they died because of

Hamilton, one way or another. You owe them something."

"I don't owe anyone anything," she cried, the pain in her voice so deep it sounded even to her own ears like someone else's.

"You have lived here in shabby gentility, shut away from the world, punishing yourself because something happened to your sight and you believed that you had no right to inflict your suffering on someone else. He called you the most honorable woman he'd ever met, Miss Cole. I have it on good authority."

"I couldn't entertain for him. I couldn't recognize faces and remember them the next time we met. I couldn't live in a strange world where I couldn't see my surroundings or find my way without someone there to help me. It would have been a burden at the very start of his career, and I couldn't bear to hear him make excuses for being overlooked for promotion or for assignments where a suitable hostess was imperative."

"And so you released him from any duty to you. Were you surprised he took that release?"

She moved as if she'd suffered a physical blow. "It took him five years to accept my answer. By that time, love tends to fade a little, and it's harder to bring someone's face back with the same clarity. The sound of the voice is not the same, and you can't quite recapture it. Five years of lying awake at night, five years of getting through the next day somehow. But in the end, he stopped writing. And I never heard from him again."

He knew she had described her own anguish rather than Hamilton's. But he said nothing, preparing to bring the interview to a close.

She rose, as if anticipating that, and he stood as well.

"Thank you for taking the time to help me through what has become the most difficult day of my life."

"I'm sorry that you've been brought into my inquiry—"

Miss Cole brushed that aside, fumbling for her cane. She found it and moved easily toward him. "I wasn't sure what to do. Now I see my way more clearly. Come with me, Mr. Rutledge, and I'll take you to Matthew Hamilton."

26

Rutledge found himself standing there gaping.

She smiled wryly, a great sadness behind it. "I can imagine what's going through your mind. But he wasn't here last night. I didn't lie to you. He was brought to my door early this morning by a very concerned lorry driver. He'd found Matthew along the road near a farm just west of Hampton Regis. I don't know what Matthew expected to do, but he was still on his feet through sheer willpower, and the lorry driver told me he was hardly sensible for a quarter of an hour or more. It was several miles before he could even tell the man where he wanted to go."

"Surely the driver must have been suspicious."

"Apparently Matthew told him that he'd been robbed and beaten, and wanted to go home. Here. To my house. The driver was all for sending at once for the police, but I persuaded him to let me find the doctor first. And instead, I telephoned you."

"Quite right."

She reached out her hand. "If I may have your arm?"

Hastily he offered it to her, and she led him to the stair-case. As they started to climb, she said, "Promise you won't upset him. I'm going against his express wishes to tell no one he's here. He will blame me for what you do."

"I understand." But he found himself wondering if she was afraid of Hamilton now, afraid that two women had died at his hands, and she might be placing herself in jeopardy. Even as she struggled to protect him.

Hamilton was lying in bed in what appeared to be a guest room, his skin gray against the stark white of bleached and pressed sheets.

Miranda Cole had opened the door quietly so as not to disturb him, but it was obvious that nothing short of cataclysm would rouse him from his exhausted sleep.

Rutledge stood there on the threshold, studying him for a moment.

His beard had grown dark shadows across his face, and his eyes seemed to have sunk deep into their sockets. The bruises had faded, a little, but the green and yellow replacing the livid red and dark purple made him seem closer to death than he had in Dr. Granville's surgery when they were still bloody. As if he were already a corpse and no one had thought to tell him.

Signaling Miss Cole with a touch on her arm to stay where she was, he crossed to the bed and called Hamilton's name in a sharp, clear voice.

It penetrated the heavy slumber. An arm, flung out to ward off a blow, was followed by Hamilton rearing up in bed, his face wild, prepared to defend himself.

Rutledge said rapidly, "You're safe, man, no one will harm you here. You're with friends."

Some of the wildness fled but Hamilton frowned at him. "I don't know you," he said, the words a rumble in his chest.

"I'm someone Miss Cole sent for. To help you, if that's possible. She's there in the doorway, ask her yourself."

Hamilton peered toward the door. "Miranda? What are you doing here?"

"It's my house," she told him in an ordinary voice, but Rutledge could see how her hands clutched the edges of her shawl. "Matthew, this is Ian Rutledge. I can't do this alone, I had to find someone I trusted. Please let him help us."

Hamilton lay back on his pillows, his eyes closed. "I'm sorry I dragged you into this, Miranda. But I didn't know where else to turn."

Rutledge said, "Do you remember how you got here, Hamilton?"

After a moment he said, "I remember lying down by the road, cold and tired. But then a vehicle was coming, and I got to my feet, trying to walk away from the road. I think he stopped. The lorry driver. The next thing I remember was being warm enough to think, and my leg hurting as we bounced over ruts."

"Where had you been before lying down by the road?"

Hamilton gave a short bark of laughter. "In someone's henhouse. I ate the eggs raw, I was that hungry. There was a cow as well, and I milked her when I felt stronger. But I couldn't stay there. They'd gone to market and were bound to find me if I fell asleep in the hay."

Hamish said softly, "The fox in the henhouse."

That complaint had been included in a report by one of the men talking to householders out on the west road. Rutledge thought he ought to be commended for thoroughness.

"Was this anywhere near the landslip?"

"My God." He groaned. "I was *in* that house. I don't know why I left it, something, a sixth sense, the way the rainwater was rushing past it—I don't know. I'd seen the family across the road leave, I told myself I could make it to their shed.

But I was hardly out the door when the ground moved the first time. Like an earthquake. When I stopped long enough to look back, there was *nothing there*."

"Why did you go to it in the first place?"

"God knows. I can't remember. I think I was afraid, I couldn't understand why I was hurt and bandaged."

"But why leave the safety of Dr. Granville's surgery? In the middle of the night?"

"Did I do that?" Hamilton stared at him. "No, you're wrong there, I was in a dark fearful place and something was worrying me. Have you ever been in a Turkish prison? No, I expect not. I was once, visiting a man charged with a serious crime. I was never so glad to be out into the fresh air again in my life."

"Where was Mrs. Granville, Hamilton? Do you remember seeing her?"

"She and Granville came to dinner—"

"No, while you were lying there, being treated by her husband."

He put both hands to his face as if he could scrub away his confusion. "I don't even know how I got these injuries, Rutledge. Or where I've been. I remember being afraid I was going to die, if I didn't do something. There were voices, and sometimes I knew what they were saying and sometimes I didn't."

"Who came to help you in the midst of everything that was happening?"

Rutledge glanced toward Miranda Cole. She was standing there, a mixture of fear and pity on her face as she listened.

But Matthew Hamilton said, "It was Felicity. It must have been."

Surprised, Rutledge stared at him, trying to determine whether he was telling the truth—or the truth as he thought he knew it.

But he was lying back on his pillows now, his face grim as he fought pain and weakness.

"You must stop," Miss Cole said quietly.

Rutledge answered her: "I can't. I don't have all the story. And it's urgent that I get to the bottom of what he's been through."

"Then let him rest for a bit, and eat something if he will. After that we'll see if he's well enough to go on."

Dedham brought food for Matthew Hamilton—eggs cooked in milk, with a little whiskey for strength, a broth rich with chicken and some rice, a custard that was flavored with sherry.

He ate slowly, stopping for stretches of time, as if his arms were too heavy to lift the spoon.

Rutledge, waiting by the window, fought his impatience. It was already dark outside, and he felt a pressing need to return to Hampton Regis.

Finally satisfied, Hamilton pushed away the tray. "You were going to tell me what happened to me. I must have fallen. It's the only way I can account for what I see here." He gestured with one hand to his body.

"You went for a walk. Down by the water, even though a sea mist was rolling in. And someone came up to speak to you."

"I don't think anyone did. I walk very early, before Felicity is awake."

"You were found on the shingle, just above the tideline. Another half an hour, less even, and as badly hurt as you were, you'd have drowned."

Hamilton seemed to listen, as if bringing back to mind the sounds of that morning. "Someone went down to the boats. I couldn't see who it was."

"He must have turned and come toward you."

"If he did, I couldn't tell. The mists muffle sound."

"And then you were struck over the head, and went down."

"I remember men's voices." He shook his head. "It's hopeless."

"But you left the surgery. Why?"

"Something was going to happen. Was Inspector Bennett there? I remember him telling me over and over again that Felicity was calling for me, and I had to wake up and help her."

Bennett, trying to rouse him as Rutledge had done earlier.

"By the bye, do you have your keys with you?"

"Are they in my pocket? Look in the wardrobe."

Rutledge had been sitting by the fire Dedham had laid in the room. Now he went to the wardrobe, his hands busy with pockets. "Yes, they're here." He quietly slipped the ring of keys into his own pocket, then said, "I must go. It's late. Will you stay here, Hamilton, or come with me?"

Miranda Cole opened her mouth to protest—whether his departure or Hamilton's, he didn't know.

Hamilton said, "Where's my wife? Shouldn't she be here soon? I've tried to think what's keeping her."

"You asked Miss Cole not to tell anyone you were here. She has followed your instructions."

"Did I? I couldn't have meant Felicity." He was tiring again, his shoulders slumped. "See if you can find out what's keeping her, Rutledge."

Five minutes later, Miss Cole was scolding Rutledge all the way down the stairs. "I thought you would stay with us. Stay here, at the house. I thought you wanted to find Matthew and help him."

"There are promises to keep in Hampton Regis as well."

He could see her uncertainty, her belief in Hamilton wavering as the night drew in. Or was she afraid of emotions that were reawakening in herself? He couldn't tell.

Rutledge tried to find the words to reassure her, but he

had no assurances to give. He thought about Casa Miranda, and Mallory there alone with Felicity Hamilton in that dark house. He knew where Hamilton was now, but what about preventing the disintegration of two people with nowhere else to go? What about a murderer still on the loose, if Hamilton hadn't killed anyone?

"Lock him in his room and brace a chair under the knob. He's exhausted, I don't think he'll wake up before I'm here at first light."

"I shouldn't have sent for you, I shouldn't have heard what you had to tell me. It's only made matters *worse*."

"You told me you couldn't believe Hamilton was a killer."

She brushed her hair back with her hand. "I don't. Not the Matthew I remember. But I see him there, the bruises, the confusion, the way he rambles. It's not like him. There's something wrong. I'm not sure I know this Matthew."

"I don't think you've anything to fear. You have no connection with Hampton Regis. And it was there that it all began."

"Then take him with you. *Please*. I'll provide you with blankets and cushions. What if he had nothing to do with the deaths, but someone else learns he's here? Three women alone—what could *Matthew* do to help us?"

Rutledge stood there, reading the anguish in her face.

In the end, he found a telephone and left a message for Inspector Bennett that he was delayed.

And prayed that he'd made the right decision.

Hamilton had nightmares in the night. Rutledge, sleepless in the room next door, heard him and went in to sit with him.

He watched as Hamilton twisted and turned until his sheets were a tangled knot. As they tightened around him, he began to call out. Most of the words were unintelligible, but there was anger mixed with fear, and then Rutledge held himself rigid in the shadows as Hamilton reared up in his bed and called, *"Who's there?"*

A garbled, one-sided conversation followed. And then Hamilton was scrambling out of his bed, struggling to rid himself of the sheets and a blanket. He stopped, his gaze on the fire. Before Rutledge could move, he'd picked up the small carpet in front of the hearth and was about to beat out the flames as if they threatened him. But even as the carpet was raised above his head, he froze and turned to stare directly at Rutledge, by the door.

Lowering the carpet, he said, quite clearly, "Stratton? What the bloody hell are you doing here?"

It took several minutes to make Hamilton understand who he was, but Rutledge, turning up the lamps, watched understanding dawn.

Hamilton looked down at the carpet he was still holding. "Good God, what's this?"

"You were about to put out the fire."

He blinked. "Was I? Yes, that's right. Stratton said he'd burn me out if I didn't burn my diaries."

"When was this?"

"Before I left London to come to Hampton Regis with Felicity."

"Did he mean it, do you think?"

Hamilton sat down in the nearest chair. "I think it was bravado. It was one of the reasons I chose a house backed up against the sea."

"Did you know that Stephen Mallory was watching the house?"

"I thought at first it was Stratton. I was relieved that it was Mallory. But I knew Felicity had seen him at least once. And that rankled."

"Were you afraid for your marriage?"

"Hardly that. But it was a snake in our Eden. I couldn't go round to his cottage and thrash him. Or ask him to move away. It was a reminder, if you like, that Felicity had loved him once. I'd have given much not to remember that."

"Did Mallory come down to the shingle and threaten you, earlier in the week?"

"I was alone. I told you." He looked Rutledge up and down. "Who are you? You've asked a good many questions. Rather personal ones at that."

"I've told you. My name is Rutledge. I'm also from Scotland Yard."

"And a friend of Miranda's." He seemed to accept that. "I see now why she said she trusted you."

"You couldn't have been alone on the strand, Hamilton. You couldn't have damaged yourself like this. Have you seen yourself in a mirror, man?"

"I didn't say no one had attacked me. I said I saw no one there."

"Why did you kill Margaret Granville?"

Hamilton raised his head. "Are you telling me that I did, and can't remember that, either?"

"She's dead. And you're here. No one took you out of that surgery and murdered you and left your body in the cottage by the sea to wash away when the land crumbled."

He studied his hands. "I'm not clear about getting out of there. Something was wrong. And I was worried, but I couldn't remember what it was that needed to be done."

"She walked into the room, and you saw her outlined against the light she'd left in the passage. You were coming out of sedation and muddled. Afraid of something but not really sure where you were or why. It could have been that her shadow was thrown against the wall, and you had no way of knowing it was the doctor's wife."

"I disliked Granville. He was there with Bennett, telling me about Felicity and Mallory. I could hear them, at a great distance, and they wouldn't stop. I wanted to shout at them, but I couldn't."

"But you were stronger when you got out of bed, caught up with Mrs. Granville in the passage, and choked her to death." Rutledge watched his eyes as he made the suggestion. For any indication that Hamilton knew this to be a lie, or saw a way of offering Rutledge a false scent to follow.

But the color had drained from Hamilton's face. "Is that true? Was that how it happened?" He dropped his hands, as if to hide them. "What am I going to do? I have to get out of here, I can't drag Miranda into this." He turned to the wardrobe and pulled out his clothing, reaching for his shoes and carrying the lot to the fire, where he began to dress. It was difficult, and in the end he had to resort to sitting in the chair to draw on his trousers. Rutledge watched him as he laced his shoes.

"All right, I'm ready." He moved on to the desk, drew paper and a pen out of the center drawer, and tried to write a message to Miranda Cole. He crumpled the first effort, tossing it into the fire. Thinking for a moment, he scrawled something across the page. Blotting it, he folded the sheet and set it on the table by the bed.

"I didn't tell her. I just said we must go to Hampton Regis tonight and then I thanked her." He tried to smile. "I always valued her good opinion. Now I've brought her trouble. How do we get there? Don't tell me we'll have to wait until her groom can drive us into Exeter?" The thought stopped him.

"My motorcar is downstairs."

"Thank God." Hamilton turned and surveyed the room. "I'm too tired to think. But all I've done since I got here is sleep. Hiding from myself, at a guess. Now I know why."

Rutledge said, "Are you sure you're up to this?"

"Let's get it over and done with." He reached for one of the pillows and then put it back. "No. I don't need it. I don't want to take anything that ought to be brought back."

They made it as far as the stairs before Miranda Cole opened her door at the end of the passage and said, "Who's there?"

"I'm going with Mr. Rutledge back to Hampton Regis, Miranda. I'm all right now, I've slept well enough and I feel stronger." It was a brave lie.

Her gaze swung to Rutledge, where he stood to one side. "Don't do this."

"It isn't my choice, Miss Cole. He has information that we badly need just now. I can't ignore it."

"Matthew?"

"It's my decision, not his. You mustn't worry, it's what I have to do."

She stood there for a moment longer, as if listening to the silence. Then she said, "I don't believe either one of you." She turned, went back in her room, and shut the door.

They went down the stairs and into the night. Outside, in the sharp air of a predawn darkness, Hamilton said softly, "I never expected to see her again. I never thought how it would feel if I did. But I always knew where to find her. I made certain of that for more than twenty years."

When he reached the motorcar, moving with a care that betrayed his pain, he spoke again. "I think I understand now how Felicity felt about Stephen Mallory. There's that question in the back of your mind. What might have been . . ."

He let Rutledge help him into the motorcar, then looked up at the lighted window he'd left behind. But he said nothing more until they were well on the road back to Hampton Regis.

27

When they reached the police station in Hampton Regis, Rutledge found the door unlocked and a message waiting on his desk.

All's quiet. What took you so long?

It was signed *Bennett*.

"Are you up to this?" Rutledge said, offering the tired man beside him a chair. "It was a long journey, and it's very late."

"In more ways than one. All right, what is it you want, a statement?"

"Yes." Rutledge found pen and paper, took Hamilton to his makeshift office, and asked him to describe in his own words what he recalled about his injuries and what he believed had happened when Mrs. Granville was killed.

He sat there, thinking it through, the scars on his face knitted with uncertainty. Then he wrote essentially what

Rutledge had suggested to him in Miranda Cole's guest bedroom.

At the end of it, he reread the statement, and then signed his name. Tossing the pen aside Hamilton asked, "Am I spending the night here? Or what's left of it?" He walked to the door and looked down the passage at the dark rooms, airless and bleak, the furnishings old, the walls in need of paint. There had been no money for refurbishing such buildings during the war, and none since. "I suppose murderers can't be fussy."

"I think, not here. Are you sure you're satisfied with what you've written?"

"Does it matter? You've told me I'm a murderer."

"It could matter, yes." Rutledge folded the statement and thrust it into his breast pocket. He led Hamilton back to the motorcar, but the man's injured leg was so stiff now that he had difficulty stepping in. Swearing under his breath, Hamilton finally managed to get the passenger door closed. Rutledge drove to the Duke of Monmouth. It was dark, but he found that the door was unlocked, and he took Hamilton inside.

The room on the other side of his was still empty, and he looked out the window for a moment, then said, "There's no way down short of a fall. And I have the key. I might remind you as well that Stratton is here in Hampton Regis. I don't think you want to meet him in the dark."

"What about Felicity?"

"She's safe for tonight. You can go to her tomorrow."

"Fair enough." He hesitated. "Do we have to bring Miranda into this business? Does Felicity have to know where I was?"

"I'm afraid the police must. And so she'll hear of it."

Hamilton sighed. "Good night, Rutledge. I hope you know what you're doing."

"So do I." After a moment, he said, "I haven't told you that Nan Weekes is dead. Someone has killed her as well."

Hamilton was not prepared for it. He said, blankly, "Good God. Are you saying to me that I did that too?"

"I hope not. Good night, Hamilton. I'll see you in the morning."

When he was certain that Hamilton was asleep, Rutledge left the Duke of Monmouth and walked as far as Casa Miranda, calling quietly to the constable on duty when he was within hearing.

"Good evening, sir." It was one of the men from outside Hampton Regis.

"Constable Gregory, isn't it? How is it tonight?"

"Yes, sir. Quiet enough. The lady refused to come for the night, sir. Miss Esterley, that was. I believe the rector stayed in her place."

Rutledge said only, "I'm sorry to hear it." He stared up at the house-front, wishing he could look through walls and judge the state of mind of the occupants. But tomorrow would be soon enough.

He bade the constable good night and walked back the way he'd come. Hamish, cross with him, was giving him no peace, and he came close, more than once, to venting his own annoyance aloud.

The sound of the voice in his mind seemed to follow him through the silent streets, an uncomfortable companionship in the darkness. The church clock behind him struck the hour. He'd forgotten how late it was. But there was no sleep for him yet.

He passed the turning for the Duke of Monmouth and walked instead to the water, his steps echoing as he neared the shops and a cat, a mouse dangling from her jaws, trotted around the nearest corner and into the shadows.

There were boats drawn up on the shingle, and others

bobbing in the tide at the end of their tethers. He walked among them, poking about here and there, looking at gear and breathing in the rich smells of the sea, salt, and fish and that almost-impossible-to-describe scent of block and tackle and nets that have long lived in the water and grown stiff with it.

It was not too many days ago that he'd gone out with Perkins to the landslip. A futile effort, but it had given him a key when he found the bandages.

Hamish said, "The church clock struck the half hour. There's naething here. And you've been away a verra' long time."

He reminded himself that Hamish was a Highlander from the narrow mountain passes of Glencoe, where eagles soared high over the Pap and screamed down the slopes. But he himself had been accustomed to the sea, he'd learned to row a boat watching his father, and he'd spent his holidays by the water more than once.

Finally satisfied, he went back to the first boat he'd come to, reached down, and pulled out the best example he'd seen of what he was looking for. Holding it close to his body, he retraced his steps.

Someone was going to be unhappy with him in the morning. But he could make that right later in the day.

He stopped at the motorcar in the inn yard, looked around him at the night, making certain that there was no one in the shadows or walking along the street at the end of the drive. Then he reached into the back, where Hamish sat, for the rug he kept there. But Hamish now was at his shoulder. Wrapping up his find, he stowed it carefully against the back of the rear seat, glanced up at the windows above him, and saw only dark panes of glass. This was the kitchen yard of the inn, where the staff slept. Neither Stratton nor Hamilton could have seen him at work.

He went round to the front entrance and took the steps two at a time. He'd had almost no sleep the night before, and it had been a wearing day.

Quietly testing the lock on Hamilton's door, Rutledge went into his own room and stretched himself out on the bed. It would be the second night he'd slept in his clothes.

In the high-ceilinged room, Hamish had full rein.

"She wasna' strangled. She was bludgeoned."

"I know that. But does Hamilton? It's the only way to find out, damn it."

"It was a trick."

"It was a necessity."

"And what will you do wi' him in the morning?"

"Take him with me to Casa Miranda. And see what transpires."

"Oh, aye? And after that?"

"For the love of God, go to sleep."

There was silence in the room, and through the walls, he could hear Hamilton twisting and turning in his bed, the springs creaking under his weight.

It was a little after first light when Rutledge woke with a start. He had set his mental clock for an hour before that and slept straight through.

Rising to shave, he listened for sounds from Hamilton's room.

Finishing dressing, he went out to the passage. He stayed there for nearly three minutes, judging the faint snores coming from Stratton's room. So far, so good. He went on to unlock Hamilton's door.

He was heavily asleep, a pillow under his bad leg, and one arm thrown across his face. Rutledge woke him with some difficulty, and said, "I want you to come with me."

Hamilton scrubbed his face with his hands. "Where am I? I don't remember."

"The Duke of Monmouth."

"Yes, of course. Give me a few minutes." But he lay there as if the willpower needed to get out of bed had slipped away in the night. "I don't have any shaving gear. I'd like to clean myself up a little before Felicity sees me. Are you going to tell her, or will I?"

"Leave it to me. Are you coming?"

It took Hamilton all of ten minutes to dress, but he walked through the door finally and said quietly, "The leg hurts like the very devil."

"It's damp out this morning. A sea mist again."

And there was a white blanket over the village, drifting in off the sea with a softness that could be felt on the skin.

There was no way that Hamilton could have walked up the hill, though it would have been less conspicuous. Rutledge held the door of the motorcar for him, but Hamilton refused his help getting in. As the engine came alive with a smooth roar, Rutledge said, "You'll do exactly as I tell you. I don't want to frighten them. Mallory is armed. He's held Mrs. Hamilton at gunpoint in that house since you were found on the strand. The rector is there with her, and I can tell you that Mallory hasn't harmed her. Inspector Bennett tried to arrest him, and he bolted. Mrs. Hamilton came home to find him in the house. Mallory told Bennett that he wouldn't cooperate unless I was brought in to get to the bottom of what was going on."

"I thought you were a friend of Miranda's. How do you know all this?"

"I'm from Scotland Yard, Hamilton. Don't you remember my telling you last night? Mallory sent for me. That's why I knew so much about the inquiry."

"You tricked me into a confession."

"Did I? I thought it was given of your own free will. Is there any part of it you want to change?"

"Sadly, no. I wish I could. How am I going to face Felicity, with this on my conscience? I've thought about that and still have no answer for it."

Rutledge put the motorcar in gear and drove to the road leading up to Casa Miranda. "Why did you name your house here and in Malta for Miss Cole?" he asked.

"As a reminder that I owed her my career."

They didn't speak again until Rutledge had pulled up before the front door.

It was several minutes before Mallory answered the summons of Rutledge's knock. He said at once, "Damn it, you weren't here last night. Putnam and I had to hold the fort."

"Any trouble?"

"No, but we couldn't know that, could we? It was a bloody long *night*."

"There was something I had to do. How is Mrs. Hamilton feeling this morning?"

"Better, if Putnam is to be believed."

"I've brought someone to see her."

Mallory craned his neck to look toward the motorcar. "If it's Miss Esterley, she's too—" He stopped, his face registering a variety of emotions, uppermost among them shock and then anger. "If you've taken him into custody, she'll have my head. Where did you find him?"

"In Exeter. It's a long story. I'd like to bring him into the house. There are things he needs. Razor, a change of clothing."

"Did he kill those women? In God's name, *why*?"

"More to the point, he doesn't remember what happened to him. And very little of the time he was under Dr. Granville's care."

"I thought you said he was being kept sedated. For the

pain. And that it had played with his mind, what he'd heard while he was half conscious. You told us that."

"What he does recall is tangled now. Will you let him in?"

Mallory said with bitterness, "Why not? It's his house, after all. Everyone else has come and gone. And I shan't be taken up now for killing him."

"You may still stand trial for the attack on him."

"I didn't touch him, Rutledge. Haven't you asked him yet?" He took a deep breath. "I don't know how to feel now that it's over. I'm so tired I can't think."

"Not quite over. Will you go and make tea? I think he's going to need it."

"Tell him—tell him I never would have touched him. Not even for Felicity."

Mallory was gone on the words. Rutledge went back to the motorcar and helped Hamilton alight. He stood there, staring up at the house, then walked to the door and inside.

"If I'm going to jail, I'd rather pack my things before I see her."

"Go ahead. You know the way. You'll find Mr. Putnam in the passage outside her door."

Hamilton found it difficult to climb the stairs but kept at it until he'd reached the top.

Rutledge heard a smothered exclamation as the rector recognized the man coming toward him. And then Putnam was greeting him anxiously, his concern for Hamilton overcoming his alarm.

Rutledge followed Hamilton up the steps and said, as Putnam turned toward him, "He needs to pack a valise. Can you help him?"

Putnam cast him a swift look, then said, "Of course. Are you in pain, man? Here, take my arm. Shouldn't we send for a doctor? It might be best."

Mallory had come back, standing by the door, calling quietly up the stairs, "The water's on the boil. Do you know what you're doing?"

In another fifteen minutes, the three men were downstairs once more. Mallory had taken the tea tray into the sitting room. Hamilton's valise was left outside the door.

Hamilton and Mallory faced each other in stiff silence.

Mallory was the first to speak. "If I've caused you worry, I'm sorry. It was all I could think of, to keep myself safe. She's your wife, and I have respected that. She will tell you as much."

Hamilton said, "Thank you." He found a chair and sat in it. "I'd like to see her now, if I may."

Putnam said, "I'll bring her to you."

But they had finished their tea before Felicity Hamilton came down to the sitting room. She had dressed herself carefully, her hair shining in the light and her dark blue skirt nearly the same shade as Miranda Cole's sweater.

"Matthew?" she said tentatively. "Are you all right?"

"As well as can be expected. I've given you a fright, I'm sorry."

"We thought you were dead," she wailed and started toward him. Then she stopped, not knowing quite what to do.

There was an awkward moment, before Putnam said, "You'll want some tea, my dear. Come and sit here, by the fire."

She hesitated, and then crossed the room to take the chair he offered her. He brought her a cup, like a good host, and went to stand by the windows, a watcher and a witness.

Mallory, his back to the wall, said, "Keep this short, Rutledge. We're none of us at our best."

Rutledge said, without preamble, "Someone has been mischiefmaking. At a guess it began when whoever it was watched Mr. Hamilton here walk down to the Mole for his morning stroll. Inspector Bennett believed it was Mallory, because there appeared to be a very good reason for him to wish Hamilton out of the way. We needn't go into that. But I've come gradually to the conclusion that Bennett is wrong. And that's why he's not here this morning. I've got the three principals sitting in this room. A witness in Mr. Putnam. I expect what is said here to stay here. Do you understand me? Hamilton, I'm offering you a list of names. Tell me which one had a reason to kill you."

Matthew Hamilton, surprise in his voice, said, "I've told you. Stratton threatened me. But I never believed he'd carry it out. If he'd been on the strand that morning, I'd have turned away and left him there. I'm not a fool. But I wasn't afraid of him attacking me."

"Who is Stratton?" both Mrs. Hamilton and Mallory asked in almost the same breath.

"A colleague," Hamilton answered. "Go on, Rutledge."

"George Reston."

Mr. Putnam moved to say something, then thought better of it.

"He's an angry man, filled with bitterness long before I knew him. He dislikes me, and I've never quite understood why. I dealt with his business partner. I still do. I rather believe that Thurston Caldwell would like to see me dead. But he daren't touch me. Too many people would point a finger in his direction. That's why I've stayed with him."

"But they haven't pointed at him, at least not here in Hampton Regis."

"Then I was wrong, wasn't I?"

"Mallory, here."

"No, I don't see that any more than you do."

"Miss Esterley."

"In God's name, why *her*? She's been a friend."

"Then we must look at your wife. Felicity Hamilton."

She smothered a little cry of disbelief.

"That's enough, man, I won't listen to any more of this!" Hamilton was angry, his face flushing with it. "If you can't be sensible about this, then it's over."

Mallory had started to his feet, then sank back into his chair, remembering that, with her husband in the room, he had no right to be Felicity's champion.

Putnam anxiously watched Rutledge.

He waited until the protest had subsided, and then said, "We haven't found the weapon that was used to strike you down, Hamilton. But I want you to look at what I'm about to bring in."

He went to the motorcar, lifted the rug from the rear seat, and carried it into the house with him.

When he held one end and let the rug unfurl, something hard and long went clattering across the floor to the hearth, nearly touching the toes of Felicity Hamilton's shoes before it was stopped by the wood basket. She cried out, and the three men, already on their feet, crowded forward to see it better, though it was nearly five feet long and made of teak with worn brass tips.

Hamilton swayed on his feet, and Putnam put out an arm to steady him. Mallory was as pale as his shirt.

A boat hook, old, battered, very likely passed down for generations through a fisherman's family, lay there in the fire's red glow.

Not quite an African execution club, as Dr. Hester had suggested, but near enough to kill a man with one blow.

Rutledge said, "You told me last night, Mr. Hamilton, that you'd heard someone over by the boats. It's in your statement. This is what he was looking for. He found it, and before you could hear him come up behind you, he brought you down with one swing. After that he was free to use it any way he liked. Or she. A woman could wield this hook as well. Now tell me, if you will, who else among your acquaintance is a cold-blooded murderer?"

Felicity asked, drawing her feet under her, away from the long, heavy length of wood, "Is— was this the one that was used?"

"I doubt we could prove it."

"Whose boat did this one come from?" Putnam asked.

"It was drawn up on the shingle, much as it always seems to be. We can trace the boat, of course. But the boat hook was borrowed, dipped in seawater, to wash away any blood, and simply put back again. Ten minutes, at most, I should think. The owner never missed it."

"I don't see why I wasn't killed," Hamilton said in wonder. "I must have a harder head than he thought."

"If you were dead, your lungs wouldn't fill with seawater as you drowned. The battering from the rocks would have masked these injuries well enough, there wouldn't be any question about what happened."

Mallory interjected, "And if there was a question, I was the scapegoat."

"I'm afraid so." Rutledge bent down, retrieved the boat hook, and rolled it in the motorcar's rug again, setting it outside the door. "Someone will be wanting this back."

Hamilton said wistfully, "I wish you could explain away Mrs. Granville's death as easily."

"Not yet. But you didn't kill her, you know. She wasn't strangled."

"Then why—? Damn it, I *confessed* to it!"

"Yes, I owe you an apology for that. It's what I told you. But your willingness to take the blame was honorable."

"What are you going to do now?" Mallory asked. "There's still Bennett to deal with."

"I want the four of you where I can keep an eye on you.

Mr. Putnam, you're needed here, if you'll agree to stay. Mallory, you and Mrs. Hamilton will go on as before, if you please. And, in a change of plans, Mr. Hamilton no doubt would like his bed. I propose that he take to it at once and stay there while I report to the world at large that he's been found, he's still not fully coherent, and we expect a specialist to arrive shortly from London to tell us more about the head injury."

He thought they were going to refuse. But Hamilton said, "I for one will do as I'm asked. I've not got the strength to argue. Am I to groan when Bennett comes? I can tell you now that the pain in my ribs and that leg will make it authentic enough even for Dr. Granville to believe."

"Yes, I'm about to address that, Mr. Hamilton. We'll do something for your pain, I promise."

Felicity said, "But, Matthew, where have you been?"

Rutledge stopped him from answering. "On the Exeter road, Mrs. Hamilton, where a lorry driver took pity on him. Are we agreed, then?"

While Putnam struggled with breakfast, Mallory helped Rutledge put Matthew Hamilton to bed, with pillows and bedding placed to ease his discomfort. Felicity hovered over him, still uncertain how to behave toward him.

Her fright had gone deep. And she was finding that her relationship with both the men she had loved was on shaky ground.

She was relieved when Rutledge sent her to eat her meal in the sitting room.

She was afraid, in one corner of her mind, that Matthew Hamilton was relieved as well.

28

Rutledge took the teak hook back to the boat it had come from. The mist had lifted inland, but along the water it still swathed the Mole in a heavy gray blanket that left a residue of moisture on his hat and shoulders. He wasn't sure who might have seen him with the boat hook, but any uproar from the owner over the loss of it would have attracted more gossip. Or so he tried to convince himself. Either way it was a gamble. Someone in Hampton Regis would know very well why he had been interested in boat gear.

Afterward, he went to the rectory to find Dr. Granville, telling him that Hamilton had been found, and that he was in pain.

"I've got just the thing for him. Do you want me to examine him? Where in God's name did you find him?"

"A lorry driver discovered him along the road west. God knows how he made it as far as he did."

"And what about my wife? What has he told you about her death?"

"I have a confession," Rutledge said. "For what it's worth. He's still rather unclear about details."

"Is he at the police station?"

"He's not well enough for that. He's in the house, and we've got a specialist coming down from London to have a look at him. Something we ought to have done in the first twenty-four hours."

"Yes, hindsight is a glorious thing. I've got something in my case that you can give him. It won't do any harm, but it should keep him quiet until your man arrives. Anyone I know in the field? Baldwin for one. Or Hutchinson?"

"We'll know soon enough, when he's here."

Granville left Rutledge standing in the entry and went up to his room. When he came back he was holding a packet of powders very like the ones Dr. Hester had left for Felicity Hamilton two days ago.

Rutledge thanked him and went in search of Bennett.

"Well done," Bennett told him, when Rutledge made a brief report. "I'll be there in a quarter of an hour. I'd like to let the Chief Constable know he's under lock and key. What's become of the lorry driver?"

"With any luck he's on his way back from St. Ives."

"Good man. We'll need a statement from him."

"Understand, Bennett, early days yet to know where we are with Hamilton."

"He's said nothing of importance, then?"

"I was able to learn two facts I can be reasonably sure of. He didn't see anyone by the water when he was walking, but he heard footsteps some distance away, closer to the boats. Whether this was a potential witness or the killer himself, we still have to determine."

"We'll send people around to talk to the men who keep their boats there."

"It's as well to ask if anything in the boats was missing or misplaced. Fact number two—Hamilton overheard a garbled version of events while he was in Granville's surgery.

Whether it was from one of us speaking too freely in his presence, or whether it was a voice outside his door talking to Mrs. Granville, I can't tell you. He's not very clear about it. But he felt for his own safety, he had to leave."

"When was this?"

"When the sedation was wearing off and he was more awake than we knew."

"Yes, well, head injuries can be quite severe. Small wonder he couldn't make sense of anything. But then he could have recognized the voice as the person who'd half killed him, and that put the wind up."

"I want to speak to Dr. Hester as soon as possible. We still have no murder weapon for Mrs. Granville."

"Here—did Hamilton have his keys with him, when you found him in Exeter?"

"He did. I've got them now."

With that Rutledge was already walking out the door. From the station he went to call on Miss Trining. Afterward he went to Miss Esterley's house.

"You didn't see fit to sit up with Felicity Hamilton last night," he said as soon as he was shown into her sitting room.

She said, "I couldn't face it. I'm no match for anyone breaking into the house. Worse than useless, come to that. Mr. Putnam was a better choice."

"I think, perhaps, a woman's company would have been more comforting. But it doesn't matter, now. We've brought in Matthew Hamilton."

"My God, where was he?"

"A lorry driver found him along the road to the west of here." He gave her the same account he'd given Miss Trining and Dr. Granville.

She listened with increasing anxiety. "You're telling me that he'll live? That in time he'll be whole again?"

"There's some hope of that, yes."

"But what about Mrs. Granville? Are you saying she was still alive when Matthew walked out of the surgery?"

"He's not clear about that. Not yet. In time, with good medical care, we'll know a little more. On the other hand, he may not remember anything, in spite of all we can do."

She smiled wryly. "Having refused to help Felicity last night, I shan't be very welcome coming to call on Matthew now. But I'd like very much to see for myself that he's all right."

"There won't be any visitors for a while. He may even have to be taken to London for care."

"At least he's being given it. I was so annoyed with Dr. Granville, you know. Miss Trining had suggested a specialist, and I agreed with her. But he told her that as long as there was swelling in the brain, rest was what Matthew most needed."

"I'm sure it was true. Now that he's awake, time will be on his side." He rose to leave.

Miss Esterley said, "Truly, I wasn't a coward, last night. You have to understand. I wasn't supposed to walk again. Ever. The doctors told me how lucky I was that the damage to my knee could be repaired, but even so they held out little hope I could use it properly. It required all the faith I possessed to go through the long, grueling weeks of treatment and exercises and manipulation. They'd learned, you see, from wounded soldiers. But they weren't entirely sure it would work for me. In the end, it did. I keep my cane as a reminder of how close I'd come to being dependent on the care of others for the rest of my life. I didn't want to take the risk, you see."

Hamish said, "She doesna' blame *him*."

"No," Rutledge answered silently. *"Not openly. But it's there, underneath. If he'd been less kind, perhaps her true feelings would have risen to the surface."*

Aloud, he said, "I should have thought the debt you owed

Hamilton would have been well repaid by helping his wife—
or as we thought then, his widow. Whatever the cost."

She blushed, the warm color rising in her face. "That's
cruel. And that wasn't the choice, was it?"

"I think you were afraid of what Matthew Hamilton might
have become."

"No, Mr. Rutledge. I saw that two innocent women had
already been murdered," she told him firmly. "And I was
afraid I might be the third. Mr. Putnam didn't face that risk.
What comfort would it have been to me this morning, lying
somewhere dead, to have you admit you'd been wrong to
ask me?"

At his next stop, Rutledge found Mrs. Reston on her way
out the door to a luncheon. She was wearing a hat that
framed her face and added a softness to it.

"My husband isn't here," she told him. "If it's George
you've come to see."

"We've found Matthew Hamilton. He's alive, but his
memory is still unreliable."

"I'm glad to hear it. Whatever you may think of me, I had
no reason to wish him ill. Do you know now who it was who
killed Mrs. Granville? Or Nan Weekes?"

"We can't be sure until Hamilton is well enough to tell us
who it was who carried him out of the surgery and left him
on a roadside to die."

"Will he recover his memory, do you think? In his shoes,
I shouldn't like to live the rest of my life knowing that I
couldn't bring a murderer to justice; no matter how hard I
tried. It's sad. What will you do now?"

"We are reasonably sure about certain points. But we
need his evidence to bring the case to trial."

"I see. And am I to tell this to George, in the hope that
he'll rush out to wherever Matthew Hamilton is resting and
finish what he started?"

"If I were you, I wouldn't put it to the test. A good barrister might see fit to ask you to testify to your role in driving him to murder."

"I remind you that I'm a very good liar. And he's the father of my children. What sort of life will they have, do you think, if he's taken up and hanged?"

"You should have thought of that before you tested him."

"He should have thought of that before he married me." She put on her gloves. "I'm late, Mr. Rutledge. You must forgive me."

She walked to the door and waited for him to hold it open for her. "I won't play your game for you, Inspector. You must do it yourself."

Rutledge ran George Reston to earth at his bank.

"I couldn't care less whether Hamilton regains his memory or lives the rest of his life as a vegetable, dribbling down his chin in a wheeled chair," the banker informed him. "He went out of his way to collect those heathen gods of his. Let him pray to them and wait for them to answer."

"That's a rather callous attitude, don't you think?"

"Is it? I think not. You must remember that we sow what we reap."

"There are two murders that haven't been solved, Reston. Mrs. Granville and Nan Weekes deserve to be offered the full panoply of justice."

"I shouldn't be surprised if he killed them both in his demented state. Mrs. Granville in his clumsy effort to reach his wife, and the maid in mistake for Mallory."

"Then how did he manage to drag himself out on the Exeter Road, where the lorry driver found him?"

"You must ask him that. I daresay he had no idea where he was going or why. I have a conference in five minutes. Is there anything else you wish to say to me?"

As Rutledge drove back to the Duke of Monmouth, Hamish said, "Ye ken, it wouldna' sit well wi' Hamilton to hear what ye've heard."

"It hasn't been a waste of time," he answered.

He found Stratton enjoying a late breakfast. Rutledge nodded to the woman serving tables and asked for a cup of tea. Then he joined Stratton at the table by the dining room windows. The sea mist was gone, and sunlight was reflecting from the glass panes of houses across the road.

Stratton was not interested in what charges might or might not be brought when Hamilton regained his memory. "I don't know these people. The living or the dead. You're barking up the wrong tree."

"That may well be." His tea arrived and he poured himself a cup. "But you can look at it another way. If Hamilton doesn't regain his memory, if he's permanently damaged by the beating he sustained, then he's not likely to take an interest in writing his memoirs."

"Yes, it turns out rather well for me, doesn't it? Not that I'd wish that on anyone. He has a very astute mind. That's what made him dangerous. He could cut through a mountain of chaff and find the seed of truth. But he wasn't the sort you got drunk with, if you know what I mean. There his brain was, still clicking away, recording, while everyone else is acting the fool."

"I don't know that he collected information to wield it, in the sense of blackmail."

"Of course he didn't. But it was *there*. Written down, you see. And in the back of your mind, it's always rubbing at you. If it doesn't matter, why put it down in black and white? Why bother with it at all?"

"Because it was his nature to remember. And he was lonely. The diaries were his companions, he talked to them and confided in them, and he kept them, as he would a friend. He told me you threatened to burn him out, once. Would you have done it?"

Stratton was caught off guard. "God, no! I was very angry with him at the time, and I wanted to make him afraid. It wasn't as successful as I'd hoped. And I was left feeling a bigger fool than ever."

"And if you'd tried again on Monday to persuade him to see reason, who's to say that your anger didn't get the better of you again? You could very well have killed Mrs. Granville, because it wouldn't have done for you to be caught in the surgery, looking for a man who'd already taken himself off in the nick of time."

"Yes, I can see how you might make that case. But I ask you, why should I go into Hamilton's house and kill his maid?"

"Because she stood between you and your safe exit from the house. And Mallory was armed. You were taking a chance, trying to look for the diaries. He'd have shot you out of hand, if you'd stumbled over him—or she raised the alarm as you were slipping out again."

Stratton's eyes were wary. "You've built a very good case. Are you telling me that Hamilton believes I've tried twice to kill him? He's truly off his head, if he has."

"I'm just saying that you've made an error in judgment here, because you've shown yourself to be obsessively worried about Hamilton's intentions. You might have been wiser to let sleeping dogs lie and see what developed." He pushed back his chair and stood up. "Think about it, Stratton, you've put yourself in an untenable position. If Hamilton tells me you're his assailant, that he left the surgery because he thought you might walk in at night to kill him, then I've got no choice but to take you into custody. It would do very little for your career, to be tried for murder. Even if there is a reasonable doubt and in the end you're acquitted."

"I trust you're a good enough policeman that that won't happen."

Rutledge smiled. "If Hamilton points his finger at you, whether or not I'm a good policeman doesn't enter into it."

He walked away, out the dining room door.

Hamish was saying, "You've made a verra' bad enemy."

Stratton sat there watching him go, his face closed with speculation.

Dr. Hester had just returned from delivering a baby. He found Rutledge waiting for him in his office. "What brings you all the way to Middlebury?" He sat in the chair behind his orderly desk and added, "Medicine is an odd business. Bury a man one day; bring a child into the world the next. I've never quite got used to seeing a mother's face as I hand her a healthy child. And this was a bouncing boy, if ever there was one. Ten pounds. *She* thinks he takes after her father, who was a good six inches over six feet. It makes up, a little, for losing him early to a cancer. The husband is just delighted to have a son to carry on his farm."

"We see only the dead on my side of the coin."

"Yes, and speaking of the quick and the dead, I've released Mrs. Granville for burial. And I'll do the same for the maid tomorrow. If you have no objections."

"None. But I think I might have discovered the weapon used to bring Hamilton down." He described his search among the boats hauled up for the night.

"I didn't examine Hamilton, but I should think you're right. Heavy enough to do the job. Long reach, no footprints close by, not much blood splattered on one's coat or shirtfront. But I'm curious, why didn't someone intent on beating Hamilton within an inch of his life simply finish the job while he was about it? At that stage it would have taken only a few more blows, surely?"

"He wanted Hamilton to drown. George Reston's brother drowned in the same place not long ago——in his case too drunk to drag himself away from the water's edge. I think our killer remembered that and was hoping Hamilton would go into the sea before anyone discovered *him*. By the time the body came ashore again, it would be so badly battered that no one would suspect he'd been beaten nearly to death first."

"Interesting point. You said *he*. You know the killer, then?"

"For want of knowing, he."

"Quite. Well, I can tell you it wasn't a boat hook in the surgery. Not enough room to wield one where we found Mrs. Granville," Hester reminded him. "And she hadn't been moved from where she fell."

"But it must have been something equally practical. We searched and came up empty-handed."

"Because the killer—he or she—took it with him when he carted Hamilton off. And a very wise decision, from his point of view."

"Then why didn't he kill Hamilton once he got him out of the surgery?"

"Do I have to do all your thinking for you?" Hester asked with a crooked smile. "If he left a body lying about, you'd *know* there was a third person in that surgery. As long as it was likely that Hamilton walked out under his own power, you've got a complication."

"And so—speaking hypothetically—our killer left him along the Exeter road, where a lorry driver could find him and save his life a second time."

"If the killer had learned that Hamilton was not clear on anything and would stay that way, he might decide to leave him alive to take the blame for Mrs. Granville." His eyes were sharp, his mind leaping ahead. "*Did* someone find him on the Exeter road?"

"Actually a lorry driver found him there. That's all I'm making public, but the truth seems to be that Hamilton walked out of the surgery and took refuge in the cottage that went over in the landslip. But he had an inkling it was in danger and hid himself next in the henhouse of a farmer who'd gone off to market. At nightfall, he tried to walk down the road and passed out."

"My God. Then he killed Mrs. Granville."

"He's confessed to it. But it's possible someone came for Hamilton, discovered he was gone, and before he could get out of there, Mrs. Granville walked into the surgery."

"Where is Hamilton now?"

"For safety, I've put him in his bed at the house, with his wife, Mallory, and Mr. Putnam to guard him."

"For safety?" Hester frowned. "Aren't you taking a chance there?"

"I don't think Mallory tried to kill him. And I don't think Hamilton killed Mrs. Granville."

"What can he tell you?"

"Precious little."

"Well, neither can I. Mrs. Granville died of that blow on the head, delivered with some force, mind you. And Nan Weekes was smothered as she slept. There's nothing new in either case."

"Hamilton is in a great deal of pain, as you'd expect. This is the sedative Dr. Granville prescribed for him." Rutledge handed the box of powders to Hester.

"Are you telling me you don't trust my colleague?" Hester demanded. "You think he's out for revenge, for what happened to Margaret?"

"I'm not suggesting anything. Hamilton is alive at the moment, and I intend to see that he stays that way. I don't want to discover too late that someone in the house took liberties with what Dr. Granville prescribed. Are these powders likely to do a great deal of harm if swallowed all at once?"

Hester examined the contents of one of the sleeves of powder. "They're stronger than the sedative I left for Mrs. Hamilton, when she was upset. Hamilton is dealing with injuries that he's very likely aggravated by activity. He'll require more help. I'm satisfied that this medication is safe, but if I were you, I'd make sure no one else had access to it. Dr. Granville told me you'd had to deal with Mrs. Hamilton. I wouldn't want her to try again and be more successful."

"I'll be certain to dole out the powders as needed. Personally."

"A very wise precaution." He got up and went to his medical bag. "How has she handled her husband's return from the dead?"

"Not very well."

"No, I thought not. Here. Take these pills with you too. If Hamilton is still having trouble with his memory and the powders seem to leave him more confused than he ought to be, or if he seems to be agitated while taking them, it might be best to have a choice. A little more pain, perhaps, but he won't be raving. And if you were hard-pressed, one of these would calm his wife as well."

Rutledge stood there, watching him work.

"Inspector?" Dr. Hester was holding out the packet of pills.

"Oh. Yes, thank you. If you come up with any suggestions for a murder weapon used for Mrs. Granville, we'll offer you the next opening at the Yard."

"I wouldn't walk in your shoes for any amount of money. I'm satisfied with my own, thank you very much."

Rutledge left, driving from Middlebury back to Hampton Regis. He ignored Hamish, who was busy with arguments of his own, and concentrated on the road.

The glimmer of an answer that had struck him there in

Hester's office had nothing to support it.

Intuition, he reminded himself, was a very unreliable gift. A burst of brilliance that showered light on one single corner of the darkness surrounding it and left the rest impenetrable.

But in the hands of an experienced policeman, intuition could sometimes lead to proof. Given a little luck.

Rutledge made good time to Hampton Regis, considered his options, and in the end went to the telephone closet at the Duke of Monmouth Inn and put through a call to London.

He had to wait more than an hour in that stuffy little room, shut in with Hamish and his own thoughts, before the call was returned.

After a while, Rutledge put in another call to London as well. This time to Inspector Phipps.

When the man came on the phone, Rutledge said, "I'm told you've found the Green Park killer."

Phipps answered, "Indeed, yes. A man named Berenson and his wife. She lured the victims there because they didn't know her, and he strangled them. Revenge, as it happened. They'd swindled him in a financial scheme and he wanted revenge."

"Berenson?" He didn't recognize the name.

"That man Fields, the one you'd had watched—he told us his sister's husband wasn't the only one cheated by the dead men. There were four others in on it, Berenson being only one of them. Fields had been of two minds about helping us with our inquiries. In the end, glad as he was to see rough justice done, he realized it would have been a better lesson if both men had lived to be clapped up in prison. I tried to make the Chief Superintendent aware of your role in turning up Fields, but he didn't like the man and would have gladly seen him taken up instead." He cleared his throat. "Mrs. Berenson is quite—pretty. And convincing."

"You're certain of your facts?"

"Oh, yes. We found the garrote amongst her knitting."

"And Constable Waddington?"

"He received a commendation for his part in the arrests. A good man, that. Chief Superintendent Bowles is impressed with him."

Rutledge said nothing. As he'd thought, Waddington had been eager to protect himself.

Phipps went on. "I'm to appear in court in fifteen minutes. Is there anything else?"

Rutledge thanked him and put up the receiver.

Bringing his attention back to Hampton Regis, he went over everything he knew, and still there was no single motive to explain both the attack on Hamilton and the two subsequent deaths. Murderers killed for a reason—out of fear, greed, jealousy, love, envy, or even sheer hatred. And none of these seemed to fit here. Unless he was completely wrong about Stephen Mallory.

Hamish reminded him, "Ye canna' judge him on the way he was in France."

"I'm not convinced he's clever enough—"

The telephone rang at last, making him jump at the loud jangle that seemed to echo around the tiny room, deafening him. He swore.

The voice on the other end of the line, apologetic for taking so long to find the information he needed, made Rutledge sit up in the narrow-seated chair and listen with concentration.

Gibson had paid a visit to the person Rutledge had named, and that led to a bank in Leadenhall Street. What he had to report was enlightening.

It came down to money, as it so often did.

But not quite in the way he'd expected.

29

Rutledge walked up the hill to Casa Miranda. The sun was strong now, and he thought he heard a blackbird singing somewhere in the distance.

"Wishful thinking," Hamish told him sourly. Yet spring came in this part of England long before it touched the Highlands, and in the air today was the scent of warm earth, mixed with the salty cast of the sea.

When he climbed the stairs to the room Hamilton was using, he found the man awake, propped with pillows. Lines of pain etched his face, but he said briskly, "On Malta the heat is already building. There's so much white stone, you see. It holds in the warmth. Even the soil is white in the summer. Limestone."

"Do you miss it?"

"In the way you miss anywhere you've put down roots, no matter how temporary they may be. It was a lovely house too. A marquis had let it to me, while he was in England. There was a porch, glass enclosed, where I took most of my meals. I could look out across the rooftops toward the Co-Cathedral and the Grandmaster's Palace." He sighed. "But you haven't come, I think, to hear me praise Malta."

"Where is Mrs. Hamilton?"

"In her bed. It's all been rather much for her. But she's young, she'll recover her balance. I'm just afraid of what's been lost. An innocence that was her greatest charm, and a sense of self that was absolutely absorbing to me. I could—almost—recapture my own youth, watching her."

"And Mr. Putnam?"

"He excused himself for a quarter of an hour to return to the rectory for a change of clothes."

"Has Bennett come to see you?"

"Mallory brought him up while Putnam was still here. He wanted to know about Exeter. I told him that my memory remained hazy at best, that I thought very likely I was continuing to run a fever."

"It could be true."

"It was. I remember how cold the wind blew as I was walking along that road. I couldn't stop the chills that racked me. I wasn't sure where I was going, only that somehow I had to get there." He hesitated. "Have you told Felicity about Miranda?"

"I'll leave that to you. When you feel you can."

"Miranda was afraid of me, wasn't she?"

"I think, rather, she wasn't prepared for reminders of the past. She had shut that door. And it's best left shut."

"I would have married her, blind or not."

"The blindness worried her more than it did you."

"What will you do about Mallory? Do you really believe he wasn't my assailant? I won't press charges, you know. It will only make for more gossip and keep the memory of these past few days alive."

"You're a forgiving man."

"No. A realistic one. Deep in my core there's a molten ball of jealousy. But it serves no purpose. And he's suffered as much as I have." He shifted his leg. "I hope you've brought something to ease *this* ache. Else I'll be drunk as a lord by teatime."

Rutledge found one of the pills that Dr. Hester had given him. "This should help. I've got stronger sedatives as well."

"This will do. I can tell you, I'm not eager to find myself in a helpless stupor while murderers climb through the windows."

Rutledge thought the man in the bed was more afraid of the outcome than he was willing to admit. But he laughed, as Hamilton was expecting him to do, as he offered him a glass of water. Then he said soberly, "I've found the killer, I think. If I'm right, by morning you'll have your house to yourself again, and it will be finished."

"I'm glad to hear it. But we shan't stay in Hampton Regis, you know. It's time to turn my back on the sea. And I expect Miranda Cole will be happy to learn I'm not as near to Exeter as I was."

"I expect she will."

He left Hamilton then, running into Mr. Putnam in the doorway. "I've just brought a few things," he said, "to tide us over. I went to Mallory's cottage and fetched fresh clothes for him."

"Well done. I'll need to speak to you later. Certainly before dinner."

"I shall have to give Dr. Granville a little of my time tonight. We're choosing the readings for Margaret's service. And the music. She was very fond of the choir."

"By all means, take as long as you need. I'll be here to spell you."

"You know now, don't you, who is behind all this?" The rector, holding his belongings and Mallory's in his arms, looked into Rutledge's face and then away again. "I didn't think you did this morning, in spite of the dramatic conclusion with that dreadful boat hook."

"I was as in the dark as everyone else," Rutledge confessed.

"Will you at least tell me what I am to expect?"

"There's not much God can do, now, Mr. Putnam. It's a matter for the law."

Rutledge found Mallory, morose and alone, in the sitting room. He raised his head when Rutledge came through the doorway.

"It's you," he said, as if he'd been expecting Felicity Hamilton to find him and offer him anything but the silence in which she'd been wrapped since early morning.

"Where will you go when this business is over?"

"Back to Dr. Beatie for a time, to work my way through everything that happened here. After that, abroad, possibly. It's my turn for exile."

"You could still marry happily and put this far behind."

"What became of the girl whose photograph you carried with you in France?"

Rutledge hesitated. "She's living in Canada now. It didn't work out for me any more than it did for you and hundreds like us."

"I watched Felicity change in just the few days we were shut in here together. I've got much to answer for. I understand now how she could have changed so much in three years. We didn't think about that, in France. We believed England was there, that it would always be just the same as it was when we left. More fools we."

"We were too busy staying alive."

Mallory took a deep breath. "Do you know yet who's behind this?"

"I've a very good idea."

"I'd like to kill him with my bare hands and save the hangman his trouble."

"Do you still have Hamilton's revolver?"

"I put it back in the drawer, where I'd found it."

"I'd keep it with you tonight. I want you to prepare yourself a pallet on the floor, the far side of Hamilton's bed. If anyone comes through that door, and you have any reason to worry, shoot first and ask questions later."

"Felicity is likely to come in there. I can't risk shooting *her*."

"Lock her in her room."

"She'll be furious with me!"

"Better furious than dead. Will you do as I say?"

"I don't have any choice. But you'd better tell Hamilton why I'm armed. He's likely to have something to say about that."

Shortly afterward, Rutledge left the Hamilton house and walked down the hill into Hampton Regis. From a vantage point well out of sight, he waited outside the rectory for an hour and a half.

At last he saw Dr. Granville leave, carrying his medical bag and walking briskly in the direction of the Mole.

Rutledge had made sure that Putnam was safely ensconced at Casa Miranda, and now, with Granville gone, the rectory was empty.

He walked up the drive, cast a glance over his shoulder, and tried the door. It was unlocked.

Inside, the rectory echoed its Victorian roots, a small house that had grown into a three-story collection of passages and rooms and dead ends to house a growing family. The rector used only a small part of the first floor, meeting his needs with a room in which to sleep and another for what appeared to be an overflow of books from his study. Furnishings in the rest of the bedchambers were sheathed in dust covers.

Granville had been given the guest room, newly aired. Rutledge, putting his head around the door, saw the doctor's valise standing under the window and a pair of shoes set neatly by the wardrobe. Granville's possessions held no interest for him, and he withdrew, continuing his search.

But Putnam's belongings did. He scoured the rector's bedroom and the adjoining dressing room, which had been converted into a bath. Then he went down the steps and repeated his search on the ground floor. He ended in the plant room.

Rutledge had just put his hands on what he'd been searching for when he heard the hall door of the rectory open and then footsteps in the hall. He put the hammer back into the wooden box with the rest of the rectory tools, exactly as he'd found it, and got to his feet.

Hamish, warning him with a sharp word, added, "He's away up the stairs."

The door to the gardens was not five feet from his elbow.

Avoiding the clutter of rakes and shovels, baskets, cutting shears, and aging Wellingtons gathering dust on either side of him, Rutledge reached for the knob, praying that the door wasn't locked. It was not. He went through it quietly and walked close to the side of the house until he reached the shrubbery. It led to the low churchyard wall. He followed the grassy path there and spent some time wandering among the gravestones, in plain sight. He hoped that he would leave the impression of a man with something on his mind, seeking solace among the dead.

As the clock over his head in the church tower struck the quarter hour, he went back to the Duke of Monmouth, stretched himself out on his bed, and slept.

Rutledge spoke to the kitchen staff and arranged for an evening meal to be prepared for Casa Miranda. When someone came to tell him the packages and covered dishes were ready, he put them in the motorcar and took them up himself after one brief stop along the way. While at the station, he gave Bennett instructions that included calling off his own watchers this night.

Darkness was just falling. To the west a long line of silvery clouds stretched out across the horizon, and under them the fading pink of sunset left a bright afterglow. Fair skies at night, he thought. Sailor's delight.

The occupants of the house, fretful after a day of their own company, fell on the food with the pleasure of people grateful for distraction.

Matthew Hamilton came down, sat in the armchair at the head of the table, and toyed with his plate.

"You aren't hungry?" Felicity asked, surprised.

He smiled at her. "I've always liked roasted ham, you know that. I was just thinking. . . ."

"About Nan."

"Yes. What do you say, my dear, to a few days in London, when I'm stronger? We might search for a new house on our way there." It was an oblique acknowledgment that Casa Miranda was haunted by ghosts, one living and one dead.

She smiled at him in turn. "I'd like that." There was no emphasis in the words, merely acceptance.

"Done, then." He turned back to his plate and ate with apparent gusto, but Rutledge could see that he was pretending. He wondered if Felicity could.

They had finished their pudding when Mr. Putnam looked at his watch and exclaimed, "I'm late. If you'll excuse me, I have an appointment at the rectory. It shouldn't last long. But I must keep it."

Avoiding Rutledge's eye, he rose from the table, thanked everyone for the meal, and went to find his coat.

Rutledge listened to the opening and closing of the outer door, then tried to concentrate on something Mallory was saying to him. Soon afterward, he went around the house and looked carefully at each of the windows and doors.

The fortress was secure. But for how long?

Between them, Rutledge and Hamilton managed to persuade Felicity to retire early, though she was certain she wouldn't sleep for hours.

"I'll feel better, knowing you're just there, through the door," Hamilton told her. "It won't be long before I'm stronger and can manage on my own."

"I wish you would remember everything," she said suddenly. "It must be very uncomfortable, not *knowing*. I shan't be able to walk down a street in Hampton Regis without wondering about everyone I pass, thinking this one or that one might have tried to kill you. How much worse will it be for you?"

"It's worrying," he told her. "What if I never remember all of it?"

"Don't think about that," she replied, and there was a thread of fear in her voice that both men heard clearly. She closed her door and Hamilton listened for the turn of the key in its lock, and then nodded to Rutledge, waiting at the head of the stairs.

Around nine o'clock that evening, someone came to the house and left a message with the constable on duty outside.

It was from Putnam.

Mr. Joyner is ill again. I'm going with Dr. Granville to see him.

When Rutledge questioned the constable, he identified the messenger as the Allen boy.

Rutledge closed the door and prepared to wait for Putnam to return.

It was almost eleven o'clock when the church bells began to ring wildly. Mallory, rushing to a window, said, "What's that in aid of? Rutledge, I don't like it."

"Nor do I. Go upstairs, Mallory, and take up your post. Tell Mrs. Hamilton there's a fire in the town and not to worry."

"Where will you be?"

"In the drive. To see what's happening."

He watched Mallory take the stairs two at a time, then let himself out the door. The night was quiet, but he thought he smelled smoke.

When he reached the constable on duty, the man said, "Must be a fire. I heard the pumps go out."

People were in the streets now, shouting and running. Rutledge walked on, far enough down the road to a point where he could see the church steeple, and to this side of it, the line of the rectory roof. Nothing. He scanned other rooftops, nerves taut now.

Hamish said, "It doesna' have anything to do wi' us, then."

In that same instant Rutledge caught the first dart of flame licking up the edge of a chimney. He realized that it was Miss Trining's house, and in the back of it, the pumps were set up and starting to work.

He called to the constable behind him not to relax his guard, then raced down to the center of Hampton Regis.

The firemen were busy, Bennett's constables helping, and the men on the pumps, their faces red in the glare of the flames, were grimly concentrating on keeping the water flowing.

He glimpsed Putnam in the crowd, then lost him in the shifting light. Dr. Granville was there as well, and even George Reston, though he was standing to one side, watching.

Rutledge made his way to Granville. "How is Joyner?"

"He died over an hour ago. Have you seen Miss Trining? Is she out of there?"

"No, I haven't seen her," Rutledge said, his gaze sweeping

the milling throng working to put out the flames.

"Damn! They tell me the fire began in the wood stacked by the kitchen door. There's been a great deal of smoke. I hope to God—" He broke off.

The bells had stopped.

Rutledge could hear people coughing and gasping all around them, but they kept working. "Where's Putnam, do you know?"

"He was looking for her as well." Dr. Granville dashed off, disappearing in the direction of the pumps.

Rutledge threaded his way across the crowded back garden, helping where he could, still searching for the rector. He finally found Miss Trining, clutching the portrait of her ancestor, watching as others brought out pieces of furniture and carpets.

He reached her, saying only, "I'm sorry."

"It's the kitchen that's burning now. The wall where the firewood was stacked to dry. God knows what started it. A spark from the chimney?"

She was stoic, her face set in a determined calm, though he could see that her knuckles were white where they held the portrait.

The shingles by the chimney were smoking heavily now, the flames doused.

"Have you seen Mr. Putnam?" he asked her.

"He's making certain all the servants are safe. I told him they were."

Rutledge made one last circuit of the property and then turned back toward Casa Miranda, walking fast.

Hamish, all the while scolding him for leaving his post, said, "It was verra' clever."

"Yes." He saved his breath for the last sprint up the hill, startling the constable, whose attention was riveted on the pall of smoke rising up in the night sky.

"Have you seen Mr. Putnam?" he called to the man.

The constable turned guiltily to face him. "Sir? I believe he went up to the house not five minutes ago." He saw Rutledge's expression in the reflection of the lights around Miss Trining's house. "You did say to let him pass at will, sir."

Damn!

Rutledge went on to the door, fishing Hamilton's keys out of his pocket. Letting himself in as quietly as he could, he stopped with his back to the door and listened.

The house was silent.

Where the bloody hell was Putnam?

Overhead Hamilton and Mallory were lying tensely in the dark, waiting. And Mrs. Hamilton, God willing, was in her own room, oblivious.

He dared not call out.

The rector couldn't have let himself in through this door—it was the one with the newest lock. But he had two keys that fit doors to the kitchen and to the servants' hall.

Still Rutledge waited where he was, his body tense with listening.

Hamish said, "Ye ken, yon fire was set."

"He couldn't have known what I'd found."

"He could ha' made a verra' good guess. Were ye seen, passing through yon shrubbery into the churchyard?"

"Possibly. Too late to worry about that now. It's done." A dialogue with Hamish was so familiar in the dark that he wasn't even aware of it. "Clever of him not to set the fire in the rectory."

The house seemed to creak and then settle around them as the chill of the night began to work through the brick and into the timbers behind.

Rutledge bent to unlace his shoes and set them to one side, out of the way. Then, moving on stocking feet, he walked softly through the door into the kitchen passage.

He listened, his eyes blind, his senses alert.

And far away down the passage, a door creaked on old hinges, then opened with only a whisper of sound.

Five minutes more and he'd have been too late.

A breath of air stirred, bringing a hint of smoke with it. Footsteps, moving quietly and without haste.

Rutledge stood there, nestling into the shadows of the wall. He could follow on the plan of the house he carried in his mind just where the trespasser must be. Through the servants' outer door. Now down the passage that led to the hall. Slowing, apparently searching in the dark for the back stairs to the floors above.

But who was it?

He thought for an instant that he'd caught the flash of a torch, as if the intruder needed the reassurance of seeing a door was open before blundering into it.

After a few minutes, a chance footfall informed him that someone had made a decision not to go up the back stairs. Rutledge took a silent breath of relief. Better a confrontation here than near Hamilton or his wife. It was what he'd hoped for.

In another twenty feet, whoever it was would be close to the room where Nan Weekes had been murdered.

He counted steps he couldn't hear.

Half a dozen more, and it would be time to show himself.

Whoever was there paused by the door to Nan's prison.

At that instant, the darkness erupted with light, brilliant, shocking, and blinding.

Rutledge swore with passion and swiftly moved forward.

Through the glass in the room where Nan Weekes had died, he saw Mr. Putnam, armed in righteousness and sincerity, standing in the full glow of a pair of lamps.

And outside, pinned like a startled insect in the brightness, was Dr. Granville.

What the bloody hell was the rector up to?

He didn't think either man could pick him out beyond the circle of light. He stopped short, keeping absolutely still, standing there like the wolf in Russian fairy tales, waiting to see what the carnage would be.

And Hamish was roaring in his mind like all the imps of hell.

Mr. Putnam said, "Doctor."

"Miss Trining told me you'd gone back to comfort Joyner's daughter, once you'd learned you weren't needed at her house." Granville tried to keep the annoyance out of his voice.

"Yes, I should have done. What did you give him, that let him die?"

"I didn't. It was coming, just sooner than he or I expected."

"But you killed your wife. In my workbox there's a ball-peen hammer I don't recognize. I expect Mr. Rutledge has already found it. Mine was my father's, with a worn blue handle. It's there as well."

Rutledge felt his anger rising. Putnam had been ordered to let Rutledge confront Granville, while he stood by as a witness concealed in shadows. Instead he was putting Rutledge's questions himself. Had the man run mad? Or had he been afraid that Rutledge wouldn't arrive in time to ask them?

"Matthew Hamilton killed her," Granville was saying. "Rutledge has a confession."

"Hamilton confessed to choking her. I told you earlier, he was muddled last night. But that's clearing up with rest and food. As you knew it must, once he was no longer sedated so heavily. Why don't we go and find the inspector?"

"The last I saw of him, he was still at the fire."

"There's the hammer." Putnam was firm. "I can swear to seeing it. The name of the hospital where you trained is on the handle."

"The hammer doesn't exist. Not anymore. It's burned up in the fire with the wood stacked outside Miss Trining's kitchen door."

"Do you feel Nan's spirit here with us? She worked for your wife. Conscientiously, as she did for everyone. She even sent you a message about the sheets left at her house."

"She'd heard us quarreling. It wouldn't have done if she'd remembered and told the world what those arguments were about."

"Money? You'd already set your sights higher. I expect when the Granville family cut you off, Margaret must have appeared to be a lifeline. She told me not six months ago that you were still repaying them what you owed them for your training. Sadly her inheritance is nearly used up. A foolish pride when there's little money to support it."

"You have no way of proving that," Granville retorted sharply.

"Mr. Rutledge put in a call to your foster father, who spoke to your bankers. On the other hand, Miss Esterley is rather well-to-do. And much prettier than Margaret. The only trouble was, she was fonder of Matthew Hamilton than she ever was of you. I'm not surprised that you were sorely tempted to put an end to him."

So far, Rutledge thought, stifling an urge to announce his presence, *the rector's keeping to the script we'd discussed.*

Granville said, "In the beginning I was set on Miss Esterley. Then I heard George Reston saying that Mrs. Hamilton would be a very rich widow. But Hamilton refused to die of his injuries, stubborn bastard that he is. I was on the point of quietly helping him to that end when he disappeared. When we couldn't find him that morning, Rutledge and I, I saw my chance, went back to the surgery and killed Margaret."

"Rutledge thought Hamilton's wounds were more grievous than they were. That was clever of you, a chance to keep him sedated and silent."

"Did Rutledge put you up to this? Are there witnesses back in the shadows?" Granville shielded his eyes with his hand and peered into the darkness. *"Rutledge, are you there?"*

"You're quite wrong," the rector answered him. "I've come here because I want to help you."

Rutledge had been on the point of showing himself just as Putnam deviated from the script. He cursed the man roundly—instead of distancing himself from Granville, Putnam was letting the doctor approach him. Closer than was safe, already. Before Rutledge could possibly reach either of them, Granville could make the decision to kill again.

What weapon did the man have with him?

"A knife," Hamish said. "It's what he kens best."

"Let me listen to your confession, Granville. It's the least I can do. Your soul is in jeopardy, man, and you will surely hang. Will you not stop now and give a thought to what is waiting for you at God's hands?"

Granville gave up searching the shadows. He stood there, a frown on his face, then walked forward. "I'm not sure I believe in God," he said slowly, as if considering the matter.

"But he cares for you," Mr. Putnam pointed out. "Inspector Rutledge will have you in custody by tomorrow morning. He knows you hid the hammer in your bag until you could leave it in my house. Make your peace now of your own free will. It will see you through the long and frightening days to come."

"You can't stop me from leaving."

"Wherever you go, you take yourself with you. And the ghosts of two women will follow you."

To Rutledge's surprise but not Mr. Putnam's, Granville said with what sounded like sincere regret, "Yes, I've already seen them at my heels." He hesitated, finally giving in to Putnam's persuasion. "All right then. Pray for me, Rector."

He fell to his knees, contrition in every line.

Putnam went down more stiffly, and reached a hand for Granville's shoulder to steady himself or to offer comfort. Rutledge never knew which.

The rector closed his eyes, lowered his head, and began an earnest prayer. Granville, on his knees, looked upward, as if to find atonement in the air above his head. Or to see if his prayers, like the King's in *Hamlet,* had failed to rise with Putnam's.

Then without any warning, he sprang again to his feet, and with an arm outflung, swept the two lamps off the table onto the floor, spilling hot oil and sending a spray of fire racing toward the back wall. Before Rutledge could move or Putnam could even cry out in alarm, Granville lifted his leg and with the flat sole of his shoe, shoved the unresisting man of God into the flames.

30

The harsh smell of burning oil and charring wool had enveloped the room and was fast reaching into the passage beyond.

Rutledge came out of the darkness with a roar of rage, his shoulder catching Dr. Granville hard in the chest before he could stumble through the door and out of reach of the inferno behind him.

Granville went backward, tripped over Mr. Putnam's sprawled feet, and fell heavily, one arm twisted behind him. As his left hand brushed the flames, he cried out and rebounded like a spring.

Rutledge didn't hesitate. He did as Granville himself had done, drawing back his knee and then delivering a blow with his stocking foot directly into Granville's sternum, pushing him backward and knocking the wind out of him. Gasping for air, Granville went down beside the struggling rector.

Catching up the blankets from Nan's narrow cot, Rutledge dragged them over the rector, smothering the fire al-

ready taking hold in the shoulder and back of his coat. Then
he pulled the rector to his feet and with all the strength he
possessed shoved him bodily, still smoking and retching,
out into the passage. Putnam bit off a scream as his burning
shoulder hit the far wall hard, and he fought to keep his feet
even as he tried to beat at the smoldering ruins of his coat.

Then in a shambling run, he went down the passage
toward the dining room, leaving Rutledge alone with Granville and the leaping blue-gold tongues of a strengthening
conflagration.

Rutledge reached down for the doctor, dodging a fist
wildly thrown in his direction. With a firm grasp on Granville's collar and shirtfront, he hauled him out of the room
and into the passage, slamming him into the opposite wall.
While Granville cursed him, he wheeled and swung the
door shut on the unbearable heat.

The fire would blow out the glass in a matter of minutes.
But just now he had Granville to deal with.

Hamish said, "You mustna' harm him!" As if he recognized the fury that was driving Rutledge.

In the distance, Rutledge could hear shouting somewhere,
and then other voices.

Breathing hard from the smoke and his anger, he turned
on the doctor. "It's over, do you understand me? Give Hamilton or Mallory half an excuse and they'll kill you with
their bare hands."

He reached for the man's belt, turned him roughly, and
secured his wrists behind his back. "Hamilton would like a
private half hour with you. Make no mistake, he's still capable of doing considerable damage. Don't tempt him."

It was a warning he hoped the doctor would take to
heart.

Feet were racing toward him, and in the light of the blazing walls behind him, he could see Mallory, with Putnam
not far behind him, and Hamilton struggling to keep up.

The constable on watch was trying to pass all three of the men. And in the rear, Felicity stopped short, eyes bright with the fire's reflection and her own fury.

They organized a rough water brigade and did what they could to stop the flames. Putnam found more blankets somewhere, and cloths for the table. They beat at the fire, beginning to make headway.

Suddenly they heard the roar of a revolver in the confined space of the passage behind them. It was deafening, stopping them in their tracks with the shock of the report.

When they turned nearly as one man to look, Dr. Granville was cowering on the floor, and Felicity Hamilton stood ten feet from him with her husband's revolver clenched tightly in both hands.

"There are five more shots," she told him shrilly. "The next one won't miss."

But he lay there, not moving, his face buried in his shoulder.

More people were coming now, Bennett leading the charge.

Ten minutes later the fire was out, though smoke still filled the kitchen quarters, and sooty faces paused long enough to catch a breath. Several of them coughed heavily before grinning at one another in satisfaction. Hamilton, exhausted, stood with both hands on his knees, head down.

Putnam was lying against the wall, his face gray with pain. Felicity had helped him take off what was left of his coat and the clerical shirt beneath it. The flesh was raw and wet, burned deeply. Putnam tried for a wan smile, saying to Rutledge, "I'll have one of those powders you gave Hamilton. It will be awhile before Dr. Hester is here. Bennett has sent young Jordan for him."

Bennett was busy with Dr. Granville. Rutledge felt in his pockets for the packet of Hester's pills and found instead the box of powders that Granville had given him for Hamilton. He looked at them, glanced up to see Granville watching him with an unreadable expression on his face, and then made a decision. He put them away. It was too great a risk, he thought. Even if only *one* was tainted . . . how was he to know which?

He found the pills then, and went to kneel by Mr. Putnam. As he gave him one to swallow dry, he found that Felicity had already fetched a glass of water from the kitchen.

"That was a bloody stupid thing to do," he told the injured man, infusing wrath into his voice. "Can't you follow orders, for God's sake? Why didn't you wait to see if I was there, why did you take it on yourself to challenge him?"

"Old fools never learn. I was afraid you hadn't come back from the fire—no, that's not true. Don't you see? I had to try to save him. I failed them all, Margaret and Nan, and even Matthew. If I'd waited for you to speak to him, I might not have got the chance. But I didn't fail you—you have what you want, a full confession."

Bennett was saying, "We lost Granville as he came up the hill. I see now why the constables never saw anything, it's bloody difficult in the dark. I went back to see if he'd given us the slip and returned to Hampton Regis. Pity he didn't try to burn the rectory down. We weren't watching Miss Trining's house. We can't prove which boat hook it was, but we've got the hammer. The handle's in a bad way, but the head is all right. You're sure of your facts, then, Rutledge?"

"We turned the surgery upside down looking for a weapon, Bennett. Remember? And all the while that hammer was in the one place we never really searched—Granville's medical bag. I was reminded when I watched Dr. Hester digging in *his* bag that it could easily conceal a weapon of the right size. Like a hammer. But Granville couldn't leave it there, he'd have to hide it again. The rectory was ideal. Both Putnam and I saw it. He could swear it wasn't his, that it hadn't been there in his box of tools before Granville came to stay."

"Granville should have thrown it into the sea," Bennett answered.

"It's possible he intended to use it again on Nan Weekes. But she was asleep and it was easier to smother her. It's a hammer to work metal, not something you'd readily find in a surgery. For all I know, Granville or his wife kept it there to deal with a rusty damper in the office fireplace or a stubborn latch on the garden gate. But there it was, the perfect weapon. Something Mallory might have brought with him and taken away again. But then Mallory never came. Hamilton walked away under his own power. Granville didn't know that when he murdered his wife. He thought in the end we'd find Hamilton dead and blame Mallory for killing him."

"He covered it over well enough. Clever bastard. Begging your pardon, Rector. But there won't be lettering left on that scorched handle," Bennett said, fuming.

"We don't need it now. We heard his confession tonight, Putnam and I, and that will see him hang."

Dr. Hester had finished with Putnam and turned to Hamilton, who shook his head and pointed to the prisoner. Hester went over to look at Granville's hand.

Watching them, Bennett confessed, "I'd never have suspected the doctor. We respected him, trusted him. It's not right." After a moment he added, "You took a hell of a chance with Putnam, you know."

"If he'd forgot for an hour that he's a man of the cloth, it wouldn't have turned nasty," Rutledge retorted. "And I needed him to look at the hammers."

He glanced around, saw that Mallory was just bringing a chair for Hamilton, who looked out on his feet, one hand pressing hard against his ribs. Felicity Hamilton was leaning against the wall by the rector, forlorn tears running down her face unheeded, the revolver shoved into a pocket of her robe.

Mallory touched Hamilton on the shoulder, nodding toward her. He roused himself, tried to stand again, and then decided against it. But he held his hand out to his wife, and after a moment she came forward to take it.

Mallory crossed to where Bennett was standing with Rutledge. "I'd like to leave now," he said tightly. "Am I free to go?"

"For the present," Bennett agreed, after a glance at Rutledge. "We'll speak tomorrow."

Mallory nodded and started to walk back down the passage alone. Rutledge caught him up. "You're not to do anything foolish. I've had enough trouble for one night, by God."

"No," Mallory said wearily. "I won't put that burden on Felicity. She doesn't deserve it. And it would fuel the gossip. You needn't worry." He walked on, then stopped just before opening the door into the hall, his back to Rutledge.

"I was the best soldier I knew how to be. We weren't all cut from the same cloth."

"If you're asking my forgiveness, you've come to the wrong person. For my sins, I have no right to judge you or anyone else."

"Every time I looked in my mirror, I saw your face. The man I ought to have been."

"It was a false mirror. What you were searching for was someone to blame. I want no part of it. I have my own nightmares. I don't need yours."

"Then, damn it, forgive me and be done with it."

Rutledge could hear Hamish's voice roaring in his ears. But he stood there for a count of ten, then said, his words clipped and raw, "I forgive you."

Mallory nodded and stepped through the door, shutting it firmly behind him.

Rutledge closed his eyes, and swore long and fluently under his breath.

Watch for
A PALE HORSE
by Charles Todd

Coming soon in hardcover
from William Morrow,
an imprint of HarperCollins*Publishers*

1

It was nearing the full moon, and the night seemed to shimmer with light.

He walked down the lane and turned to look up at the hillside.

The graceful white horse cut into the chalk by ancient Britons galloped across the green slope without stirring from its place.

He couldn't see it without remembering. That was the only reason he had chosen to live in this godforsaken place. To torment himself until he couldn't bear it any more.

The horses had died too, in that first gas attack. It wasn't just the men. The poor beasts couldn't know what the low-lying mist wafting toward them brought in its wake.

An eyewitness had likened the cloud to a great horse moving across a barren meadow, ambling toward the barn for its dinner. Not hurrying, not drifting, just moving steadily, without apparent purpose, without apparent design, following the wind as the horse followed the scent of its stall and the fresh hay heaped in the manger. But like the pale horse of the Apocalypse, on his back rode Death. And Hell had truly followed them.

He smiled grimly at the imagery.

He hadn't been there when the Germans unleashed the chlorine attack against the Allies at Ypres. Yet it had changed his life in ways no one could have foreseen.

He wished he'd never heard the name of that medieval Belgian town. He wished the Germans had never reached it. Or that the British had left well enough alone and let them have the wretched place.

There was a silver flask of brandy in his pocket, and he felt for it, uncapped it, lifted it to his lips, then paused.

What if he drank it to the dregs and crawled into the ruins of Wayland's Smithy to die, like a wounded animal hiding itself away until it either healed or breathed its last?

Would anyone care?

A shadow was coming up the road toward him. It was Andrew Slater, the smith. It was impossible not to recognize him, even at this distance. Andrew was built like a church tower, tall and broad and solid. But the man didn't turn at the lane. He passed by without speaking, as if sleepwalking, moving on toward the Smithy. Like to like.

It would be crowded inside with the two of them there, he told himself with black humor. Not counting whatever ghosts lingered in that narrow Stone Age tomb.

I envy Andrew Slater, he thought, there in the darkness. *He* lives only in the present, while I have only the past.

He drank a little of the brandy, for courage, saluting the pale horse with his flask. Then he turned and trudged back to his cottage and turned up all the lamps for comfort.

2

I an Rutledge walked into his flat and sat down in the darkness. He was too tired to deal with the lamps. It had been a long and trying day. The hours he'd spent searching for a murderer had ended in the man's attempt to leap through the tenement window on the wild chance he could still elude capture. It had taken Rutledge and two constables to prevent it, and all three of them bore bruises to show for their efforts. Rutledge's shoulder ached, and the top of his left thigh felt as if it had been kicked by a horse. But then desperation had lent strength to the man.

In the darkness the voice of Hamish MacLeod answered him. A dead man's voice, but for nearly four years now it had seemed to Rutledge as real as his own. He had never grown used to hearing it, and yet with time he had come to terms of a sort with it. It was either that or madness. And he feared madness more.

"Ye nearly went out yon window with him."

It was true, he'd been faster than the stunned constables, and got there first. He'd read the flare of intent in the man's eyes, and reacted to that just as the man's muscles had tightened to turn his back on them and race for the casement.

"A better death than hanging," Rutledge said, "if he'd succeeded. But he'd have gone scot-free if he'd been lucky enough to land on that shop roof just below and to the left. I couldn't chance it. He'd have killed again. It was in his nature."

Rutledge let the silence wrap him, closing his eyes and resting his head on the back of his chair, waiting for jangled nerves to find solace if not peace.

He had nearly let himself drift into a shallow sleep when there was a knock at his door.

Shaking off the torpor of exhaustion, he got up reluctantly and crossed the room. When he opened the door, he found his sister Frances standing there.

"Ian? Are you all right?" Her gaze went beyond him to the dark flat, and that sixth sense of hers seemed to catch the atmosphere like a sleek cat scenting danger.

"Tired, that's all. Come in. I've yet to turn up the lamps. I haven't been home long."

"Well, I'm here to dig you out of your cave. I'm meeting friends for dinner, and I need an escort."

"Frances. There must be half a hundred men who would gladly take you anywhere, including Paris. What's happened to them? They can't all have decided to throw themselves off Westminster Bridge in despair."

Laughing, she followed him into the flat and waited as he lit the lamps and made the shadows retreat. Those in the room, she found herself thinking, as well as those of the spirit. Her instincts to come here had been right.

"Yes, well, they're none of them as handsome as you, Ian, and I might as well take the veil. It's hopeless."

Beneath the humor, her voice betrayed her. Either she was lying, or there was something wrong that she wasn't ready to talk about.

"Is there truly a dinner party?" he asked quietly.

"As a matter of fact, there is. You remember the Farnums. They're taking Maryanne Browning out to dinner, invited me and included a friend of yours. At least I think you count her among your acquaintances if not your friends."

Maryanne was a widow, her husband Peter a victim not of the war but of the Spanish flu. Rutledge had spent New Year's Eve at her house, at a party that he didn't care to remember.

"You aren't matchmaking, are you?"

"Good God, no! I'm truly fond of Maryanne, but I'm harboring no hopes in that direction. We've been trying to keep her busy, Ian, rather than leaving her to mope. And so all of us in her circle take it in turns seeing to it that she's not forgotten. Or left out of things."

He believed her. It was a kindness Frances would think of—and do.

"I'm tired, I told you. Do you really need me to make up your numbers?"

He caught something in her expression as she said offhandedly, "Simon can't come tonight. He's in Scotland."

And that was the nub, of course. She was growing quite fond of Simon Barrington. She hadn't shown a preference for any of her suitors, not for years. Not since Richard, who never was her suitor, but possibly the only man she'd loved. She was clearly disappointed that Barrington was out of the city.

More than usually disappointed.

He made a mental note of it, then answered, "All right, I'll come, if you give me a quarter of an hour to change. Help yourself to a drink, if you like."

She gave him a swift embrace. "I knew I could count on you."

As he walked into his bedroom he called, "Who is the other person? You mentioned that I knew him?"

"It isn't a him—it's a her. Meredith Channing. She and Maryanne have become friends."

He stopped on the point of taking off his coat.

Meredith Channing . . .

An attractive woman who knew far too much for comfort. About him, about the war, about—

He'd almost said Hamish, but he was nearly certain she hadn't read that nightmare in his mind. He'd blocked it for so many years now that it was habit to keep the Somme and Hamish and the firing squad shut firmly away where no one could find it.

Hamish said, "Don't go."

And Rutledge caught himself just in time, before he answered aloud. "I've already promised," he said silently. "I can't go back on it without explaining why. And that I shan't do."